The Secret of Eden
and the Founding Fathers

The
Secret of Eden
and the
Founding Fathers

J. Andrew Jackson

First published by Takin Five LLC 2022

First edition

Book design by Stewart A. Williams

Print ISBN: 979-8-9860474-4-7
E-Pub ISBN: 979-8-9860474-3-0
Paperback ISBN: 979-8-9860474-5-4

For my Mom and Dad

PREFACE

For the first time in my life, history seems to be a moving target. With the onslaught of traditional and online media, there appears to be a move to rewrite history to fit a person's or group's agenda. As a result, attempting to teach a young student the lessons of history has become more challenging than ever. Alternative and even completely contradictive viewpoints of our past have muddled our collected viewpoints, at least here in America.

My research, as I have been writing my *Secret of Eden* series, has taught me that history has been written through the eyes of the victors. Since the dawn of man, tribes or nations have conquered their neighbors. One common fact amongst the conquered nations is that their cultures and histories have been eradicated. How much of the recollections of our actual past have been burned, and their memories have been forbidden? In many cases, only folklore has survived. The ancient secrets stored in places such as the Library of Alexandria are probably forever lost.

While this all is true, I believe there is hope. Over the last several years, my eyes have been opened to the reality of reincarnation. I believe that many of us have lived through the most tumultuous times since mankind first started to roam this planet. I believe that many of us have the true history hidden within our conscience. The key is learning how to access the real truth.

ACKNOWLEDGEMENT

The amazing part of writing the second book in my *Secret of Eden* series is that I started writing Book Two first. I then decided to stop and tell the backstory first. This resulted in my writing *The Secret of Eden and the New World*. I needed to tell the story of how the treasure of the Knights Templar made it to North America.

I have always been fascinated by the American Revolutionary War and baffled by the fact that a ragtag army consisting of only three percent of the male population defeated the largest military in the world. Several times, I have posed this question on social media. The quick answer I always get is that the French joined the conflict. A quick search on the web results in the conclusion that other than supplying a few shipments of arms, the French didn't join the war effort until February 6, 1778, when the Treaty of Alliance was signed. The war started on April 19, 1775. That's almost three years with few armaments, supplies, and, most importantly, no financial support. How can this be? I do believe there was divine intervention. I also believe that the Founding Fathers, who were almost all Freemasons, knew of a secret treasure they could use to underwrite their currency. This book, while being a work of fiction, tries to explain this mystery.

I want to thank my wife, Julie, and my children, Melissa, Nick, and Rachel. They have given me the time and space to explore my passions of both history and writing. Also, Julie opened my eyes to the supernatural surrounding us every day. My life changed the day that she convinced me to read a book by a noted Psychiatrist named Dr. Brian Weiss. My eyes were forever opened to the reality of reincarnation. Julie and I attended a conference in Chicago where Dr. Weiss explained Past Life Regression Therapy. Through hypnosis, I learned of a past life memory that shocked me to my core. What I saw that day was not imagination. It was not a Dream. It was a look into a past real-life situation. The character that I saw will be a dominant person in this book. The story around this character is fiction, but his being was a past manifestation of myself.

Lastly, I would like to thank my parents, to whom I have dedicated this book. My parents were both students of history. They were part of history themselves. They lived through the Great Depression, World War II, the Korean conflict, and many other trying times that our nation has endured. They both served in the Marine Corp. during World War II. They indeed were part of America's greatest generation.

I had a very unique childhood. I am the youngest of five. While my parents were facing an empty nest, they decided to follow their aspirations of understanding American history. My dad was what they refer to as a "Civil War Buff." Instead of camping or visiting Disney like most of my friends, we traveled to virtually every Civil War Battlefield in the north and south. While my friends were riding roller coasters, I rode in chartered helicopters just to take in the terrain at storied battlefields such as Gettysburg and Vicksburg. After the Civil War tour was complete, we started the Revolutionary War tour. We started in Boston, spent a long weekend in Valley Forge, and ended up in Yorktown.

I am blessed to have parents that taught me why this place we call America is truly special. For this, I am thankful and shall cherish those memories forever.

CHAPTER 1

THE SIEGE

THE SOUND OF cannon fire was relentless. The good news was that most of it was coming from the Patriots. The feeling amongst the soldiers was that victory was within our grasp. This was the first time since this awful war commenced that I could see confidence in the eyes of the soldiers. Most of them have lived through victories at Princeton and the loss of New York City. Some went as far back as Lexington and Concord, but then had to survive sickness and starvation at Valley Forge. Finally, it all seemed worth it. All seemed well for the revolution, but I had a horrible feeling about my situation as this day moved on. The ominous cloud that surrounded me was getting worse as the day went on.

The stage for the final Siege was set. Our leaders had come up with a brilliant strategy of smoke and mirrors that resulted in the British Commander, Lieutenant General Cornwallis, being trapped.

As I stood outside the Command Tent and waited for my

orders, I heard an argument ensuing that became very heated between the Marquis de Lafayette and Alex. Since Alex is my closest friend, I naturally favored his opinion in this argument. The two great men went back and forth about who would lead the charge against Redoubt #10. The Redoubts were small, hastily built fortresses where the Redcoats could hunker down and avoid enemy fire. Redoubt #9 and #10 were the last strongholds of the British here at Yorktown. If these Redoubts fell, Cornwallis would be surrounded. I believe that Marquis was trying to protect Alex from a suicide mission. The three of us have been close friends for many years. However, Alex was having none of it. He felt that he had earned the honor of leading the Siege through his exploits in previous battles.

After a few minutes, the tent flap opened, and out stepped General Washington. He was followed by the Commander of the French Troops, Comte de Rochambeau. There was no man anywhere that had the presence of General Washington. Wherever he went, he commanded everyone's attention. The General intervened on behalf of Alex and stated, "Lieutenant Colonel Hamilton has earned this honor and will lead the Siege on Redoubt #10. He will lead roughly four hundred Americans. The Siege of Redoubt #9 will be led by the French Count of Deux-Ponts, who will have four hundred French Infantry. The French will also lead a diversionary attack on the Fusiliers Redoubt. This will draw the attention of the British. I am ordering this camp and all soldiers to silence throughout the night. The attacks on Redoubt 9 and 10 will be commenced in utter silence. No musket is to be loaded during this time. All men are to have bayonets at the ready. This will be a battle won by hand-to-hand combat. Gentlemen, victory is at hand."

This decision would possibly seal my fate and also would explain the darkness that surrounded me. I was officially an Intelligence Officer and reported directly to General Washington. However, I needed to be at Alex's side during the Siege. May my lovely wife, Hannah, and my son John forgive me for what I am about to do. There was no guarantee that I was going to make it out alive.

After nightfall, Alex prepared his men for the Siege on Redoubt #10. The night was very cloudy, and the moon was hidden behind the clouds. The complete darkness allowed our approach to go undetected. This was another sign that we were receiving help from above. We began the March toward the Redoubt. Seemingly, the only sound that I could hear was my own heart beating. Finally, we arrived at the wall without the British spotting us. Alex ordered his men to surround the Redoubt, which they quickly did. We estimated that the British had somewhere between seventy and ninety men. The numbers were clearly in our favor.

Via hand signals, Alex gave the order to attack. What I saw next was a scene from hell. As we began to climb over the wall, the British quickly became aware of our presence and began to fire their muskets. The first volley killed ten of our men. The young private climbing next to me took a musket ball directly to his face, which removed most of his head. I kept trying to move as fast as I could, but the feeling that the next musket ball would hit me at any second gripped me. The fear was overwhelming. Somehow, I needed to survive this and make it back to my family. The good thing about musket fire was that it took about eight seconds to reload. Eight seconds might not seem like much, but it is an eternity when the enemy is sprinting at you with a bayonet. As I breached the crest, I could see the hand-to-hand combat that ensued. We clearly outnumbered the British. Most were surrendering. Through the smoke from the British muskets, I saw a British Colonel making his retreat into the command tent at the center of the Redoubt. I led several men after him. As we entered the tent, several of the men who had joined me were instantly killed by musket fire. That just left me and a very young Private to take on the British Colonel. I had clearly made a mistake. The crazy life that I have led was about to end. Most of the British soldiers were escaping through a tunnel that led from the tent. Everything was going in slow motion. The Private was frantically trying to load his musket. I knew that the Colonel had to kill me, or I would have followed him into the tunnel. I withdrew my knife and tried to get close enough to make an accurate throw at the Colonel. I watched as he raised his musket and placed his finger on the trigger. I attempted to dive, but then I heard that most ghastly sound. His musket had fired. Complete terror took over my being....

My Father was shaking me and telling me to wake up. He said, "It is just a nightmare."

I was soaking wet from sweat. I have had this Dream many times, but the details became clearer with each occurrence. When will this ever end?

CHAPTER 2

MAY 1ST, 1858

HAVE YOU EVER had a feeling that you know is true, but you can't prove it? I have been having this feeling since my Dreams started roughly four years ago. It is more than just a feeling. It is at the core of my being. The creator has given me an assignment that I am only beginning to understand.

My name is Nathaniel Mayfield Briggs. My friends and family call me Nate. When I first told my sister Jane about my Dreams she suggested that I write them down. I did this for several years. Jane then categorized my Dreams by both timeline and content. What emerged was astonishing. My Dreams were very vivid. It was as if I was a participant in what I was witnessing in the Dreams. The first set of Dreams detailed the life of a 12th century member of the Knights Templar. The second set was about the life of an aide to a very prominent 14th century Scottish Lord. Shockingly, the third set was about my great grandfather, Jeremiah Briggs and his role with the Founding Fathers. Jane and I spent a summer turning my notes into three separate stories. We corroborated as much as we could with historical accounts. The common theme amongst all three stories was that they all contained a secret that threatened the very survival of mankind. I was desperate to find out what all of this had to do with me. I had to go outside my comfort zone and get some help. So, at Jane's insistence, I agreed to meet with a very special elderly women named Felicia.

A few months ago, Jane and I met with Felicia to discuss my Dreams. Felicia has many gifts that set her apart from everyone else. Not the least of which is that she can communicate with the spirit world. Many in my hometown of Birmingham Michigan have no understanding of her gifts. For most, the convenient and lazy way to understand Felicia is to cast her as a witch. Once you get to know her, you realize that she is not only a devout Christian, but a very charitable person. This meeting changed my life forever.

This first meeting with Felicia will be etched in my memory forever. My recollections are as follows:

As we entered her home, I noticed Christian symbols everywhere I looked. There were crucifixes, statues of Mary the Mother of Christ, and sayings from the New Testament posted on many of her walls. This conflicted with the impression that she was a witch. She simply was misunderstood. She was a bit of a hermit and only rarely left her home. I have learned over my eighteen years that I should not pre-judge anyone. On that first visit to Felicia's house, we immediately bonded. There was a connection that I couldn't explain. She seemed to know my whole life story. Jane had given her the three stories ahead of time so that she could prepare for our meeting. I asked Felicia, "How did you know that you had a gift?"

She explained, "I was blessed with the skills to speak with the spirit world as a young girl. After my younger sister died from Small Pox, I suddenly had a new world opened up to me. I was so distraught over the death of my sister that I was unsure how I would go on. Somehow, her death enabled me to tap into a skill that is inherent to all of us. Suddenly, I was able to communicate with the spirit world. These spirits assured me that my sister was doing great and was very happy. Unfortunately for many like me that have this sixth sense, it comes after they have been stricken with a great tragedy." She continued, "Oddly enough, I have never been able to talk to my sister. I have seen images of her where she is smiling. I know that sooner rather than later I will be joining her. This brings joy to my heart."

I asked, "Why can't you speak with her?"

She responded, "I don't know why, but there seems to be rules and guidelines in the afterlife. You will understand as we move forward. Some beings are guardians of the Spirit world. Some call them Angels. Others say that they are beings that give direction to wayward spirits. They have one thing in common, they all praise the Creator. Everything that you have learned in the Bible is basically true. Some power hungry leaders have made changes to the written word for their own benefit. When you join the spirit world, you will understand everything. You will come to know Jesus and you will understand the mission of your Soul." She asked me, "Do you understand what the soul is?"

"I understand that the soul is what leaves our body after death and goes to Heaven." I said.

She said, "That is correct in a general sense. I will start at the beginning. There is a concept known as reincarnation where the soul leaves a body at the time of death and can be reborn into a new body. This can happen immediately or can happen several hundreds of years later. The soul has a specific task that it must complete before it can go to heaven. Sometimes, souls can complete their mission after just a few lives, and sometimes they may be reincarnated hundreds of times. To expand on this concept, many times, souls work in concert with other souls. For example, in this life, these souls can be your sibling or a perfect stranger. In the next life, these same souls may be your mother or father. Sometimes there are lifetimes where not all souls from the past join in. Maybe the circumstance dictates that they are not needed. However, they are still there. Some refer to them as Guardian Angels. Sometimes they speak to us through what we call intuitions. For the fortunate ones, they have a soulmate. This means that they have been blessed with a special soul on most or all of the journeys. They usually are a wife or husband. They may be born into situations where they may be in different parts of the World. But somehow in every life, they seem to find each other. At a very deep level that a human cannot understand, there is a magnetism that draws these souls to each other. When they find each other there is a very special love that is beyond words. When we are born into a new body, at some point we have intuitions, or even more strongly, Dreams that guide us. One of the most misunderstood concepts is Dreams. Some think they are meaningless drifting that the mind goes through while asleep. What people don't understand is that many of our Dreams are memories from a past life. Sometimes they make sense, but most of the time they don't. In your case, I believe that your Dreams are very forcefully trying to guide you. I believe that you are part of a very old and sacred mission that involves many other souls. I have learned a very effective technique called hypnotism that allows me to speak with your inner being. Sometimes it allows for me to speak with the Masters who are guiding your soul. I assure you that it will not cause you any harm. You probably won't even remember being hypnotized. Your sister will be here to witness the entire thing. I believe that it will bring you answers."

I looked at Jane and she nodded that it will be okay. She said, "You know that I will not let anything bad happen to you. Also, I trust Felicia. She is the kindest person that I have ever met."

I agreed to let Felicia perform the hypnotism.

We moved into her living room where she guided me to her couch. She said, "Sometimes it is easier if you lay down."

I said, "I can't promise you that I won't fall asleep, but if I start to snore please wake me up. My brothers claim that I snore all of the time."

Felicia laughed and said, "You need not worry about snoring." That was the last thing that I remembered.

Seemingly two minutes later Felicia woke me up. I asked, "How long was I asleep?"

"Roughly an hour and a half." Jane responded.

I asked Felicia, "Did it work. Were you able to learn anything?"

She nodded yes and said, "I will let your sister explain to you what we discovered."

I said to Jane, "Please tell me everything that happened." She said that she would. She seemed distraught by what she had heard.

She began, "Felicia instructed you to look up at the sky as if you were looking through a see-through Cathedral ceiling. Then she asked you to look down towards your feet and tell her what you saw. You responded in a voice that wasn't yours, "I am wearing a white tunic with a red cross on it."

Jane continued, "She asked you your name and you responded, "Jacques Courtier". She asked Jacques what his mission was and he responded in a heavy French accent, "My mission, as always, is to be a Guardian of the Secret of Eden. She asked him several questions in French that I couldn't understand. He seemingly responded. She requested to speak with Ian MacIntyre. Suddenly, a Scottish voice came forward. She asked him what his mission was and he gave the same response, "I am the Guardian of the Secret of Eden." She asked him about his mission to the New World. He told the story exactly as we had recorded it."

Jane paused to collect herself then continued, "Felicia asked Ian, "Is Clara with you?" Ian responded, "She is always with me." He continued, "Just as I am on my next mission, so is she. We will be together again soon."

Jane said, "Then Felicia startled me by asking for our great grandfather, Jeremiah Briggs. Just hearing his name sent a shiver down my spine. It brought back memories of our father telling us his tales. Now I am about to hear his voice."

Felicia asked, "Are you Jeremiah Briggs?"

He responded with a hint of a British accent, "Yes." Felicia asked, "Do you understand that you are speaking through your great grandson Nathaniel right now."

He responded, "Yes." He continued, "Nathaniel will be a very important person on this mission".

Felicia then asked, "Is there any guidance that you can give Nathaniel?"

The voice responded, "Everything was recorded in my Diary."

Felicia then asked one final question, "Is the Secret of Eden still hidden?"

The voice responded, "Yes, but we moved it from its resting place in

New Scotland. It is recorded in the Diary. Nathaniel will need to learn the code. But he needs to be aware that others are on a mission to stop him." After these last couple of questions, Felicia woke you up."

I sat quietly for several minutes. I was trying to digest what I had just heard.

I asked, "Am I part of this mission? Am I safe? Is my family safe? Do I have a soulmate currently walking this earth? Am I to carry on the mission of Jacques, Ian, and Jeremiah?"

Felicia then shocked me to my core. She said, "My dear boy. You are not only here to carry on their mission. You are Jacques, Ian, and Jeremiah. You are all the same soul."

We all sat very quietly for several minutes when Jane finally spoke. She said, "Our great grandfather left a Diary?"

CHAPTER 3

REINCARNATION

A T THE CORE of my story, I am detailing something that all of us have lived through. I am speaking about reincarnation. Most of us have no recollection of these past lives. While this belief is at the core of religions of the Far East, such as Buddhism and Hinduism, it is not accepted in America in 1858. You must understand that America was founded on Judeo-Christian beliefs. These beliefs traveled with the settlers to the New World. In Europe, the Church in Rome still held dominion over its societies. If the Church wasn't teaching about a subject such as reincarnation, then no one was going to touch it. For a teenager like myself, I found this very confusing. As I was learning about this topic, I turned to the Holy Bible. I was shocked to find out that in Matthew 11:11-15, Jesus inferred that John the Baptist was Elijah reborn. There it was in black and white. How can this subject be taboo? Are we doubting the words of Jesus Christ? I wanted to take this up with Reverend McKay at our Church, the First United Methodist Church of Birmingham, Michigan. My

Sister Jane, however, asked me to keep my thoughts on reincarnation between the two of us, and of course Felicia, for now.

The Dreams that I have been having are not just ordinary Dreams. According to Felicia, they are my sub-conscience mind revisiting previous life experiences. As I have mentioned, in my past lives, I have been a Knight Templar, an aide to a Scottish Noble, and my great grandfather, Jeremiah Briggs, who worked closely with the Founding Fathers of America. Those are just a few of the incarnations. I'm sure that the other lives will soon enter my Dreams. What a tall tale this is. Will anyone believe this? Will my parents have me committed? I am here to tell you that not only is the story true, but there is a more extensive back story. As crazy as it sounds, there is a dire warning in my Dreams. The secret of my Dreams comes with a set of rules that threatens humanity if these rules are not followed. The story goes all the way back to the time of Noah. It seems that Noah had similar warnings before the great flood. Should I set out to change humanity or start building an Ark? My parents want me to be a typical eighteen-year-old. Not the protector of the world. I now realize that a normal life is not in the plans for me, for I am, along with all of my previous incarnations, a player in a story that protects the very survival of mankind.

Through my Dreams, I have determined that my soul's mission began in the time of Noah. I have learned that my soul was a grandson to Noah in that lifetime. The descendants of Noah and his wife Na'amah grew in number after they made landfall. They lived in rudimentary huts, which gave them shelter against the elements, but little else. The beasts had returned to what was left of their habitats. Survival was extremely difficult for these survivors, but they were from hardy stock. In that life, my name was Peleg, and my brother's name was Joktan. God had protected our father, Shem, who was the eldest son of Noah, from the great flood that had stricken all of humanity. At the time, for all they knew, they were the only survivors. Therefore, it was incumbent on us to rebuild a world that was righteous and good.

One of the central tenets of this new tribe was to be fruitful. The Lord had deemed at least one of each gender of species was to survive on the Ark. This included humanity. As a man and woman came of age, they were paired together to do God's work. The Tribal leader, which was still our grandfather, Noah, prayed to the Lord for guidance, leading him to call a man and a woman together as man and wife. This marriage was sacred, and the bond was only broken by death. Peleg considered himself to be the most fortunate man alive. He was wed to Tytea. She was the daughter of Japheth, Noah's third and youngest son. Tytea was fair-skinned and the most beautiful woman that any man had ever seen. She was a very happy and optimistic person by nature. Even when a crop had failed, or a fellow tribesman became ill, she always came to aid the person who needed help with a smile on her face and an optimistic view of the future. She became my soulmate for all eternity. Tytea, Joktan, and Peleg were to be referred to as the Children of the Flood and were given the sacred task of being the Guardians of the Secret of Eden.

CHAPTER 4

THE BRIGGS FAMILY OF BIRMINGHAM, MICHIGAN

I WAS BORN ON January 20, 1840, in Detroit, Michigan. My mother, Sarah Briggs, and my father, Andrew Briggs, are the parents of eight children. A ninth, Emma, had died in childbirth. Emma would have been a year older than me if she had survived. I am the fourth of the eight children. My parents were both born at the place that was simply known as the Compound. The Compound was located in southern New York State on the Susquehanna River. It was a Plantation that also served as a Milltown. Originally, it was co-owned by Founding Father Samuel Adams and Peter Adams, brother of the Second U.S. President John Adams. The Adams Trading Company was in many ways its own town and was a very prosperous business during the Colonial days. As my story will tell, the Compound was far more than a milling and lumber town during the American Revolution. At its core, it was one of the centerpieces of the revolt against Britain.

It will never be remembered that way because everything done regarding the Revolution was done in secret, which meant that it was never to be recorded. History shows that Philadelphia and Boston were the centers of the Revolution, but for those Patriots directly involved, the Compound was just as important. Once the Revolutionary War had ended, the Compound's value began to deteriorate. Even though it was owned by one of the most prominent families in America, the Compound had outlived its usefulness because the lumber business had become highly competitive, and the farming business was spotty because of severe weather fluctuations. The horse ranch was the only business that has continued to prosper. The Revolutionary War and the subsequent battles with the British were a thing of the past. Hence, my parents looked for greener pastures, as they say.

My parents, Andrew and Sarah, decided that they were going to move to Michigan after my father's close friend John W. Hunter convinced them of the virtues of Michigan. Mr. Hunter established a farming community in a place that went on to become known as Birmingham, Michigan. Some say it was given that name because it reminded them of its namesake back in England. It was a day's ride from Detroit, which was a growing seaport. In 1839, the railroad tracks connecting Pontiac and Detroit added a stop at Birmingham. This meant that you could have a day trip to Detroit anytime you wanted. In addition, two steam locomotives stopped at Birmingham daily. From Detroit, you could reach the Eastern U.S., Europe, and beyond.

My family lived on a twenty-acre farm a few miles west of Birmingham. While loving their new home, my parents were still New Englanders at heart. They moved to Michigan, like many others, because Michigan represented freedom and opportunity. The wars with the British were over, and the conflicts with the Indian Tribes had been settled mainly by Treaties. My father was also a great outdoorsman, and Michigan was very bountiful concerning deer, elk, and other game.

My parents were very happy with their farm, but some of the

basic necessities they had counted on back at the Compound were nowhere to be found. So after my sister Emma died during childbirth, my parents decided that all future children would be born in Detroit, where better medical care was available.

My grandparents, John and Mary Williams Briggs, remained at the Compound until that fateful day in 1835. A fire had started at the sawmill and quickly spread to the entire community. As the story goes, the region was under the grips of a major drought. Once the fire started, it was over quickly. The Compound had burned to the ground and was never rebuilt. My grandparents barely escaped with just the clothes on their backs. My grandmother was from Hanover, Pennsylvania. Most of her family was still there, and she knew they would always be welcome. My grandparents moved to Hanover and would spend the rest of their days there. My father never believed the accidental fire story. He knew that the Compound had many secrets. The secrets would never be revealed. The mysterious building at the Compound, known as the Hall of the Freemasons, had been the subject of many rumors. Somehow this building, along with the horse ranch buildings, survived the fire. Supposedly, this building was one of the main meeting spots of many of the Founding Fathers. However, there was never any evidence of this. It was like the stories that many of the Inns in the Colonies told that either George Washington or Benjamin Franklin had slept there. While it made for fanciful stories, most of it was not based on any facts. Either way, my father believed that the fire was intentionally set to hide some things that certain people wanted to keep hidden forever.

My older siblings had left the farm to start their careers and families. Our house seemed much less crowded without them. Even though there seemingly was an emptiness, we moved on. We would still get together as a family very often. I soon realized that my family had not become smaller. It actually had become larger. Our home was a safe and happy place. My mother was a saint. She always had a smile on her face. She always made time for us. Also, if anyone from the greater Birmingham Community needed help with a meal or having a roof over their head for the night, my mother was the one to reach out to. We often thought that she was so giving that certain people would take advantage of her. She would often respond to these comments by saying, "That is for the Lord to decide."

My father was a very jovial man. He would always make us laugh. He thought that a good laugh could always overcome any sadness. My favorite memories were sitting around the fireplace after supper. There were plenty of stories. Many involved my great grandfather and his many tales of glory. Even though I had heard them a million times, I still loved hearing them. The amazing part was that they were different every time, depending on whether my father had wine with supper. My older siblings would just chuckle. My father was having such a good time telling them that no one ever tried to correct him.

My parents' seemingly happy world was about to be rocked. So Jane and I decided to tell our parents about the true nature of my Dreams.

CHAPTER 5

JANE'S HOUSE

J ANE AND I had taken some time to let what Felicia had told us to sink in. The subject of reincarnation was a complicated one. As Christians, we have a firm belief that if we live a righteous life, we will go to heaven when we die. Being reborn into another body is not part of the teachings. If reincarnation is real, why doesn't anyone remember their past lives? Doesn't everyone have Dreams? What makes me deserving of this special recollection? Felicia had mentioned that there were Masters or Angels that guide your spirit. Is my soul's mission so special that I have been granted this special view into my soul's past? And most of all what is the Secret of Eden? Of course, I have heard the biblical story about the Garden of Eden and how Adam and Eve had violated God's only rule about not eating from the tree of knowledge. As the story goes, Adam is told that he can eat freely from all the trees in the garden, except for a tree of knowledge. Subsequently, Eve is created from one of Adam's ribs to be his companion. A serpent deceives Eve into eating fruit from the forbidden tree, and she gives some of the fruit to Adam. God then cast Adam and Eve from the Garden of Eden for disobeying his rules.

I thought that this was one of those stories that we are not to take literally. Rather we should fully understand the message being conveyed through the story. Jane calls it an allegory. Is there some secret regarding Adam and Eve that affects mankind's survival? Obviously, there is much more to this story. Like any story, I must start at the beginning and in this case, it appears that the starting place is with my great grandfather's Diary.

Jane and I agreed to meet on the following Saturday. Her husband, Jonathon, would be at work all day. Jane and Jonathon Willits had known each other since they were small children and wed as soon as Jane reached eighteen. Jonathon was the son of a very wealthy and prominent businessman named Elijah Willits. They owned a beautiful home on the Rouge River.

As far as my visit to Jane's house, I would simply tell my parents that I going there so that she can help me with my studies. My parents were very happy that I had been working so hard on my schoolwork. My Father even commented, "Maybe we will have a Veterinarian or even a Lawyer in the Family." I hated to disappoint them, but my passion was to someday own a horse ranch, not further schooling.

It was Saturday morning. I fed the horses as usual. Goldie, my beautiful Morgan, was very happy to see me. I packed up my school supplies and mounted the saddle onto Goldie. We set out for Jane's house. Before we arrived, I took Goldie for a hard run. The Willits land had wide-open expanses that were perfect for a fast ride. After the run, we made our way to Jane's. I made sure that Goldie had plenty of water. It was very warm for this time of year. As I entered Jane's house I could smell the bacon.

Jane said, "I saved you some bacon and eggs." Even though I had already eaten breakfast, there was always room for bacon. I thanked her and made quick work of the breakfast.

We shared some small talk for a few minutes and then she

said, "I have given this a lot of thought. You are going to have to tell our parents. First of all, father may have some knowledge of the Diary. Second, I think we are going to have to make a trip to Hanover this summer to try to get our hands on this Diary."

I said, "How do you think they will react to all of this?"

She said, "At first, I think that they will be shocked, but eventually they will come around. I think you should let them read the stories first. We can tell them about Felicia after." She went on to say, "Jonathon and I are planning on coming over for supper this evening. It is Rachel's birthday. I think we should pull them aside and give them the stories and ask them to read them. We should tell them the truth. We should tell them that these stories are written from your Dreams and detail how some content has been added from history books to give the stories their proper context. We will ask them to read them as soon as possible and then, at a later time, we can meet with them to tell them about our great grandfather's involvement, as well as, Felicia's thoughts."

I reluctantly agreed. I wish this would just go away, but I knew that there was no chance of that.

CHAPTER 6

THE TALES

MY FAMILY GATHERINGS were wonderful events. This one was no exception. It was my youngest sister Rachel's birthday. After the celebration was over, we sat and shared stories as we have always done. The adults enjoyed a glass of wine or two. This seemed like to appropriate time to hand off the stories to my parents. I made eye contact with Jane. She was thinking the same thing.

Jane asked my mother to meet her near the front porch. I went to retrieve my father. We all met in the front yard.

My mother said, "You two look so serious. What on God's green earth is going on?"

Jane spoke first, "As you knew, I told Nate to start writing down his Dreams. He did this for quite some time. We painstakingly organized these notes. We did some research around what Nate had written. We added some historical context to give the stories clarity. They tell a fascinating story or stories. Nate and I would like you both to read the stories. Let's meet again in a few weeks and discuss the stories."

My mother replied, "Jane are you trying to tell me that Nate has a wonderful imagination. I already know that."

"Nate has many gifts. Writing is one of them." Jane said. My father did not say a word. I think somehow he knew what was coming.

Jane handed them the stories that she had bound into a book. Then, finally, I said with a smile, "Let's get back to Rachel's party. It's time to make a bonfire." With that, we all returned to the party.

Later that evening, I could hear my parents talking while I lay awake in bed. My father said, "I hope this doesn't involve the Compound. There were many secrets there. My father had to live amid all the secrets. I was only ten when both of my grandparents died on that awful day. Even as a youngster, I knew some of the secrets. These secrets were never spoken of again after my grandparents passed. While I don't think any of them were bad per se, you must understand that the Compound was one of the focal points of the American Revolution. My father always told me that there were times when you weren't sure if Redcoats would break your front door down or burn down your house. It was a great time for America, but also a very terrifying time for the families living at the Compound. I have never told you this, but a secret was held at the Compound that had existed since the dawn of man. It went back to the times of Adam and Eve. It involved someone called the Watchers who warned man to correct his ways or another catastrophe like the great flood would be cast upon us again. It was said that the Founding Fathers declared independence not only because they needed to escape the tyranny of the British Empire, but also because the Watchers thought they were the last hope. There was always talk about my grandparents being conduits to the Watchers. All of this talk with Nate has brought this back to the surface for me. I have prayed that this curse is not passed to my children. I hope I'm wrong."

My mother said, "Andrew, our son has written some stories. Let's read them before we jump to any conclusions."

CHAPTER 7

THE STORIES

T HE NEXT MORNING was Sunday. We all rose early and went to the eight o'clock mass at the First United Methodist Church as we have done every other Sunday. We usually attend a later service. The Reverend said, "Nothing finer than seeing the entire Briggs clan at our early mass."

My mother said, "The children wanted to go for a long ride today so we figured that we would give thanks to the Lord a few hours early this week." We ventured up to our usual spot in the front row, but it seems that we have outgrown it. Some of us moved to the second row.

Across the church, I saw a familiar face. It was Felicia. We made eye contact and she gave me a big smile.

My mother noticed and said, "I didn't know that you knew Mrs. Baldwin?" I thought quickly. I had no idea that her last name was Baldwin. Was she related to the Baldwin Family that founded Birmingham with Mr. Hunter?

"Jane introduced me to her while we were doing our research."

I responded.

My mother responded, "She is a wonderful person. She is a bit eccentric, but a wonderful person. She often helps me feed the poor." After mass, we all went back to the farm where my mother and sisters made a huge breakfast consisting of eggs, bacon, sweet rolls, and cider. Rachel already had her new riding pants on that I had given to her as a birthday gift. Everyone told her that she looked like one of those cowgirls in the rodeo. She took this as a compliment.

Jonathon decided to join us on our ride. He said, "It has been a while since I have gone on a long ride. It will give me a chance to tell you about the new race horses my father is evaluating." This sounded great to me. We agreed to meet him at his and Jane's house. I knew that this would give my parents the entire day to read the stories.

Rachel and I met Jonathon at his house about an hour later. We decided to head south down what used to be called the Saginaw Trail. This was a former Indian Trail that grew into a well-traveled road by the 1850s. It is now called Woodward Avenue, but everyone I know still calls it the Saginaw Trail. Jonathon said, "If you head north on it you can go all the way to a place called Mackinac at the top of Michigan."

I said to Jonathon, "Someday, I would like to venture all the way to the top of the State. Mr. Hunter always told my father that northern Michigan is the most beautiful place he has ever seen."

We made our way south to a little village known as Royal Oak. Our brother Nick told us about this place at Rachel's Birthday Party last night. Evidently, his wife Ella's grandfather, Lewis Cass, saw a magnificent oak tree and had given the village its name. We stopped and had lunch at an old German restaurant that turned into a tavern at night. I never had German food before, but it was delicious.

Rachel and I arrived home just before dark. We led the horses to the barn and fed them. They both had to be very tired. Today's ride was very long for them.

I looked at Goldie and I swear I can read his mind. He is saying, "Can we do this again tomorrow?" After seeing that all of the horses were fed and watered, Rachel and I went into the house where my parents were there to greet us.

My father asked, "How was the ride?"

Rachel replied, "Jonathon took us to a place called Royal Oak where he treated us to German food."

My mother said, "How did you like it?"

Rachel replied, "It was a different flavor than anything I have ever tasted before. I liked it very much."

My mother said, "It's always good to explore and try new things." Rachel then went off to bed.

My father then stated, "We read your stories. They both tell quite a tale. What do you think they mean?"

Before I could answer my father, he said, "Somehow my grandfather's story had made its way into your Dreams."

My mother soon joined us. She said, "What does this all mean. It reminds me of stories I heard at the Compound when I was a young girl. When we moved to Michigan we had hoped for a new start. We left there because it was a dead-end for us. Why are we being drawn back in?"

My father said to my mother, "We are not being drawn in. Nate is." My mother began to cry. My father comforted her. They both sat there very quietly.

My Father finally spoke, "The British are no longer a threat. There is nothing left of the Compound after the fire, except for the ranch. Maybe you are just a messenger of some kind. I don't necessarily see a danger. We need to meet with Jane and get her thoughts about these stories." They both returned to reading the stories. They figured that they need to finish reading the entire stories before meeting with Jane.

We bid each other good night and I went to my room. I was exhausted from the long ride. I will be asleep before my head even hits the pillow.

CHAPTER 8

THE DISCLOSURE

WE ALL AGREED to meet at Jane's house this Thursday after school lets out. Both Jane and I decided to tell them everything. The truth can set us free, as they say. I am hoping that they see the positive side of this. Our family can make a significant impact. The messages that I have dreamed about tell of some extraordinary beings known as the Watchers. The message of the Watchers resonates in the Abolitionist movement, which is very important to all of us, but is especially paramount to my mother. I think I may dedicate myself to the anti-slavery movement after all this is over. That would place me in lockstep with what the Watchers had requested. This is a lot to digest. I'm just starting to get my arms around the Secret of Eden. America winning the Revolutionary War and instituting a Constitution that declares all men are created equal was a big first step. It now must become a reality. Slavery must end.

As planned, we all met on Thursday at Jane's House. Jane started by explaining our sources for the stories. She said, "I needed to verify that the events of Nate's Dreams were historically accurate. I was able to verify that the Knights Templar were digging under the Temple Mount and that there was a prominent Clan in Scotland named the Sinclairs. This was the easy part. What they did with the treasure and the Secret of Eden was more difficult. This was because they were holding secrets. No one is going to publicize the fact that they have a treasure in their possession. As of right now, I can't verify the treasure part of the stories. However, there is a possible solution."

My father said, "Unless you have a way to go back in time, there is no way to prove any of this."

"We may have a solution," Jane said.

Jane had definitely grabbed everyone's attention. She continued, "This next part will be the hardest part for you to hear. I consulted with the older woman from Church named Felicia. I believe that you both know her. What you may not know is that she has a special gift. She can communicate with the spirit world. She sees things that we can't see. Anyways, with Nate's permission, I let her read the stories. She quickly established a theory. She asked if she could meet with Nate. He said yes. We met with her, and she explained that she could perform a procedure known as hypnosis. She explained it to Nate, and he agreed to proceed. Nate had just turned eighteen and was old enough to make his own decisions. Besides, I have done some research on hypnosis, and I believe that it is completely safe. Felicia then placed Nate into a dream state where she could hear the voices of The Knight Templar and the Scottish Aide. The voices were coming from Nate's mouth, but they were not his voice. Both barely spoke English. They both said that they are Guardians of the Secret of Eden."

Jane paused for a moment and said, "This next part might be the hardest part of all. The next voice that spoke was your grandfather, Jeremiah Briggs. He knew that he was speaking through his great-grandson, Nate. He also said that he was a Guardian of the Secret of Eden. He went on to say that Nate is going to do great things. When asked if Nate was also a Guardian, he responded, 'Yes.' Felicia then brought Nate back. He didn't remember anything. We recounted the entire story for Nate. He then asked Felicia I asked 'Am I part of this mission? Am I safe? Is my family safe? Do I have a Soul Mate currently walking this Earth? Am I to carry on the mission of Jacques, Ian, and Jeremiah?'

Felicia then shocked us by saying, "You are not only here to carry on their mission. You are Jacques, Ian, and Jeremiah. You are all the same soul."

My Parents sat dumbfounded. I'm not sure if they have ever heard of the concept of reincarnation. I took a few minutes and explained it. I even used the example from the New Testament. My father finally spoke.

He said, "I would think this is far-fetched if it wasn't for the fact that I was born and raised at the Compound. I have heard and seen many crazy things." My mother said nothing.

Jane concluded by saying, "There is one more fact that you have not heard. The voice of Jeremiah said that he left a very detailed Diary for Nate. That Diary is our way to look back in time."

My father said, "I never heard of any Diary."

CHAPTER 9

THE LETTER

THE FOLLOWING WEDNESDAY, as School was letting out, my father was there to greet me. He said, "Let's find your sister. You're mother, and I have come to a decision." Jane was the teacher at the schoolhouse. Actually, with the help of Jonathon's father, she was the founder of the schoolhouse. The Birmingham School had now grown to three rooms. When we walked into the room where Jane was sitting with one of the younger students, she showed her the correct way to perform additions. My sister was a natural-born teacher. She had the patience of a Saint. She wrapped up her discussion with the young girl and noticed my father and me standing near the door. She motioned for us to come in. My father marveled at all of the teaching aids that covered the wall.

He said, "Janey, your room would have even inspired me as a young student. Your mother and I always knew that this was your calling, and we are very proud of what you have accomplished with this new school here in Birmingham."

Jane smiled and said, "Thank you. The example you and mother have shown all of us is paying dividends. Now, I'm sure that the school is not why you came today. Do you have more thoughts or questions about Nate's stories?"

My father said, "No questions, but I think as soon as school lets out, we need to make a trip to Hanover to see if there is anything to this Diary matter. You are welcome to bring Jonathon as well. I would like to send a letter to your Aunt Andrea to let her know we are coming. The letter will take a week to arrive, so I would like to send it out immediately."

He went on to say. "The late spring/early summer is the opportune time for me to have a few days away from the farm. Everything is planted already. Your brothers will have to pick up the slack while I'm gone. I don't want to be gone for more than five or six days. Your mother can handle things for that long, but we don't want to push our luck."

Jane said, "School finishes on June 4th. I will need two days to wrap everything up. I will be ready on the 7th. I will speak with Jonathon this evening. I do hope he can join us. He loves an adventure. I don't believe that he has been through Pennsylvania. He will love the rolling hills and beautiful landscapes."

My father said, "Let me know tomorrow if you can, but either way I will send a letter to your Aunt Andrea tomorrow. I already took it upon myself to check the train schedules. There is a daily train that leaves Detroit at 7:00 AM that, after a few connecting trains, will get us to Hanover the same day."

Jane said, "Sounds like a great plan." I boarded our delivery wagon that my father used to deliver the goods we were selling. He had already made his daily deliveries, so we just headed home.

After supper that evening, my father wrote a letter to Aunt Andrea to inform her that we were coming to Hanover for a visit. My father tried to get to Hanover once a year. My grandmother, Mary Briggs, lived there with my Aunt Andrea. My grandfather, John Briggs, passed away roughly five years ago from what the

Doctor called 'Hardening of the Arteries.' His last years were very rough because he was confined to bed or, at most, the rocking chair on the porch. My father always told stories about my grandfather being a mountain of a man who ran the Mill at the Compound. He always said that my grandfather was larger than life itself. Like the others at the Compound, their lives were immensely impacted when the great fire occurred. My grandparents then moved to Hanover, where my grandmother was born and raised. My grandfather was hired at the local Mill, but life was not the same. The people from the Compound were a significant part of America's History. The Founding Fathers held regular meetings there. America's future was planned there. The only problem was that no one outside of the Compound would ever know of its history because of the secrets that the Compound held. I wondered if we could make a side trip to the Compound while we were in Hanover. I would have to bring this up with my father.

The following day my father took the letter to the Birmingham Post Office and sent it off to Hanover. The mail system was one of those things that improved dramatically over the last 100 years. This was in great part due to Mr. Benjamin Franklin. Mr. Franklin held many positions before the Revolutionary War. The highest of which was that of Postmaster General for the Colonies. This position reported directly to the Crown back in England. Mr. Franklin traveled extensively throughout the Colonies and established efficient locations for Post Offices. Many were in Taverns or Inns. They did not have to have their own establishment. They only had to be convenient and adequately placed. The mail would be delivered via carriage and have many transfer points throughout the Colonies. Mr. Franklin spent years visiting Post Offices to establish standard practices in processing the mail. He also produced a standard rate sheet that charged each customer based on the parcel's weight and how far it was going to travel. I wondered whether Mr. Franklin had developed many of the Postal Services' ideas while visiting the Compound. Evidently,

Mr. Franklin was at the Compound so often that he had a permanent room above the Tavern. The ironic thing was that the Compound never had its own Post Office. All of its mail was routed through nearby Binghamton.

— 26 —

CHAPTER 10

HANOVER

IT WAS THE beginning of June, and the school year was coming to an end. For me, it was the complete end. I didn't want to go to secondary school as my older brothers did. My dream was to own a horse ranch with my father. I have been drawn to horses my entire life, and now it was time to make the life of a horse rancher a reality. I have to admit that Jonathon's idea of raising race horses was very intriguing. My knowledge of horses currently was confined to workhorses and transport horses. The trip to Hanover would give Jonathon, my father, and I plenty of time to discuss these ideas.

This was a very exciting time for me. My entire future was just ahead of me. I have a very loving and supportive family who will assist me in all that I do. I had one problem. I needed to properly understand the Dreams and all that goes with them. Supposedly I am a Guardian of some ancient secret. Could my goal of being a horse rancher and my calling of being a Guardian of the Secret of Eden coexist? I certainly hope so.

The late 1850s were a tumultuous time. Several southern states threatened to secede from the Union if the Federal Government in Washington DC declared slavery illegal. First of all, I'm not entirely sure what it means to secede from the Union. Second, how could these supposed Christians want to continue with the practice of slavery? These same people would pray to Jesus Christ every Sunday as if slavery was a God-given right. I believe that someday, I may have a role in abolishing slavery. Would this prohibit me from being a rancher? My life already seems complicated. As my mother always says, "If you have a large task ahead of you, the best plan of attack is to take it one step at a time. Your instincts will carry you forward. The task will get smaller every day."

Finally, the day we were to start our trip to Hanover was here. We made our way to the Michigan Central Train Station in Detroit. This place was a modern marvel. The nearby Detroit River had to be partially filled in to accommodate such a large train station. From here, you could travel to anywhere on the East Coast and as far west as the Mississippi River. The station was mammoth. I thought it would be very easy to board the wrong train. My father quickly purchased our tickets, and we boarded a train bound for Cleveland, where we would change trains and board the Philadelphia Express. We would take this only as far as Harrisburg, Pennsylvania, where we would board a local train for the short ride to Hanover. The entire ride would take fourteen hours. It would be a long day. Most of the time was spent looking out the window. We had passed by mountains and over rivers too numerous to count. The villages were often just several buildings and a small train station. Each town had its own history and its own story to tell. I noticed that the thriving towns were neighbors to a rail yard or near water. The towns that had neither were seemingly on their last leg. We did pass some large horse ranches that caught both mine and Jonathon's attention. Someday I would like to make this journey on horseback so that I can see the towns and their people.

Immediately, I was taken back to a nightmare I had several months ago. It was unlike the other Dreams because it involved me. In this Dream, a horrible war was taking place in scenes similar to what I was seeing out of the train window. The Battle was vicious and involved fighting against other Americans, sometimes brother against brother. I never told Jane about this Dream because it was a one-time occurrence and involved me. Perhaps I should tell her. I hope the Dream will never come to fruition because the carnage I saw was beyond description. There was no mention of the Secret of Eden, at least none that I could remember.

Finally, we were getting close to Hanover. The Conductor announced that it was the next stop. We gathered up all of our belongings and prepared to finally get off the train. The ride was very beautiful but very long. Hanover didn't seem that far on the map I had seen but was much farther in reality. By horseback, this would have taken a week or better.

We stepped off of the train at the Hanover Station. My Aunt Andrea's home was a short walk from the train station. We arrived a few minutes later. We were warmly greeted by my Aunt Andrea and my grandmother. My grandmother was shocked when she saw me. I thought that perhaps it was because she hadn't seen me since I was ten years old. It had been a long eight years in which I had grown into a man. It wasn't that. She said, "You are the spitting image of your great grandfather Jeremiah." I had never heard this.

My father said, "Now that you mention it, he does look like him. I never thought of this before."

Her attention then went to Jane. She said, "What a beautiful woman you have grown into." Jane blushed and thanked her for the kind words. Next, Jane introduced Jonathon to our aunt and grandmother. Jonathon thanked them for opening up their home to us.

Aunt Andrea said, "Please make yourself at home." So we all retired to the dining room, where my Aunt Andrea served everyone chocolate cake and coffee or red wine. There was a lot of catching up to do. My father brought them up to speed regarding life at our farm in Michigan.

My grandmother said, "How wonderful it is to have a school founder in our family. Especially since you are a woman."

Jonathon responded, "Anyone who knows this particular woman knows that it is better to stay out of her way when she is determined about something." Everyone laughed. Jane blushed.

My father went on to say, "She is very quickly becoming a community leader that all of the male leaders not only respect, but seek her counsel."

My father then asked how they were doing.

My Aunt Andrea responded, "Honestly, it has been very difficult. When we were still at the Compound, we had friends and family that we had known our entire life. Here in Hanover, we have few friends that we can turn to. Mom's family and friends have mostly died off. So when the fire happened, Hanover was an obvious choice for us. George was still with us even though his military service often caused him to be away."

My father then said, "Why don't you move to Michigan. It is a beautiful place with lovely people. Besides, you would be surrounded by family. I would love to have you nearby. This business of seeing you once every other year or so is unacceptable. Mom, I know you weren't happy when Sarah and I moved to Michigan, but it was the right move. The Compound was my grandfather's story. Dad was born into it. There was no future in it for Sarah and me. We have built a family and thriving farm in Michigan. I think you would be very happy there."

My grandmother responded, "You have given Andrea and me something to consider."

My father continued, "If you decided to move, we could rent space on one of the cargo trains to move your belongings. Then, I could come back with my boys to help get you both packed up."

My thoughts went to my Aunt Andrea. She had what I consider to be a sad existence. She met her husband George back at the Compound. George, like many others, felt like there was more out there. The Revolution had been won by the Patriots. The Compound had played an essential role in the Revolution, but going forward, it was a dead end. The fact that no one could even tell you what had happened there made it a dead end. It would be a wonderful place to live if it had its proper place as a National Shrine of Honor. The fact that the surviving Patriots wouldn't even acknowledge its existence made the inhabitants that were still there feel that they were being shamed. George's way out was by joining the Army.

The Battles with the British ended after the War of 1812, but the various Battles with the Indian Nations were still underway. The Iroquois had joined the Mohawk, Onondaga, Oneida, Cayuga, and Seneca to become known as the Six Nations. From the time that the Pilgrims first set foot in what is now known as America, the Six Nations had been embattled to save their homeland. During the Battles between the French and the British, the Six Nations seemingly supported the British at one time or another. During the American Revolution, the Six Nations sided with the British. This did not end well for them. The victorious Americans subsequently pushed the Six Nations off of their lands little by little. Many of the Warriors in the Six Nations fought back. George fell victim to this fight. His small Army Platoon was sleeping on the shores of Lake Champlain and was viciously attacked while they slept. All of the soldiers were killed. The U.S. responded and wiped out any remaining Six Nation members in the area around Lake Champlain. Aunt Andrea learned the news when she received a letter from the Army Commander. He said that George died admirably and would be considered a hero. Andrea's life would never be the same. Andrea and George never had any children. She always thought they would start a family, but that was not to be.

CHAPTER 11

THE CRATES

THE NEXT MORNING I woke up to the sound of voices having a heated discussion in the dining room. I walked out to discover my father, aunt, and grandmother in a heated debate regarding my great grandfather's belongings. Finally, my grandmother said, "We need to keep the past in the past. No good will come from bringing any of your grandfather's items to light."

My father said, "I understand how you and Dad wished to forget that time. It was a tough time. The memories of losing both parents the way Dad had was extremely difficult."

"Your father had nightmares about this for years. This was no way for a family to live." My grandmother said.

My father said, "I understand this. I remember it very well myself. Many years have passed. It is my birth rite to understand and possess my grandfather's artifacts. I want to see them. You have them, but they are not yours. They belong to our family. We all have the right to see what he left behind."

I had to speak up. I had to very carefully select my words. "Grandma, I am the one who has asked to see my great grandfather's artifacts. I know this sounds crazy, but he communicates with me through my Dreams. He told me that he left a Diary with a message for me."

Just then, Jane walked up and said. "Grandma, I have been helping Nate with his journey, and I can confirm that what he is saying is true."

"Jane, how can you confirm what Nate experiences in a dream?" My grandma said.

Jane explained, "There have been many Dreams. Nate has been writing them down. I have verified the facts such as location, names, and historical facts surrounding his Dreams. Furthermore, Nate has been seen by a Seer who confirmed that Jeremiah left a message for Nate."

The room fell silent for a few moments. Then, finally, my grandmother spoke, "I will not stop you from your pursuits. You seem to have done your homework on this subject. I am not exactly sure what I have because John forbid me from setting my eyes on it. He thought the secrets his father possessed had brought down enough wrath on this family. There are two crates up in the attic. This is all that we could escape with when the great fire ravaged the Compound. John believed these crates possessed some very secret items that were better left hidden. The keys to unlock the crates are in a mason jar in the cellar."

Aunt Andrea finally spoke up, "I agree with Andrew. It is time we look into the past. So far, our family legacy has been kept secret. Maybe our family's story is still unfolding. I have always felt that our family was special. The stories of our grandfather working with the Founding Fathers are special for us. It is high time we find out the truth."

My grandmother left the room momentarily and returned with the Mason jar. She said, "May God protect us all."

My father went to the attic and spotted two very old trunks that were under several other crates. He yelled for Jonathon and me to come and help lift the crates. They were heavy. The plan was to bring them down and take them out onto the covered sitting room that was attached to the house. This was an open-air covered room where you could sit and enjoy a lemonade or tea on a nice afternoon. We were able to carry the crates down the narrow staircase and navigate our way to the sitting room. We all sat down and stared at the crates for a minute before Jane finally said, "The curiosity is killing me. Are we going to open the crates or just sit here and stare at them?" My father finally took the keys out of the jar and opened the first crate. When the lid opened, a musty smell permeated the room.

My grandmother said, "These crates haven't seen the light of day in 40 years." The first crate must have been my great grandmothers. The first item was a beautiful wedding dress.

Jane lifted it and said, "Look at the detail on this dress. I have never seen anything as beautiful as this."

My grandmother said, "You should have seen her. She was the most beautiful woman that I have ever laid my eyes on. She had long blondish brown hair with crystal blue eyes. Even as she aged, she maintained her beauty. Her beauty was not only skin deep, but she was a deeply caring person who always was looking to help others. When I first met John, or for you two – you're grandfather, she welcomed me from the first instant. She could have been different. She was the daughter of a very well-known person. Her father was Founding Father Samuel Adams and the cousin to the second President and Founding Father John Adams. She could have looked down on others, but she didn't. Your great grandparents had a wonderful love affair. They were always holding hands and had that look in their eyes as if they had just discovered one another. Your great grandfather holds a very special, although secret, place in this Country's history. Your great grandmother, Hannah, is right there beside him."

Jane continued going through the crate. She came across what looked like their wedding invitation. It was describing a grand event at the home of General and Mrs. Phillip Schuyler in Albany, NY. She passed this around. There were also several pieces of art in the crate.

My grandma said, "She was a rather terrific artist in her day. There are three of four sketches of what we believe were the Adams homestead. It was a sprawling estate. Her uncle, John Adams, was one of the most prominent men in America at the time. The estate was called Peace Field if I'm not mistaken."

The painting on the bottom stopped all of us in our tracks. It was the painting of a young man standing next to a horse. We were all taken back by the fact that the painting appeared to be of me. The person in the painting was dressed in brown nickers with white hose and a brown jacket. My grandmother said, "This is Jeremiah Briggs. You can see why I was so taken back when I first saw Nate last evening." For me, the only thing that I could think of was that the horse looked just like Goldie.

The next picture was equally startling. It was a painting of a handful of men enjoying tea at a table in a garden setting. Upon closer inspection, the painting showed Jeremiah seated with Benjamin Franklin, George and Martha Washington, Thomas Jefferson, John Adams, and a younger man who I believe was Alexander Hamilton. Jane said, "This belongs in a museum."

We all sat in stunned silence. The family folklore appears to be true. Our great grandfather was involved with the Founding Fathers. Jane said, "We have already found a treasure, and we haven't even found what we came for yet. This is astonishing." We had finished reviewing the items from the first crate. Jane suggested that we return everything to the crate. "The air may degrade the artwork." She said.

Next, we moved to the second crate. We opened it to find a Revolutionary War uniform. We presumed it was Jeremiah's. It had a bright blue coat with red trim, white pants, and a white vest. We were looking at history. In which battles had this uniform been worn? Hopefully, the Diary would shed some light on Jeremiah's wartime exploits.

Next in the crate was a regular-looking brown outfit with a

white shirt and white hose. Jane said, "I believe that is the outfit he was wearing in the painting with him and the horse that we just looked at. It must have been special. Maybe he was wearing it when he met Hannah."

At the bottom of the crate were two smaller boxes. The first one that we inspected was the smaller of the two. Upon opening it, we discovered that it contained letters and other keepsakes. Most of them looked like letters to Hannah. There was also a ring box. Jane opened it up to find a beautiful ring. It must have been Hannah's. Under it was a note that said, "To be saved for great grandson. He will carry on our legacy." We all sat in stunned silence. Was this referring to me? Was I supposed to give this to my wife when I get married?

We saved the letters for later. I almost felt like we were prying into Jeremiah's personal space even though they both had been deceased for many years. There also was a ticket that seemed to grant passage on a vessel. My father said, "This may be his ticket when he first moved to the Colonies from England." We returned the letters to the box. We were looking for a Diary.

The last box was a heavy wooden box that was very ornate. It was locked. There was a codex lock mechanism. It required you to know the seven-letter passcode to gain entry. Jane said, "I have read about these locking boxes. In old Europe, very special documents were kept in them for safekeeping. They can only be opened with the passcode. If someone forces the box open, several glass vials of acid will pour onto the documents, thus destroying them."

We sat there for hours trying to open the codex. We tried all common family names. Revolutionary War terms. Terms from history. All to no avail. Jane said to me, "We should scour your notes. There must be a clue in there."

I said, "Let's stop for today. Let me sleep on it. Maybe something may come to mind." She agreed.

As we walked to the other end of the house. I said to Jane, "When I saw that painting of the Founding Fathers sitting with our great grandfather, I was startled because I have had that Dream. I saw that scene in my Dream as it was happening. In the scene, the Founding Fathers teased Jeremiah about being so smitten with Hannah." Many of them seemed to be living vicariously through Jeremiah.

We finally bid each other good night and agreed tomorrow would be a new day.

CHAPTER 12

ARCADIA

THE FOLLOWING DAY I woke up at sunrise in a cold sweat. In My Dreams, I believe that I have uncovered the secret code. I quickly rose and got dressed. The locked ornate box was sitting on the table in the dining room right where we left it. I sat down, pulled the box towards me, rolled the Codex letters to the position I wanted, and heard a click. The lid to the box opened. I peered into the box and saw a large pile of letters and several books. On the bottom of the box was a thick book that, upon opening, revealed daily handwritten accounts. I had found my great grandfather's Diary.

I started to read the Diary. It started back in England, where Jeremiah was by himself. He had no family, and there were no jobs. I continued to read for about an hour. So much of what I was reading was confirming my Dreams.

In many cases, I felt as if I could finish the sentences. Then a startling thought came to me. According to Felicia, my soul and Jeremiah's soul were the same. So, technically, I wrote this Diary.

Shortly after that, Jane joined me. She started the morning by warming up some tea. When she walked into the dining room, she stopped dead in her tracks and said, "Nate, you figured out the passcode."

I said, "Yes, my Dreams guided me once again."

"Please explain what you saw in your Dreams." She said.

I started by saying, "Do you remember in the Sinclair set of Dreams, there was a fisherman named Antonio who was lost at sea and lived in a faraway land for twenty years. He then returned to Scotland where he was introduced to Henry Sinclair."

Jane responded, "Of course, he went on to guide the mission to the place where there was a Gold River."

"Then, I'm sure you remember what Antonio called this place," I said.

She thought for a moment and finally said, "Arcadia?"

I said, "Yes, Antonio told Henry Sinclair, "If you guide your ship towards the Great Swan, you will find Arcadia."

I detailed how I rushed out to the dining room and was able to open the codex on the first try by using A-R-C-A-D-I-A. Then I said, "I found the Diary." I handed it to her and said, "There must be two hundred pages of handwritten notes." I then told her my thoughts about Felicia saying that Jeremiah and I were one in the same soul and how that means that I was the author of this Diary."

She smiled and said, "I am going to need my tea to digest that thought." We both laughed.

When she returned with a full teapot and two cups, she said, "The fact that Jeremiah and probably some of the Founding Fathers used the term Arcadia means that they thought the New World was indeed the place that Aristotle and Plato had described in their writings. The New World was to be the "New Atlantis." This is why the Patriots fought so hard for America's independence from Britain. America had to stand on its own as that shining city on the hill." She further stated, "Jesus spoke of a place that he called the "City on the Hill" in his famous parable of Salt and Light in the Sermon on the Mount. The Founding Fathers believed that America was this city. In the parable, Jesus said that all eyes will be on this city to set the example of how to live a righteous life. This city was to be a beacon of light for the entire world."

I said, "This lines up perfectly with what the Watchers had asked for on the stone tablet that details the Secret of Eden."

We moved to the other contents in the box. There were seemingly dozens of letters. We both decided to try not to hold them with our hands. We believe that we are staring at history. These items should be on display somewhere for all Americans to see. There were numerous letters from Benjamin Franklin, George Washington, Thomas Jefferson, John Adams, and Alexander Hamilton. They were all relatively mundane. There was nothing new or explosive in any of these letters. Instead, they discussed the day's events or, most likely, how each other's families were doing.

Jane said, "There has to be more. Maybe there is a stash of letters somewhere where they discuss the Revolution.

I said, "No. These are the letters that detail the founding of America. You just need to know how to read them." I went on to tell Jane that I had several Dreams where Mr. Franklin taught Jeremiah how to communicate using secret codes. These letters somehow also include a cipher. One common way that Mr. Franklin taught Jeremiah was to have a hidden sequence of numbers with each letter. The numbers would then refer to a third document. For example, let's say you are given the numbers 2, 56, 38, & 42. You would go to the third document and select the word corresponding to the number. For example, the number 2 would correspond to the second word in the cipher document. They had many different coding methods. This was a common but simple one. For most of the early days of the Revolutionary War, Benjamin Franklin was in France. These letters were the only way he could get word back to the other Founding Fathers about what was going on with the negotiations with France. Mr.

Franklin was a student of the masters of secret coding in Europe. One such master was a British Nobleman named Sir Francis Bacon. Mr. Bacon was often involved in endeavors that were in opposition to the Crown. He learned many different ways of sending messages. Many times he used codes such as these. Other times there were hidden messages in the artwork."

Jane sat in stunned silence. She finally spoke, "How do you know this. I don't recall seeing this kind of detail in the Jeremiah Briggs Dreams notes. I know you certainly didn't learn this in school. So where does this knowledge come from?"

"I am not sure. I just somehow seem to know these things. Maybe there are still new Dreams that are yet to come." I said. We both sat quietly, reading the letters.

One by one, the others began to join us. With each new person, I had to share how I came up with the word ARCADIA. Everyone sat in quiet astonishment, and Jane and I showed them the Letters from these famous Founding Fathers. It wasn't easy to glean anything of consequence from these letters. That is true for all the letters except those from Alexander Hamilton. These pre-date the Revolutionary War and are very playful. They sound more like two best friends sharing funny personal stories. Some were discussing Jeremiah's upcoming Wedding. Evidently, Mr. Hamilton served as Jeremiah's Best Man. One detailed how the men would have one last night of "Drink and Song," as Mr. Hamilton put it.

My Aunt Andrea said, "These letters are a national treasure. Should we be telling anyone that we have uncovered them?"

Jane said, "Someday, for now, this story is not yet finished. Nate has a historic journey in front of him. We must let this story ride out first. As we have learned from Nate's Dreams, there are always adversaries who look to stop the Guardians." Not everyone in the group understood the term, Guardians.

I told Jane, "Why don't we let Grandma and Aunt Andrea read the stories." We agreed, and Jane passed the copies of the stories to my aunt. Jane thankfully had written another copy of the stories that she left back in Michigan.

After the group finished breakfast, my grandmother and aunt went to freshen up. I said to my father, "I still want to visit the Compound."

He said, "I am not sure if there will be anything left to see, but you are on a mission that is beyond my comprehension. I will get you to wherever you need to go." He went on to say, "Why don't you, Jane, and Jonathon go explore what there is to see in Hanover. It is a pretty little town with its own history. I would like to speak alone with my mother and sister. We will plan on leaving for the Compound tomorrow. Perhaps, while you are out, you could stop by the train station and see when the train heading to Binghamton departs. We will hire a carriage from Binghamton to take us to the Compound."

CHAPTER 13

ANOTHER SEER

THE FOLLOWING MORNING we said our goodbyes at around eight o'clock. The train was scheduled to depart at eight-thirty. Jonathon had already purchased our tickets, so all that we had to do was show up, stow our luggage, and climb aboard. The train ride was scheduled to take roughly three hours. It's not that Binghamton was that far, but there were numerous stops along the way. Namely, there was a twenty-five-minute stop in Harrisburg. Once we arrived in Harrisburg, Jane noticed an open-air market right next to the train station. I went with her and Jonathon to buy some snacks for the ride. They had everything from jerky to apple pie. We loaded up enough for all of us to have a feast on the rest of the ride. We purchased enough jerky to last us the entire day and then some. We didn't know what awaited us at the Compound. It was doubtful that there would be any food nearby. The plan was to get there as soon as possible, spend a few hours there, and then go back to Binghamton, where we would stay at an Inn.

While on the ride, Jane asked our father, "Did you speak to Grandma and Aunt Andrea about moving to Michigan?"

He said, "Yes. They want to think about it. I told them that if they would like to move, it needs to happen before school starts again in September. I will need to have the boys assist with the move. I told them they could stay in the guest cabin for starters." The guest cabin was an existing cabin that was on the farm when my parents first moved there. Mr. Hunter thought it had been someone's hunting cabin. My parents lived there for the first year while my father and Mr. Hunter built our farmhouse. It was small for a family but would be adequate for the two of them. They could stay there if they wished, build something bigger, or move to Birmingham, where everything was within walking distance. He further said, "I believe Andrea would like to make the move. It gives her a fresh start in a new place. Birmingham is an exciting place to be because of all the transplants still arriving from the east coast. On the other hand, my mother is firmly entrenched in Hanover. This is where she and my father have made their home since the fire. She will need some convincing."

As the train crossed into southern New York State, my father explained that the train was going to pass right by the Compound. At least within a half-mile. During the times when Jeremiah lived here, there were no trains. By the time train tracks were being installed everywhere, the Compound no longer had enough activity to warrant a train stop. My father was looking out of the window and said here it comes. I looked up and could see the remains of a former town in the distance. Then I saw the sign. It read, "Home of the Adams Trading Company." I immediately felt weak-kneed.

Memories of the past flooded my mind. Images of Hannah were before me. I remember her like it was yesterday. I also could see the Compound in its heyday with a flurry of activity. I could see the building with the letter G on it. Then I came back to the present. Will any of this still be there? I asked myself. Will it be as I remember? Then my father said something that neither

Jane nor I had considered. He said, "While we are here, we need to visit the cemetery to visit your great grandparent's gravesites. Tears immediately began streaming down Jane's cheeks. This revelation of the cemetery had caught both of us off guard. Neither of us was ready for this. For both of us, Jeremiah and Hannah were alive. I knew I was intimately connected to this story, but Jane's reaction caught me off guard. As we were stepping off the train, Jonathon and our father had gone ahead to gather our belongings. Jane said, "Please forgive me for not telling you earlier, but for the past few months, I have been having Dreams also. My Dreams are not through Jeremiah, but seem to be through the Mary from the Templars Dreams, Agatha from the Sinclair Dreams, and Maria from the Dreams regarding our great grandparents. I am dreaming of the Seers."

I said, "Somehow, I knew that you and I were always connected. It was always beyond being brother and sister. There is nothing that you need to apologize for. I didn't ask for any of this either. Somehow, we were both chosen for this life."

CHAPTER 14

THE COMPOUND

SHORTLY THEREAFTER, WE arrived in Binghamton. My father went to arrange for a carriage to take us to the Compound. He returned after a few minutes. He said, "I had to explain where the Compound was to this young fellow. He questioned me as to why I wanted to go there. He said that there is a wooden fence around what used to be the town. In order for us to walk around the Compound, we will have to get permission from the person who owns the ranch on the far end of the Compound. I explained that I grew up there and I wanted to show my children my childhood home. Something was odd about this conversation. The Adams Estate still owns the Compound, as far as I know. We are part of the extended Adams Family. Therefore, I have every right to visit whenever I want."

We climbed aboard the carriage. The Compound was about a thirty-minute ride. I swear that I know every inch of this trail. I don't think that I even needed a guide. Finally, we arrived at a gate. Nearby was a worker who was cutting up a fallen tree. Our driver and this man seemed to know each other. He jumped on his horse and rode back to the ranch to get the ranch owner. After roughly twenty minutes, we could see a horse-drawn wagon heading our way. As the wagon got closer, I could see a smile come over my father's face.

When the carriage finally arrived, my father said, "Thomas, is that you?"

The man smiled back and said, "Yes, Andrew, it's me." My father introduced us to his childhood friend Thomas Wright. They hadn't seen each other in thirty years. They used to play together as children.

Thomas said, "It is so nice to see someone from the old days. What brings you here?"

My father answered, "My children are studying our roots and wanted to see the fabled Compound."

Thomas said, "I apologize. There isn't much to see since the fire swept through here. That was such an awful thing. I still think it was intentional. As you can see, the nearby forests went untouched by the fire. It only burned the structures. I don't know how many fires you have been around, but they usually don't burn selectively. They usually burn everything in their path."

My father said, "I thought your family left at the same time my parents moved to Hanover?"

Thomas said, "Your father offered my father a deal to manage the ranch, and we never left. The Adams still own everything here at the Compound, but I manage it." He also said, "I assume that you met my nephew Matthew. He transported you here."

Matthew said, "I'm sorry for asking so many questions, but occasionally we have a treasure hunter show up claiming that a vast treasure is buried here. Of course, we just laugh it off. I usually explain that my family has been here for over a hundred years. So if there were a treasure here, we would have dug it up long ago."

My father said, "No problem. This place has always held a mystery for some people. I have never looked back until my children inquired about the Compound."

"Spend as much time as you like, then come up to the ranch house. Dolores will make us supper. It is a special occasion when we have company. Especially when it's an old friend." Thomas said.

"Well, we planned on staying in town tonight, so we probably need to head back in a few hours." My father said.

Thomas said, "Nonsense, you will be our guest here tonight. We have the vacant guest house that hasn't been used in almost a year."

My father looked at Jane and me and said, "Thank you, we will accept your invitation."

We then parted company with Thomas and began to walk around. First, we ventured over to the area that used to be the Town Square.

I said, "I remember all of this. The Adams Company offices were to my right. The blacksmith and tannery were down the way on our left. A row of homes was behind us, including what was a majestic country house that was owned by Mr. Samuel Adams."

My father said, "I think you have better memories of this place than I do. The original home of Jeremiah and Hannah was just down past the Adams home. Across from Jeremiah and Hannah's original home was the Tavern which also had six rooms on the second floor that were reserved for special guests. A little farther down was the only structure that remained standing—the building with the G on it. As I got older, I learned that this building had a name. It was called the Hall of the Freemasons."

As we approached the Freemason's Hall, we noticed that the windows were broken out and boarded up, and the door was sealed shut. We walked around the building and realized that all entrances and windows were boarded up. Jonathon noticed that the cellar entrance was not locked. We opened it and walked in. The entrance to the building from the cellar was locked. We pushed on the door, and the wood door gave way. I hope Thomas wouldn't mind, but we were going to have a look around.

After all, as he said, this was still owned by the Adams Estate. We were part of the Adams Family. He was not. As we made our way around the building, I was having flashbacks about the meetings that took place between the Founding Fathers. The founding of America took place here, not in Philadelphia. No one outside this small group of men could know of this place. The British would have destroyed it instantly if they had ever become aware of it. I had a significant premonition that a second basement was on the far side of the building. The Secret of Eden was nearby. I am not sure where, but I sense that it is close. This journey here to the Compound was not about discovering my roots. It was about officially setting out on my journey to be a Guardian of the Secret of Eden.

THE CEMETERY

WE CONTINUED TO walk around the Freemason's Hall. To think that the Founding Fathers also walked these same floors was overwhelming. Our tour was about finished when I discovered a movable wall. Jonathon and I pushed against it with all of our weight. It finally began to move. The hardware that the movable wall rested on was well rusted and dilapidated. We decided to venture down what appeared to be a hallway. There were steps at the end of the hall. They led down to another door that seemingly was locked but gave way as Jonathon put his shoulder into it. It led to an underground tunnel. I said, "I believe this was an escape tunnel underneath the Freemason Hall. The tunnel probably led out into the woods where the escapees could make a run for it. The tunnel probably included a small armory so the men could arm themselves on the way out. Jonathon and I agreed that we would like to return with lanterns and venture further into the tunnel. I was reasonably confident that the treasure was not in this tunnel. I'm sure that it was better hidden than just being somewhere within this tunnel.

We backtracked and found our way back to the cellar door and exited the building. I kept thinking to myself, "If these walls could talk, what a wonderful tale they would tell." Jonathon lagged behind because he was trying to secure the cellar door.

Jane was waiting outside for us. I took the opportunity to speak with her. I said, "I had a very strong premonition that the treasure is still in there. It was somewhere near that second basement that we visited. I believe it is safe for now, and we shouldn't look any further." As Jonathon exited the building, the carriage driver Matthew appeared.

Matthew said, "I'm sorry, but this building is off-limits. We don't feel that its structural integrity is capable of carrying much weight."

Jonathon said, "This building was made of stone and steel. It could last through many direct hits from a cannonball."

Matthew said, "Sorry, those are my orders."

I said, "Matthew, I appreciate your concern, but as you heard, my family is one of the owners of this former community. We don't need anyone's permission to visit and walk wherever we desire. Also, orders from who?" I felt that I needed to take a harsher tone with Matthew. He said nothing. There was something that was off about him since we first met. He turned and walked away. We walked along and joined up with my father, as he stood on the site of his former home. It was next door to what used to be his grandparent's original home. I could see from his facial expression that being at the sight of his childhood home caused him heartache. We continued down the road until there was a split.

My father said, "The mill was to the left, and the farms and the ranch were to the right." We knew which way we needed to go. I could see the headstones directly ahead. The cemetery was straight ahead. My father didn't need to say anything. As we entered the cemetery, somehow, I knew where to go. Back in the corner, there was a beautiful spot. I saw two crosses. They said:

HANNAH ADAMS BRIGGS
Born June 21, 1756
Died: May 28, 1821

JEREMIAH MICHAEL BRIGGS
Born: August 1, 1753
Died: May 28, 1821

To see this was shocking yet somehow very peaceful. I had never realized that they both died on the same day. Jonathon asked my father, "Were they in some kind of accident?" But, of course, I already knew the answer.

My father said, "I was only a young boy, but the way I remember it was that my grandmother died in the morning from what seemed like some sort of influenza that had ravaged the Compound. It was said that my grandfather died from a stroke later in the day."

This was just how our grandmother had described Jeremiah and Hannah's love affair. He did not want to go on without her. We sat and stared for several minutes. Not to ruin a great love story, but I remember Dreams where my great grandfather was injured during the War. I wondered if he suffered from significant health issues from those injuries. Usually, I would be saying a prayer for the soul of the departed. But, in this case, I thought to myself, "Wouldn't that be rather self-serving."

Behind the crosses, a magnolia tree was giving off the most beautiful essence. Jane could smell the essence also. None of the others could. Jane said, "That fragrance is beautiful, but I don't think it is magnolia. I'm not sure what it is, but it is not easily forgettable." Jane and I exchanged a glance. Could this be the essence that Ian smelled before his death? Or the same question about Jacques? Both men smelled this fragrance shortly before their deaths. It meant that their soulmate was there waiting for them.

I finally said, "The essence is Lavender." Jane just stared at me with a bewildered look. I said, "If you recall the Dream from the Templar story where Jacques had the realization regarding the beautiful fragrance. It seems that back in Noah's day, there was a time when Tytea was very ill, and Peleg was terrified that her death was near. As they had done almost daily, they walked to the Great River. The Great Flood spawned all kinds of new growth near the Great River. These plants were not known to be in this region before the Great Flood. There was one plant in particular that always drew Tytea to it. Its fragrance was unforgettable. It was a soft purple color, and one sniff of the fragrance had a calming effect over Peleg and Tytea. The fragrance, combined with the flowing water, would soothe any ailment. That is why Peleg still brought Tytea to the banks of the Great River daily. He was hoping for a miracle. In the Dream, Tytea turned to Peleg and said, "My days here in this lifetime are drawing to a close, but as the Watcher told us, we will be together for eternity. This fragrance will be part of my soul going forward. You will know I am with you whenever you smell the purple flower." The plant was known as Lavender."

As we were leaving the cemetery, Jane looked to her right at a tombstone and seemed as if she was going to faint. She saw the following:

MARIA ALPOLISI
Born: unknown
Died: May 29, 1821

I said, "Maria died the day after Jeremiah and Hannah passed."

Jane seemed unusually startled by this site. Then it dawned on me. I now know what Jane's role is in the drama unfolding right before us.

We finally left the cemetery. Jane gathered herself. Finally, Jane asked my father, "How well do you know Thomas? His Nephew Matthew seems a little off. He didn't like that Nate and

Jonathon entered the Freemason's Hall."

My father said, "I knew Thomas as a young boy. We were both born and raised here and knew of the Compound's history. Most of us escaped this place. But Thomas did not."

I finally spoke up, "I think that they know that something of great value is hidden in that building. They may have chosen to stay here because of this knowledge. From what Jane and I have uncovered about the treasure, the Guardians have always gone to great lengths to hide and protect it. If it is like several of its other hiding spots, treasure hunters who get near it and don't have the final clues will be brutally dealt with. It could be poison arrows. It could be weights falling and crushing the treasure hunters. I believe the treasure is safe for now."

My father said, "I don't think we should even bring up the Freemason Hall or the treasure during supper tonight. Let's be courteous to our host tonight and start to make our way back to Michigan tomorrow."

CHAPTER 16

THE RANCH

W HEN WE ARRIVED at the Ranch, I was delighted to find a beautiful horse ranch with roughly twenty horses ranging from young colts to old workhorses. I talked at length with Thomas about his horses. Then, finally, I asked him, "How do you manage all of this?"

He said, "It has become very difficult. Every year the work gets more challenging. At some point, I will probably have to give up the Ranch. My nephew doesn't seem to have the drive to manage a ranch of this magnitude. He wants to get rich quick. Unfortunately, as of right now, he is all I have left. Dolores and I never had any children. Matthew is my sister's son. She passed when the boy was five. He has been with us ever since. He is very passionate about the history of the Compound. He seems to believe the treasure hunters. He thinks that there is something valuable hidden in that building.

We walked to the ranch house. My father stunned Jane and me when he said, "Jeremiah and Hannah built the Ranch House.

This was their home." It was like somehow I already knew that. The memories of the Ranch House being built began to flood my thoughts. Those were very happy times for Jeremiah and Hannah.

We enjoyed a lovely meal of venison and creamy potatoes. The conversation was mainly centered on boyhood stories of the Compound. Most of them were very light-hearted. Dolores commented," It is so nice to have visitors from the past. Please come back with Sarah next time. I would love to see her again. She and I were schoolmates together. As we all did, we made the best of our life here."

After supper, we thanked our hosts and retired to the guest house. We arrived there, and all the beds were already made and waiting for us. We made a fire and rehashed the day's events. We all agreed that the day pulled at all of our heartstrings. Everything from seeing what was left of the Town's Square to the Freemason's Hall to the Cemetery. I said, "It was great to see what is here and try to imagine what it must have been like."

The conversation finally made its way to the treasure. I said, "Thomas mentioned that he could no longer handle the Ranch. So where does that leave us and the treasure? I see two possible choices in front of us. We take over the Ranch, or we move the treasure."

There was a long pause, and then Jonathon finally spoke. He said. "This Ranch has great value. There is more than enough land for grazing and expansion. Perhaps, we may collectively want to take over this Ranch. We could man the Ranch with trusted ranch hands and then rebuild and repurpose the Freemason Hall."

I said, "That still leaves us with Matthew. However, there may be others that are aware of the treasure."

As always, my father was the voice of reason. He said, "This treasure has survived here for nearly 100 years. As Nate explained, any treasure hunter who gets near the treasure must know the secret clues, or they will meet their demise. I think that we should not do anything rash. Let's travel home and come up with a plan."

I knew that the most secure solution was to move the treasure to a place where only the chosen few would know of its location. Sneaking into the Compound and unearthing this treasure would be a tall order. But maybe to Jonathon's point, it would be easier if we lived here on this land.

We all ventured off to bed. Once again, I had nightmares about the cataclysmic war that was about to unfold in America. Would the Compound be engulfed in this war? Would our land in Michigan be involved? This thought terrified me.

The next morning we all awoke just after sunrise. We wanted to get an early start on our journey home. Thomas said that he would take us to Binghamton. We loaded up our belongings which included the lockable chest that was the home to my great grandfather's Diary. I so looked forward to reading his Diary. Even though I experienced his life through my Dreams, I want to see his written word. Would he recollect situations different than I had? Some of my most memorable Dreams are of his courtship of Hannah. Would he describe in detail the "Love at first sight" relationship that I witnessed? I understood what no one else could even begin to understand. Hannah was both Clara from the Henry Sinclair Dreams and she was the mystery woman from Jacques Dreams in the Templar Story. When would Hannah, or whatever her name is in this current life, enter into my story? This is a very exciting thought. I thought to myself, I better not expect this woman to appear out of nowhere. I need to let everything happen naturally.

We arrived at the Binghamton Train Station. We had roughly one hour before our train was ready to depart. We said our goodbyes to Thomas and thanked him for his hospitality. My father exchanged addresses with Thomas. If we decide to take over the Ranch, at least we will know how to reach him.

CHAPTER 17

BACK IN MICHIGAN

W E ARRIVED BACK in Michigan a week ago. My brothers had done a good job caring for the horses while I was away. After I said hello to my mother and siblings, I rushed to the barn to say hello to Goldie. He was so excited to see me. I promised him that we would go for a long ride the very next day. Before we arrived, Jane and I discussed the Diary. Since I had to catch up on my chores, we agreed to have her read the Diary first. We planned on seeing each other tonight because it was my brother Abraham's birthday.

Jane and Jonathon arrived early for the birthday celebration. She said that we needed to talk. So we walked off to the barn, where we were out of earshot of anyone, and she told me about the Diary.

She said, "It tells the complete story of Hannah, the treasure, and the Founding of America. This could be turned into a classic novel. Many facts about the Founding Fathers and the Revolutionary War are different from what we have been told in the history books. Many seemingly coincidental actions changed the outcome of the war. It affirms my belief that America was chosen by God. Only God could have managed to make the day's events go the Patriot's way. The Diary is a love story about Jeremiah's and Hannah's courtship, marriage, and family. Every historical situation is detailed as though he was telling Hannah the story. There are secret codes between Jeremiah and Benjamin Franklin. Jeremiah was the messenger between Ben Franklin and George Washington. He managed to keep them informed on everything that was happening from Paris to Boston to Philadelphia and beyond. He also speaks at length about the treasure. The Diary also shows that Benjamin Franklin spent a substantial amount of time with Hannah, Jeremiah, and Alexander Hamilton, or Alex as they referred to him. He taught them the ways of the Freemasons. Both Jeremiah and Alex subsequently joined the Freemasons and quickly rose through the ranks. Jeremiah spent several years working directly for General Washington during the war and helped steer the great General through many difficult decisions. The communications that Mr. Franklin had secured the pledge from the French King to join the war effort was passed on to General Washington by Jeremiah. This was what turned the war in favor of the Patriots. Jeremiah decoded Mr. Franklin's message and delivered it to General Washington. The Diary also tells the story of Jeremiah and Hannah after the war and how his wounds scarred him and probably shortened his life. It shows that both Jeremiah and Hannah were true American heroes.

I wasn't shocked by anything Jane had said. My Dreams told a similar story. She asked me to stop by her house tomorrow to pick up the Diary. The plan was for me to read it and compare it to the notes from my Dreams. We would then sit down and write the complete story. We would fill in any missing details by consulting various history books. We would have to be careful not to blindly trust anything we read in history books. After we completed the story, we planned to have another meeting with Felicia to discuss our findings.

I was ready to go and join Abraham's Birthday party when she said, "There is one other matter. As I told you on the train ride from Hanover to Binghamton, I have been having Dreams myself." She went on. "I believe I am seeing things through the Seer's eyes."

I said, «Welcome to the club. You will find out that this can be a burden at times. Now, I will tell you what a wise person once told me. Write everything down.»

She said, "My own words are returning to haunt me." We both laughed.

CHAPTER 18

THE DIARY

THE FOLLOWING MORNING Rachel and I decided to go on another long ride. This time we would head towards Pontiac. This was roughly five miles each way. I wasn't sure who was more excited, Goldie or Rachel. It was a beautiful late June morning. I was sure to take lunch money because we would be gone for most of the day. I had told Jane that we would stop by her house later in the day to pick up the Diary.

After our ride, we stopped by Jane's to pick up the Diary.

She handed me the Diary and said, "We are receiving a very loud and clear message. We need to figure out what we are going to do with the treasure. I want to talk it over with Jonathon."

I said, "Let's talk it over with Mom and Dad as well."

She then handed me the Diary, which I stowed in my satchel. I told Goldie we needed a smooth ride back to the farm. Somehow, he seemed to understand me. The ride home was very slow and steady.

Over the next week, I read the Diary in its entirety. Even

though I knew most of it already from my Dreams, to read Jeremiah's handwriting was astonishing. Jane and I met several more times to review the Letters. They were priceless. The letters to and from Benjamin Franklin and George Washington were collectors' items and probably should be on display somewhere.

For the remainder of the summer, Jane and I wrote the story of our great grandparents, which was a compilation of my Dreams, recorded history, and, most notably, my great grandfather's Diary.

When we finally finished the story, we expected tales of glory, first-hand knowledge of historic battles, and, of course, a classic treasure hunt. But that was not what jumped off of the pages at us. Instead, the stories of the Founding Fathers, the Patriots winning the Revolutionary War, and even the Secret of Eden were merely a backdrop for the centuries-old love story between our great grandparents, Hannah and Jeremiah Briggs.

CHAPTER 19

THE STORY OF JEREMIAH MICHAEL BRIGGS

HE FOLLOWING IS from my great grandfather's Diary, his notes and letters, and of course, from my Dreams, which corroborate the Diary. I have written this story in the first person because, due to my Dreams, I feel that I was there for most of it:

My name is Jeremiah Michael Briggs. I immigrated to the American Colonies in 1771. The promise of the New World was too much for me to pass up. When the Europeans first started to immigrate to the Colonies, the promise of the New World was very attractive. The first to arrive quickly realized that there were many hurdles. The first obstacle was the cost of passage. Many families wanted to make the journey, but the costs of transporting your family and their possessions put the dream out of reach. On average, the cost for an adult was five pounds sterling, a child over twelve was half price, under twelve was free, a horse was ten pounds sterling, and one ton of your possessions was three pounds sterling. A typical British laborer would make less than twenty-five pounds sterling per year. Immigration was only for the wealthy. Many wealthy Europeans moved to the Colonies in the early 17th Century. One of the most prominent settlements was Jamestown in the Colony of Virginia. Many early settlers in Jamestown soon discovered that even though the land was vast and the soil was fertile, there were not enough people to work the farms.

Like many times through history, necessity spurned new ideas. The wealthy landowners needed to find people to tend to their needs, or the venture would fail. The Indian Tribes were initially thought to be the answer to the workforce problem. However, many conflicts ensued because the Indian Tribes felt the land had been theirs for many generations. While the Indians would not help with the farming workforce issue, they offered the new settlers a lucrative opportunity—this involved fur trading. The beaver and deer pelts were sold to the settlers, who sold them to their partners back in Europe. The fur-trading marketplace extended through the Colonies and into the Hudson Bay Territory in Canada. However, the lucrative fur trading business in Canada had one big downfall; the Canadian Territory was owned by France. France and England had been fighting for years over this land and the goods produced on this land.

For the time being, the relationship with the various Indian Tribes was stable. This still left the farming workforce problem unsolved. As I mentioned earlier, when a necessity arises, industrious people find solutions. The answer was a concept known as Indentured Servitude. This concept involved a loan in return for service. In this case, the wealthy landowners offered to pay for passage, housing, and food in return for a commitment to work for the landowner for anywhere from 3 to 7 years. The laborer was often promised 25 acres of land or more at the conclusion of the agreement. The downside for the workers was that this commitment came with a very rigid set of rules. Any infraction such as breaking the law, or running away resulted in additional time being added to the contract. This option was desirable for many unemployed workers back in England, but not all.

The times were very tough in 18th century England. The 30 Years War caused significant unemployment and poverty throughout Europe. This option of committing to a servitude contract was attractive for many. Many young men had previously committed to going into military service, but were either killed in battle or left destitute at the end of their military commitment. The offer of moving to the Colonies had a tremendous upside as compared to the other options. This practice of Indentured Servitude was very successful, especially in the Northern Colonies. Unfortunately, many Landowners in the Southern Colonies discovered that they could have continuous servitude by purchasing slaves. The slaves provided a workforce indefinitely for little cost, and no promises for land or other assets were needed. This practice was the scourge of the Colonies.

CHAPTER 20

THE OPPORTUNITY

WAS LIKE MANY British young men of the time. I was 18 and held no prospects for gainful employment. My two older brothers, Abraham Jr., and Lemuel, were killed during one of the many battles on behalf of the House of Hanoverian, otherwise known as King George I, II, and III. I was not about to enlist when I wasn't even sure what the cause was which we were fighting for. My mother, Ellen, died while giving birth to me in 1753. My father, Abraham Sr., had passed from a heart condition when I was 12. My brothers had raised me after that. My neighbor, Mrs. Crabtree, took it upon herself to teach my brothers and me how to read and write. This would prove to be my most valuable asset.

I was living in Southampton, England. My days were spent searching for day labor jobs. This was very difficult. I was living day to day. There were days when I barely had anything to eat. I was way too proud to beg for money. I wanted to earn it the proper way. While reviewing the job posting board, I noticed a paper describing an opportunity to move to the American Colonies for a long-term opportunity. I did not have anything to write on, so I memorized the name and address of the person looking for workers. Later that day, after having no success finding work, I decided to at least find out more details about the work in the Colonies. I went to the office of the Adams Trading Company and asked a worker who I could speak to regarding the notice. An older woman came forth and described the opportunity. She said, "Mr. Adams of the Massachusetts Colony would pay for his passage, room, board, and 10 pounds sterling per year for your services. In return, Mr. Adams would require you to sign a five-year contract. If the prospective worker does as they were told and follows all of the rules, there would be an option for 25 or more acres of land for free." She further said, "I will warn you that Mr. Adams is a Puritan and is looking for people who are hard-working and obedient to the rules of the Good Book. The work will be difficult, but the end result could be a great opportunity." I thanked the woman and told her that I needed to think about it.

While waiting for scraps that would usually be fed to the dogs at the back door of a tavern, I began to review my options. I thought the opportunity sounded too good to be true. But, on the other hand, I was currently fending off dogs for food. What did I have to lose? It was then that I made the decision that would change my life forever. The following day I returned to the office of Adams Trading and signed the agreement. Two days later, on June 15, 1771, I, Jeremiah Briggs, formerly homeless and destitute, was gainfully employed and on a ship headed to the New World.

Two years after my arrival in America, I found myself working for both Mr. Samuel Adams and Mr. Peter Adams. Mr. Peter Adams was the brother of John Adams, who was a prominent statesman from Quincy, Massachusetts. Samuel was their cousin. Peter and Samuel co-owned a large plantation in the New York Colony.

The Compound, as they called it, was on the Susquehanna River. This location provided the opportunity to ship lumber, fur, and cured meat to the rest of the Colonies and Europe. The Compound was more of its own city rather than just a plantation. It had its own Printing Company, Trading Post, Blacksmith, Tannery, Grist Mill, Iron Mill, Saw Mill, Glassworks, Arsenal, Horse Ranch, Twenty acres of Tillable Land, and last but not least, a Tavern. The workers not under an indentured servitude contract had the option of on-site housing in one of the large homes built for the workers. At the south end of the Compound, there was a building shrouded in mystery. It had no visible name on it. Just the letter capital G surrounded by a square and compass. Very few people ever entered this building. Meetings held there usually involved out-of-town guests and members of the Adams Family. The one time I asked about the building, I was very sternly told to tend to my own affairs.

Peter Adams was rarely at the Compound, while his partner Samuel was there at least once a month. Peter spent most of his time at the family estate in Braintree in the Colony of Massachusetts. I reported directly to Mr. Gordon Smith. Mr. Smith was a nephew of Samuel Adams. After two years of my servitude agreement, I was promoted to leader of the workers. I would plan the daily schedules and ensure all required supplies were where they needed to be. When the person in charge of all the milling operations, Jonathon Pierce, took ill and subsequently died, I took over his duties as well. Even though I never had formal training on technical matters, I quickly showed that I had a very intuitive mind. One by one, I restructured all of the mills so that the material flow made sense. The productivity of the mills increased at least fifty percent due to my advances. Gordon Smith began to take notice. Most men would have been happy that the operation was more efficient and thus more profitable. Unfortunately, Gordon was not one of these men. He resented the fact that an English servitude worker was outshining everyone at the Compound, including himself.

CHAPTER 21

THE ACCIDENT

IT WAS A cold October morning, and Henry Walker was getting prepared to go to his loading job at the Saw Mill. Henry, his wife, Beatrice, and their two small children lived just outside the Compound. Henry's mother, Ingrid, had recently joined his family at the Compound. Henry had completed his Servitude Agreement. The Compound Manager, Gordon Smith, made the acreage offer to all workers after they had successfully completed their contract. Henry opted for a cash bonus instead that would allow him to build himself a small house and also provide enough money to pay for his mother's passage from London.

Today was a huge day at the Saw Mill. The pressure was on. The Mill had been down for two days while the blacksmith and other metalworkers were repairing the main blade shaft. Henry had noticed the previous week that the shaft was out of balance and would soon break. Henry knew all of the inner workings of this Mill. He has worked at this Mill since he arrived ten years ago. He knew if the blade broke free, it would shoot across the

Mill, destroying anything in its path. Henry also knew that the Mill had to make up for the lost time. There was no room for error today. He knew that after the lumber was cut and processed, it was loaded onto a barge where it was transported perilously down the Susquehanna River. The journey down the river would take one week under normal conditions. The water level was lower this year due to a late summer drought. When the water level was too low, workers would have to assist the movement. They would have to use setting poles to assist with navigation. Great care had to be taken to ensure the barge was never grounded. With the weight of the wood and the barge, it was a certain disaster if they ever struck ground. When you couple this with the cold and windy late October weather, you were asking for trouble. Also, the large barges waiting for our lumber were making their last trip of the year. The water in the Chesapeake Bay becomes too rough in November. Three years earlier, an entire barge was lost due to rough seas.

I had overseen the rework and installation of the new shaft on the previous night. Henry tested the blade and shaft with one log. While the saw was unassembled, I had the Metalsmith sharpen the blade. The blade was now ready to cut through the thickest wood that anyone could find in New York. The saw worked perfectly. The wobble in the shaft was gone. It was ready for this last load of lumber.

As the workers reported for the day, Henry noticed that George Smith was not there. George was the younger brother of the Compound leader, Gordon. George was a very nervous man, and Henry assumed that he just couldn't handle the pressure that was expected today. They were used to working without George because he tended to miss many days. Everyone knew he could get away with it because he was the boss's brother. No one talked about it, but George was a heavy drinker. Drinking by the employees was heavily frowned upon. The tavern was mainly for the management and their guests. Only a few people knew that George and Gordon had their own still for making homemade spirits and the like, that was located in a very well hidden hut at the far reaches of the Compound. Many had seen both Gordon and George excessively drunk on many occasions. Everyone looked the other way because Gordon was an Adams.

The shift was ready to start. The saw speed was controlled by a cam system. The smallest cam would rotate the saw at the slowest speed. I engaged the smallest cam, and the blade began to rotate. If the shaft had a problem, it would not be noticed until the high-speed cam was engaged. The first log was positioned on the table and readied to be moved towards the blade. I reached for the lever to engage the high-speed cam. As the cam was engaged, I heard a snap, and the saw blade immediately flew out of its holster. The blade hit Henry in the chest, and blood splattered everywhere. I immediately disengaged the cam. I then ran over to Henry, where I saw a gaping wound in Henry's chest. Blood was coming out of his mouth. I knelt near Henry's face. Henry's last words were, "Please tell my wife and children that I love them."

At that instant, Gordon walked into the Mill. He saw what had taken place. He began screaming at me. He blamed me for this accident. He noted that I was the person responsible for the repair the night before. He told everyone to return to their homes. After everyone left except for Gordon and me. We began screaming at each other. I was certain that Henry had replaced the shaft. I walked away from Gordon. I could smell the whiskey on his breath. My thoughts quickly returned to Henry and how his family would be heartbroken. Henry was a great worker and a better father and husband. How could this have happened? As I began to leave the Mill, something caught my eye. I turned, and much to my surprise and shock, the broken shaft we had replaced the night before had been reinstalled. I was sure that Henry had changed the shaft. We even tested it. It was time to leave and travel to Henry's house to tell his family the tragic news.

CHAPTER 22

THE TRUTH

L ATER THAT DAY, I sat waiting for Mr. Samuel Adams to arrive at the Compound. He would no doubt want to know what had happened to poor Henry. I couldn't help but wonder if I was to lose this job would I be forced to go back to England. The whole situation was very troubling. I watched Henry replace the broken shaft. Somehow, the broken shaft had been reinstalled. There had to have been foul play. Since it was my word against Gordon's word, I assume that I will lose this fight. Even though I will lose, I will defend my integrity. Gordon and his brother George were not good people. They were drunk more often than not. I have nothing to hide. If I am fired from this position, I will leave with my head held high. I believe that all of the other workers liked working for me. They often said derogatory things about Gordon. I prayed that Mr. Adams was a fair man and listened to both sides of the story. I would soon find out. His carriage had just arrived.

Mr. Adams entered the office building as he usually does.

He was immediately greeted by Gordon who told him about the deadly accident at the saw mill earlier in the day. I could hear him, although quite muffled, blaming me for the accident. I could hear yelling. Mr. Adams was yelling at Gordon. Then I clearly heard him say, "I want to speak with Mr. Briggs, ALONE!" Gordon came and informed me that Mr. Adams would like to speak with me. As I stood up, Gordon was about two inches from my face. The smell of liquor and bad hygiene was overwhelming.

He said, "If you try to throw this back at me, I will have your head."

I said, "Its right here. No one has ever provided you with the very important lesson of "Don't pick a fight that you can't win."" I had already accepted the fact that I probably had lost my job, but if this drunken idiot thought he could threaten me then he was in for a major surprise.

I entered Mr. Adams's office and stood while he was filling out some paperwork. Finally, he said, "Sit down." Which I did. Then he said, "Tell me exactly what happened. I don't want you to fear any repercussions from telling me the truth." This statement told me that he suspected that Gordon's version of the story was not accurate.

I said, "Thank you, sir. We had a broken shaft on the large saw. Henry Walker, the unfortunate man who lost his life earlier today, worked together with me late into the night last night to repair the shaft. We knew that today was critical for making the last shipment of lumber down the river. The blacksmith had repaired the shaft and we cut an entire log with the repaired shaft last night without incident. The saw worked better than it has in years. We knew we were ready for today. We came in this morning and started the shift. On the first cut, the blade snapped and the blade flew and hit Mr. Walker in the chest. He died moments later. I was distraught because I knew that we had fixed the shaft. As I was leaving the scene, I decided to look at the shaft. To my shock, I realized that someone had reinstalled the broken shaft. This was not an accident."

He said, "George also works at the saw mill, correct?"

I said "Yes".

He said, "Please get him for me."

I said, "Right away, sir."

I went outside where Gordon was standing and said, "Mr. Adams would like to speak with George. Where is he?"

Gordon said, "Who do you think you are talking to?"

I said, "Someone who is about to be implicated in a murder, that's who. Now go fetch your brother or I will." I was not about to go down without a fight. I have worked too hard for this opportunity. Roughly ten minutes later, Gordon appeared with George. He appeared very drunk. Gordon was trying to coach him through what to say. The two entered Mr. Adams's office.

The next thing I heard was Mr. Adams screaming "I will speak with your brother alone." Gordon left the office and glared at me.

I said, "Your drunk idiot brother is about to rat you out. You are not very smart." He then lunged at me which I easily stepped out of the way. When he did this, the repaired shaft fell out of his pocket. Several witnesses saw this entire encounter. Gordon Smith was caught red-handed.

Mr. Adams's door finally opened and George stumbled out. I walked in and told Mr. Adams what had happened and showed him the repaired shaft that had fallen out of Gordon's pocket. He summoned Gordon and George to the office. He asked me to stay. The two brothers then entered the office and Mr. Adams said, "You aren't even smart enough to destroy the evidence. I hired the two of you as a favor to my sister. Pack up your belongings and remove yourself from the Compound immediately. Mr. Briggs, see that they are off the premises within thirty minutes and then return to my office."

I escorted the two back to their home and waited while they gathered up their possessions. After they came out of the home, I escorted them to the edge of the property and said, "If I ever see either of you again, you will find yourself at the wrong end of a musket."

I watched as the two walked down the trail that led to Binghamton. Somehow, I knew that this was not the last of Gordon. I immediately returned to Mr. Adams's office. He asked about Henry Walker's family. I told him that he had a young family and that his mother had just emigrated from England to join them.

He said, "Let's go to their home and pay respects to his widow."

We walked to the Walker home which was on the edge of the Compound.

As we arrived Mrs. Walker walked out to greet us. She was clearly distraught. Mr. Adams said, "Mrs. Walker, I am extremely sad for your loss. Your husband was a fine worker and even a better man. I will take care of the burial expenses. Also, I will continue to pay your husband's wage for five years. In addition, if you would like gainful employment, we will find a place where you can fit."

She thanked him and said, "Thank you, sir. I didn't know how we were going to make ends meet without Henry's wage. We always felt that the Adams Trading Company was a family business. Now you have proven it." We paid our final respects and returned to his office.

He said, "Jeremiah, I was ready to make a move here at the Compound. I hear wonderful things about you. I would like you to join me for supper this evening where we will discuss your new position."

I said, "Thank you, sir. I look forward to joining you."

CHAPTER 23

THE TAVERN

A S I RAN back to my quarters, I thought, what a day today has been. It started with the pressure of knowing we would need to get the last load of lumber on its way down the Susquehanna River and onto the Chesapeake Bay. I have prided myself that we have not missed a scheduled ship date for this entire year. Even when that buffoon Gordon and his idiot brother seemingly were in my way, I still managed to get things done. Now with them out of the way, I believe that I can implement all of the improvements that I had proposed. Early on, Gordon listened to my ideas. Only when it became apparent that the improvements around the Compound were not of his doing he stopped listening. Actually, there were certain instances where I would suggest something, he would say no, and then weeks later, I would notice my idea was being implemented. Of course, Gordon would take the credit. Some men would have stopped submitting ideas. I was not one of those men. I was being paid a wage, and I was going to earn it. Withholding ideas was not in my makeup. I just prayed that someday, I would be recognized for my creativity. Today was that day.

I needed to heat up some bathwater. I was beginning to smell like Gordon. Minus the whiskey breathe, of course. I had only a few minutes, but I needed to clean up. I had no idea what this new opportunity held. I have heard the term "Dress for how you want to be treated." I fully understood this, but unfortunately, I lacked proper clothing. I promised myself that on my next trip to Binghamton, I would purchase some clothing that was befitting such an occurrence as I was about to have with Mr. Adams.

A few minutes later, I gave myself a clean shave and combed my hair back into a neat ponytail. I put on the only clean outfit that I had. I hurried over to the office to meet with Mr. Adams. I was greeted by his assistant Mrs. Williams. She was always very stern with me, but tonight I noticed a subtle difference. She actually smiled when she greeted me. She said, "Mr. Adams said to tell you that he is at the Tavern. He is waiting for you." I hurried down the street and went into the Tavern. It is funny that I have lived at the Compound for years, and this is only the second time that I have stepped foot in the Tavern. The first time was to deliver a shipment of new dishes that had arrived. I always felt that this place is for the guests of Mr. Adams.

I approached the table where Mr. Adams sat with a gentleman I had seen around the Compound many times. Although come to think of it, the only time I ever saw him was when he was entering the mystery building with the G on it or on his way to this Tavern. I know that he is a visitor, but I believe that he has semi-permanent quarters set up for himself above the Tavern. The strange thing about this man was that he knew my name, but I did not know his. He would often greet me by saying, "Good day, Mr. Briggs, or How nice to see you, Mr. Briggs." He was an elderly man who always wore very unique spectacles. He had a very distinctive and prominent look. I always wanted to stop him and properly introduce myself but never did. I could tell they were close friends because of how Mr. Adams and his friend were carrying on.

Mr. Adams saw me and said, "Mr. Briggs, thank you for finding your way to me. I trust that Mrs. Williams told you of my whereabouts?"

I said, "Yes."

He said, "May I refer to you as Jeremiah. I would like to dispense with the formalities."

I said, "Of course, sir, but to me, you will always be Mr. Adams."

He laughed and said to his friend, "See, I told you. He is already off to a good start." Both men laughed. I could tell that they had had a few drinks before my arrival. Mr. Adams summoned over our server and ordered another round of drinks. I truly hoped that there was food soon. With all of the day's chaos, I had seemingly forgotten to eat. I took the bold step of asking the server to bring some bread.

Both men laughed, and Mr. Adams's guest said, "Jeremiah, you will soon learn that many of our meetings involve a healthy dose of spirits." I had never really been a drinker. Mainly because I could never afford it. Once I was settled here at the Compound, I finally had enough money to afford some libations but never had the time. The two men continued to make small talk regarding their group of associates. They referred to it as their Consortium. I played along. I laughed when they laughed. I was a perfect guest at their table, even though I didn't have the faintest idea what they were talking about. Finally, they started to direct their conversation at me.

I didn't know how to address Mr. Adam's friend, so I finally said, "Sir, I am afraid that I don't even know your name."

The guest looked at Mr. Adams and said, "I apologize for Mr. Adams's uncivil behavior." This caused Mr. Adams to smile. The guest continued, "Please allow me to introduce myself. My name is Benjamin Franklin. You may call me Ben."

I said, "Nice to meet you, Mr. Franklin." Both men found humor in my response.

CHAPTER 24

THE BEGINNING

WAS AWESTRUCK WHEN I heard the name Benjamin Franklin. This man was famous, but I didn't have the slightest idea of why he was famous. So, I will take it upon myself to learn about Mr. Franklin. Mr. Adams went on to say, "Please understand that anything we tell you is extremely confidential. You are not to speak of it to anyone outside of the men that I will introduce you to."

I said, "I fully understand, and you can count on my confidentiality."

Mr. Adams went on to say, "Ben and I are part of a larger group of men that share common business and political goals. Our business goals involve growing the Adams Trading Company to include endeavors in which my fellow Consortium members have an interest. These will include fur trading, land management, lumber trading, printing, and many other worthwhile business activities. Our common goal is, of course, profit. We aim to profit not for the usual reasons. Our profit will help us grow politically. We want to grow to the point where the Crown has no choice but to recognize us and the Colonies as worthy of their attention. Many within the Royal circles believe that the American Colonies are nothing more than a financial drain. They don't understand what potential this New World possesses. There are enough natural resources to be self-sufficient. The Crown, in effect, will not need to support the Colonies in the future. Our Consortium will grow into a collaborative venture that will get the Crown's attention. Someday, this land will be governed by its citizens."

Supper finally arrived. I thanked the Lord. We shared three rounds of drinks, and I was quickly losing my wits. The dinner was something that I have never had before. The server called it "Pot Roast." It consisted of beef that had already been removed from the bone. The beef had been slow-cooked with potatoes and carrots. I was so hungry that I would have eaten anything, but I must say that this was truly one of the best meals I have ever had.

After supper was concluded, our drinks switched from whiskey to brandy. I thought to myself, I hope that not all the meetings involved such a heavy dose of spirits. But, somehow, I knew that I was wrong. Mr. Franklin finally returned the conversation to me.

He said, "Jeremiah, I have been watching you as you have developed on this Compound. You started as a servitude employee who has worked to the leadership position of the entire Compound in a matter of several years. I don't mean to offend you, but you have come to the Colonies with nothing but hope. You literally left your family's hardships back in England. You came to this Compound looking for a chance to have a life. Had you stayed in England, you probably would have joined the military, where you would have been directly sent to a battlefront and probably would have been killed. Instead, you chose to accept the opportunity in the Colonies. Somewhere deep inside you, there was a feeling that you would never succeed at anything worthwhile in England. The system that is in place in England pre-determines your value based upon your family name. You chose to come to the Colonies because an opportunity had presented itself that had nothing to do with your family name or your place in society. You are the best example of what these Colonies offer. Through your grit, you have created your future. If anyone told you that you were not capable of doing something, you quickly proved them wrong. We recognize this virtue and wish to help you and, at the same time, help us. We believe that you and people like you will be the basis for the civilization that we intend to build here."

This was a lot to take in. I knew in my heart that everything Mr. Franklin had said was true. The problem was that this would probably be considered treason by the Crown. But, somewhere deep inside, I knew this was my destiny. When I coupled this with the very real but crazy Dreams that I have been having, I knew that God had led me to this moment.

Mr. Adam's said, "I would like you to take over the leadership position for the Compound, at least for the short term. We have a much larger opportunity that awaits you when the time is right. We are entering the winter season, where the workload lessens. Ben plans on spending time here this winter. We would like to have you learn our ways. There is no better teacher than Ben. He will conduct your training in the Freemason's Hall."

I said, "Excuse me, sir, but where is the Freemason's Hall?" They both laughed.

Mr. Adams said, "It is that building across the street with the G on it. No doubt you have been told to stay away from that place. We did this so we would not bring any unwanted attention from any busybodies. Sometimes, we also refer to it as the Masonic Temple. If you accept our offer, this will undoubtedly become your home away from home, at least for this upcoming winter."

There was a pause. All of us needed to visit the lavatory, which in this case was behind the building. When we all returned, Mr. Adams said, "How does all of this sound to you. Of course, you will receive a wage increase, and if all goes well, you will actively participate in the Consortium's Profits."

I said, "I am teeming with excitement and am ready to start this evening. I will be unable to sleep, so I may as well get to work."

Mr. Franklin said, "Spend the next two weeks wrapping up your Compound activities. I must travel to Philadelphia to meet with several of our partners. I will return after my business is complete. Also, if I get my way, there will be another joining you for the training. Mr. Adams does not currently agree with my assessment of this young man, but I think I can convince him after a few more glasses of brandy." Mr. Adams rolled his eyes.

What Mr. Franklin said next startled me. He said, "I have a very special friend here. She has gifts that I can't begin to explain. She has been watching you as well. She says that your destiny is to be a very important member of our team. I believe that you already know who I am referring to. Her name is Maria." I was shocked when I heard this, although I shouldn't be because deep down in my heart, I knew that Maria and I have a very special connection.

I thanked them for the wonderful evening and told them that I looked forward to this opportunity. I left the Tavern and began the walk home. I began to think about Maria. I visit with her nearly every day. She was more like a mother or grandmother to me. She took me in shortly after I arrived at the Compound. I knew that she was special, but I never understood why. That mystery would soon be cleared up.

Also, I wondered who this other trainee was. I was confident that it was not someone from the Compound. I haven't seen anyone who quite fits the Consortium's needs. I also thought about the leadership of the Compound. They had said that they had a more prominent position for me. That means that at some point, I must find adequate leadership to take the reins in my absence. This was a lot to consider. Then suddenly, a deeper thought came to mind. Did any of this have anything to do with the "Secret of Eden" that I have dreamt about so many times? My mind was racing, but I fell asleep as my head hit the pillow. Thanks to that last brandy that Mr. Franklin had ordered.

The following day Mr. Adams departed for Massachusetts, and Mr. Franklin headed to Philadelphia. I bid them farewell and once again thanked them for my new position. I also told Mr. Adams, "I will give the Widow Walker your regards at the Burial Ceremony today."

CHAPTER 25

Maria

ECENTLY, I HAVE had many startling things happen to me. First, the death of Henry Walker was an absolute tragedy. Telling Henry's wife and mother of his demise was one of the hardest things I have ever had to do. Next, dining with Mr. Adams and Mr. Franklin was a special thrill. Then, being named Compound Manager was a complete surprise. The thing that I think about most is that somehow, Maria is part of this story. I have never seen Mr. Adams even speak with her. From my viewpoint, she was a lonely middle-aged woman who I enjoyed spending time with. Our tradition was that she would invite me over for supper every Sunday. She was an outstanding cook and was the most insightful person that I had ever known.

On the Sunday following my meeting with Mr. Adams and Mr. Franklin, I arrived at precisely five o'clock at Maria's home. I always managed to show up with fresh bread or perhaps a bottle of red wine. I looked forward to these suppers all week. It wasn't because of the outstanding food. It was because of the spirituality that Maria possessed. She always told me that good things awaited me here at the Compound. I always thought that she was just trying to be positive, but as time passed, I began to understand that she had an insight into another realm that I could only begin to understand. This Sunday was no different.

We sat and mainly discussed the previous week's activities at the Compound. We also discussed the autumn season that was coming quickly. She expressed that the fall was her favorite time of the year. She said, "Autumn is when nature must transform itself to prepare for the upcoming winter. The trees shed their leaves. The animals secure their winter sustenance and make their nests sturdy and resilient. The transformation is significant. Most people take nature for granted because it just seems to happen. I have learned that there is a force that governs all things. Humans just seem to think that they are the only ones with forethought. Everyone should stop what they are doing in the autumn and wander to the woods." She paused briefly, then continued. "If you sit quietly and just take the transformation in, you will better understand the life force that God has created for all of us."

We sat quietly for the next several minutes. Finally, she broke the silence by stating, "This autumn will be you're greatest."

I assumed that she said this because of my new position at the Compound, but on later reflection, I knew that she was referring to something else.

As we were saying our goodbyes, she caught me off guard. She said, "Soon, you will be joined by the other Children of the Flood. This brings great joy to my heart."

Usually, I would question her on what she was referring to with the Children of the Flood statement, but I decided just to smile and say goodnight. This was because the term, Children of the Flood, has been a subject of my Dreams for as long as I can remember. The real question is, how did Maria know any of this?

CHAPTER 26

ALEX

S EVERAL WEEKS HAD passed since my meeting with Mr. Adams and Mr. Franklin. Mr. Adams was scheduled to arrive over the next two or three days. I had been very busy preparing the Compound for the upcoming winter. The first task was to return to the sawmill. Just walking in there took me back to that horrible event that had cost Mr. Walker his life. We repaired the saw and blocked the area where the blade had discharged. If a catastrophic incident happened again, the blade would hit either a woodpile or the mill wall. Sadly, it has come to this, but the tragedy has caused me to look at all of the Compound's operations. What would happen to each operation if something broke loose? I had also instructed the Blacksmith, and the other people responsible for operating the machines to evaluate each process and make a spare part for any item they feel will wear out or break. By next spring, I wanted the machines to be in tip-top shape and have a regiment of spare parts that would minimize any lost time. The lumber that was supposed to have shipped on that last barge was stored under a cover. The plan was to keep it outside where it would maintain its moisture. If the wood was placed in a heated environment, it would dry out and warp.

The next task was to cut and split enough firewood to last an entire winter for the Compound. This was a very large endeavor. There were roughly thirty buildings, with each having at least two fireplaces. They needed enough wood to keep the fires going twenty-four hours a day until next spring. The workhorses and work carriages were very busy transporting all of the firewood. Finally, I made sure that we had taken care of Henry Walker's widow. This winter would be hard enough without her husband and the father of their children. Even though Mrs. Walker was technically off of the Compound, I provided her with enough wood to last her an entire year.

The Farm had completed its harvest several weeks earlier. The hay needed to be processed for the livestock. Our hay consisted of Alfalfa, Clover, Oats, and Millet. Our soil seemed to be conducive to growing these items. The livestock seemed to flourish with this hay in their diet. Our farmers would collectively work together to collect the hay and transport it to the livestock barn. The women would spend these days canning the year's harvest. Each family was given its portion of canned vegetables and fruits.

Any repairs to houses or Compound structures needed to be completed before the winter. Carpenters and laborers were extremely busy during this time of year. I wanted the Compound to be completely winter-ready when Mr. Adams arrived. We were pretty close. After the winterization process was complete, many workers would return to their families in nearby towns such as Binghamton. Some came from as far as Scranton in the Pennsylvania Colony.

The date was October 20, 1773. Usually, the Compound wasn't completely winterized until mid-November. I thought that the Compound had never looked better. Hopefully, Mr. Adams would take notice when he arrived. I knew that ending the winter preparations early would save on labor costs. Mrs. Williams was still "Finishing the Books," as she liked to say. I am very confident that the Compound was finishing a very profitable year.

The following day, Mr. Adam's carriage had finally arrived. He stepped out of the carriage and was followed by a young man who, if I had to guess, was just exiting his teenage years. Mr. Adams greeted me very warmly and commented that everything looked orderly. I said, "Yes, sir. We have completed all of our winterizing tasks weeks ahead of schedule."

He said, "Job well done. However, it will be painful when you have to move on to the larger assignment that we discussed on my last visit."

I said, "I am implementing new procedures that will make the transfer to the new leader very painless."

He looked around and said, "Let's head into the office where we can speak privately."

We sat in Mr. Adam's office, and he said, "Jeremiah, I would like you to meet Alex. He was an orphan who was born in the Caribbean. He made his way to my family by way of a cargo-carrying vessel with which we do business. He has been living with my cousin John Adams and his family until now. It seems that there was a major disturbance at my cousin's home. Alex thought it would be a good idea to build his own still in my cousin's barn. My nine-year-old nephew Quincy was serving as Alex's assistant. One thing led to another, and a fire broke out, which subsequently burned down my cousin's barn. The decision was whether to take him out back and shoot him like a lame mule or send him back to the sea. We came up with a third option. We decided to send him to the Compound, where he will work at your direction. I apologize, but this task may be the tallest order that we assign you."

Alex finally spoke up. He said, "In my defense, the still was producing a fine Gin that would have captured the marketplace."

I tried not to laugh, but I could see controlling Alex was like riding a wild stallion. He would need to be broken, in a nice way.

Mr. Adams further stated, "Ben thinks that Alex has a brilliant mind. I quickly reminded Ben that more of his experiments have failed than have succeeded. Anyways, Alex will be joining you when Ben begins your training in a few days. Please keep Alex occupied with anything that is not flammable."

Mr. Adams said, "Let's plan on meeting for supper this evening to discuss some upcoming matters. Yes, Alex, you can join us." We parted ways, and I had to think of things for Alex to do. Perhaps I could just have him shadow me for the time being. I started to ask Alex about his skills, and he responded in a sarcastic accent that I recognized as the Queen's English. I could see that this one was going to be a handful.

As we left the office, Mrs. Williams said, "If he is going to be working here, I will need his full name."

Alex responded once again in the Queens' English, "Madame, my full name is Sir Alexander Hamilton, Esquire." Mrs. Williams just rolled her eyes.

I said, "His name is Alexander Hamilton minus the Sir and Esquire."

CHAPTER 27

THE ORIENTATION

A s we parted the office, I decided that the proper thing to do was to give Alex a tour of the Compound. The first stop was to drop off his belongings at my house. There were several extra beds, and I told him to take whichever bed he liked. We then ventured around the Compound, and I introduced Alex to everyone we encountered. As we made our way through the Compound, I noticed that many of the single ladies were congregating and going out of their way to meet Alex. I thought it was my imagination at first. As we approached these young ladies, Alex would have a flirtatious line for each of them. Before long, Alex had met every young lady in the Compound. As we would exit a building, I would notice that there was a group of girls giggling as we passed by.

This had gone on long enough. So I thought that I better straighten this matter out right now. So I said, "Alex, what is going on with all of these young women?"

He said, "I am not sure, but I love them all." I wanted to laugh, but then I thought about the fathers of these young girls.

I said, "Alex, I know each and every one of these girls' fathers. Most of them work for me. If you cross one of their daughters, they will use you for target practice with their muskets. Then they will take what is left of you and feed you to the dogs." I further said. "Whatever you do outside of this Compound is your business, but everything here is my business."

Alex said, "Ok. I was just having a little harmless fun. Trust me. I understand where I stand with the entire Adams clan. You have my word that I will stay away from these ladies."

I said, "Thank you." Then I had to ask, "Were there many ladies where Mr. John Adams lives?"

Alex said, "Yes, I had to be careful there. Every girl seemed to have an angry father as well. But, on the other hand, I was accustomed to traveling throughout the Caribbean where the wine and women flowed with abundance."

I said, "Sounds like fun."

Alex said, "It was, but as they say, all good things must end. While I was at the Adams estate, I stayed away from all women, not because I didn't want to see any women, but because the Adams' are puritans, and they don't think you should be near a woman until you are married. Then there is Samuel's daughter, Hannah. They thought for sure that I was trying to seduce her. But, unfortunately, they had it all wrong. Her father chased me down with a musket. Hannah had to explain that we were just friends. Even though I thought Hannah was the most beautiful woman that I had ever seen, she was like a sister to me. Besides, if I ever crossed Hannah, I would be more afraid of her than Mr. Adam's musket. She is beautiful but tough. She is an expert marksman with both the rifle and the bow. She is not the person you want to be on the wrong side of. She also competes in equestrian events in Boston. At first, all of the men laughed at her, but she got the last laugh after she won every event. Her father, however, wasn't buying that I wasn't interested in his daughter, so he shipped me off to here."

Later that afternoon, we met Mr. Adams at the tavern for supper. As usual, we had several rounds of whiskey before supper was served. Most of the conversation was about the Compound. Mr. Adams said he had a preliminary look at the books. He said, "The Compound had a record year. I commend you on your performance."

I thanked him and said, "I think we can do better. I have some ideas concerning expansion. I think we can clear the balance of the land to the north. The soil is very similar to the existing farm. We could use it for additional farming or perhaps expand the horse ranch. My research into horses tells me that proper grazing land is one of the limiting factors. We have plenty of land. It just needs to be cleared. Much of this could be done in the off-season. The other area that we could improve on is the milling operation. There is vacant land on a wider expanse of the river on the east end of the Compound. This would require us to purchase the land and build a new mill. The water flow at this location is much greater than our current location. We could double our production." Mr. Adams listened intently to my ideas.

He said, "Let me consider this, and I will get back to you. I will need to speak with my partner Peter as well."

The conversation then moved to our upcoming training with Mr. Franklin. Mr. Adams said, "Ben will no doubt take you back into the history of our operation. Then, at some point, you both may be asked to join our organization."

Alex asked, "What is the name of your organization?"

Mr. Adams responded, "They have called us many things. The name we prefer is the "Sons of Liberty." This is short and concise."

I asked, "How large is your organization?"

He said, "Overall, there are roughly seven to eight thousand members who don't regularly attend meetings but would be available in a call to arms situation. The senior leadership consists of about twenty of us. Many are business and community leaders. They are the best and brightest that the Colonies have to offer. You two will be meeting them over the next few months. We are looking to expand our leadership team to some younger members. Ben often jokes that our senior team must convene our meetings earlier than we used to because it is past our bedtime for most of us. Our battle to change how England deals with the Colonies is fast approaching a crescendo. Either we will get what we desire, or there will be conflict." He went on to say, "That brings me to my next point. We will be celebrating our annual Harvest celebration in two weeks near my Cousin John Adams' Braintree Estate at a large home that is referred to as the Peace Field House. Many of our associates are scheduled to attend. This is a splendid celebration that would allow both of you to meet everyone and for them to meet you. Many bring their spouses so you will get to know them as well. I will warn you that the wives have their husband's ear regarding who they should associate with. Your membership will be taken to a vote. It is incumbent on you two to make a good impression." Mr. Adams continued, "Also, I would like you two to see my tailor in Boston upon your arrival. Plan on coming a day early. Both of you need some presentable clothing. Ask for Henri. I will let him know that you are coming. You two need to "Dress for Success", as they say."

Supper arrived, and the cook had outdone himself again. This time we were served steaks with potatoes. We devoured our meal and then retired for the evening. The next day would mark the arrival of Mr. Peter Adams. He was making his once-a-year pilgrimage to the Compound. He was not nearly as involved as his cousin but made the journey to check on his investment.

The next day arrived, and I spent most of the time with the leaders of the various operations. We were reviewing their performance. We talked about what we could do to improve the performance. As scheduled, Mr. Peter Adams arrived midday. I met with both of the Owners and reviewed the year's performance. They both seemed happy but were distracted. I didn't dare ask what was wrong. I hadn't achieved that level yet. I'm sure they would tell me if they wanted me to know.

CHAPTER 28

HARDSHIP

EVERAL WEEKS LATER, Mr. Franklin arrived at the Compound once again. We were scheduled to travel to Boston the following day for the Annual Harvest Festival. All of my tasks at the Compound were complete. Both Peter and Samuel Adams were still at the Compound. Most of their time was spent reconciling the books for the entire year. The British tax collector knew of the Adams Trading Company and wanted its share. Mr. Samuel Adams spent some of his younger days serving as a Tax Collector, so he knew the rules and how to get around them. The good thing about the Compound was that it was so far out in the country that it was very rarely paid a visit by the British.

I needed to finish all of my daily tasks for the next few days so I could spend as much time with Mr. Franklin as possible, so I opted out of dinner that evening. Alex was a great help. I wondered if Mr. Adams' assessment of Alex was based more on getting Alex away from his daughter than any of the other reasons he had mentioned. So far, I found Alex to be a quick study and a great problem solver as long as there were no young ladies around.

The following day Alex and I met Mr. Franklin outside the Freemason's Hall. We were both very eager to get started. We entered the mystery building, but quickly discovered that we were only allowed into the lobby and the adjacent anteroom. Mr. Franklin said, "Only members of this sacred organization are allowed past those doors." I wondered what could be in there that required so much secrecy. Mr. Franklin gave us his apologies and added that maybe someday we would be invited to join the organization. He brought many books with him. Some were law books, but most were historical.

Mr. Franklin started by saying, "I feel that it is important that you fully understand our current predicament first. You need to understand why certain Colonial men act out the way they do. It is said that the Pilgrims came to the New World to escape religious persecution. While this was true, it was not the only reason. The New World represented unlimited resources, unlimited farmlands, unlimited game, and pristine lands. They came here to escape the heavy taxation that all Europeans faced. They came here to escape the system where you gained an advantage because of your birthright, not because of hard work. The Pilgrims were of moderate means. They brought everything they had with them. Many intended on never returning to England. They came to America to provide for themselves. They did not need anyone else to feed, cloth, or protect them. It was understood that they were here on their own. The British could not aid them in any way from across an ocean. Over the next 150 years, more and more people arrived in America. Most of them were here for what I just described. Things started to change rapidly once the message began to spread throughout Europe. A new breed of men descended upon America. We shall refer to them as the Profiteers. They recognized that the rugged natural landscape of America made it attractive to both the fur traders and lumber barons. The fur traders made obscene profits from the southern Colonies up to the Hudson Bay in the French-controlled territory of Canada. The British Parliament began to take notice. Enormous profits were being generated in the Colonies, and the Crown saw very little of it. Couple this with the fact that many in Britain believed that the Colonies were supposed to purchase all of their goods from Britain. When the British Parliament found out about all of these profits, a major problem began to fester. The British felt that they were not getting their fair share. As the shipping routes were expanded, the Colonists realized that they could buy these same goods for a fraction of the price from places such as the West Indies. The Colonists found much cheaper places to purchase basic staples such as tea, sugar, molasses, and the like. This new trade situation grew overnight. Shipments from the West Indies replaced shipments from Britain."

Alex added, "This explains why my home in the West Indies went from a minor port to a major shipping port over a very short period. People went from barely getting by to living in lavish homes seemingly overnight. Even at a young age, I recognized that I could live a nice life where I was in the West Indies. However, I left what was my home because I felt that there was something larger out there for me."

Mr. Franklin said, "Yes, Alex, there was something larger out there. Fate and destiny played their hand when you had the opportunity to set sail to the Colonies. Your life was changed forever. As for you, Mr. Briggs, fate also played a hand in your future. Had you not noticed the flier advertising the opportunity in the Colonies, you would probably not be among the living right now." He went on to say, "I believe that all of us, including myself, are here for a purpose. This purpose is very difficult to grasp. We must follow our intuitions and let them, along with the history lessons that I am passing on to you, guide you on your mission. Many people have a mission, but they don't understand what the goals are. I believe that you two young men are special.

Mr. Adams also recognized this. That is why we are sitting here today. We will return to the subjects of fate and destiny later. I will now return our focus to the circumstances surrounding us this very day."

A server brought us some tea, fruit, and fresh bread, as Mr. Franklin had instructed. He thanked the server and said, "There is nothing finer than enjoying a cup of tea while discussing the place that I have come to love." The server smiled and left us. He continued, "As you will no doubt surmise, I like, many of my associates, believe that far better days lie ahead for the Colonies. We share a common belief that this land is indeed special. We believe that Jesus referred to the New World when he talked about the city on the hill in the famous Sermon on the Mount speech. Jesus described a special place that would serve as a Beacon of Hope to the oppressed throughout the world. The New World represented a place where you could prosper because of your own sweat, not because you were born into something. You can pray as you like and not worry about repercussions from the Church in Rome. We believe that the government should run on its own course and not be subject to the blessings of the Church. Please don't mistake this for a lack of reverence for the Holy Bible. We believe that when governing ourselves, we will be guided by the teachings of Jesus Christ, but not beholden to any Church Leader who may disagree with our plans." We took a break to get some air. It was a rare late fall warm day.

When we returned, Mr. Franklin detailed all the hardships the British Parliament inflicted on the Colonies. He talked about tax after tax. As I knew since I had spent my first eighteen years in Britain, their problems were of their own doing. King George III, just like his father, George II, never met a war in which he didn't want to get involved. As history has taught the world, wars cost a lot of money. Especially the wars that have no clear-cut victor. The wars of the 1700s rarely resulted in vast amounts of Gold being seized by the victors. The British thirst for conquest has nearly bankrupted them. One solution for the British was to heavily tax the Colonies. The vast profits that Mr. Franklin talked about earlier today were easy targets for a financially strapped nation.

Mr. Franklin then discussed the reasons for the British military presence. He said, "The French and Indian War required massive amounts of British forces to be stationed here in the Colonies. This was their war, not ours. As loyal subjects to the Crown, we sent many of our young men to fight on behalf of the Crown. We spilled much of our own blood. The cost to the Colonies was beyond measure. How did they thank us? By implementing new taxes, of course. They argued that since British forces were required to stay in the Colonies, taxes were justified to pay for them. We wanted the forces to return home, but that was not to be. It seems that the sight of mass amounts of the Military would cause unrest in Britain. The easy solution was to leave them in the Colonies, out of sight of their citizenry, and make us pay for them."

Mr. Franklin shuffled his papers and continued. He said, "This building and organization that we currently find ourselves in came to prominence because it was a place where people from different backgrounds could meet and openly discuss the Crown's attempted muzzling of our free thoughts while draining our treasuries. I began to travel around the Colonies and meet people who were outraged by the activities of the Crown. I urged calm with all of these people. I had many contacts within Parliament and I thought that I could help fix this problem. In 1766, I boarded a ship bound for England to make my case. I was allowed to speak before Parliament. I gave a speech that detailed the Colonist' viewpoints on taxes and British oversight. I tried to explain that England would gain and the British Empire would grow if the Colonies were allowed to grow and prosper. They were having none of what I was offering. Their viewpoint was that the Colonists were nothing more than a mosquito on their buttocks.

I could see that Mr. Franklin was pained by just talking about the British and their rejection of his ideas. We decided to take a break for a few minutes. Alex and I walked outside to get some fresh air. Alex said, "Why do you think they are spending so much time with us? What is so special about the two of us that has these leaders making us a priority? They can find two chaps anywhere to buy into their message."

I said, "I have been wondering the same thing."

What Alex said next shook me to my core and made me understand our purpose. He said, "The only thing I think that I have that is special is that I have Dreams about special hidden treasure and about history that has taken place in faraway lands."

I stood there speechless. How was it that Alex and I had similar Dreams? We just met each other. Were we part of some great play that had been pre-written in the heavens? Just then, I recalled Maria's statement about the Children of the Flood. Had I just met one of them?

I finally spoke. I said, "Alex, we need to talk. I have had similar Dreams my entire life." He looked dumbfounded.

Mr. Franklin spotted us and said, "Come along you two. We have much to cover."

I sat through the ensuing discussion, completely distracted by what Alex had told me. I wondered, did Mr. Franklin and the others know that Alex and I had this gift? I could hardly wait to speak with Alex this evening.

Mr. Franklin returned to the discussion of the Stamp Act. He said, "After I returned from England, I called a meeting with anyone who concerned themselves with this matter. A friend of mine introduced me to Mr. Samuel Adams. He said he was a member of a group called "The Sons of Liberty." He described them as like-minded business and community leaders who shared my concerns about the British over-reach. He scheduled an introductory meeting at a tavern called the Green Dragon in Boston. At this meeting, I met the following leaders: Patrick Henry, John Hancock, John Adams, Paul Revere, John Brown, and John Jay. While we didn't agree on everything, we had a special bond. This bond was our love for what we were building in the New World. We were all committed to seeing this thing through. However, we disagreed on how to get there. Several of the men wanted to immediately revolt against the British. They claimed they could quickly assemble an army of seven thousand men if needed. I pleaded for patience. I told these men, "I believe our time to revolt may be coming, but that day is not today. I have many powerful friends in the New York, Pennsylvania, and Virginia Colonies that I would like to bring into this group. They are powerful men who are titans of their chosen businesses. One of these great men is the finest military man that the Red Coats have in their Army. I am speaking about Lieutenant General Washington. I have met with him several times and had this discussion. He receives the same treatment from the British that we do. The fact that he was born in the Colonies prevents him from moving up in the ranks of the Military. There are men who can't hold a candle to him that outrank him. This caused him to resign and return to his homestead at Mount Vernon in the Virginia Colony."

After a long pause, Mr. Franklin continued, "As you may know, I am very involved in the Postal System. I believe that getting our message out to like-minded people will be the strength of our group. We can use the Postal System to spread our word. The British don't participate in any oversight of the Postal System. They only are concerned that they get their precious tax from anyone that chooses to mail anything. This was referred to as the Stamp Act."

Mr. Franklin further explained to Alex and me, "I feared that the British were treating us like children. They would repeal a tax only to replace it with something more costly. Even worse, they would replace a tax with a tariff. This just sent the Sons of Liberty into a frenzy. I had all I could do to keep these men, especially Samuel Adams, at bay. Then, to worsen matters, the British placed the Custom Office or the American Board of Customs Commissioners to collect the tariffs in Boston, just one block away from Samuel Adams's home. It almost seemed that the British knew of the swelling rebellion and were poking it with a stick.

By then, it was afternoon, and Mr. Franklin said, "It is afternoon, and I'm sure the tavern owner is wondering where I am. Let's adjourn for today. I will be having supper with Samuel Adams. I think it would be in both of your interests to attend. Now that you know the backstory, everything that happens moving forward will be written about in history books."

I agreed to meet for supper. I have many Compound matters to check on before supper. Alex offered to help me, and I accepted his offer. It seems that Alex and I have much to talk about.

CHAPTER 29

PARTNERS IN DREAMLAND

ALEX AND I left Mr. Franklin at the Freemasons Hall. I had to tend to matters at the horse ranch. It seems that one of the older horses had taken ill. He was a Morgan that was in his twenties. When we arrived we found him lying down in his stall. The closest Veterinarian was in Binghamton. Our Ranch Manager had sent for him early this morning. He still hadn't arrived yet. I have always been drawn to horses, but I had no skills when it came to caring for them when they were sick. I asked Mr. Henry Jones, our Ranch Manager to let me know when the Vet arrives. We parted ways and I headed back to the Compound office where I told Alex that I would meet him. He had gone to the Widow Flanders house where it appears that a raccoon had burrowed his way into her home. Not only was she was afraid of the raccoon, but she now had a gaping hole in her roof where snow or rain would pour through.

Alex said, "When I arrived, Mrs. Flanders was sitting there with her musket at the ready. I must have startled her because she pointed the musket at me. I hit the deck instantly. She apologized profusely, but I may have to change my trousers."

I laughed and said, "Well, at least it wasn't an angry father this time."

Alex said, "Very funny. I will be leaving any future visits to Mrs. Flanders's home to you. Anyways, we will need to send one of our carpenters over there to fix the hole."

We left the Compound office and walked back to my home where we both wanted to get cleaned up. I sincerely hope that Alex did not change his pants for any other reason besides the fact that they were just a little dirty.

On the way back to my home, we ran into Maria who was on her way back from the General Store. As usual she very warmly greeted me. Before I had a chance to introduce her to Alex, she said, "Alex, it is so nice to meet you. My name is Maria. Welcome to the Compound. You will have to join Jeremiah and me for our weekly supper get together."

Alex said, "Maria, it is so nice to meet you as well. I would love to join you two for supper." We finished sharing pleasantries and Alex and I continued on our way home.

The walk was quiet when Alex finally said, "I feel as if I have met Maria before."

I said, "I was surprised that she knew your name."

"I assumed that you saw her earlier today and told her of my arrival", Alex said.

"No. I haven't seen her in days. I believe that she is a Seer. She lives in between the spirit world and our living world. She has made comments to me that lead me to believe that she has supernatural abilities", I said.

We both cleaned up and headed out of the door. I said, "I wonder how Mr. Franklin is feeling. We parted with him several hours ago. He would no doubt be keeping the tavern owner busy. Once we were out of the house and I was sure that no one could hear us. I decided to get directly to the point. I said, "Have you ever dreamt of the Secret of Eden or the term Children of the Flood?"

He paused for a minute and said, "No." I was both happy and sad at the same time. I wanted someone to share this Dream, or should I say, Nightmare with. He then said, "Not unless you are talking about a Secret that was discovered by the Knights Templar then subsequently moved by Henry Sinclair."

I knew that I would not get an answer out of Alex that was not surrounded by a healthy dose of sarcasm. I said, "What do you think all of this means. Do you think this is why we have been chosen by Mr. Adams and Mr. Franklin?"

Alex said, "Why don't we discuss this with Mr. Franklin when we have a minute alone with him. I think he will keep this matter confidential. After all, what he has shared with us today is nothing short of treason."

I said, "Hopefully, he is alone when we arrive."

As we entered the tavern, we immediately saw Mr. Franklin sitting with Mr. Samuel Adams. It seems that Mr. Peter Adams left earlier that day for the return trip to Boston. Both men seemed to be rather well-watered, as they say. Mr. Franklin saw us and said, "Ah. My prize students have arrived. Please join us for a libation or two before we order our supper."

Alex replied, "I am going to hold off for a while." All of us sat there in shock when Alex said, "Well, that was long enough." You would have thought that this was the funniest thing that Mr. Franklin had ever heard.

He said, "I will have to use that one for my own purposes at a later date." One thing for sure, there was always levity when Alex was around.

We sat and discussed today's lesson over a few drinks. Alex and I switched to Ale. Otherwise, I would have needed someone to carry me home. Mr. Adams said, "Ben tells me that he explained what we are up against with the British. One thing you must realize is that those of us who live in Boston are taking the brunt of the onslaught. We are the closest major city in the Colonies to Nova Scotia."

I asked, "Why does Nova Scotia matter?"

Mr. Adams said, "Halifax, Nova Scotia is a major Garrison for the British Military. They have a large contingent of soldiers and weaponry there. We are within striking distance." He went on to say, "I have been an outspoken critic of the Crown in these matters. They in turn have directed their henchmen to make my life miserable. They have falsely convicted me of civil violations where they claim that I have stolen money. These claims are completely fabricated, of course. The end result for me is that they have the means because of the conviction to place a lien on any property or asset that I have."

I asked, "What about the Compound. Isn't this an asset?"

He said, "My Cousin Peter and I recognized this early on. I sold my shares of the Compound to Peter. Even though I technically run the Compound, I am just an employee. Therefore, the British cannot seize Peter's assets. They can only seize mine. I informed them that the funds that I received from the sale were lost due to a gambling debt. Meanwhile, the funds secretly have been given to our cause. Ben, I hope that I have not told these two too much."

Mr. Franklin said, "They already know a great deal. If I didn't trust them, I would have never confided in them." The server brought our supper to the table. It was the Pot Roast again. I have never been so happy to see a meal.

I noticed that Mr. Franklin's plate didn't include any of the meat. I had to ask. "Mr. Franklin, don't you care for their meat?"

He said, "No, I can see that their meat looks delicious, but I am what is known as a vegetarian. I do not eat meat. I do it for financial and ethical reasons."

Alex said, "Next time please just order the meat. I will take it from your plate and add it to mine." Everyone laughed.

We completed our supper and continued with the steady stream of Ale when Mr. Adams said, "I almost forgot. Ben and

I have an urgent matter to attend to in Boston. You two need to accompany us to Boston a few days earlier than we had planned. A situation has arisen that requires our immediate attention. We will be leaving tomorrow around noon. Upon arrival, we will have a few very hectic days. We should arrive on Wednesday. As we discussed, go to my Tailor, Henri. You are to purchase three new outfits each for our upcoming meetings. Henri already knows to charge it to my account. You two will be meeting some very important people throughout the weekend. Please look and act as you belong in the company of these great men. On Thursday evening, we will be meeting at an establishment known as the Green Dragon in Boston. There, you will meet our Boston-based associates. Then on Friday evening, we will celebrate our annual Fall Harvest Extravaganza at Peace Field in Quincy. There you will meet many of our associates from the Southern Colonies."

Mr. Adams said, "Please take the opportunity to deal with all Compound matters in the morning. Hopefully, seeing that the season is basically over for the Compound you should be able to leave for a week without the place falling apart. Mrs. Williams is already arranging an express carriage for all of us tomorrow. Please don't be late." We continued with the Ale for several more hours. Our questions about the Secret of Eden would have to wait. The Carriage ride may present the opportune time to discuss the Dreams that both Alex and I have been having.

CHAPTER 30

BOSTON BOUND

S USUAL, I woke up at sunrise. My pounding head reminded me quickly of the previous evening at the tavern. Then
it hit me. I am traveling to Boston later this morning. I was
told to plan for at least a week. Thankfully, my clothing was
washed the previous day. I pay Miss Katherine Crawford to wash
my clothing for me. At some point, I suppose I should start doing
it myself, but Miss Crawford enjoys the extra money, and I enjoy
doing everything other than laundry.

I woke Alex up and told him to get dressed. We had a lot to
get done before noon.

Alex said, "On behalf of my swollen head and upset stomach,
I respectfully request that you let me sleep for a few more hours."

I said, "While I respectfully acknowledge your request, I very
firmly advise you to get out of bed before I pour a bucket of cold
water over your head." He begrudgingly rose and got dressed.
He thankfully had listened to me and hired Miss Crawford to
wash his clothes. As luck would have it, we were both essentially

ready to travel. We would need to return and pack a bag for the week-long journey.

Just then, I heard a knock on the door. It was Mr. Jones, the Ranch Manager. He seemed very troubled.

He said, "The horse that we call Captain Jack passed during the night." He said he has been with this horse since Mr. Adams hired his Father, Joshua Jones, to manage the Ranch. I said that I was very sorry. Even though this was one of the many workhorses that resided on the Ranch, I felt a tremendous loss. It was hard to reconcile. The hardest part of when a horse, cat, or dog becomes ill is that they cannot describe what ails them. I know that many horses die in battle, which is horrifying, but these ranch animals seemingly become part of the family. I thanked him for the update, and he assured me that the horse would be properly buried in the pasture that lies on the edge of the farm.

Before he left, I said, "I need to meet with you and all the other leaders at nine o'clock. It seems that I have been asked to accompany Mr. Adams on a trip to Boston. Therefore, I will be gone for at least a week."

Henry said, "You are probably very busy this morning. Would you like me to pass on the message to the other leaders that you need to meet with them?"

I said, "Yes. That would be a great help." Henry then left. I knew the morning would go quickly, so I would take all the help I could get.

I quickly grabbed some breakfast tea and bread with jam and headed for the Compound office. I looked behind me and saw Alex moving very slowly behind me. He looked like one of those monsters portrayed in the various fiction novels floating around the Compound. I entered the Compound office, where Mrs. Williams waited for my arrival. She had gone to the trouble of brewing another pot of tea for us. I said, "I thank you. I will not decline a cup of tea this morning more than ever."

She laughed, "I know that when Mr. Franklin is visiting, I am to have tea at the ready all day long." We both laughed. Alex then joined us.

Mrs. Williams said, "Alex, do you feel alright?"

He said, "Yes. Perhaps I ate something that did not agree with me last night."

I said, "Perhaps it was the food, or was it possibly the two gallons of Ale that you consumed last night?" Mrs. Williams was chuckling.

Alex said, "I'm never doing that again."

I said, "At least not until this evening."

One by one, the leaders began to show up. I thanked Henry for gathering everyone. I explained that Alex and I would be traveling to Boston with Mr. Adams today. I said. "All of you know your operations better than I could dream to. Please carry on like you always have. I believe that some of you are done for the season. Please help your fellow managers who haven't quite finished everything up yet. I would like all of you to make a pass through the Compound and check on all of the homes. During the summer and fall, holes in roofs and walls aren't noticeable, but when winter finally arrives, they will become a major issue. It is much easier to perform a repair now versus when there are two feet of snow on the ground. If any problems arise that are bigger than you are comfortable handling, please bring them to Mrs. Williams's attention. As I have learned, she is truly the glue that holds this place together."

A voice from the back room spoke out. It was Mr. Adams. He said, "Mr. Briggs, I knew you were a quick learner. I dread to think of this place without Mrs. Williams." Mrs. Williams thanked Mr. Adams.

Mrs. Elizabeth Williams has resided at the Compound for nearly twenty years. Her husband, James, was the Manager of the farm. One fall roughly ten years ago, Mr. Williams threw out his back while bailing hay. He has not been able to work ever since. He remained in bed for six months. He now can stand up and walk short distances, but that's it. Now, he is an avid reader and occasionally writes short stories. This was a very stressful time for the Williams Family and their five children. Mr. Adams recognized this immediately and offered Mrs. Williams a position in the Compound office. He soon noticed that she had a proficiency with numbers. Everything happens for a reason. I have heard people say that when one door closes, another one opens. No one wanted to see Mr. Williams injure himself, but without it, the Compound would have never gained Mrs. Williams. I knew the Compound was in very good hands while I was away.

Alex and I arrived back at the office at eleven-thirty. Earlier, I had the chance to take a long hot bath. There was nothing quite as refreshing as warm water to refresh your soul. I had no idea when the next opportunity would arise for me to clean up properly. Alex took my advice and did the same. Shortly after that, Mr. Franklin and Mr. Adams arrived.

Maria walked up to us as we were ready to board the carriage. Unbeknownst to me, Maria and Mr. Franklin were old friends. I am surprised that she never mentioned it in any of our Sunday suppers. After they said their goodbyes, she came up to me with a big smile and said, "Soon, all of the Children of the Flood will be together once again. Enjoy every minute of it."

I still didn't completely understand the meaning of this.

We loaded our bags onto the carriage and began the long journey. Alex and I chose to sit in the row that was right behind the driver. I had not left the Compound for anything other than a quick trip to Binghamton since my arrival years ago. I thoroughly enjoyed the scenery and the small towns we were passing through.

The trip in its entirety would take roughly thirty-six hours. The Carriage Company, which was owned by Mr. Peter Adams, had stables conveniently located along this entire journey. The horses were trained to travel about forty miles and then would be changed out for fresh horses. The driver would also change out several times. Our first major stop was in Albany.

We changed horses and driver there, and Mr. Franklin and Mr. Adams wanted to have a quick meeting with General Philip Schuyler. The General was one of their associates who happened to live in Albany. He was a hero of the French and Indian War and was very sympathetic to the cause. Mr. Adams sent a messenger to the General's home stating that he had an urgent message for the General. He told the messenger to tell the General that we were going to the Bradstreet Tavern for supper. A few minutes later, we arrived at the tavern. It was like every other tavern that I had seen. We enjoyed a few pints of Ale while we were waiting. About thirty minutes later, the General arrived with his wife Catherine and his daughter Eliza. Mr. Adams apologized for the surprise visit but said he had urgent business to discuss. They sat and joined us for supper. Mr. Franklin was his usual charming self. Mr. Adams and the General walked outside to discuss the urgent matter. Something came over Alex. He was the perfect gentleman and spent the next 30 minutes or so talking to Mrs. Schuyler and Eliza. He seemed to have a spark in his eye. I could tell that he was very attracted to Eliza but was not using his usual tactics. I thought to myself, "Maybe Alex is changing his ways." Mrs. Schuyler informed Alex that she and the General would attend the Annual Harvest Celebration at the Peace Field House on Friday Night. She said that they look forward to it every year.

Alex finally overcame his shyness and asked, "Will Eliza be coming to the party?"

Eliza said, "I don't believe so, but I would love to." He went on to tell her that it had been a wonderful time the previous years. Then he promised that he would personally introduce her to all of the other young people in attendance.

She turned to her mother and said, "Please, can I go?"

Her mother said, "I will talk to your father, but I don't see why not. The fact that these young men are friends of Mr. Adams and Mr. Franklin speaks very loudly of their character."

I thought to myself, "Alex better be on his best behavior. I could tell that the General was not someone to anger." We finished supper and had to get back on the journey again. Alex spent the balance of the time talking to Eliza and her Mother. He said that hopefully, he would see both of them on Friday. We bid farewell, and the carriage started to head out of town.

Once we were out of earshot, Mr. Adams said to Alex, "I know that young lady's father very well. If you miss-treat her in any way, your head will be mounted to a stake that will greet everyone as they enter Albany." We all laughed. Somewhere deep in my mind, I knew that Alex just had a life-changing moment. I'm not sure why I was feeling this way. Alex was the type of young man that met young women everywhere he went. Yet, I was feeling something different about this encounter. Why did I have this ability to sense things? I wondered if somehow I was being guided by some unseen force. Was this God or someone else? Fate and destiny were hard at work. If we had taken another route to Boston, then Eliza and Alex would have never met. I eagerly waited for this encounter with Eliza to play out. Alex spent the next hour or so asking about Eliza and who her father was. Mr. Franklin provided as much information as he could.

We left the Albany city limits a few minutes later. The roads between Albany and Boston were paved. Albany had served as a garrison in the French and Indian War. The fact that significant troop movements came through the Port of Boston and made their way to Albany meant that money needed to be spent to ensure that military schedules had been met. We were thankful. The horses could move considerably faster, and the ride was much smoother. I was able to sleep through much of the night. We made another stop to change out the driver and horses again. The name of the town was Northampton, Massachusetts. Evidently, it was the site of many battles with the various Indian Nations during the early years. This time we all slept through the exchange. I finally woke up, and the driver informed us that we were about an hour away from Boston. The sun was just about to rise.

Finally, we arrived in Boston. We were all staying at Mr. Adams' Boston home. It was a relatively small home, but that didn't seem to matter because his family lived at the place they referred to as Peace Field in Quincy. Mr. Adams feared for his family's safety here in Boston. At the Peace Field Estate, his family was surrounded in every direction by members of the Adams Clan. They were all neighbors. They protected each other. Even the British knew to stay away from this place. Mr. Adams was away so much that he knew he couldn't protect his family properly. Even though he knew that his daughter Hannah was perfectly capable of defending herself, she would not be able to defend his wife Elizabeth and his son Samuel. His son Samuel was a very peaceful and quiet person. He planned on joining the Seminary after his 18th Birthday.

CHAPTER 31

HENRI

MR. ADAMS HAD made arrangements with a neighbor to allow Alex and me to borrow horses for a few days. We made our way into the City Center, where both of us were amazed. We had never seen so many people. Even though I was born and raised in England, I had never actually stepped foot into London. Even when I first immigrated to the Colonies, I had arrived during the night in Boston and was quickly rushed to a wagon where I made the ride to the Compound. I never saw anything in Boston. Now I am seeing this city in its full glory. People were walking everywhere. Most looked like they had a mission that they were on, and some looked as though they were just there to enjoy the show.

We tied up the horses and decided to walk a bit before we went to Henri's. Off to our left were several Red Coats who were seemingly harassing an older gentleman. Alex wanted to come to the man's defense, but I cautioned against it. The Red Coats were moving on. Alex said, "What gives them the right to harass an old man like that."

I said, "I don't know, but I imagine we will hear many worse tales over the next few days."

To our right, there was a preacher who was pronouncing that the end is near. He said, "If the Colonies don't change their ways, God will reign fire and rain upon them."

We walked up and listened for a minute. When the preacher noticed Alex and me, he stopped dead in his tracks. He sat quietly staring at us for a minute, at least. He finally said, "Praise God. The Guardians are finally here to save us." Everyone began to look at us. They had a look of fascination on their faces.

I grabbed Alex and said, "Let's move on."

When we got far enough away, Alex finally said, "What in the hell was that?"

I said, "I don't know, but we need to speak to Mr. Franklin as soon as possible."

We walked at a brisk pace to Henri's Clothing Emporium. We walked in and asked for Henri. After a few minutes passed, a short French Man approached us and said, "You must be the two young men that Mr. Adams told me to expect."

I said, "Yes, we are. We have been instructed to purchase three new outfits each for some very important meetings that we have coming up."

Henri and his assistant began to measure us for our new clothing. We then picked out our new outfits. I picked two blue and one brown outfits. All three came with white stockings and shirts. Alex selected something similar. Instead of the Brown outfit, he chose an all-white outfit. We next moved to the hats. We each picked two hats that were of the latest fashion, at least according to Henri. He then wrote everything up and informed us that our new outfits would be ready for pickup tomorrow morning. It was midday, and we decided to head back to Mr. Adams's house.

We arrived back at the house where Mr. Franklin and Mr. Adams were having a heated debate. I asked what was wrong, and Mr. Franklin explained, "We were recently notified that the

British Parliament had enacted what they call the Tea Act. This forces the Colonies to purchase their tea from the British-owned East India Tea Company. This tea, of course, is exempt from all taxes and levies that the teas that we provide to the Colonies are required to pay. The British know that this will bankrupt the companies owned by our associates. So they are making moves that are seemingly directed at breaking up our resistance movement."

Alex said, "Mr. Franklin, even I recognize that war is inevitable. We must start to make preparations. It may take us a year or two to prepare, but it is inevitable."

Mr. Adams said, "Alex, I always knew that I liked you." The levity broke the tension.

Alex said, "I know that I am just an orphan that tends to burn down barns, but the time for talk with the British is quickly coming to an end."

I was just starting to understand who this man, Alexander Hamilton, was going to be. We have been told that we will be meeting great men over the next few days. I have a feeling that Alex will become one of them. I am just happy that we have become close. Watching this man grow will be a thing of beauty.

Mr. Adams had to leave for several hours. We decided to meet at the Green Dragon for supper. Mr. Adams said, "The environment there is friendly to our cause, and the food is pretty good." We bid goodbye to Mr. Adams and told him that we would see him shortly.

After Mr. Adams left, we decided that what Mr. Franklin referred to as Happy Hour was upon us. So, we each poured a drink, and Alex proposed a toast.

He said, "To the Sons of Liberty. So may we prevail in our quest." This brought a big smile to Mr. Franklin's face.

I told Mr. Franklin, "We need to discuss a very important matter with you." So we retired to the sitting room, where I began to explain the Dreams that I have been having since I was a child. Recently, I found out that Alex is having similar Dreams. I said, "How can this be?"

Mr. Franklin explained, "You two young men are probably wondering what has brought you together." He continued, "This is a subject that I planned on discussing with you in great detail back at the Compound. I will give you the short version for today. There is a belief in many parts of the world that when a person dies, their soul passes into another body. Their soul is on a mission that will not allow them to go to heaven until the mission has been completed. I believe that you two are on such a mission. I believe that you have been together for many lifetimes. The question is, what is your mission? Why have you been placed in my path? Very few people know that I have a gift. I can read people's auras. I could tell right away that both of you are special. I believe that both of you will play a significant role in the upcoming revolution. I believe that the answers to your questions are in your Dreams." He paused briefly and continued, "Jeremiah, I know that you have become quite close with Maria. Has she explained how I know her?"

I said, "No, she hasn't."

Mr. Franklin said, "I first met Maria in Philadelphia. She was a close friend of my late wife, Debby. After Debby's death, Maria came to me for help. She explained that several Catholic Priests accused her of being a witch. I investigated the matter and found out that they were trying to have arrested. I intervened and, during the middle of the night, had her secreted to the Compound where she would be safe. I knew she was special, but I had no idea how special she was. While checking on her on one of my visits, she explained that she believed that she is a reincarnated soul that has assisted in protecting a secret that I may have some interest in. She also explained that there is a special young man working at the Compound who will help make America the home of all that is right and just. That young man that she referred to is you, Jeremiah."

I said, "Hopefully, all that she says is true. She actually refers to me as one of the Children of the Flood. I have heard this term numerous times in my Dreams."

Mr. Franklin said, "She has mentioned that term to me before, but I don't exactly know what it means. I assume that the flood refers to the Great Flood in the time of Noah."

I asked him, "Have you ever heard of the Secret of Eden?" A big smile came to his face.

He asked, "Let me throw it back at you. Do you know of the Secret of Eden and where it is?"

Alex chimed in, "It is hidden under a small castle somewhere. I don't know where that Castle is, but I believe I was one of the people who helped hide it."

I said, "For some reason, I remember the treasure and Secret of Eden, but I don't remember it being hidden. I remember that the treasure included chests filled with gold and silver, a Chalice, and a large golden candle holding device."

Mr. Franklin looked like he was going to faint. I helped him find his seat. After a few minutes, he finally said, "You are speaking of the Holy Grail and the Golden Menorah. The Holy Grail is the Chalice that Jesus used when he first performed the Sacrament of Communion at the Last Supper. The Golden Menorah was carried by Moses on his journey in the desert. Supposedly, it is located in the Temple of Solomon in Jerusalem. I believe that this Menorah is a replica. I believe the real Menorah that Moses held with his own hands is still missing. You're telling me that you know where it is?" Mr. Franklin went on to ask, "What do you know of the Secret of Eden?"

We both said we have visions of it but don't understand its purpose. Mr. Franklin said, "The Secret of Eden is the foundation of our revolution here in the New World. I know that this is a lot to consider, but you two may be the most important people in the Colonies right now. Although, I think there be one or two more who will join up with you at some point in the near future. Do not discuss this with anyone. We will only speak of this back at the Compound."

Alex said, "I have one other thing to add." Then, after a long dramatic pause, he continued, "I need another drink." We all laughed. We enjoyed a few more drinks before it was time to head out to meet Mr. Adams.

My purpose was beginning to become apparent. I always knew I had a special purpose, but I didn't know what it was. Now I am beginning to understand.

CHAPTER 32

THE ENCOUNTER

Alex, Mr. Franklin, and I set out for the Green Dragon to meet with Mr. Adams. We kept the conversation very light. Alex returned to inquiring about Eliza. I could tell that he was quite taken with her. Hopefully, she would come to the Harvest Celebration this coming Friday. I didn't know what to expect. Mr. Franklin said you will meet the leaders from several of the Colonies at the party.

He said, "The Festivities will be attended by all of the Boston Socialites. You must be very careful what you say because many of these high society types work for the Crown and hence are very loyal to them. No public thoughts about insurrection or impending wars. The party is about celebrating another harvest. It will be complete with the finest wines in the Colonies and the most elegant dancing on this side of the pond."

I said, "Dancing? I hope you don't expect me to dance. I have never danced in my life."

Alex said, "I am in full agreement with you on this. No one

said anything about dancing."

Mr. Franklin responded, "Miss Eliza will be very disappointed if you don't dance with her."

I said, "For this, I must have a front-row seat. This will make this entire journey worthwhile." We all laughed, except Alex of course.

Just as we came upon the Green Dragon, we noticed that roughly ten Redcoats were standing near the entrance. As we approached, we could see that they were hassling a young gentleman and his wife. Having been from England, I was used to being around soldiers. I have never seen any soldiers in all of my years in England behave as badly as the soldiers that I have seen today. Alex and I had witnessed the Redcoats roughly up that poor gentleman in the City Center today and now these soldiers were publicly humiliating this young couple. As we approached Mr. Franklin said, "What is going on here? Has this couple caused a disturbance or broken some law?"

One of the Redcoats stepped forward and said, "Old Man, why are you making this your business?"

I have heard this voice before. Then it hit me. It was Gordon Smith. My former boss and Manager of the Compound. I had just enough whiskey in me to say, "What kind of Army would let a man like you in?" I said to his companions, "Are you aware that you are keeping company with a murderer. I am sure that your Commander would love to hear that." Just then he withdrew his sword from its sheath. Unbeknownst to me, many of Mr. Franklin's associates had gathered behind us. All of them withdrew their knives and swords. The Redcoats were outnumbered two to one.

Mr. Franklin said, "Come now. There is no need for swords. We are just trying to get some supper. So please be on your way."

The second Redcoat who appeared to be their leader said, "Old man, who do you think you are. You would be wise to not speak to us in that manner."

Mr. Franklin said, "I am the Head Postmaster for the Colonies which makes me a Superior Officer to you hooligans. I was appointed by King George III himself. If you are still here when I finish speaking, I will summon General Thomas Gage who I had lunch with this afternoon." The Redcoats immediately disbursed.

I hadn't noticed Mr. Adams behind us. I walked over to him and said, "Sir, I am very sorry for my outburst, but I became crazed with anger at the sight of Mr. Smith. I immediately thought of the beautiful family that Mr. Walker left behind after the mill incident."

He said, "No apology necessary. Many would have hung Gordon for his atrocity. The fact that he is my sister's son is the only thing that saved him."

We all entered the establishment. One by one Mr. Adams friends and associates came up to offer congratulations for standing up to the Redcoat the way I had. The anger gradually wore off as I was toasted by the men in our group. Mr. Adams introduced the men. I met Patrick Henry, Paul Revere, and John Hancock. They joined us for supper. We had wide-ranging discussions throughout the evening.

Mr. Franklin pulled Alex and me aside and whispered to us, "Not everyone here can be trusted. Be very careful what you say. Tomorrow evening we will return here for a meeting of the Sons of Liberty. There are secure rooms in the basement. You can speak your mind then." We both completely understood.

We stayed at the Green Dragon until most of the patrons had departed. I sat and thought to myself, "I came to the Colonies as a British Subject. A few years later, and now the British are my enemy. My father and brothers had fought for the British. My brothers gave their lives for some irrelevant British cause. I firmly believe with all of my heart that these brave men that I am surrounded by are part of the plan that has been laid out for me. They are all here to assist me in my role as Guardian of the Secret of Eden. This was a comforting thought."

As I sat there finishing my ale, my mind returned to Gordon. Somehow, I knew that this was not the last of him.

CHAPTER 33

THE POSTMASTER

THE NEXT MORNING, we all rose early. Mr. Franklin invited Alex and me to accompany him as he tended to his Postmaster business. We slowly ate our breakfast and drank our tea while Mr. Franklin arranged all the paperwork he had brought with him. Finally, we all departed Mr. Adams's house and agreed to meet him back at the house later that afternoon.

Alex said, "Please explain to me what the Postmaster does. I have heard that the term Postmaster is held in high regard, but I don't know exactly what their mission is."

Mr. Franklin said, "Excellent question, Alex. The Postmaster first and foremost develops an efficient and accurate method to deliver letters and packages to their desired location. This can be in the Colonies or anywhere else in the world, for that matter. This is about controlling the flow of information. During times of conflict, the only consistent way that info or intel can travel is via an organized postal system. During the middle ages, couriers carried messages to and from the various Crowns. Often the messenger was killed before the message could arrive. Wars could change course because a document that included a settlement or peace offering never made it to its intended recipient. In England, the leaders realized that there was a critical need for the safe transfer of the mail. During the Crusades, the Knights Templar played a major role in delivering messages from the Holy See in Rome to Paris, London, and other centers of power. The Knights delivered the messages for a fee just as they charged a fee for protecting Pilgrims or serving as a bank."

Both Alex and I exchanged a glance when we heard Mr. Franklin mention the Knights Templar.

Mr. Franklin continued, "The Postmaster must develop efficiencies that speed up the delivery of messages. For instance, my colleagues and I have come up with a delivery service that has horse transfers that take place much in the same way that our carriage changed horses and drivers during our transport here to Boston. These horses are specially trained to travel fast. I have developed precise schedules where you can accurately tell how long it will take to send a letter from Charleston to Boston or New York to Philadelphia. We have precisely preplaced the horses and drivers at locations that made sense. This would dramatically reduce the time it would take to deliver a letter. Freight and packages are shipped more often on land than by the sea. Sending messages by ships could be a little less predictable. The weather, as well as inexperienced captains, could make the system less than productive.

Mr. Franklin continued, "Many were unaware that the Postmaster also lends a hand in managing shipping. All of the Harbor Masters communicate directly with the Postmaster. The Postmaster manages the schedules, fees, tariffs, and levies."

Alex asked, "If you are in charge of collecting the fees, can you just not collect the fees that are egregious?"

Mr. Franklin smiled and said, "I could do that, but once my superiors back in London found out, I would be out of a job and probably be placed under arrest. The one thing that I can do is discuss shipping schedules. I know when particular freight is scheduled to arrive or depart. This gives our associates a distinct advantage for now. I know when troops are scheduled to arrive, and when troops depart, I know precisely where they are going. The role of the Postmaster is unheralded, but keep in mind that no one else in the Colonies has as much information as I do."

I asked, "If this leads to conflict, will you have to give up your position?"

Mr. Franklin said, "Yes, but I intend to ride it out as long as possible. After conflict starts, I believe my role will shift to that of a Statesman. We believe the only way we can win such a conflict is to have the French on our side. I will probably spend most of my days in Paris, where I have numerous avenues to access King Louis XVI. His biggest weakness is his hate for the British. You must understand that the hatred between the two kingdoms has gone on for hundreds of years. This has often turned into war. There was the Hundred Years' War which the French won, and then there was the Seven Year's War, in which the British were victorious.

Alex said, "I would wager that King Louis XVI would like nothing better than to see his arch-enemy, the British Throne, lose the Colonies."

Mr. Franklin said, "Yes, Alex, that is what I am wagering my entire career on. Without the French standing behind us, it would be impossible for the Colonies to secede. The first and foremost task for me will be to secure loans. Wars are very expensive endeavors. The side with the deepest pockets and best logistics usually wins. History usually depicts wars being won on battlefields. Many don't realize that someone behind the scenes had figured out the enemy's troop and supply movements. The victorious side usually will create a tactical advantage by cutting off supply routes and slowing down troop movements. Once supply routes are cut off, munitions and necessities such as food and gear never reach their intended destinations. Nothing will slow an army down quite like going without food."

Alex said, "I have wondered how the militias here in the Colonies could defeat the world's largest Navy. I am beginning to understand that by controlling the flow of information coupled with knowing the landscape, the militias can perhaps catch the British off guard. From what I know of warfare, it usually involves large armies facing off against each other, and the more valiant side wins. For the Militias to succeed, they will have to turn a decided disadvantage into an advantage."

Mr. Franklin said, "Alex, please continue."

Alex said, "By knowing where British troops are heading, the militias can have surprise attacks that will make their small numbers an advantage. They will be able to sneak up on their enemy. Furthermore, if you know where the troops are heading, the supply movements won't be far behind. Cutting off and seizing the supplies will level the battlefield. Otherwise, all will be lost if the militias try to fight the British head-on in a traditional battle. The British will quickly overwhelm us."

Mr. Franklin said, "Alex, you are one hundred percent correct. The next step by the British will be to flood the Colonies with the British Army. If I do my job properly with King Louis XVI, he will see this as an opportunity to attack his lifelong foe. The British will not be able to send a large force here to the Colonies if its homeland is threatened by its arch enemy."

I said, "Back at the Compound, I have several men working for me that were in the French and Indian War. The Indians have notoriously fought on both sides of this War. My friends described the warfare that we are discussing. The tactic the Indians used against the British in the French and Indian War brought terror to the hearts of these men. Many of their friends died when the Indians attacked during the night. The British would have sentries posted throughout the camp, but the Indians would move so silently through the woods that by the time the Sentry noticed them, it was too late. The Indians knew and controlled the woods. The British became so disheartened that many troops tried to abandon their posts. This would usually re-sult in a charge of treason and a very quick death. The tactics of surprise are our only chance to defeat the British. We must learn these tactics."

CHAPTER 34

THE SONS OF LIBERTY

WE FINISHED MAKING the Postmaster rounds with Mr. Franklin and returned to Mr. Adams's home. The plan is to meet Mr. Adams and Mr. Franklin's associates at seven o'clock at the Green Dragon. My thoughts went to the previous evening's encounter with Gordon. Hopefully, I had not made matters worse. My anger got the best of me. I just remembered going to Mr. Walker's house to inform his wife of his passing. He was such a good man. The loss was so unnecessary. I will never forgive Gordon for what he did. Deep inside, I knew that our paths would cross again. Would I have the courage to avenge Mr. Walker's death? I wonder how many other atrocities Gordon had committed now that he was a Redcoat. I need to leave these thoughts behind for the moment. I need to focus on my mission.

Mr. Adams summoned us to the sitting room. I'm sure it was what Mr. Franklin referred to as 'Happy Hour'. When I walked into the room, I noticed that there was no alcohol anywhere to be seen. Mr. Adams had a very serious look on his face. He finally spoke. He said, "You may have wondered why Ben and I have brought you on this trip. Why we have been teaching you very valuable lessons, some of which, are at our own peril."

Alex tried to lighten the air in the room. He said, "I thought you needed friends to drink with?"

Mr. Franklin tried his best not to laugh. He said, "Alex, I understand why Mr. Adams gets angry with you at times, but I do believe that your attempts at humor will be a strength for us at some point. You will be able to diffuse troublesome situations. Don't ever stop trying to be humorous. A change in temperament can ultimately change the outcome of a conversation. Although this may be true, there are times also when you should say nothing. This is one of those times."

I said, "What Mr. Franklin is saying in the kindest way that I have ever heard is "Shut up and listen"."

Mr. Franklin said, "Touché."

Mr. Adams continued, "Tonight, if you choose to join us, you will meet some very serious men who are ready to put their life on the line for our cause. Neither Ben nor I have asked you, "First, do you believe in our cause, and second do you wish to join us?"

Without missing a beat, I said, "I do not speak for Alex, but I believe that I have been placed into this situation by God to achieve a goal that I don't quite understand yet, but with every fiber of my being, I know that the proper move for me is to join with you and crush the oppression that we are witnessing."

Alex spoke next. He said, "I have been an orphan my whole life. I feel that I have finally met my family. Your cause is righteous and justified. I too wish to be part of it."

This brought a smile to both Mr. Adams and Mr. Franklin's faces. Mr. Franklin said, "Now to the important part. We shall share a toast to your acknowledgments."

Alex said, "Well, if you insist." We all had a good laugh.

We shared a toast then Mr. Adams said, "Tonight, you shall be asked to give your oath to the Sons of Liberty. Over the next few days, you may be asked to swear to a slightly different oath."

I wasn't sure what he was referring to, but I knew that I would find out soon enough.

Soon after that, we walked to the Green Dragon. This name seemed somehow appropriate. Our legion was going to be formidable but cagey just as the fabled Dragon was said to be. This time as we arrived at the Green Dragon, there were no Redcoats there to cause trouble. However, I could see a group of Redcoats assembled about a block away. I was reasonably certain that Gordon Smith was among them.

Mr. Adams, Mr. Franklin, Alex, and I entered the Green Dragon as we had the previous evening. This time we made our way through the kitchen to a stairway that led to a large room in the basement. I'm sure that this room had been originally built for storage. A smaller structure was built behind this building last summer that is used to house the food and drink products.

As we entered the room, it appeared that we were the last to arrive. Mr. Samuel Adams said, "Gentlemen, let me introduce you to these two young men who wish to join our cause. The one on my right is Mr. Jeremiah Briggs. He currently manages the Compound for me and has turned a struggling operation into a very profitable one. The young man on my left is Alexander Hamilton. He is also now working at the Compound. Alex, as we refer to him, possesses extraordinary intelligence who will no doubt be an asset at some point."

From the back of the room, a voice spoke up that I would later learn was Mr. Paul Revere. He said to Mr. John Adams, "John, isn't this the young man that burned your barn to the ground last summer?"

Mr. John Adams responded, "The one and only."

Alex responded, "One little incident appears to have become my trademark. I promise to not start any fires, but you may want to keep me away from the munitions." The room broke out in laughter. I could see that Alex was already winning them over with his charm.

Even though we met several of the men the previous evening, the men stood, one by one, and gave a brief introduction of themselves. The man to our right rose first. He said, "Very pleased to meet both of you. My name is John Hancock and I'm a proud merchant that specializes in imports and exports. I am from Boston"

The next man rose. He said, "My name is Patrick Henry. I am an attorney from Virginia."

The man to his right rose. "I am John Jay. I am a Statesman from the New York Colony."

The next man stood and said, "My name is Paul Revere. I am a Proud Silversmith and Blacksmith from Boston."

The next man rose and said, "I am Robert Morris. I am a Banker from the Pennsylvania Colony."

The next rose and said, "I am Richard Henry Lee. I am a Politician and Statesman from the Virginia Colony."

The next man rose. He said, "My name is James Otis Jr. I am an Attorney from Boston.

The last man was the man who spoke first, "My name is John Adams. I am an Attorney from right here in Boston. I am also the chair of this meeting. We have been told by Ben and Samuel that you wish entry into the Sons of Liberty"

Both Alex and I said, "Yes, I do."

Mr. John Adams continued, "You understand that our motives are in direct opposition to the Laws of the Crown of England."

We both said, "Yes I do."

Then John Adams asked Mr. Franklin to hold the Bible that was behind him so that each man could place his right hand on the Holy Bible.

We both placed our right hands on the Bible. Mr. John Adams said, "Do you solemnly swear an oath of allegiance to the Sons of Liberty. To hold the principles of Life, Liberty, and Justice for all in the highest regard."

We both said, "Yes. I do."

Mr. Adams said, "Welcome to the Sons of Liberty." Everyone

stood and applauded our membership.

Mr. Revere said, "It is about time we brought some young blood into this group. As Ben has stated many times. We are getting a little long in the tooth for this."

Mr. John Adams then said, "We have another very important matter to discuss. As you no doubt are already aware, the British enacted a Tea Act last May. The word of it just made its way to us this fall. They are expecting us to not only abide by this new act, but they expect us to pay a fine for our sales of tea from our alternative sources all the way back to May. A reasonable government would have approached us like civilized people and worked out an arrangement. Gentlemen, this is not about tea. This is about them putting down our rebellion. Many of us have opinions on this matter and they need to be expressed today."

Patrick Henry spoke first, "I believe that the time has come for us to rebel. If not now, when? We need to make a very clear statement. Perhaps we should take the East India tea when it arrives."

John Hancock chimed in, "More tea in our marketplace will hurt all of our merchants. The only ones that will be happy are the owners of the East India Tea Company. We need to destroy the shipment. Maybe Ben could confirm this, but I believe that a large shipment of tea is scheduled to arrive in mid-December?"

That's when I spoke up. "No doubt that the British know all of you and would suspect you immediately. When the shipment arrives, all of you make yourselves scarce and make sure that you have a provable alibi. Alex and I will sneak into the Harbor at night and destroy the tea." I then looked at Mr. Franklin and said, "As we discussed earlier today, this impending war must be won by surprise attacks. The British will look to all of you, but you will all make yourselves very publicly seen as these events occur. The British will be dumbfounded. This will be the first of many attacks that will eventually lead us into a conflict that we can win if we stick to a very strict plan." Everyone sat there quietly thinking about what I had just proposed.

Alex then ended the quiet by stating, "Perhaps I will start a fire." The entire room broke out with laughter. Mr. Franklin's comment to Alex earlier this afternoon where he told him that his levity would solve problems was already working.

Mr. John Adams then said, "As all of you know, many of our associates will be attending our Annual Harvest Festival at Piece Field tomorrow. I propose that we confer with them regarding this plan regarding the East India tea matter. I remind you, do not speak openly regarding any of our plans at the party. There will no doubt be sympathizers to the Crown in attendance. This meeting is adjourned."

The meeting then became much more social as pitchers of ale were served. The discussions broke into smaller groups. Many of the men wished to get to know Alex and me. We all drank and ate a delicious Beef Tenderloin supper that was beyond description. I had time after supper to really get to know some of these gentlemen. I had a long conversation with Mr. John Hancock. He detailed how back in 1768, British Customs Officials had forced their way onto his ship, the Lydia, with no written Warrant.

I said, "This is only going to get worse. I heard a story earlier today about how several young ladies have been raped by British Troops in Boston."

Mr. Hancock said, "I know one of their fathers. The Redcoats had claimed that she was a prostitute. I have known this young lady since she was a little girl. She is not a prostitute. The other thing that is happening is that, as additional troops arrive from their base in Nova Scotia, they just seize our horses. They say that the soldiers have the right to seize horses during times of unrest."

I said, "Where I live you would find yourself at the wrong end of a musket if you tried to steal someone's horse. This is just plain wrong. I am sorry to say that I believe war is on the horizon."

Mr. Hancock said, "Don't be sorry. At the other end of that war will be our freedom."

Everyone really embraced Alex and me as the new members of the Sons of Liberty. In many ways, I also was also an orphan. These men would become my extended family.

CHAPTER 35

THE RIDE TO PIECE FIELD

THE NEXT MORNING, Alex and I slept a little longer than usual. When we finally rose and joined Mr. Franklin in the Dining Room, he was working diligently scouring reports of inbound ships to the Colonies. He tracked the Bills of Lading from the East India Tea Company. He said, "It seems that there are seven vessels heading for the Colonies carrying the East India Tea. Four are headed for Boston, one each for New York, Philadelphia, and Charleston."

I said, "Why so many for Boston?"

He said, "It denies logic from a business sense. The census that I reviewed last month in Philadelphia showed that there were 40,000 people in Philadelphia, 25,000 in New York, 15,000 in Boston, and 12,000 in Charleston. The normal course of business dictates that you ship your products to where your customers live."

I said, "They are sending a message. They are looking to rub our noses right in it. They want the Sons of Liberty to take the bait. As I said last night, they don't know Alex and me. The Senior Members of the Sons of Liberty should be seen as peacefully protesting. A team of young upstarts like Alex and myself can move quietly and destroy the tea. The only problem is that Alex and I can't pour four ships' worth of tea into the Harbor. We are going to need help. It is hard to believe that the Colonies, all together, drink that much tea."

Mr. Franklin said, "Believe it or not, tea is the number one drink of choice both here in the Colonies and worldwide."

Alex finally joined us and said, "Are there any ships carrying Whiskey or Rum that we can ransack?" We all laughed.

Mr. Franklin said, "We will leave the flow of spirits untouched. We will have more rioting than we wish otherwise."

Mr. Franklin said, "While I like the idea of having outsiders destroy the tea, I cannot have you two risk being captured or worst during this operation. We have much bigger plans for you two."

Once again, I wondered, "What kind of plans are they referring to?"

We then talked about the day. The ride to Peace Field would take a little over two hours. We planned on departing at two o'clock. I said to Mr. Franklin, "After breakfast, Alex and I are going to the Boston City Center to take it all in one more time."

We agreed to meet back at the house around one o'clock. Mr. Franklin reminded us to wear our finest and cleanest outfits this evening. I would even take a bath before our journey. It just hit Alex that he may be seeing Miss Eliza this evening.

Alex said, "You may be in line behind me for the bathtub. I need to look my best this evening."

I said, "You are going to bathe. Is it the first of the month already?"

Alex said, "Very funny."

Mr. Franklin sat and chuckled while we went back and forth. I believed that we were keeping him young.

We arrived back at Mr. Adams's house shortly after noon.

Alex prepared the bath for himself. I decided to get some rest. It was going to be a long night.

Precisely at two o'clock, we loaded onto the carriage and started to make our way to Peace Field. Alex seemingly was getting more restless by the moment.

I finally said, "I do hope that Eliza is there for your sake. Otherwise, you will be miserable for the foreseeable future."

Finally, we arrived at Peace Field several hours later. Alex and I were informed that we would probably be sleeping in the storage barn this evening. Mr. Franklin would no doubt be staying in a nice, warm, cozy bed.

Mrs. Adams came out to greet us. She said, "Samuel, I'm so glad you are finally home."

Mr. Adams said, "It's wonderful to be home. Dear, I would like you to meet Mr. Jeremiah Briggs. Jeremiah, this is my wife, Elizabeth."

She said, "So lovely to finally meet you. Samuel has spoken so highly of you."

Piece Field Estate

I said, "Your husband is a great man. I am learning much from him."

Samuel said, "Of course, you know Ben and Alex."

She said, "Ben, I always look forward to our encounters. You always bring clarity to the dark and muddled. And Alex, I hear very good things about you as well. Hannah will be so excited to see you."

I had a feeling that this would be a night to remember.

CHAPTER 36

WHERE DESTINY MEETS FATE

THERE WAS SOMETHING very familiar about Peace Field. I couldn't quite put my finger on it. Was it from one of my Dreams? Most of my Dreams seemed to be in Scotland, France, or even the Holy Land. Not in Quincy, Massachusetts. On rare occasions, I have Dreams that are seemingly in the future. These Dreams are not as clear and are very difficult to remember. I do recall one such Dream about the future where I woke up in a state of euphoria. I wanted to go back to sleep so that I could rejoin the Dream. Unfortunately, my Dreams don't work that way. However, I do believe that this place was in that euphoric Dream.

A carriage soon arrived that contained Mr. John Adams and his family. His young son sprinted to Alex, where he jumped up onto Alex for a piggyback ride. The young boy said, "Alex, I missed you so much. Are you coming back to live here?"

Alex said, "Quincy, I missed you as well, but unfortunately, I am now living elsewhere. However, I promise to visit you often."

Mr. John Adams said, "Jeremiah, I would like you to meet my wife, Abigail. My other children arrived several hours ago to help set up."

I said, "Very nice to meet you, Mrs. Adams."

She said, "Please call me Abigail. My husband has spoken very highly of you. Welcome to Quincy."

I said, "Thank you."

They ventured into the Estate. I discovered that neither John Adams nor his Cousin Samuel owns Peace Field. It seems that the Estate is owned by Mr. Leonard Vassall, who is a very close friend of John Adams. Mr. Vassall is a famous sugar plantation owner from Jamaica. Mr. Vassall and his wife spend most of their time in Jamaica. The nearby Boston marketplace is Mr. Vassall's largest Customer base. He had bought the Estate on one of his many trips to Boston. He allows the Adams Family to use Peace Field. Mr. Vassall is happy that it was being used by his close friends. Mr. Samuel Adams and his family have been living here for the last few years. This worked out well for Mr. Samuel Adams, seeing that he technically could not own a home because of his legal issues with the British. Mr. Adams only had to pay for the staff and upkeep of this grand old mansion.

I ventured over to where Alex was playing with Quincy. I said, "Quincy, how old are you."

He responded, "I'm just turned ten this past July."

Alex said, "Quincy was working with me when I had my mishap at Mr. John Adams' barn. Quincy is his middle name. His full name is John Quincy Adams. To avoid confusion with his father, many of us simply call him Quincy."

I said to Quincy, "That makes perfect sense. Are you looking forward to the party tonight?"

Quincy said, "Yes. I only hope there will be other children to play with. Otherwise, sitting and watching the adults dancing all night is boring."

Once again, the thought of dancing also sent a shiver down my spine. What if I meet a young lady here tonight that wants to dance? The thought terrified me. Fortunately, or unfortunately, depending on how you look at it, I find myself to be rather shy when it comes to meeting women. Not that I wouldn't like to meet a young lady, it's just that I don't know what to say. So, perhaps, I should just watch what Alex does and then do the opposite.

As we sat outside the Estate, many carriages began to arrive. I greeted all of the men I had met the previous night at the Green Dragon and their spouses. Finally, we went into the Estate. It was very crowded, so Alex and I found a spot near the rounded staircase. We exchanged pleasantries with the people that we met. A server went by, and Alex ordered both of us a red wine. He further instructed the waiter to bring a new glass of wine every ten minutes. Whether he was standing or not.

A few minutes later, I said to Alex, "What is that fragrance. It is very familiar. It is the most beautiful thing I have ever smelled." I was immediately taken back to my Dreams.

Alex replied, "I don't smell anything. The wine must be going to your head. I will tell the waiter to switch you to whiskey instead."

I said, "If I switch to whiskey, you will be carrying me out of here at some point."

Just then, I looked up the staircase. My world came to a screeching halt. I was staring at the most beautiful woman that I had ever seen. But, it wasn't just her beauty. There was a feeling that I somehow knew her. All of the memories from my Dreams came together at the same time. Just then, I had the realization that while I am here to assist with the Revolution and be a Guardian of the Secret of Eden, my real destiny is to connect once again with this very special person.

Alex said, "Quit staring and close your mouth. I told you that she was beautiful."

She came down the stairs. I will never forget that image. She was wearing a blue dress that matched her eyes perfectly. Her curly blondish brown hair rested below her shoulders. She carried herself with the grace and elegance of a royal.

She saw Alex and quickly came to say hello. She said, "Alex, how wonderful to see you. I hear that you are now living at the Compound. I trust that you haven't burned anything down yet."

Alex said, "One little incident. I will have a noteworthy life, and on my tombstone, it will read 'Great man, but once burned down a barn while building a still'". She laughed and said that she misses his humor very much.

She said, "Alex, are you going to introduce …" She had stopped mid-sentence when we made eye contact. Somehow, something special had just happened. She was sensing it too. I could see tears welling up in her eyes. The look of shock suddenly turned into the most beautiful smile I have ever seen. She then said, "I am so sorry. Have we met? I feel as though I already know you."

I smiled and said, "No matter how much I wish it were true. I am from England originally, and now I run the Compound for your father."

She said, "Oh, you must be Jeremiah Briggs. My name is Hannah. I hear your name quite often. My father speaks very highly of you. He even says there is still hope for Alex because of you."

Alex just rolled his eyes. I said, "Alex has been a wonderful addition to the Compound. He has become like a brother to me. Look, he has even instructed the waiter to bring us a glass of wine every ten minutes. Would you like one?"

She said, "Yes, thank you." She grabbed her glass and then had to leave to greet other guests."

As she was leaving, she smiled and said, "Please save a dance for me later."

I said, "Certainly."

Alex and I just stood there meeting and greeting these beautiful people. I pondered back to a time not so long ago when I walked the streets of Southampton looking for scraps to eat. I had nothing to eat and nowhere to sleep. Had I not noticed that sign for the Compound, I wouldn't be in the wonderful position

I find myself in. Now my biggest concern was whether or not I would have to dance with the most beautiful woman that walks God's green Earth. Things are looking up for me. I realized that Mr. Franklin's fate and destiny that he had so eloquently spoken of had just intervened in my life.

Alex then noticed Eliza walking through the front door with her parents.

Alex said, "You are on your own. My beauty has arrived." I walked over with Alex to greet Eliza and her parents.

I said, "It is so nice to see you again. And Eliza, you were able to join us after all."

We continued to make small talk. I looked across the room. Hannah was looking at me and smiling. The important thing was that she wasn't paying attention to all the men giving her attention. Seemingly, every young man at the party was trying to get her attention, but she was smiling at me. This happened several more times. We looked at each other like we had met in some fairy tale that was now intertwined with our current life.

I finally had enough wine in me to get up the courage to walk across the room and talk to her again. I said, "Alex tells me you are an expert marksman with the long rifle and bow. That is very impressive."

She said, "Yes, I enjoy these affairs, but I am happiest when I'm bird hunting or on a long ride on my horse. Actually, I spent most of today hunting pheasant with my Cousin. We took eight birds."

I said, "That's great. It's funny that you mentioned that you are happiest when you are outdoors. That's exactly how I feel. My entire life has been spent in the wild. As a matter of fact, I have never been to a party such as this. It's wonderful, but I am less afraid of encountering a mountain lion than having to dance in front of all of these people."

She laughed and said, "Have you ever danced before?"

I said, "No."

She said. "Then I have a new mission. I am going to teach you how to dance tonight."

"I think we should remove anything breakable first," I said. She laughed. Her attention then turned towards Alex.

She said, "I've never seen Alex so enamored with a girl before. He has had many opportunities, but there seems to be something different about this one."

I said, "Yes. We were on our way here the other day with your father when he had a chance meeting with Eliza. He has been a bundle of nerves ever since."

She said, "It's funny that you referred to Alex as your brother a few minutes ago. I feel the same way."

I said, "That can't be true because that would make you my sister, and God would not commit such a wrong."

She looked at me and said with the most devilish smile. "You would not like to have me as a sister?"

I could feel myself blushing, and I said, "No. That would be a rather sad day."

She said laughingly, "I have made you blush."

I said, "It must be the wine." Just then, Mr. Franklin waved me to come over. I said to Hannah, "Even though it terrifies me greatly, I look forward to meeting you on the dance floor later."

She smiled at me, and I then made my way to Mr. Franklin.

He said, "Jeremiah Briggs, I want you to meet Mr. Thomas Jefferson from Virginia. He is a prominent businessman and one of our associates."

I said, "Very nice to meet you, sir." We made small talk, but I couldn't get my mind off Hannah. Hopefully, I didn't make too big of a fool out of myself. Once again, I looked across the room. Hannah was talking to some of her father's friends. It was like she knew I was looking at her. She turned her head and smiled at me.

For the next little while, I spent time with the associates that I had met last night. There were several toasts in my honor as the newest member of the Sons of Liberty. We toasted to our battle for Freedom. My mind quickly returned to happy thoughts as I saw Hannah on the far side of the room. She had her back to me. As if on cue, she turned around and caught me staring at her. Did this woman have eyes in the back of her head? Or perhaps, were we speaking on a whole other level. It was like we knew each other's thoughts.

It was finally time for the music to start. Mr. Samuel Adams had hired a six-string band that played along with a fife and bugle corps that played flutes and percussions. The band surrounded a grand piano. They started the festivities by playing a song that all Patriots know, Yankee Doddle Dandy. This brought everyone to their feet. This song transcended the simple lyrics it possessed. It spoke to the American spirit.

This was followed by a Waltz from someone I had never heard of. His name is Wolfgang Amadeus Mozart. It was very lovely. I knew that my time of avoiding the art of dancing had come to an end. I was speaking with Mr. Paul Revere when suddenly I felt someone grab my hand. Without even turning around, I knew it was her.

She said, "Excuse me, Mr. Revere, but Mr. Briggs has a very pressing matter to tend to."

Mr. Revere laughed and said, "I'm sure that Mr. Briggs would rather spend a moment or two with you than sitting here listening to my ramblings about the Redcoats."

We found a nice wide spot on the Dance floor, and Hannah said, "Now listen closely. It is actually very simple. Step forward with your left foot. Then step sideways to the right with your right foot. Then bring your left foot next to your right foot. Then step back with your right foot. Step back sideways with the left foot, and then bring your right foot next to your left foot. Then repeat the entire process."

This didn't seem that difficult. The drinks and toasts that I had celebrated with my new brothers in rebellion probably gave me more difficulty than the dance moves had.

We started slow. I began to get the hang of it. I noticed that Alex was nearby. Eliza was giving him similar instructions. We both looked at each other and shared a laugh. I thought to my-self, 'If you want to start a rebellion, Alex and I are the proper choice. If you want to learn how to dance, we are not.'

My gaze returned to Hannah. Not only was I dancing with the prettiest woman in the room, but it was like we were part of some cosmic ballet. It was like someone from above was orchestrating my every move.

Hannah said, "See, you learned how to dance to a Waltz. Was that so difficult?"

I said, "No, the key is to have such a wonderful and beautiful teacher."

She said, "Thank you for the kind words." She continued, "I don't want to seem forward, but tomorrow I plan on going for a long ride on my horse. Would you like to join me?"

I said, "Absolutely, there is no place I would rather be."

She smiled and said, "Do you think you can keep up with me?"

I said, "Is that a challenge? I have heard the tales of how you beat all of the men in Boston. I am fortunately not one of those men."

She said, "Meet me at the horse barn after breakfast tomorrow morning."

I said, "At least I won't have to travel far. Alex and I are sleeping in the barn right next door this evening."

She laughed and said, "I'm sorry for the meager accommodations, but as you can see, we have many people to house."

I said, "No worries. Now while I'm sleeping in the freezing cold, I can at least strategize about how to keep up with you tomorrow."

She said, "It is settled then. We will race to the point. It is a beautiful spot that overlooks the ocean. Will you be able to accept defeat?"

I said, "Win or lose, I will be the winner because I will have had the chance to spend more time with you."

She said, "Good answer."

We continued to dance the night away. I never thought I would enjoy dancing, but I also never thought I would meet anyone like Hannah. Even though we just met, I feel as if I have known her forever.

Mr. Franklin called me over to meet another one of his associates. I told Hannah that I would return shortly. I found my glass of wine and took a sip. I was walking backward while gazing at her. Suddenly, I bumped into Mr. Franklin, which caused me to spill my wine all over the shoes of Mr. Franklin's friend. A server was nearby. He quickly cleaned up the spill. I apologized profusely. My mind was clearly elsewhere. I met Mr. Franklin's friend and his wife. We talked for several minutes, but I could only think about getting back to Hannah. I returned to her several minutes later.

She said, "I saw your mishap. Alex was standing with me. We both had a good laugh."

I said, "Wonderful, not only have I stained that poor man's shoes, but I will hear about this from Alex all night long."

The night was regrettably coming to an end. I have never had a more enjoyable evening. I thanked Hannah for the dance lessons and said, "I look forward to your challenge tomorrow." I grabbed her hand and kissed it.

She gave me that devilish smile and said, "Please don't bring anything that you may spill. I just bathed the horses today. I would hate to have to do it again."

I met Alex outside. He was saying goodbye to Eliza and her parents. He had a huge smile on his face. He said, "I see that you had a lovely time with Hannah. You seem to forget that she is your Boss's daughter."

I said, "I am sorry about that, but Hannah and I have a bond that is beyond description."

Alex said, "Hopefully, you won't spill any wine on me this evening."

I said, "Go ahead. Get it out of your system."

Alex said, "I would prefer to save it for tomorrow."

I said, "Perfect, I will be gone for at least part of the day to-morrow. I am scheduled to go riding with Hannah tomorrow."

Alex said, "Don't let her talk you into a race. She will wipe the course with you."

I said, "Too late. Also, I must find that gentleman and his wife that I spilled my wine on and apologize once again. I didn't even catch their names. Do you know who they are? I hope that he will not play a prominent role in my future. Otherwise, I am not off to a good start."

Alex said, "I believe that was General George Washington and his wife, Martha."

CHAPTER 37

THE MORNING AFTER

I WAS AWOKEN PRECISELY at dawn by a rooster that seemingly was just inches from my ear. Alex was nearby, lying underneath a blanket of hay. I'm sure if I had asked Hannah, she would have given us some blankets. I retrieved a bucket of water from the well to clean myself up. Even though I was half-frozen, I chose to pour the bucket over my head. I disrobed and prepared myself for the shock. The cold water seemingly stopped my heart for a minute. I quickly dried off and brushed my hair back into a perfect Ponytail. Thankfully, I still had one of the new outfits I had not worn yet. I was going to spend the day with Hannah and wanted to look my best. Alex had witnessed me pouring the ice-cold water over my head. He said, "Have you lost your mind?"

I said, "I am spending time with Hannah today. So I want to look my best."

He said, "I won't see Eliza today. She is leaving early this morning with her parents for the journey back to Albany. No need to pour cold water over my head." He continued, "I have plans to visit Albany in a few weeks to visit with her."

I said, "I will have to find an excuse to get back here very soon."

He said, "Let me guess. There will be some emergency or other urgency that causes you to come up to Peace Field where, oh, let me see, Hannah lives."

I said, "Something like that."

Alex went back to sleep under his pile of hay, and I went for a walk. I hadn't taken notice of what a beautiful place this is. Peace Field is the perfect name. I walked up to a nearby hill that Mrs. Abigail Adams told me about last night. She said, "Some nights, I take Quincy for a walk up to the top of the hill. You can see for miles in all directions." Once I arrived there, I looked out in the direction of Boston. Suddenly, I saw a disturbing image. There was a major battle taking place several miles away. Why was I seeing this? Was someone from above trying to warn me? I sat up there on the hilltop for several more minutes.

The vision slowly faded away. The next vision was of Boston growing tenfold. There were buildings that seemingly reached the sky. Was this Boston's future. Was this a British Colony or an American City? Why was I given this gift of being able to see things? I am pretty certain that Hannah also has this gift. I could sense that she has similar capabilities. Fate had placed both of us on a collision course that finally ended last night. Somehow, I knew that I was destined to be with her, but there were many complications. Not the least of which was that we lived two hundred and fifty miles away from one another. Would fate somehow fix this for Hannah and me?

I headed down the hill and returned to the mansion. I needed to focus on today only. These complicated future ideas were just thoughts that tended to make me nervous. My time here in the Colonies has been relatively simple until now. I have heard Mr. Franklin say, "How do you eat a large beast? One bite at a time." He had many wise sayings. They reminded me of the Proverbs in the Bible. Rumor has it that he once published his sayings or proverbs, as I like to call them, in what is known as

Poor Richard's Almanac. Evidently, he has another ruse where he posed as a woman named Silence Dogood. He did this because it was the only way he could get his brother James to print any of his thoughts in his publication. Miss Dogood was so convincing that several men offered to take her hand in marriage. Mr. Franklin had to stop the charade. Someday, I need to speak with him about his aliases.

As I approached the house, I noticed Mr. Franklin was having tea with several of our associates. Seated at the table were John Adams, Thomas Jefferson, George and Martha Washington, Mr. Franklin, and Alex. Once she saw me, Mrs. Washington said, "Jeremiah, please join us."

I pulled up a chair and said, "General and Mrs. Washington, please let me give you my most profound apology for spilling that glass of wine on you last night." The server came by, and I ordered myself a cup of tea.

General Washington said, "Please bring his tea in a cup with a lid. One never knows when Miss Hannah will wander by." Of course, Alex thought that was the funniest thing he had ever heard.

Mrs. Washington said, "First of all, please call me Martha. Hopefully, we are shedding the formal ways in which the British handle everything. You, gentlemen, are about to change the world together. At least we can refer to each other by our first names."

With a very straight face, John Adams said, "Alex, you can continue to refer to me as Mr. Adams." Everyone laughed.

Martha continued, "As far as last night's mishap, it was worth every minute. There is nothing as romantic as seeing a young man being so smitten with a young lady. George, I remember when you had that look about you."

The General said, "Yes, I remember those days fondly."

Martha continued, "And John, I'm sure Abigail could tell a tale or two."

John Adams replied, "Yes, but that would be called a Fairy Tale." We all laughed.

I said, "Please keep me in your thoughts. Miss Hannah has challenged me to a horse race today."

John Adams replied, "You will need more than our prayers. George, I would say that she is as good on a horse as any of your cavalrymen."

The General said, "Mr. Briggs, your demise today will most likely be a sight to behold."

I said, "So everyone tells me."

Mr. Jefferson said, "Ben, when are you leaving? Perhaps, we could share a carriage? I have much that I would like to discuss with you."

Mr. Franklin replied, "A wise man once said, 'Both Fish and visitors begin to stink after three days. So, I plan on leaving to-morrow." Both Alex and I laughed.

Mr. John Adams said, "Wise man? Let me guess, Miss Do-good also agrees with Mr. Saunders regarding this assessment?"

Mr. Franklin said, "Of course, she is wise beyond her years." Everyone was laughing. I had no idea why, but I played along as if I was in on the joke.

The General said, "Ben, I think the reason that you spend time with these young men is that they laugh at your old insidi-ous humor."

Mr. Franklin said, "George, the next time I see you, I will have all new insidious humor."

CHAPTER 38

RACE DAY

SHORTLY AFTER, I headed to the horse barn where Hannah was waiting for me. She was wearing her riding clothes. She was just as beautiful as she was the night before in the formal evening dress.

I said, "Good morning. How lovely to see you again. My associates just informed me that I stand no chance in a race against you."

She said, "Is that so. I will try to go easy on you. You probably are tired from all of our dancing last night."

I said, "Tired would be the wrong word. Excited would be more appropriate."

She said, "Come over here. I want you to meet my two prize horses. In this stall is my stallion, Mark Anthony, and the other stall is my mare, Cleopatra. I call them Mark and Cleo for short. I have had them since their birth. Their lineage has been with my family for over a hundred years."

I said, "They are beautiful. Are they both Morgans?"

She said, "Yes, you will be riding Mark. We will race down the south road for roughly five miles. You will see the Point once you get near there. The views are breathtaking." Here comes that smile. She said, "I will be waiting there for you."

I said, "I love your confidence. See you there."

Both horses were already saddled and ready to go. So I took my mount and prepared to head south.

Hannah said, "We should both go at a slight jog to let the horses warm up. The horses will be ready to run once we arrive at the willow down at the property line."

The first thing that I noticed was that she was not riding side-saddle. She is the first woman I have seen ride a horse by straddling it. She seemed to have the horse's confidence. I have been around enough horses to tell when they are happy with their driver. Cleo seemed excited and happy. Mark wasn't quite sure about me yet. We talked all the way to the willow tree. It was primarily small talk about how she started riding when she was five. She asked me if I get to ride much at the Compound. I said, "I ride every opportunity that I get. As a matter of fact, I'm trying to convince your father to expand the horse ranch."

She said, "Really, perhaps you could hire me to help."

I said, "Nothing would make me happier." She smiled at me, and the next thing I saw was a cloud of dust. She broke off of the road because she knew the fields. There was at least a three-foot fence coming right in front of her. The horse took the fence in full stride like it wasn't even there. I was trying to push Mark to go faster, but he was content running at our current speed. Come to think of it. Mark was moving as fast as any horse that I have ridden. The problem was that Hannah was clearly pulling away. A few minutes later, I had lost sight of her. I thought, "I hope this horse knows where he is going because I surely don't." Then, finally, she came into view. She was at the top of what appeared to be a cliff. She had just dis-mounted Cleo. I finally rode up and dismounted.

She said, "I almost had enough time for a nap."

I said, "Ha Ha, very funny. I will admit that your ride was a thing of beauty. You took that jump with no effort at all."

She said, "Cleo and I have been jumping that fence since she was a young Filly." We tied the horses up and walked up to look at the beautiful view.

She said, "Do you believe in soulmates?"

I was caught completely off guard, "I said, "Yes."

She said, "I am referring to the horses. They were born one day apart. They have been together literally since they could stand. I used to spend hours watching them run and play together. They sleep standing almost face to face. When they are out grazing, they stand almost always touching each other. It is very romantic. When you had lost sight of me, there was no need for concern. Mark will always find Cleo."

Our conversation turned to last night. We were standing face to face. She had that smile again. She said, "Alex seemed to be taken with Eliza. One would possibly say he was smitten. What exactly does that mean?"

I started to answer her, "It means…wait a minute. Where else have you heard that term recently?" She had obviously overheard my conversation with Mrs. Washington.

She said, "You are not supposed to answer a question with another question."

I said, "Hasn't anyone ever told you that you shouldn't eavesdrop?"

She said, "Eavesdrop? The conversation was so loud that I am sure the next farm had heard it. I was being teased by the house staff all morning." She paused and said, "So you still never answered my question."

I said, "To be smitten means that you want to spend every second of every day with that person. It means that you have let your guard down enough for that person to come in and get to know the real you."

Just then, I grabbed her hands. Instantly, we were both whisked away into a Dream that took place in the days of Noah.

We saw the two young children, Tytea and Peleg, standing on the deck of the Ark, looking at the vast sea that was in all directions. Suddenly, we were whisked away to a different place. We saw the Knight named Jacques standing on the cliff in Scotland. The beautiful maiden with him had pointed west and told him, "Your future lies west." Next was the Celtic Chieftain and his Princess, pointing west over the endless sea. The image changed, and it was Hannah and me all of a sudden. Then we were both back on this cliff in Quincy. We both felt the wave of emotion that went right through our beings. We could sense the hopes and dreams of everyone who had moved to the New World. Just like those who traveled before us, we knew that we were in Arcadia, or the New Atlantis as Plato had once called it. Hannah and I were looking back at our past incarnations just to tell them, "We have arrived."

Then I looked deep into Hannah's eyes. We were speaking, but our lips weren't moving. We were speaking with our souls. She said, "You found me."

I said, "Yes. And I am never going to let you go." Suddenly, a tear ran down her cheek. We were coming back to the present.

I said, "I didn't mean to make you cry."

She said, "Haven't you ever heard of tears of joy." This warmed my heart.

We stood hand in hand, looking at the beautiful scene in front of us. The sea was crystal blue and seemingly went on forever. Suddenly, I understood the correlation to the ocean. Hannah and I have been together forever, just as the sea seemingly goes on forever. What a wonderful thought.

She said, "This has always been my favorite place. I haven't told you yet, but I love to paint. So I often come to this spot and try to capture its beauty."

I said, "I would love to see some of your work."

We stood there quietly for a few minutes when I said, "I have not thought about it for a long time, but when I was a young boy, my father took me to a place called the Isle of Wight on the

English Channel. I stood at the top of a cliff similar to this one and stared at the beautiful water scene before me for hours. My father said that I was in a trance. I have always been drawn to water." I looked into Hannah's blue eyes and said, "Now I know why."

We mounted the horses, and she said, "Let's climb down to the stream and let the horses get a drink. I'm sure they are thirsty."

We continued to share our innermost thoughts that day. To think that I just met her yesterday is inconceivable. After the vision that we shared, I believe that we have known each other for a very very long time.

Hannah said, "Truth be told, I didn't even want to go to the party last night. I went pheasant hunting with my cousin Boylston yesterday. I was having so much fun that I lost track of time. By the time we returned, the guests were already arriving. I was mud from head to toe." I laughed. She continued, "My mother said, "Hurry up and get bathed and dressed. You never know. You may meet Prince Charming this evening." To which I said, "The only young men who show up at these parties are city boys. I doubt that I will find my Prince Charming this evening."

Hannah then stopped, looked at me, and said, "My mother was right." I could feel myself blushing again. She said, "I have made you blush again."

I changed the subject slightly. I said, "I feel that we are in some cosmic play. I have Dreams where we both are different people, but somehow we seem to find each other. It's like we are always meant to be together. Some of these Dreams were in ancient times. Some were in the middle ages in Europe."

Hannah said, "It's funny that you say that. I had a Dream last night that was seemingly from Noah's time where he paired me with a boy that I grew up with. We were to be married. He said that we would be together for all of eternity." She paused and finally said, "That boy was you."

I said, "I have had that same Dream. In fact, in each of the

Dreams, you look different but beautiful." I paused to collect my thoughts. I finally said, "I knew it was you when you descended that staircase last night."

I continued, "I'm not sure if you have met a lady named Maria at the Compound yet, but she is a Seer. Before I left for this trip, she told me that soon all of the Children of the Flood will be reunited. I now fully understand what she was saying. You and I have been together since that fateful day when Noah married us. My brother, who was with us in that lifetime, went by the name of Joktan. You now know him as Alex."

She said, "I have always felt that there will is a special bond with Alex. As we both said last night, he is like a brother to both of us."

I laughed and said, "We will not be short on laughter." We both laughed.

We finally started heading back to Peace Field. Finally, we arrived at the barn and removed the saddles. The horses' evening' meal was waiting for them. They had all they wanted out of life. They had food, a daily ride, grazing time, and most important of all, they had each other.

She grabbed me by the hands and said, "Do you really need to return to the Compound tomorrow?"

I said, "Unfortunately, yes. I was thinking about it. Your father makes the journey to the Compound at least every other week. Maybe, you should start to join him. We could say that you are helping me expand the ranch."

She smiled and said, "My parents will see right through that. Remember, they were this age once."

I said, "I'm not sure if you have any plans tomorrow, but we aren't leaving until around two o'clock. I would like to spend every possible moment with you."

She said, "That sounds wonderful. Let's meet for tea just after sunrise."

Just then, Alex barged into the barn.

I said to Hannah, "See you in the morning."

She leaned forward and kissed me on the cheek. Here comes that smile again. She said, "See you for tea. I will make sure that the server brings a lid for your cup."

Alex burst out laughing. He said, "Hannah, that was brilliant. Jeremiah, where have you been? There is a meeting going on in a few minutes that we are supposed to attend. Remember. We are here to join the Sons of Liberty, not court the boss's daughter. I am supposed to be the irresponsible one. Not you."

I could hear Hannah giggling on her way out of the barn.

CHAPTER 39

THE RURAL LODGE

A LEX HAD A carriage waiting to take us to what was known as the Rural Lodge. It is not a Masonic Temple or Freemason Hall, even though many Freemason meetings occur there. The reason is that there are not enough potential members in the Quincy area at this point. Many of the meetings there happen after a party at the Peace Field House. When Alex and I arrived, we were told to wait in the vestibule. I could hear shouting from within the Main Hall.

Alex said, "Wonder what all of the yelling is about. Obviously, there is some disagreement taking place."

The doors finally opened, and Mr. Franklin appeared. He said, "Sorry for all of the cloak and dagger activities, but we are considering you two for membership to the Freemasons. Unfortunately, new members must undergo a lengthy initiation process, but we don't have time in both of your cases. So instead, the members inside would like to ask you a few questions. The questions don't directly have anything to do with the Freemasons, but are relevant to our current predicaments. So please follow me."

Mr. Franklin said to the collected Patriots, "There is no doubt that you have already met Jeremiah Briggs and Alexander Hamilton. They have recently joined the Sons of Liberty. Now I would like to consider them for an Apprentice Level Membership in the Masonic Lodge or what we all call the Freemasons. Now is the time to ask questions. The members proceeded to ask Jeremiah and myself many questions mainly focused on our feelings toward the British. Mr. Franklin then asked Alex and me to wait out in the vestibule.

About ten minutes later, Mr. Franklin came out and welcomed us to the Freemasons. He said that our actual induction ceremony would take place back at the Compound when we return. He said that the vote was unanimous. We entered the hall, and the atmosphere had changed dramatically. Several kegs of ale were rolled into the room, as well as a keg of whiskey.

I found myself quickly surrounded by the members. They all congratulated me and said, "Well thought, considerate young men are our future."

I stood there admiring all of the hunting trophies that were mounted to the wall. There were deer, elk, and moose heads mounted all the way around the room. Suddenly, one of the men placed his arm around me. It was Mr. Samuel Adams. He said, "Usually when a father meets his daughter's potential suitor, he always sends a clear-cut warning that the suitor better not hurt his daughter. This case is a little different. If you hurt my Hannah, she will make sure that your head makes that hall of fame."

I had to laugh, "Sir, I fully understand. I saw her ride today. I saw her take a fence that most men would shy away from."

Mr. Adams said, "I once watched her take a ten-point buck while riding her horse at top speed."

I said, "I have nothing but the best intentions for not only Hannah, but also for you and your family. I am sincerely worried about you after hearing stories of retribution by the British. I think you should have your family move to the Compound for at least this winter. If you don't want me in such close proximity to Hannah, I will live in Binghamton and commute to work every day."

He said, "I appreciate your concern. I have already discussed this with Mrs. Adams. I think moving my family would be wise at this juncture. My wife is not thrilled about it. My son, Samuel Jr., may try to join the Seminary early. I have not spoken of this with Hannah yet. Please allow me to be the one to tell her of the move. It will not be necessary for you to move to Binghamton. As I said earlier, if you try anything that makes my daughter unhappy, there is an open spot waiting for you at the end of the wall."

"Well, that went well," I thought.

Mr. Franklin then approached and said, "Now that you are a member of the Freemasons, you will learn about your actual mission."

I said, "I have another mission outside of leading a rebellion?'

Mr. Franklin said, "Believe it or not, you and Alex have a far larger purpose going forward. I'm not sure at this point, but it may also involve Hannah. I believe that the three of you share a very unique history."

I thought, "He knows. How does that wily old man know so much? How can he know that Alex, Hannah, and I have been together for multiple lifetimes?"

General Washington then walked up to me and said, "Mr. Briggs, I would like to formally invite you to my home in Mt. Vernon in the Virginia Colony. We have slightly different issues that we are facing in Virginia. Slavery is one of them. I would like to see this practice end. Yes, I own slaves, but I offer them freedom when the time is right. I think that we must fight the British as a united front. We will have to reconcile our differences on slavery if we are to secure our freedom."

I said, "Sir, I welcome the opportunity to travel to your home. Mrs. Washington was so gracious this morning at our morning tea."

He said, "She got you in trouble, didn't she?"

I laughed and said, "It was a good kind of trouble."

He said, "Well, write to me when you plan on visiting. And bring Hannah. Martha absolutely loves her."

I said, "Thank you, Sir. I will definitely bring Hannah if her father allows it."

Well, it didn't take Alex long to be inebriated. Then, finally, he came up to me and said, "You know Hannah will have your head hanging on that wall if you don't treat her right."

I said, "That is the second time I have heard that tonight."

The party went well into the wee hours. What started with a very serious discussion ended with Alex leading everyone in song.

CHAPTER 40

THE DRAGOONS

THE NEXT MORNING came soon enough. I dreaded the thought of leaving Hannah, but I definitely looked forward to sleeping in my bed. I'm not sure if it was because of a lack of comfort or that wretched rooster. He is even closer to my ear than he was yesterday. It was time to get up and get cleaned up by pouring an ice-cold bucket of water over my head as I had done yesterday. Although it was extremely shocking, I was awake for the day. I had to re-wear the outfit I had worn for a few hours the day we arrived. I needed some fresh laundry.

Once again, I was looking forward to seeing Hannah again. I was a little nervous, but not as bad as yesterday. I went to the outdoor garden patio. Just as I arrived, Hannah came out the patio door. Each time I see her, I am frozen for a brief second. Not only is she beautiful, but scenes from previous lives together rush through my conscience like a nice breeze on a spring day.

She said with a big smile, "Good morning."

I said, "Good morning. How is it that each time I see you are even more beautiful than the previous day?"

She said, "You are way too kind." We both ordered tea. I promised her that I would do my best not to spill it.

She said, "How was the meeting?"

I said," It was interesting. It started with a lot of heated debate, but it ended with a very well lubricated Alex leading everyone in song." She laughed.

I said, "One interesting little tidbit from last night happened while I was admiring the hunting trophies of deer, elk, and moose heads that circle the entire room. I had two separate people tell me that I better not ever cross you because you would surely add my head to the collection."

She laughed so hard that she almost spit out her tea. She said, "Who would say such a thing?"

I said, "None other than Alex and your father." This caused her to laugh even more.

She said, "You know they are probably correct."

I said, "Then you have my solemn vow that I will never cross you."

I reached out and grabbed her hand and said, "You must give me the tour of the entire property today."

She said, "That sounds great. I want to make the most of our precious moments together today. Who knows how long it will be before I see you again."

I said, "I promise you it won't be that long." She obviously hasn't spoken with her father yet about leaving Peace Field.

We sat quietly, enjoying the sounds of birds singing and the wind moving the wind chimes ever so slightly. Then, out of the corner of my eye, I noticed some movement coming from the north. On closer inspection, I could see that it was a small troop movement of British Cavalry known as the Dragoons. They were trained to fight with swords and pistols while riding a horse. They were the most fearsome opponent in most battles because they could move about the battlefield quickly. A soldier who has horse-riding ability must work his way up the ranks for an opportunity to be a Dragoon.

I said, "Hannah, please run into the house and tell your father to hide."

She turned her head and saw what I was looking at. She gasped and said, "Should I get some weapons?"

I said, "No. That may make matters worse."

I walked out towards the road that they were approaching on. They made their way to where I was standing. At least eight of them were on horseback. The other six were on foot.

The lead Dragoon said, "Out of my way. We are here for your horses, and we will be taking over this residence as our quarters."

I noticed that there were about 80-100 locals following behind them. Most of them had swords. I'm sure some were hiding pistols. I said, "You will do no such thing. This is a private residence, and you have no right to do this."

Just then, I heard a bellowing voice from behind the Dragoons. It was General Washington. He said, "Banastre Tarleton, what is going on here?"

The Lead Dragoon turned and was startled. He said, "General Washington, I had no idea that you were here. I thought you were retired?" It turns out that Lieutenant Tarleton was under General Washington's command in the French and Indian War.

The General said, "I have taken a short leave. I plan on returning when the Crown needs me, which seemingly will be sooner rather than later because your antics are going to ignite this like a tinderbox. Have you learned nothing? Look around you. Those men may only have swords and possibly pistols. You would no doubt be killed if you tried anything here today."

Tarleton said, "But sir, I have my orders to take up residence and secure Quincy."

The General said, "Get off your mount when you speak to me." Tarleton quickly dismounted and stood at attention.

He said, "I apologize, but I didn't know that you were at this house. We have received word that one Samuel Adams is staying here."

The General said, "Tarleton, do you have a warrant for his arrest?"

Tarleton said, "No. But we wish to question him."

The General said, "Tarleton, have you read your handbook lately as to how we are to treat the Colonists? You are not allowed to take over a man's home and confiscate his horses without any kind of court order."

Tarleton said, "I read the handbook back in my training days."

The General stood about six inches away from Tarleton. The General stood roughly six foot five inches tall and towered over Tarleton by almost a foot. He said in a loud stern voice, "Tarleton, I have read the handbook. As a matter of fact, I WROTE IT."

Tarleton said, "I am very sorry. I will turn the men and head back to Quincy."

The General said, "You will stand at attention until I tell you otherwise."

He further said, "I am dining with General Thomas Gage this evening. Do you know what the subject of our discussion is supposed to be? Well, let me tell you. We are set to discuss how to calm down tensions in the greater Boston area. Should I tell him that you were trying to take the estate where not only I have been staying but also the Postmaster of all of North America (looking over at Mr. Franklin)? Now, I want you to take your men and set up tents outside of Quincy like you have been trained to do. If I hear of another criminal act being attempted by you, I will see to it that you are swinging by a rope from that tree over there. UNDERSTOOD?"

Tarleton said, "Yes, sir. It won't happen again."

The Dragoons turned and left the area.

General Washington returned to the house where he found Mr. Samuel Adams and said, "Samuel, you need to take your family and escape to a safer place today. After I leave, they may come back with the proper paperwork."

Mr. Samuel Adams said, "Understood."

All of the guests began to leave Peace Field. Mr. Adams thanked them one by one. General Washington and his wife, Martha, were headed to Boston to meet with General Gage.

Mr. Franklin pulled Hannah and me aside and said, "I believe Hannah's father is going to send both of you and Alex to the Compound. I will meet you there in roughly two weeks to continue your training. It is extremely critical that we prepare you for your mission as soon as possible. Our entire future depends upon it. I will see you then. He shook my hand and hugged Hannah."

Mr. Franklin and Mr. Jefferson climbed into their carriage and began the long journey to Philadelphia first and then onto Mr. Jefferson's home in the place he called Monticello in the Virginia Colony.

Hannah's Father then summoned us to the second-floor library, where he said that we needed to have a discussion.

CHAPTER 41

The Library

About ten minutes later, Mr. Adams, Mrs. Adams, their son Samuel, Hannah, and I met in the Library. The first thing Mr. Adams said was, "Where is Alex?"

And just then, as if on cue, the door burst open. It was Alex. He was covered with hay that was stuck to his clothing. He said, "Did I miss something?"

The morning had been very stressful, but you can always count on Alex to provide some comic relief. We all laughed for a brief minute. Mr. Adams said, "Alex, Jeremiah will fill you in later. Evidently, the British have deemed that I am a threat. I already know how this plays out. They will start by questioning me, and then suddenly, I will find myself in a jail cell. They will hold me on a made-up charge while they put together a larger made-up case against me. Therefore, here is what needs to happen. Elizabeth, I will need you and Samuel to depart this afternoon on an express carriage to the Compound. Hannah, Jeremiah, Alex, and I will depart shortly after dark on horseback. We must get the horses out of here before those Dragoons come back for them. Since the horses that we are riding will have to rest for at least eight hours per day, it will take us many days to get back to the Compound. I would like to use this opportunity to spend time in the major towns that are on the way. We must tell all of the Patriots that war is on the way. Everyone must be ready."

I looked around the room. Mrs. Adams was crying. She said, "I hate to leave this old home."

Mr. Adams said, "Elizabeth, you know that Mr. and Mrs. Vassall are scheduled to return in December. So we would have probably been headed to either Boston or the Compound at that point anyway."

Young Samuel spoke up. He said, "What of my plans to go to the Seminary next year?"

Mr. Adams said, "Nothing has changed. You will enroll in the Seminary of your choice next year. But, right now, I need you to help your mother pack up. I will have two or three carriages travel with you to the Compound. We must move quickly."

Mrs. Adams said, "Come, Samuel, let's get all of the house attendants to help us pack." They left the Library.

I said, "Sir, I have a suggestion. I think you should clear all of the horses and carriages out of the Adams Trading Company Offices in Quincy. The Dragoons will no doubt raid the office and take whatever they like."

Mr. Adams said, "That's a good idea. I will send a messenger to the office so that the stable manager clears out all of the livestock and sends it to Albany. Also, I would like to send a message to Mr. Phineas Stearns, who lives in Watertown. I would like to meet him in Framingham in two days. That will be a stop on our escape. Mr. Stearns is a very staunch Patriot and will no doubt have the other Patriots ready to meet with us. I will reach out to the other Patriots in the other towns along the way. They will be eager to join us."

Mr. Adams and Alex left the Library. Hannah looked at me and said, "Last night, I cried myself to sleep because you were leaving. Now, we are going to be together for the foreseeable future. Is this the fate and destiny that you spoke of yesterday?"

I said, "It would seem so."

We stood up as to leave the room and stood face to face. After a few seconds pause, I said, "The only thing that matters to me is that I have you by my side."

She leaned over and kissed me on the lips. It will be a moment that I will never forget.

CHAPTER 42

THE DEPARTURE

THE WHOLE MATTER caused unease at the Peace Field House that morning. The thought of these Dragoons just coming and taking whatever they wanted was very disheartening. I am not sure what would have happened if General Washington had not been there. I suppose Mr. Franklin could have helped diffuse the situation. Having a Senior General from His Majesties Royal Army was a nice person to have on our side. That is until they find out that he supports the Colonists. Then he will be enemy number one.

The house was in absolute chaos. Crates were being packed at a frantic pace. It was hard to believe that all of these crates would fit on three carriages. Mr. Adams had told his wife, Elizabeth, to leave some of the larger furnishings. He would have his office staff come over and pack that up at a later date. Clothing and family keepsakes were the critical things to focus on.

The trouble with trying to leave before nightfall in November is that the days are very short. The carriages needed to be on their way before five o'clock. Those of us leaving on horseback could wait until at least seven o'clock. Mr. Adams needed to make his escape from Quincy under cover of night.

Alex and I were helping wherever we could. Moving crates and wrapping up artwork was the task at hand. I came across a watercolor painting that was from the lookout where Hannah and I had our special moment the previous day. It immediately took me back to that instant. Just by looking at the painting, I swear I could hear the sounds that would forever be in my heart. The sounds of waves breaking, seagulls cawing, the wind gusting through the trees. Then I saw the image of Hannah's hair blowing ever so gently in the wind. This image will be in my thoughts forever.

Mrs. Adams walked up and said, "Hannah painted that a few years ago. She calls it "The View of Scotland."

I said, "Really, we were at that exact spot yesterday. The painting really captures it. Is there anything that Hannah is not great at?"

She laughed, "Not really. Neither Samuel nor I know where she gets all of this skill. It's not from me."

I said, "Mrs. Adams, Hannah surely gets her charm and grace from you."

She said, "Thank you. I have tried very hard to pass down what my mother taught me about living an honest and dignified life. Hannah instantly excelled at horseback riding, shooting both the bow and rifle and other skills usually reserved for men. No other girls were doing these activities. Most of her friends were boys. The skill that impressed me most was Tai Chi. When she was around ten, Samuel had brought a Chinese sailor to our home. This man's name was Qi Jingli. Everyone called him Jingley. Anyways, he taught Hannah the art of Tai Chi. He taught her this art, which is a form of self-defense but watching her perform Tai Chi is like watching a ballet being performed. It is also a form of meditation and is supposed to have great health benefits. As a parent, I am comforted knowing that Hannah can take down multiple men at a time if she is ever threatened. I wanted young Samuel to learn it, but he had no interest. His interests have always been in religious endeavors."

I said, "That is a noble profession. You must be very proud of both of your children."

She said, "Thank you for your kind words. I must get back to my packing."

I sat there dumbfounded as to how I had found Hannah. She was perfect in every way. I had known about the artistic skills, but to see this painting was very meaningful. The fact that she called it "The View of Scotland" just confirms that we are both tied together in some mystical play. I decided to go and see if she needed any assistance. She was getting the horses prepared for the long journey.

I arrived at the barn to find her talking to Mark and Cleo. Their heads were right next to hers. She was whispering to them. Then, she saw me walk up and stopped whispering momentarily. "I am just telling these two of the extraordinary journey we are about to embark on. I told them that they are moving to a new country home where they will have endless trails to ride on and a huge field to graze in."

I said, "How did they receive the news?"

She said, "I'd be lying if I said I knew their every thought, but they seemed calmed by the conversation. They both know that I would never let anything bad happen to them."

I said, "Do you have a similar relationship with the other two horses?"

She said, "Not as close, but I think they trust me. I believe all four of them will like their new home."

I said, "I know this uncertainty is very hard on your entire family, but I will do anything you ask to make them adjust to their new home. I believe we are just starting a new chapter of a classic tale for you and me."

She said, "I feel it too."

I said, "Not to change the subject, but both Alex and I were only prepared for a three or four-day trip. I would like to launder our clothes."

She said, "Do you know how to wash clothes?"

I said, "Yes. I hand them to Miss Katherine Crawford. She washes them, and then I pay her." She thought this was very funny.

She said, "First, it was dancing, now laundry. Does it ever end?"

I said, "Somehow, I think the dancing was much more fun. Just show me where I can find the soap and washboard if you please. Alex and I will figure it out."

She said, "One of my aides is finishing my laundry. I will send her to the barn after she is done."

I said, "What else needs to be done with the horses. Do they need to be shoed?"

She said, "No. They were shoed and groomed last week. Other than loading up our bags, I think we are ready to go. I need to finish packing my crates."

As she was leaving, I said, "I was admiring your beautiful artwork with your mother. Please don't forget to bring your art supplies. There are some exquisite scenes at the Compound that I'm sure you will capture in a painting or two."

She said, "Already packed. I already have several sketches of you that I would like to paint. One is from when I was eavesdropping on your conversation with Mrs. Washington, and the other is of you while you nervously waited for our ride to start."

I said, "I can hardly wait to see them."

Later that afternoon, we started to pack the carriages. As I feared, there would need to be three carriages. Moving a family nearly three hundred miles was not easy.

Just then, a carriage pulled up. It was Mr. John Adams, his wife Abigail, and their son Quincy.

Quincy said to Alex and me, "You weren't going to leave without saying goodbye, were you?"

Alex said, "Not a chance."

I said, "Quincy, you should visit us at the Compound. The hunting and fishing are endless. I'm sure you would have a grand time."

Quincy said to Abigail, "Mother can we go to the Compound."

She said, "Sure. We will have family there now. So we will definitely visit."

Alex took Quincy to show him something out behind the house.

John Adams wished to speak with Samuel, "He said, Jeremiah, you need to hear this as well. I found out that several Redcoats had received information that you would somehow damage an inbound tea shipment. That's what they were coming to question you about. Do we have a traitor in our midst?"

Samuel Adams said, "I'm not sure, but it would seem so. We must keep our eyes and ears open for any sign of a traitor."

John Adams said, "One proven way of finding a traitor is putting out false information to anyone who is in question. If the information makes it into British hands, we will know who the traitor is. I will begin working on this."

Samuel said, "I am going to disappear this evening. I will be back in a few weeks to publicly discourage anyone from destroying the tea. Then, they won't be able to blame me. This confusion will be the first of the thousand cuts that Jeremiah so eloquently detailed last evening." The two men hugged each other and told each other to stay safe. Elizabeth and Abigail also said their goodbyes.

As they were parting, Mr. John Adams said to Hannah, "Be sure to go easy on these men on your journey."

Hannah replied, "I will let them keep up with me." Then, she turned to me with that devilish smile that I was becoming accustomed to.

A few minutes later, Mrs. Elizabeth Adams and young Samuel said their goodbyes. Mrs. Adams said to Hannah, "Please keep your father safe."

She said, "All of us will keep him out of harm's way."

Mr. Adams replied, "I can hear you. Am I that old that my daughter is now my guardian?"

Mrs. Adams, young Samuel, and Hannah all said in unison, "Yes." We all had a good laugh.

They mounted the lead carriage and headed towards the Albany road."

Mr. Adams said, "As soon as nightfall arrives, we will take our leave. Hannah, we will depart on what we always very appropriately called the escape path behind the mansion. Since you are very familiar with the path, you will be in the lead position. We will proceed as quietly as possible. No talking or lanterns until we are clearly out of town. Try to keep the horses off of any gravel roads. We will make our leave in about one hour. Please be ready. Alex, please help me bring out all of the weapons to the barn. Everyone will have two pistols, a sword, and two or more knives. Hannah, I want you to carry the long rifle."

CHAPTER 43

THE DARKNESS

NIGHTFALL WAS FAST approaching as Alex and I packed the last of our freshly laundered clothing into our travel bags. We also loaded as much ammo as we could carry. We were both going to ride the larger stallions. I figured that they could handle the extra weight. Suddenly, a thought had occurred to me. I needed to find Mr. Adams.

I went into the house where he was packing up his belongings. I said, "Sir, do you think Gordon had somehow listened to our conversations at the Sons of Liberty meeting the other night. I know a Redcoat couldn't make it down the staircase unnoticed, but there were open windows high up on the walls."

He said, "It is possible, I suppose." He paused for a few seconds and said, "Many employers would have turned him over to the Constable for his actions at the Compound or, even worse, hung him right on the spot. Now, this is how he repays me."

I said, "I am just speculating, but I believe our secret regarding the tea snuck out that evening. We certainly didn't speak of it at the Harvest Festival. At the Freemason meeting, we glossed over the subject. It had to be that night. Do you trust everyone that was in that room on that night?"

He said, "Yes, those men and I have been lifelong friends. They all have been hurt by the British. They would not turn on their friends. So your theory has some credence. Let's see what my cousin John discovers."

I left the room and saw Hannah closing up her bags. I said, "Let's see, you taught me how to dance. You thoroughly embarrassed me in a horse race, and you helped me with my laundry. The least I can do is carry your bags for you."

She smiled and said, "That would be very kind." So I picked up her bags and proceeded down the stairs and out to the barn."

It was finally dark enough to leave Peace Field. I told Hannah, "I have only been here for two days, but I have had some of the greatest moments of my life here at this old house. Hopefully, we shall return someday."

She said, "I have had highs and lows here. There was always the concern of my father being arrested at any moment. Then there were the high notes, such as meeting you and having our first dance here. Yes, I will miss this place, but I'm looking forward to starting my new journey with you."

I smiled and said, "Time to make some new memories together."

We all mounted our horses and headed to the back of the house. It was a cloudy night, so there wasn't even the Moon to give us a little light. I'm not sure how Hannah could even see where she was going. I suppose that the horses can at least see the trail. We moved slowly and remained very quiet. The path through the woods was very narrow. During the day, I'm sure it was easy to navigate, but not in the total darkness. I was hit in the face by tree branches several times. This narrow trail continued for about a mile. It finally opened up to what I believe was the road that took you into nearby Quincy. We all pulled up near each other, and Hannah said, "Across the way, there is another path that will lead us to the road to Milton. We will have another half mile or so of narrow paths. We crossed the road and began down the path. We continued for a while. The only thing I could hear was the horses breathing. Their hoofs were apparently on grass. We were approaching an opening, then suddenly Hannah pulled up on her horse. We all immediately stopped. We could hear voices and the sounds of hoofs. We remained very quiet. Suddenly six Dragoons passed us. We remained as quiet as possible. We thought the road was clear, but there must have been one straggler. As he approached us, one of our horses shuffled its hoofs. The straggler yelled to his comrades, "Did you hear anything?"

We sat as still as possible. I could see that Hannah had taken the long rifle from its holster. The Dragoon dismounted and tried to light his lantern, but was struggling with the darkness. He finally got it lit and began walking in our direction. I had my hand on my sword. My pistol was not loaded. I will not make that mistake again. The Dragoon stood still for what seemed like an eternity. We were outnumbered six to four, but we had the element of surprise, and the darkness was our friend. The chances of us coming out of this encounter unscathed were minimal. Finally, his comrade yelled, "I don't hear anything. Let's go. We have whiskey waiting for us."

The Dragoon walked back to his horse, placed the lantern back in his satchel, and rode away. We all exhaled. We waited about ten minutes and then began to proceed. We guided the horses to stay off of the road. The slightest noise could give up our position. After a few more miles, Mr. Adams said, "We should be okay now. The British Patrols will not travel more than a mile or two out of town." He also said, "Milton should be no more than a mile up the road. I have many friends there. I don't think the British would place any men there. It would be far too dangerous. We now felt comfortable having the horses on the road. Alex, Hannah, and I were walking side by side. It was easier to talk that way. Mr. Adams was roughly twenty feet in front of us.

I said, "This night reminds me of one of the Dreams that I have had about Scotland. We were riding horses into the cemetery when it was equally dark and…"

Alex said, "We went to a burial chamber where we removed a treasure that included the Secret of Eden."

I said, "That is amazing. You and I have been having the same Dream. Is it possible that somehow we were both there?"

Alex said, "It would sure seem that way."

Hannah said, "Now you two are even scaring me."

I said, "Hannah, do you have a recollection of this burial chamber?"

She said, "I have vague memories, kind of like I was there, but I wasn't. If that makes any sense. I have far more vivid memories of the treasure in other situations."

Alex said, "Is there something wrong with us?"

I said, "No, just the opposite. We have been given a special gift. I have especially been given a gift. I believe that Hannah and I have been together in many lifetimes."

Hannah said, "I also feel like we have known each other forever."

Alex said, "We may have to set up some rules if you two are going to be all mushy all the time."

Hannah said, "Too bad. You are outvoted two to one."

I said, "I can't argue with that. Remember you told me to never cross Hannah. I'm just taking your advice." We all laughed.

Just over the ridge, we could make out a small town. There were several lanterns that guided us in. Mr. Adams said, "There is a Tavern up on our left. The owner is a friend and a fellow Patriot. He has several rooms for rent on the second floor. I will speak with him regarding where we can water and feed the horses for the night."

Mr. Adams went into the tavern and returned a few minutes later with Mr. James McTavish. He was a Scot. He was happy to meet all of us. He said that we were all welcome to stay in his rooms for the night. He said that there is a stable across the street that he owns where we can feed and water the horses. He said, "They will be very comfortable in there. However, I must warn you that we have several bounty hunters that frequent our town. They are part-time bounty hunters and part-time thieves. If they come in the tavern, just keep to yourselves. They know not to push me too far. I have chased them out with my musket on several occasions."

We thanked him and proceeded to tie up the horses. Alex and I then grabbed the bags and proceeded into the tavern. Mr. McTavish directed us to the rooms at the top of the stairs. Each room had two beds. Mr. Adams and Hannah took one room, and Alex and I took the other.

Alex said, "I never thought I would be so excited to sleep in a real bed."

I said, "I could sleep anywhere as long as there is no bloody rooster." We shared a laugh. We met Hannah and her father downstairs, where the owner had served us with four mugs of ale.

We sat and had a few rounds of ale. Mr. McTavish's helper was making us some supper. I was so hungry that I would eat anything. For the last few days, I have been treated to some excellent food. My expectations were lowered this evening.

Just then, the tavern door burst open. There were two very drunk men walking in. They looked around. Everyone pretended to ignore them. Then, they sat at the next table from us and began to make comments about Alex and myself.

Hannah said, "Just ignore them."

The larger of the two men must have heard Hannah. He said, "Sweetheart, you couldn't ignore me if you tried. You know I am a bounty hunter. I can handcuff your two friends for no reason at all."

We just continued to ignore them. Finally, Mr. McTavish came over and told them that if they don't keep quiet, they will have to leave. This quieted them down for a minute. We talked peacefully for several minutes. I was conscious of their every move.

Alex said, "I need to excuse myself."

As he walked by, the shorter man stuck his foot out and tripped Alex. He tumbled to the floor. He stood up and was ready to take a swing. The larger man stood up and said, "Go ahead. I will beat you to a pulp and then throw you in the brig."

I raised out of my seat. I wasn't going to let this happen to Alex.

Hannah also stood up and walked over to the large man and said, "Perhaps I can give you something in exchange for leaving my friend alone."

The large man said, "I bet you can."

Then out of nowhere came a flurry like I had never seen before. Hannah threw several punches and a kick or two that left both men bleeding and unconscious on the floor. All of the other people in the tavern stared in stunned silence. This woman had destroyed these two men. Then, she stood over them and said, "I told you that I would give you something." All of the patrons stood up and cheered.

Mr. McTavish said, "Lassy, I have never seen anyone, man or woman, fight like that."

Mr. Adams sat at the bar and watched the entire event unfold. He had a smile on his face like he knew what was coming.

Mr. McTavish asked several patrons to help him drag the two men to the brig. He returned several minutes later and said they were now under lock and key. Please enjoy yourselves. We sat and ate our supper. The locals would not let us pay for a thing. We had several more drinks, and then it was time to call it a night.

Hannah asked me if I would like to join her while she checked on the horses. I said, "Of course."

We walked over to the stable hand in hand. I said, "After that adventure, I don't know if I should be terrified of you or even be more smitten." She laughed.

She wrapped her arms around my neck and said, "I would prefer the latter." I then gave her a very passionate kiss.

I would soon learn that checking on the horses would become my favorite part of the day.

CHAPTER 44

ON THE ROAD AGAIN

WE WOKE SHORTLY after sunrise the next morning. Mr. Adams didn't tell us of our next stop until we were on our way. This was just in case we were intercepted by the British. As he said, "You can't be forced to tell someone something that you don't know yourself." I fully understood this. I cleaned up and put on one of my freshly laundered outfits. Alex did the same. I went downstairs to find Hannah and her father sipping tea with Mr. McTavish.

Mr. Adams said to his friend, "I'm sorry that I didn't get a chance to tell you last night, but war is on the horizon. The British are, for some reason pushing us in this direction. Therefore, we must have all of the Militias ready."

Mr. McTavish said, "How soon?"

Mr. Adams replied, "It is difficult to say, but I would speculate sometime within the next year."

Finally, we were back on the road again. We all rode quietly for the next hour or so. Mr. Adams and Alex were twenty yards or more in front of Hannah and me. She reached out to grab my hand. We rode hand in hand quietly for several more miles. She finally said, "My more recent images of the treasure are foggy at best. The older images that I believe are from the Holy Land are crystal clear."

I said, "I think I know why. In the Scottish set of Dreams, which I believe are the Dreams where we moved the treasure to its current resting spot, you were not among the living. The Dream that I have has you dying from a Black Plague outbreak. But, even though you were dead, I knew you were always with me. Our mission was joined by a Seer, who I believe was named Agatha. Agatha, or her spirit to be precise, has been with us since the days of Noah. She is and always has been our guide. She has had many names and always seems to appear as a mentor to us. She gave me the ability to communicate with you more directly in the Scottish lifetime. In fact, after Agatha helped me recognize your presence, I would know you were there because (I paused and looked at Hannah) I could smell your beautiful Lavender scented aura."

She said, "Lavender? I love the smell of Lavender." Then, she looked at me and said, "You look like you have something else to add."

I said, "At the party before we met, I smelled this incredibly beautiful fragrance before you came down the staircase. It was Lavender. I asked Alex if he could smell it, and he said no. He was certain that the wine had gone to my head. Then you appeared on the staircase. As have been many of our encounters, it was very magical. If you recall, you also thought that you knew me. Anyways, I just realized that the fragrance was the same that I smelled in the Scottish Dreams. I would imagine that if I searched my thoughts, I would find many encounters with that fragrance. The beautiful aroma is only matched by your beauty."

She said, "Thank you. You are too kind." She went on to say,

"As a young girl, I was surrounded by other girls who dreamed of meeting a Prince Charming. I, on the other hand, only wanted to be outdoors practicing with my bow or perfecting my Tai Chi routine. Don't you find some irony in that I now find myself in a real-life fairy tale where I have discovered my Prince Charming, whom I have seemingly known for generations?"

I said, "Yes. We should write a book about this someday. Otherwise, no one will believe it." I went on further, "When I look back at my situation, I now know that I was guided by some force that I could not see or explain. Can you imagine if I had not seen that posting to join the Compound? I would have never met you. What a tragedy that would have been. When Mr. Franklin first discussed fate and destiny, I will tell you that I didn't believe it. Now I am a living example of it."

I further stated, "There is something that you don't know about me."

She said, "I doubt that. Remember, we have been together so long that I believe that I can read your thoughts. Are you about to tell me that you are an avid writer?"

I laughed and said, "I should have known that you already knew this. When we finally arrive at the Compound, I have much to add to my diary. I have this image of us sitting there on a cold winter night with a fire blazing in the fireplace and a pot of tea at the ready. You will be working on your artwork, and I will be busy with my quill and my journal, writing the glorious tales of Hannah Bri… I mean Adams."

She had that devilish smile on her face. She said, "You know some say that when you make such a slip, you are giving away your true thoughts."

She said, "Have I made you blush again?"

I said, "How much further do you think Framingham is?"

She said, "Nice change of subject."

I said, "Caught red-handed." We both laughed.

CHAPTER 45

FRAMINGHAM

THINK WE WERE approaching Framingham. The farms were suddenly more numerous. Many of these towns were surrounded by large farms. They wanted their crops to be close to the trading posts where they could ship anywhere in the Massachusetts Colony via horse-drawn wagons.

Alex pulled back and joined Hannah and me. He said, "I haven't had a chance to discuss this with both of you yet, but Mr. Franklin and I had a long talk about my future. At some point in the near future, he would like me to enroll in Kings College in New York City. He said that he would pay all the fees and see that I have a stipend for living expenses."

Hannah said, "Alex that is wonderful news. You have some God-given talents that most of us couldn't dream of."

Alex said, "Thank you, but please understand that I have been an orphan basically my entire life. As far as I know, my father is still alive, but I have not heard from him in years. I finally feel that I am part of something very special. I don't want to give it up already. It seems that I just have met the both of you."

I said, "Alex, first of all, you have known Hannah and me virtually forever. The time that you will be away will go quickly. You can come home to the Compound on Holidays, and Hannah and I will promise to visit you often. I have never been to New York City, but I'm told it is a hotbed of activity. You will always be a part of us. Take this opportunity and make the most of it."

Hannah said, "Do you know how many taverns there must be in New York City?" We all shared a laugh.

Alex said, "Now, you have talked me into it."

Just ahead, I could see the city of Framingham. It had been a long ride. I'm sure that the horses are ready for a rest.

We arrived and dismounted. Mr. Adams went into the Inn to secure us a couple of rooms for the night. Alex joined him with all of the bags. I helped Hannah lead the horses to the stable that was behind the Inn. We checked them in with the Stable Master and led them to their stalls. The Stable Master said, "There is a wonderful grazing area out back if you would like your horses to graze."

Hannah said, "That sounds great. I will return in a few hours to take them to graze."

We thanked the Stable Master and joined Alex and Mr. Adams at the Inn. I went to my room. I decided to take my boots off and rest for a minute. I laid down on the soft bed, which felt terrific. In a matter of seconds, I was fast asleep.

Suddenly, I was awakened by Alex. He said, "You have been sleeping for nearly two hours. Mr. Adams is preparing to speak to a large gathering of militia."

I quickly cleaned my teeth with the charcoal-covered rag that I have been carrying. I hated the taste of it, but it cleaned my teeth. I also chewed on a few Chew Sticks that were covered in fresh herbs. I knew at some point I would share a kiss with Hannah this evening. Without this, Hannah probably would run back to Quincy if she got a whiff of my breath.

Alex said, "Are you about done prettying yourself up for

Hannah?"

I said, "You could probably use the same. After bacon for breakfast and probably some whiskey after our arrival, I'm sure your breath would knock a buzzard off a manure wagon."

He said, "Very funny. However, I will take your advice."

After we both freshened up, we set out and headed out of the Inn, where we discovered a large gathering of men. At the front, we found a stage where Hannah and Mr. Adams stood waiting to address the throng. Hannah saw me and reached for my hand as I climbed onto the stage.

She said, "Did you have a nice rest? I was going to wake you, but I figured you needed the rest."

I said, "I intended to take a five-minute nap. But, in reality, had Alex not awoken me, I probably would have slept right through to morning."

She said, "You smell very fresh."

I said, "I figured you would probably need my help checking on the horses tonight."

She smiled and said, "I look forward to it."

We stood there hand in hand while Mr. Adams started to speak.

He said very loudly, "The British do not think you are their equals. They think you lack the courage to wage war for your secession from the British Empire. They think that you are too religious to wage war. I stand before you to proclaim that nothing could be further from the truth. The truth be told, the British have over-extended themselves because of so many useless wars with the French. They don't understand that nothing is as fearsome as a man with a cause. Freedom is our cause. We live in a land where we don't need anything from the outside. Our resources are greater than any land in the world. We just need to be left alone, and we will prosper." He paused for a second to let everything he had said sink in.

"We all left Europe for a reason. None of us are from royal bloodlines. What we are proposing here is that every man will have an equal voice and an equal opportunity to lead. Every man will have the opportunity to have his voice heard. Our revolution will not be easy. It will cause many hardships, but we will push through these hardships for future generations. We will fight to the death so that our descendants can live in a land that is theirs. A land that owes no provenance to any far away puppet masters."

"In closing, I ask you to join the local Framingham Militia and train hard. The day of our revolution is fast approaching. The day when you will be asked to leave your farm and head off to battle is coming soon. Then, we will push the British back into the sea and tell them to return to where they came from."

A voice sprung from the audience, "Will there be a stipend paid so that we can continue to feed our families during the war."

Mr. Adams said, "Yes, we are working on the details, but you will be paid for your service. Also, those of you who join us will be given a large plot of land that you can call your own at no cost to you." The crowd roared.

Mr. Adams concluded by saying, "Tell your neighbors and friends that the battle for their freedom from oppression is fast approaching."

Mr. Phineas Stearns, who had organized this rally, invited everyone to join Mr. Adams at the Buckminster Tavern, which was directly across from the Inn.

Hannah said, "I am going to freshen up and then check to see if the horses are back from their grazing session."

I said, "I will meet you at the stable shortly."

The crowd squeezed into the tavern. There was an overflow that went out into the streets. I managed to make my way up to the bar, where Alex was waiting for me with a pint of ale that was for me. He said, "That was quite a speech."

I said, "The best speeches are the ones that come from the heart."

Alex agreed. He said, "Here is to Mr. Adams." We drank our ale.

I said, "I need to finish this quickly. Hannah is waiting for me at the stables."

Alex said, "I am beginning to notice a pattern. She never invites her father or me over to the stable. It always only you."

I said, "Be quiet about this, and I will buy you several rounds of ale when I return."

He said, "What stable. I don't know anything about any stables." I laughed and left him there.

I hurried across the street to the stable. Hannah was leaning against the stall fence. She was watching the horses dive into their afternoon feeding. I snuck up on her. Before I got there, she said, "Don't the horses look content?"

I said, "Yes. How did you know it was me?"

She said, "Don't you remember. I have eyes in the back of my head."

I said, "I should have known that surprising you by sneaking up on you was out of the question. By the way, our secret of meeting at the stables has been figured out by Alex. I had to bribe him with rounds of free drinks for his silence." She laughed and said, "I will miss him when he moves away to College."

I said, "So will I."

She said, "I was wondering about what we were going to do when we get to the Compound."

I said, "A little bit of this (as I kissed her neck) and a little bit of that (as I kissed her on the cheek) and a whole lot of this as I turned her around and kissed her on the lips."

She said, "That sounds wonderful, but I was wondering about the ranch. You mentioned expanding it."

I said, "Yes. There is a large plot of land adjacent to the current land that just needs to be cleared of stumps and large boulders. Then we would plant grass seed, and the next season we will have a new area for the horses to graze. In the meantime, we can start allowing the horses to breed."

She smiled and said, "We better join the others before you owe Alex any more drinks."

I could have stood there with her in the stable for hours.

CHAPTER 46

THE MISSION

We rejoined Alex at the Buckminster Tavern. The night was joyous and long. They had a piano in the corner. An accomplished piano player was showing off his talents. Some local string players joined in after supper. I had a chance to show everything I had learned about dancing back in Quincy.

Hannah said, "Practice makes perfect."

I said, "I never thought that I would say this, but I am rather enjoying myself. It has more to do with my company than anything else."

Hannah smiled and asked, "Is there a piano at the Compound?"

I said, "Yes, there is a piano that is in desperate need of tuning. Also, there are a handful of musicians living there full time."

She said, "We should have the piano tuned, and then we should have a music night filled with glorious music and dancing."

I said, "That is a splendid idea. I will put Alex in charge. He always loves a good party."

Alex was having a glorious time with the local Patriots. They all were toasting him. They all listened to him not only because he was funny but because you could see that he was a natural-born leader.

Hannah and I sat down at the far end of the tavern, where there was less noise. I said, "I have been meaning to tell you about the Dream that I had while I was napping this afternoon. It was the Dream that tied everything together. I believe that it foretold our mission. Recently. I have been asking, why us? What is the purpose of bringing all of us together? It is almost like my mind released the answers that have been locked away."

Hannah said, "Did you receive answers?"

I said, "Yes. I believe that I have. This Dream was set back during the days of Noah."

She said, "I have had many vivid Dreams about being on the Ark. Before you tell me about your Dream. Let me tell you about my recent Dream. As always with my cousin, who we now know was you or your spirit. We were young children. We were both stricken with fear as the Ark began to float. Our family members were not able to comfort us. They all had tasks to perform. All we had was each other. I believe that this is where our bond was formed. From that point forward, we were always together. Our wedding made it official in the eyes of the almighty, but it all started in the presence of horses, goats, pigs, and other animals that we were tasked with tending to." We both laughed.

I said, "I have had the same Dream. Even though we were terrified, I agree with you that this was the beginning." I paused, sipped my ale, and then continued, "The Dream I had a few nights ago involved the Watcher. I believe this was where we were given our assignment of being a Guardian."

"Please refresh my memory," Hannah said.

I recalled the Dream as follows: *We were adults by this time and presumably married to each other. I recall that we were standing on the shores of the Great River as we had done so many times. We discussed its beauty with my brother Joktan when a large being came up behind us.*

The being said, "Do not fear. I am one of the ones that your family patriarch, Enoch, spoke of. He called us the Watchers." He went on, "We have been sent from the Almighty to steer humanity on its course to salvation. Before the Almighty created the Great Flood, we were here in numbers. Our brethren lived amongst the people for the purposes of educating humanity as to our ways. After a short period of time, some of our brethren turned to evil. They were enchanted by the women of this place. They gave in to temptation. This angered the Almighty and caused him to inflict the Great Flood onto the people and the wayward Watchers. Your Grandfather, Noah, is one of the righteous and was given instructions on how to save his family and the beasts of this world. You three are the offspring of the righteous. You are indeed "The Children of the Flood" and shall always be referred to as such. We have been watching you and have determined that you all are the worthy ones. We are giving you the task of spreading our message and protecting a treasure that contains a secret that will explain everything. All of man's questions about the Almighty and "Why we are here" will be answered when man is both ready and has followed the Almighty's rules. This secret will return mankind to the Garden of Eden and will grant access to the Tree of Knowledge once again." He continued, "I will give you a stone carving that will list these rules. You must keep it hidden from the evil doers. In addition, we have hidden the great treasure under the Great Lion that my predecessors built for mankind."

Joktan asked the Watcher, "Our time here is limited to our lifetimes. So how can we protect this secret when we are dead?"

The Watcher said, "You will never die. Of course, your physical body is limited, and, of course, it will die, but your souls are eternal. You will be reborn into new bodies when the message is in danger. Your souls will be tasked with a very sacred mission. You three will be together forever. In addition to being Children of the Flood, you are the Guardians of the Secret of Eden."

The Watcher continued, "My message to you also comes with a warning. You will have an adversary. He is already present in your lives." He paused briefly, then continued, "The sons of Adam and Eve were named Cain and Abel. Out of jealous rage, Cain killed his brother Abel. God *cast him out to wander the desert. He was forever scorned in the eyes of the Almighty." The Watcher continued, "As was told in Enoch's vision, God cast the fallen one, Azazel, out of heaven. Azazel will come to be known for future generations as Satan or Lucifer. Azazel adopted Cain as his disciple. Cain's children grew to be followers of Azazel. The descendants of Cain were then killed in the flood. This forced Azazel to start anew. Azazel has already corrupted a member of your family as he did with Cain."*

Peleg said, "Is it Canaan? We discuss Canaan amongst ourselves. He has a very dark presence." Canaan was the son of Ham, Noah's middle son, and a cousin to Peleg, Tytea, and Joktan.

The Watcher said, "Your instincts serve you well. Someday, Canaan will be cast out by your grandfather, Noah. He will grow strong with the evil one. Dark souls will flock to him. He will be a formidable adversary for you three. His offspring will be known as the Children of Canaan. Canaan will be reborn as you three will be reborn. His mission will be to stop you and plant seeds of evil everywhere. He will be a very cunning enemy, but you will have the Watchers and the Almighty on your side."

Hannah said, "I have never had this Dream in so much detail." Then, she paused and asked, "Do we know who this enemy is?"

I said, "The only enemy that I have encountered thus far is your cousin Gordon. While I believe that he can cause us some grief, I don't believe that he has the cunning to be the enemy that the Watcher described."

CHAPTER 47

PHINEAS STEARNS

THE NEXT MORNING started very early again. Somewhere in the distance, I heard a rooster giving everyone their wake-up call. I thought about making a pronouncement at the Compound stating, "I hereby ban anyone from owning a rooster". I am sure that Alex would second my motion. I freshened up and joined the others downstairs. We proceeded to the tavern for breakfast. Mr. Phineas Stearns joined us. We soon learned that he was going to accompany us on our next stops which were going to be Auburn, Springfield, and then Albany. He knew the Militia Leaders in these towns and wanted to make sure that there was a large turnout to hear Mr. Adams speak.

We got on the road to Auburn shortly thereafter. Both Hannah and I commented on the beautiful countryside that we were traveling through. Several hours later we arrived in Auburn. We checked in at the Inn and we boarded the horses at the stables next door to the Inn. Mr. Stearns went to find the local Militia leader. We made our way to the tavern. A few minutes later, Mr.

Stearns joined us. He was joined by a Patriot by the name of Artemas Ward. We exchanged pleasantries. Mr. Ward was looking at all of us and finally said, "Were you in Milton a few nights ago?"

Mr. Adams asked, "Why do you ask?"

Mr. Ward, "Excuse me, but I will be right back.

We were slightly alarmed at his sudden departure but Mr. Stearns said, "No worries. I have been good friends with Artemas since we were young boys."

He returned a few minutes later with a copy of the Boston Gazette.

The Boston Gazette started to be published in 1719. It is often referred to as the paper of record for the Patriots. During the 1770s, it has been used as a way to transfer messages. Many were written in hidden code. The printing presses were in Boston, but the messages could be transferred anywhere in the Massachusetts Colony very quickly because of Mr. Peter Adams Carriage Service. Messages could be sent the entire length of the Colony in under two days. As the war drums started to beat louder and louder, the Boston Gazette would be the primary source of spreading the news of the impending revolution.

Even though the British knew about the Gazette, they could do little to stop it. There were many printing locations. Virtually, anyone who owned a printing press operation could print the Gazette. Many of the articles were written anonymously. The British had a pretty good idea who was behind the publication, but did not have enough evidence for a conviction. They simply would destroy any printing press operation that was found to have printed the Gazette. For the determined Patriots, this was not enough to stop them.

None of us had seen the latest version of the Gazette yet. It had just arrived this morning in Auburn. Mr. Ward handed the Gazette to Alex and pointed at an article that appeared on the bottom of the front page.

Alex read the article and immediately had a big smile on his face. Mr. Adams said, "Alex, please read the article aloud so the rest of us can understand why you are smiling from ear to ear." Alex began to read the article out loud. It read as follows:

MILTON MELEE

It seems that the usually sleepy town of Milton was the scene of an incident on Sunday night. The town has been frequented of late by two hooligans who claim to be Bounty Hunters for the Redcoats. At a nearby table, one of our most beloved Patriots sat with a small group. One of them stood and began to walk to the door when one of the hooligans tripped him. An altercation was about to start when a woman stood up and tried to calm the situation down before any fights broke out. One of the Hooligans made a critical mistake by mouthing off to the women. In a flurry that lasted no more than three seconds, the woman had knocked both men unconscious with a flurry of punches and kicks. Her identity is unknown, but one of the locals gave her the nickname of the "Angel of Death." Another called her "Miss Freedom." No one is exactly sure of her identity, but one thing is for certain, if the Redcoats had witnessed her in action, they would all run back to their ships and return to Merry Old England. The Constable subsequently arrested the two men for Disturbing the Peace.

We all sat in stunned silence. Mr. Ward finally said to Mr. Adams, "Was this your group?"

Mr. Adams said, "Yes, unfortunately, this was us."

Mr. Ward looked at Hannah and said, "You don't look like an Angel of Death to me. So going forward, I will think of you as Miss Freedom."

Alex then said, "I should have been given a nickname. If I hadn't been tripped, the entire incident would have never happened." We all laughed.

I said, "How about the "Klutz from the Compound"?"

He said. "Very funny. As I recall, you owe me several rounds for my silence last evening."

Mr. Adams said, "Silence. Alex, I don't ever recall you being silent." He continued, "Our friend here, Mr. Ward, is not with us to hear about our trials and tribulations. Instead, he is here to discuss the impending war."

Mr. Adams went on to discuss the situation with Mr. Ward and Mr. Stearns. Hannah, Alex, and I made our way up to the bar, where Alex began to recoup the fee for his silence.

The afternoon wore on, and it was time for Mr. Adams to give his speech to the Auburn Militia. I said to Hannah, "Your father's speeches are inspiring, but these days have begun to blend together."

Hannah said, "I agree, but when I think of how it was supposed to be, I will take this any day."

I said, "How do you mean."

She said, "By now, you would have already been back at the Compound, and I would have been stuck in Quincy. We would maybe have seen each other every two weeks. That would have been awful."

I said, "Yes. That would have been terrible."

Alex chimed on, "When are we going to Albany."

Hannah said, "I think the day after tomorrow. My father said that he has so many people that he needs to meet within Albany that we may need to spend another night."

I said, "Alex that should be music to your ears. Eliza doesn't know that we are coming. Does she?"

Alex said, "Not exactly. I told her I would try to get there within a few weeks. So this is a little ahead of schedule."

Hannah said, "My father tells me that there is a wonderful City Center area with many shops. He says that there are even a few boutiques from Paris there."

Alex said, "Sounds expensive."

I said, "Perhaps I could have let you borrow some money if I didn't have to buy you so many pints of Ale."

Mr. Adams gave his speech later that afternoon. Afterward, Hannah and I chose to walk around the quaint little town.

We were both exhausted and decided to call it an early night. So we kissed goodnight and went to our separate rooms.

That night I had a nightmare about being out to sea when a major storm rolled through. A huge wave came over the bow and caused us to be underwater for a few seconds. When the water washed away, I could no longer see Hannah. I was so panicked that I woke up in a cold sweat. It took me an hour or so to fall asleep again. What was this Dream trying to tell me? Should Hannah and I stay away from ships? I woke up so fast that I didn't figure out what had happened to Hannah. Had she washed overboard? I was frantic. Finally, I fell back asleep.

I woke up just after sunrise. I cleaned up and went downstairs. No one was there yet. I sat for what seemed like an eternity. Finally, Hannah appeared. She looked beautiful and rested. Obviously, my nightmare wasn't true. For Hannah, Alex, and myself, Dreams have a much bigger purpose than for everyone else.

She said, "What's wrong. You have a troubled look on your face?"

I said, "I had a nightmare where we were at sea and waves were overtaking our ship. Then, a large wave crashed over the bow, and suddenly I couldn't see you. I woke up in a panic. I almost came and knocked on your door."

She said, "I wonder what this means. Our Dreams seem to have special meanings, but this one is different from the rest because it is from the future. All of my Dreams are from the past."

I said, "Perhaps it is a warning of some kind. It may be telling us to do something a little different. We should discuss this with Mr. Franklin when we see him."

She agreed and said, "Look at me. I'm here right now. We should heed this warning, but we must continue on our mission. When we were on that cliff in Quincy, you said you would never let me go. Perhaps if we are on a ship heading somewhere, we should take extra caution to secure ourselves together and to the ship if rough seas are upon us."

I said, "Either we will survive together or perish together. Either way, we will be together."

She said with a smile, "I don't see any waves here, so let's go prepare the horses."

CHAPTER 48

CHILD OF CANAAN

THE NEXT TWO towns of Springfield and Pittsfield blended together. We started to cross through the Berkshires Mountain range. The landscape was breathtaking. The small towns and villages were warm and welcoming. Many of the settlers that we met didn't know much of the impending revolution. They were tending to their farms and minding their own business. The British barely ventured into these areas.

Even though it was only November we were seeing snowflakes as we passed through several of the mountain passes. Hannah and I agreed that after everything settles down that we wished to return and explore this area. The region where the Compound resided was similar, but not nearly as mountainous. With the extra climbing required, we made some additional stops to water the horses. The first place that we arrived in was Springfield.

Mr. Adams said, "General Washington likes this location for an Armory. He likes the fact that Springfield resides on the Connecticut River which flows to the Atlantic Ocean. The fact that there is no major port at the mouth of the Connecticut River means that it is often left unprotected by the British."

This was the last leg of the journey for Mr. Phineas Stearns. As we arrived in Springfield, we located the Inn where we would spend the night. As usual, Hannah and I led the horses to the stable. You could see in their eyes that they were getting tired. A good night's rest would do wonders. That could be said about all of us except Alex of course. He managed to find the tavern and proceeded to already make friends. We joined Alex. It didn't take long before someone said, "Are you the ones that were involved in the Milton incident." We denied it. We were becoming famous. Times were such that the people were latching onto anyone that was perceived to be a hero. Another asked Hannah, "Are you the Angel of Death?" I could tell it was beginning to wear on her.

I said, "How about if we just change the name to 'The Angel of the Rebellion'."

She laughed and said, "I'm not sure that is quite deserving either, but "The Angel of Death" sounds like I'm a horrible person."

I said, "By the end of the winter, no one will even remember the incident. They would have a much better chance of remembering 'Alex's Tavern Tour through the Massachusetts Colony'."

She said, "That is a very fitting title."

Mr. Adams wished to have a private word with Mr. Stearns. They no doubt were discussing the upcoming Tea Party. As we have learned in the past, it's not that Mr. Adams wants to keep secrets from us. He wants to both keep operational details to only the people that need to know and to protect us. Once again, we can't disclose details that we don't know.

Shortly thereafter Mr. Henry Knox arrived. He is a friend of General Washington. He was leading the efforts in securing the armaments. Mr. Adams called us over for this discussion. We exchanged pleasantries. Mr. Knox apologized for missing the Annual Fall Harvest Party.

I got right to the point. I asked, "What is the plan to arm our forces?"

Mr. Knox replied, "For starters, we are asking everyone to bring their rifles and muskets from their homes. Many of our men are veterans of the French and Indian War. They took their firearms home with them. Second, one of the reasons that I wanted to meet with Samuel is that we need to have production facilities for swords and bayonets. I believe that you, Mr. Briggs, manage the Compound. How quickly can you start producing weaponry?"

Mr. Adams said, "Mr. Franklin has these three slated for a special mission that will take priority over everything else. We want the Compound to remain a ranch and mill town. It's a perfect cover."

Mr. Knox said, "Ok. We will need to discuss setting up more armament production sites. We need to enlist every blacksmith and silversmith for this endeavor."

Mr. Knox looked around to make sure that no one was within earshot. He then said, "One of the other ways that we plan on arming our troops is to steal them. Currently, we know where all of the British Armories are located. We will send in our best agents and we will simply steal their arms." He continued further, "Can you imagine how angry the British will be if we attack them with their own weapons."

We enjoyed our conversation with Mr. Knox. He told glorious tales from the French and Indian War. After supper, Hannah and I decided that we wanted to take in the town. We walked hand in hand and took in the sights. There were breathtaking views from high on the bluffs overlooking the Connecticut River.

We returned to the City Center just in time to hear Mr. Adams's speech to roughly one hundred Patriots. Once again the subject of stipends came up. Once again Mr. Adams made the promise of both stipends and land.

Afterwards, we sat down for supper. I said to Mr. Adams, "We must solidify our plans regarding armaments. The task of defeating the British will require significant arms. Whether they are stolen or built by blacksmiths is not the question. The question should be, "How is this going to be paid for?""

Then Alex shocked us all when he said, "Yes, but I believe those that call themselves the Watchers are on our side. We need to tap into their wisdom. They will help lead us to victory."

Mr. Adams said, "Who the hell are the Watchers?"

Alex said, "They are part of my Dreams. Mr. Franklin is aware of the Watchers and my Dreams. Their wisdom will lead us to success." Mr. Adams sat there with a blank stare on his face.

I finally said, "I also have the Dreams of the Watchers. I believe that we are a small part of a large overall story. A small part but a very important part."

Mr. Adams asked, "Hannah do you have these Dreams as well?"

She said, "Yes. I have had many Dreams since I was a little girl. Most didn't make any sense. They didn't make sense until I met Jeremiah. Now, they are much clearer." She went on to say, "I know it will be difficult for you and mother to hear, but I believe that I am part of an age-old story where Jeremiah, Alex, and I are on a special mission."

Mr. Adams said, "A few years ago I would have said this is a bunch of hogwash, but as you will learn when you are officially inducted into the Freemasons, the supernatural surrounds us."

Just then the door of the Tavern burst open and six very rough looking characters walked in. They looked like the sketches of Pirates that I had seen as a boy. Why would they be so far inland?

Mr. Knox walked over to our table and said, "Stay away from those scoundrels. They are said to be fur traders, but their main mission seems to be trading of spirits and muskets. Their leader is the large one. His name is Anders."

I said, "Why here? We are a long way from the sea."

Mr. Knox said, "They like this town for the same reason that General Washington likes it. There is virtually no British oversight on the Connecticut River. They steal and pillage their way up and down the River. They are based in Nova Scotia and operate freely right under the nose of the British Fleet that is stationed in Halifax. They have figured out how to bribe the proper authorities both in Halifax and here in Massachusetts. Please stay out of their way. Nothing good can come from an encounter with them."

I sat there trying to place the leader of these Pirates. I know him from somewhere. Suddenly, we made eye contact. The face changed to that of our cousin Canaan from the Noah Dreams, then he was Abdul from the Templar Dreams, then he was Oleg from the Scottish Dreams. One by one, his face changed to the face of all of our adversaries. It was like I was staring at Satan himself.

I believe that Alex and Hannah had sensed the same thing. The question of who our adversary was going to be in this lifetime had just been answered. He is sitting across the tavern from us. His name is Anders.

We decided to head back to the Inn. As we rose and began walking towards the door, Anders, stood and blocked our way. Suddenly, Hannah's face had the look of absolute terror on it. Then terror was replaced by anger.

One of the Tavern's patrons yelled out, "The Angel of Death has arrived."

Hannah finally spoke. She said, "I should kill you right now while I have the chance. Unfortunately, that would be viewed as murder. I beg you to attack one of us. I have centuries old rage that would be unleashed upon you."

Anders and his men laughed. He said, "I am not a drunken bounty hunter like the two that you encountered in Milton. I am not afraid to kill a woman. Especially a woman who is threatening me."

Hannah replied, "You are the scourge of humanity. You are too stupid to even understand who you really are." She paused briefly, then continued, "You were evil when you were known to us as Canaan, you were evil to my friends here when you were the beast known as Oleg, and for me your incarnation that was known as Simon de Montfort will haunt me forever. As I told you before you killed me in that lifetime, "Victory will be mine the next time we meet. I will kill you in this lifetime."

Just then, Mr. Adams arrived with the Constable and the confrontation ended just as quickly as it had started. A calmness came over Hannah. In this lifetime, she was prepared for this adversary. For her, her future was now clear. For Alex and me, we still had much to learn.

Somehow, I knew of nothing with regards to this Simon de Montfort person. We must speak with Maria when we arrive at the Compound.

As I laid in my bed recounting this encounter, I kept coming back to the fact that Ander's demeanor completely changed when Hannah mentioned the name Oleg. This had meant something to him. The encounter in the New World happened hundreds of years ago. Then I came to the realization that just like us, he was Oleg in that lifetime. That was the simple solution. There was something beyond this. The name Oleg was special to him.

CHAPTER 49

ALBANY

T HE NEXT MORNING arrived just as every other morning had arrived, with a rooster waking us up. Both Alex and I cleaned up quickly and met Mr. Adams and Hannah downstairs. Mr. Adams went to pay for the rooms which gave the three of us a chance to talk privately.

Hannah said, "I know that we must discuss what happened last night, but I would like to wait until we are back at the Compound."

I said, "I agree. We should include Maria. She always is able to see the complete story."

Alex said, "Allow me to say one thing." He paused for effect then continued, "On behalf of Jeremiah and myself, let me say how good it is to have you on our side." We all laughed. Hours earlier we had a very dramatic encounter with our adversary for the first time in this lifetime and once again Alex was able to diffuse the stress. He has a gift that will work well throughout his life as long as he continues to use it.

We were back on the road to Albany just after a quick breakfast. All of us were well-rested. Alex seemed very anxious this morning.

Hannah jogged my memory when she said, "Alex is going to be on his best behavior this evening. I'm sure at some point he is going to see Eliza."

I said, "How could I have forgotten."

Alex said, "Hopefully, we will have somewhere to freshen up. I don't want Eliza to see me this way."

Hannah said, "I am sure Eliza will understand that you have been riding on horseback for better than a week now. All of us could use some freshening up. I would give a King's ransom for a hot bath."

Mr. Adam's said, "I was holding the surprise for when we arrived, but now is as good of a time as any. I sent advanced word to General Schuyler about our arrival. I told him that we would be spending two days in Albany. I received word last night back from the General that he not only insists that we stay at his home, but that he is going to throw a party in our honor tomorrow evening, The last time Mrs. Adams and I were here, the men went to a special club where they have a Finnish Sauna and a large bathhouse. The women went to a salon that is the equivalent to any salon in Paris where you will be treated like a queen. After that, you will be treated to some of the finest shops in the Colonies. I suggest everyone get new outfits for the Party. You will be meeting some people who are very important to our cause."

Several hours later we arrived at the banks of the Hudson River. This river was very important because it led to New York City and then the Atlantic Ocean. One of the conversations that I had with Mr. Jefferson was how men he knew had drawn up plans for digging a canal that would connect Lake Erie to the Hudson River. This would make the lands to the west much more desirable. The goods from the western lands could easily be shipped to New York City and beyond. I felt as though Mr. Jefferson is a visionary. He understands the much larger picture. The fact that this land is so vast and so valuable is lost on many of the settlers. Their views have been beaten down by the fact that it is so difficult to move west. The Indian Nations have laid claim to much of the land. I believe that there is enough land for all of us. I thought to myself, it's great to have these wonderful visions, but first, we must successfully secede from Britain.

We boarded a barge that carried us across the Hudson River. On the other side, there was a sign that said, "Welcome to Albany". On our way to Boston, it was already dark so I didn't get to see any of this. As we stepped off of the barge a man approached us and said, "Welcome to Albany. I will escort you to the Schuyler Mansion." We followed him to a Grand Mansion that sat up on a hill overlooking the Hudson River.

The Schuyler Mansion

Upon our arrival, we were immediately greeted by General Schuyler, Mrs. Catherine Schuyler, and of course, Eliza. We thanked them for their hospitality. Next, the servant showed Hannah and me to the large horse barn. It seems that even the horses would spend a few days in luxury. The barn was constructed of beautiful mahogany.

Hannah told the horses, "Don't get too used to this. We are leaving in a few days." The horses all looked at her like they knew what she was saying.

We returned to the Mansion, where another servant showed us our rooms. The servant said, "The General and Mrs. Schuyler wish to invite you to dinner at six o'clock. Cocktails will be served at five-thirty." Both Hannah and I parted ways at that point with our assigned servant. Each of us was asked if we would like to take a nice hot bath. I said, "That sounds great." I'm sure Hannah did the same. I had roughly two hours to freshen up before dinner.

I bathed and got into my last clean outfit. The servant took all of my dirty clothes to be laundered. I can't imagine living like this every day. I looked as presentable as I have looked since the wonderful night at Peace Field. I went to a waiting room that was just outside Hannah's room. Finally, Hannah and Eliza stepped out. Hannah looked beautiful. She was wearing a spectacular Green dress.

I said, "You look beautiful. You certainly don't look like someone who has been on a horse for the last week."

She laughed and said, "You look handsome as ever. Thankfully Eliza let me borrow this beautiful dress for tonight." The three of us went downstairs to the Main Study, where everyone was waiting. General Schuyler had invited another couple to join us. They were a recently married young French couple. The gentleman spoke English reasonably well, but his young wife didn't speak a word of English. The General introduced them as Marquis de Lafayette and Mrs. Marie Adrienne de Lafayette. Marquis said, "My full name is Marie-Joseph Paul Yves Roch Gilbert du Motier, Marquis de Lafayette, but my friends call me Marquis."

Alex said, "My Lord, you have enough names for the whole lot of us."

Marquis laughed and said, "I come from a long line of

Warriors. My mother wanted all of her favorite saints to protect me, so she included all of them in my name." We all had a good laugh.

Alex said, "Then, for your safety sake and to calm your mother's fears, we will have a toast for each and every one of those saints."

Marquis said, "I like the way you think."

Hannah turned to me and said, "I believe that Alex has finally found his long-lost brother. They must have been separated at birth." We both had a good laugh.

It turns out that Eliza speaks French. She served as the translator for Marie.

We all sat down for dinner in the main Dining Room. Dinner included Roast Pheasant with a variety of vegetables and roasted potatoes. The conversation was terrific. The people in the Colonies typically have contact with only the British. Hearing the perspective of an adversary of the British was enlightening. The French and the British have been fighting on and off for centuries. Many emissaries, such as Mr. Franklin, quietly try to make the French understand that siding with the Colonists is the right move. If the Colonists win, the French would have special rights as a trading partner. That would be a significant asset if the French understood that America has boundless natural resources. Currently, England and Spain have the most significant footprint when it comes to trade.

Marquis made it very clear that he loved America. He also loves a good cause. He said, "Many of the European wars are fought without a true cause. Not liking someone is not a cause. Battles over the freedom of a nation is a worthy cause." He promised to do his part when he returned to France.

After dinner, we all adjourned to the study, where we played the game of Billiards. Alex said he often played the game when he was touring the Caribbean. I had only heard about it. It took a little bit, but I soon began to make a shot or two.

Hannah and I sat with Eliza. She was a remarkable young

debutante. She wanted to hear how Hannah and I met.

Hannah said, "I have to look no further than Alex to find the person that introduced us. When my father first sent Alex to the Compound, I thought my father was doing so because he thought Alex was trying to court me. Nothing could be further from the truth. As I have said to Jeremiah many times, "Alex has been a brother to both of us." I'm drawn back to a statement that my father had made just before Alex left for the Compound. He said, "I want him to have Jeremiah Briggs's influence. Perhaps the greatness Mr. Franklin sees will rise to the surface." That was the first time that I heard Jeremiah's name. I heard it many other times after that, but that was the first. I remember a flame deep inside of me was ignited. I didn't know why, but I wanted to meet him. One time when my father was home for a few days, he was discussing the Compound and how well things were going. I told him, "You speak so highly of Mr. Briggs. I would like to meet him someday." He said that he would invite him to the Annual Fall Harvest Party. The rest is history."

Eliza said, "You just met at the Harvest Party? I would have guessed that you two have been together for years."

Both Hannah and I just smiled.

Eliza said, "You two seem right out of a fairy tale."

Hannah said, "I often think that myself. I wake up every morning wondering what adventure lies in front of us today."

Hannah and I went to check on the horses as we had done every other night. Mark and Cleo were sound asleep when we walked in, as were the other two horses.

Hannah said, "I enjoy coming to dinner parties such as this, but I would not like to have this lifestyle all of the time."

I said, "Thank goodness. We may play an important role in what is forthcoming, but I never see myself living in this kind of opulence. However, I believe I will have the good fortune of attending many such affairs as we did tonight. Mr. Franklin sees me traveling the Colonies delivering secret messages and such. There will be many evenings such as this along the way."

She put her arms around my neck and said, "Would you like some company, Mr. Briggs?"

I said, "Of course. I'm not going without you. As I told you on that cliff, I don't ever intend on leaving your side."

She said, "My mother will have to join us as a chaperone."

I said, "That won't be necessary."

She said, "Whatever do you mean by that."

I smiled at her and said, "It's getting very late. We should be getting some sleep."

She said, "I am on to you. You are very good at changing the subject."

I said, "Let's end this wonderful evening like this. So I leaned in and kissed her."

We walked back into Mansion and retired to our separate rooms.

CHAPTER 50

THE PAMPERING

ENERAL SCHUYLER HAD breakfast served precisely at eight o'clock. His servants served everyone tea in their rooms at seven-thirty. I could tell that this household was operated with military precision. I arrived a few minutes early to find General Schuyler and Mr. Adams discussing the upcoming party. We exchanged pleasantries. I thanked the General for a wonderful evening last night. Soon we were joined by Marquis and his wife, Marie. Shortly after that, Alex joined us. Mrs. Catherine Schuyler and Eliza followed him. Then finally, Hannah.

Marie said something in French that Marquis translated. He said, "How is it that all of us look like we just woke up, and then Miss Hannah shows up and looks even more beautiful than she did last night."

I said, "She is amazing. I have been very fortunate to have her with us on this long journey. Every morning, she is a breath of fresh air."

Hannah said, "Thank you for your kind words." Then, she

turned to Alex and said, "Hopefully, you recovered from your overwhelming defeat on the billiards table at the hands of Eliza?"

Alex said, "I got better as the night wore on. At the end of the night, I was at least able to sink one or two balls before she cleared the table."

Mr. Adams said, "Maybe we should obtain a billiards table for the Compound. It would give us something very enjoyable to do on those long winter nights."

I said, "I will look into it."

General Schuyler said, "If you are in town today, stop into Mr. Hannity's Emporium. It may seem like he only has books, art supplies, and custom jewelry, but he can get anything. Make sure to tell him that you are my guests."

The thing that caught my attention was the part about the custom jewelry. Hopefully, Mr. Hannity would have something that I could afford.

We enjoyed breakfast, and we sat quietly and enjoyed our tea. Mr. Adams finally spoke. He said, "Be careful what you say to anyone this evening. There will be people sympathetic to the British cause in attendance this evening." We all noted that.

A few minutes later, we all went our separate ways. I accompanied Hannah to the top of the stairs, where I said, "I look forward to going to that Emporium later today. I do need some writing supplies. I'm sure that there will be some artwork that will catch your eye."

She said, "That sounds lovely. Enjoy your morning at the bathhouse." Then, she leaned up and kissed me goodbye.

I said, "You do the same. I'm sure the salon owner will be sad when he sees you. There will be nothing that she could do to make you more beautiful."

She said, "You are too kind."

Several hours later the men returned from the bathhouse. The

Ladies' day at the Salon took much longer than the men's. I took this time to consider my finances. I was thinking about a significant purchase today. What could I afford? What was proper? My living expenses at the Compound were basically included as part of my salary. I had laundry expenses but little else. I would need an advance for all the travel Mr. Franklin expected. I'm sure that this would not be an issue.

Several hours later, the women returned to the Mansion. Hannah said, "We had a wonderful time. I loved the pampering, but the best part was just talking with the women. It made me miss my mother. Even though we don't have many common interests, I value her wisdom."

I said, "I had a similar experience. I enjoyed the sauna immensely, but it was more about the friendship among the men. Now I am very excited to spend the afternoon with you exploring Albany."

She said, "Then let's go. I have been waiting all afternoon for you."

I said, "Ha Ha. That's a good one."

We set out on foot to the Albany City Center. When we arrived, I could see that there were shops for everything. There was a large Trading Post that flowed into the streets as a farmers' market. There were so many flavors of jerky. We bought several flavors. There was a French Bistro where we decided to have tea and a French pastry.

I said, "I'm sure there are similar shops in Philadelphia, Richmond, Charleston, and New York."

She said, "These are all the places I am supposed to accompany you to, somehow without a chaperone."

I said, "Isn't this pastry wonderful. I wonder if Marquis eats like this all of the time."

She said, "There you go again."

I looked at her and said, "There are wonderful things ahead for you and me, but I need to have some mystery. Believe me when I say, "You and I will always be together."

She said, "I feel like a princess in one of those fairy tales."

I said, "You are the perfect princess. You are smart and beautiful. You also can bring down a large buck while riding full speed on horseback. I shall never go without food." We both laughed.

We finally came upon Mr. Hannity's Emporium. We entered and were greeted by a young lady that welcomed us. I introduced both Hannah and myself to the young lady. I told her that we are out-of-town guests staying with General and Mrs. Schuyler. She said welcome, and please give me a minute. She returned one minute later with an older man and said, "Father, this lovely young couple is from out of town and are guests of the Schuylers."

The Man said, "Welcome, I am Michael Hannity, and this is my daughter Elizabeth. Please feel free to gaze at all of our one-of-a-kind merchandise. As guests of the General, you will be given a substantial discount."

The jewelry counter was right in front of us. I could see that Hannah was mesmerized. First, she tried on Pearl Necklace, which was beautiful. Then she noticed the rings. She said, "That beautiful ring looks like something a Queen should wear."

Mr. Hannity laughed and said, "You have a good eye. The Royals in England often wear something similar. It has a two-carat diamond at its center and six smaller diamonds surrounding it. Would you like to try it on?"

Hannah said, "No, I shouldn't. I will become too attached to it."

I said, "Go ahead and try it on." So Mr. Hannity slipped it on her ring finger. It was stunning. It matched her beauty perfectly.

Mr. Hannity said, "This is size six. It's a little loose. You are no doubt a five and a half."

Hannah said, "It's beautiful. Thank you for letting me try it on."

We walked over to the book section. She said, "Please don't feel that you ever need to give me such a ring. I would be just as happy with a tin ring as long as I know it is from you."

At that very instant, I knew that somehow I was going to

purchase that ring. There was no way that Hannah was going to wear a piece of tin on her finger. Even though we had just met, I knew we had been together for hundreds if not thousands of years. For most young men, this purchase would not be appropriate. For Hannah, this was the right decision.

We continued over to the books. There was an art book in front of us that showed copies of the works of famous artists such as Leonardo Da Vinci and Michel Angelo. They were a new form of art known as print. One could recreate the artwork and then simply use a special printing press to reproduce it. The book included roughly 150 prints of the most famous artwork ever produced. This book cost 25 shillings but was priceless. I needed to buy this for Hannah. I had enough money on me to pay for this. She was enthralled with this book.

I said, "I am going to discuss the cost of a billiard table with Mr. Hannity while you look at that book." I don't even think she heard me.

I walked up to Mr. Hannity and said, "I am talking to you under the guise that I would like to purchase a billiards table, but I am here to inquire about that ring. How much does it cost?"

Mr. Hannity said, "With the General's discount, that ring will cost 200 shillings."

I said, "That loud crash you heard was me fainting."

He said, "A beautiful woman such as Miss Hannah deserves to have that ring on her finger."

I said, "That is all that I have in savings. I work at a place that is known as the Compound. It is a wonderful place to live, but I don't make much money."

He said, "Oh. You work at the Compound. You must know Mr. Adams."

I laughed and said, "Yes. He is my boss, and Hannah is his daughter."

He laughed and said, "I will sell you the ring for 150 shillings. I will resize it today. Will you be at the party at the General's Mansion tonight?"

I said, "Yes, He is throwing the party in honor of Mr. Adams and his traveling companions, of which both Hannah and I are part."

He said, "Wonderful, I will bring the ring tonight. I will hand it to you discretely. Then you can send the money when you get back to the Compound. Furthermore, since this is for Samuel Adams's Daughter, you can pay me over the next year."

I said, "Thank you very much. I will never forget your generosity."

I almost forgot, "How much for a Billiards Table?"

He said, "A good 8-foot slate table will cost you 50 shillings."

I said, "Thank you. I must cover my tracks. You wouldn't believe the intuitive abilities that Miss Hannah has."

He laughed and said, "There is no point ever trying to deceive a woman. They have skills that men can only dream of." We laughed and shook hands.

I said, "I believe today I am going to purchase that art book for Hannah, as well as some writing supplies for myself." I grabbed a new journal, some fresh ink, and a handful of new quills.

He said, "Wonderful. That book is truly a classic."

Hannah said, "Thank you. What a wonderful gift. Somehow, I need to get it to the Compound."

I said, "Your father has carriages traveling back and forth to Albany from the Compound daily."

We then made our way back to the Mansion. I told her in great detail about the billiards table. I finally found a way to distract Hannah. Distract her with a great piece of art. I was supposed to buy a new outfit, but the staff at the Mansion had already finished my laundry. I had already spent a lot of money today. Hannah had already stated that Eliza had another beautiful dress she could borrow.

CHAPTER 51

THE GRAND BALL AT THE SCHUYLER MANSION

THE PARTY WAS scheduled to start at six. Dinner was at seven, and the musical entertainment was scheduled to begin at eight. I knew that everything would be right on time. The General was in charge of this party. Once again, I stood at the bottom of the staircase with Alex. This time we had Marquis as a welcome addition. I had told Marquis how Alex instructed the waiter to bring a fresh glass of wine every ten minutes whether he was standing or not at the Harvest Fest. Marquis thought this was hilarious and gave our waiter the same instructions. Alex and Marquis were like two peas in a pod. They were both only eighteen years old and had a bright future in front of them. I would bet anyone that these two men would be great leaders someday. Today, they were two young men having a great time. For the time being, I would join them.

Alex said, "At that last party, you should have seen Jeremiah's face when he saw Hannah for the first time. I have never seen him so tongue-tied. The great news today is we can all stand here and celebrate while we wait for all three beauties, Hannah, Eliza, and Marie, to come down that staircase."

Marquis said, "To the three luckiest men on the planet." Then, we each finished our wine. It wasn't quite ten minutes yet, but the waiter seemed to understand our predicament.

A few minutes later, all three women came down the staircase. Hannah had a stunning red dress. I said to Hannah, "I don't think there is color in the rainbow that doesn't work for you."

She said, "Thank you. You are looking very dashing yourself."

The guests were starting to arrive. The General introduced us to several very important people. The first was an elderly man by the name of Phillip Livingston. He was a well-known merchant from New York City, but was born here in Albany. I could tell by the way he spoke that he was sympathetic to our cause. I made sure to keep the conversation away from the rebellion. I didn't know who the British spies were. Also, some on our side could be just testing me. I thought it would be a good practice to stay away from the subject of the rebellion unless we were in the confines of the Compound.

Next in line was Mr. Benedict Arnold. He was a merchant who had vowed to join the General when it was time for the battle. He struck me as being very negative. Everything in our discussion was centered on less than pleasant topics. There was nothing, in particular, to refer to, but somehow the conversation worked its way into something negative. At that instant, Hannah said, "Alex is calling for us. Very nice to meet you, Mr. Arnold."

We walked over to Alex, and Hannah said, "Alex, you called us over to make a toast."

Alex said, "I did… Of course, I did."

Hannah looked at me and said, "There is something that bothers me about that man. I can't put my finger on it, but there is something off about him."

We made our toast with Alex. Mr. Adams joined us with a

gentleman named Arthur St. Clair II. We were introduced, and then I said. "Mr. St. Clair. I can tell from your accent that you are Scottish. Is your family related to the Sinclairs from Scotland?"

He said, "They are a distant cousin back in Scotland. They were a famous clan back in the 13th and 14th centuries. Some say that Henry Sinclair founded North America, not Christopher Columbus."

I said, "Oh, that's very interesting." Even though I knew it was true because I was the top aide for Henry Sinclair in another lifetime. I went on to say, "It would be wonderful if that were proven."

Afterward, I told Hannah, "Don't you find it a great coincidence that we should meet a Sinclair or St. Clair as he calls himself."

Hannah said, "It's like we are the main characters in a great story playing out right in front of us."

We joined Alex, Eliza, Marquis, and Marie, who were continuing with toasts. I saw Mr. Hannity enter the room. I said to Hannah, "I will be right back. I had a few more questions for Mr. Hannity about the billiards table."

Mr. Hannity greeted me warmly. As he shook my right hand, he slipped the ring box into my left Coat pocket. He did this very smoothly. Now I must find a reason to go to my room and deposit the ring into my satchel.

I returned to Hannah. She once again had that devilish look on her face. She said, "Whoever knew that billiard tables were so complex."

I said, "Believe it or not, it is like a large piece of furniture that has to properly fit into a space. I think we are all set. I need to get your father to approve the 50 shillings expenditure."

She looked at me with a smile and said, "Uh-huh."

I said, "Ok, you caught me. I was trying to order you another book of artwork secretly."

She looked me in the eye, still brandishing that devilish smile, and said, "I promise you that I will act surprised when I get another art book."

I said, "Excuse me, but I need to freshen up before dinner is served. I will be right back."

I went to my room and quickly hid the ring in my satchel. I then returned just as we were being called to be seated for dinner. We were then treated to the best piece of beef that I have ever had. They called it Standing Rib Roast or Prime Rib. The meat melted in your mouth. The entire meal was outstanding.

After dinner was over, Hannah and I made our way around the room. We wanted to make sure that we had met everyone. We met Alex, who was having a very deep conversation with a man from the Iroquois Nation. He introduced himself. He said, "Good evening, my name is Thayendanegea. The white men call me Joseph Brant.

I said, "Which do you prefer?"

He said, "White men typically call me Joseph, but my name is Thayendanegea."

I said, "Then Thayendanegea it is."

Alex went on to explain how the Iroquois have developed a very fair and effective constitution. He went on to say, "Our new friend, Thayendanegea, is telling how they established this and how it works for so many different Indian cultures."

Thayendanegea said, "The Iroquois Confederacy is made up of the Mohawks, who call themselves Kanienkehaka, the Onondaga who were from the hills, the Cayugathey who came by canoe, the Oneida who were the people from the standing stone, and the Seneca, who were from the big hill." We decided that we needed to set our differences aside when the white man first arrived. Our cultures are still strong and proud. So we developed a system whereby each nation manages itself with its own rules. Then we have common rules in place for all of the sub-nations to follow such as a common defense, trade agreements with the British, and skirmishes with the settlers."

Alex said, "I believe that the settlers and the Iroquois can live together peacefully if both sides take the time to learn each other's cultures."

We thanked him for his wise words and went over to say hello to some other guests.

I said to Hannah, "I think that we can learn to live peacefully with the various Indian Nations. One thing that will help is for the Indians to be fighting on the right side this time. They seem to find themselves on the wrong side of every conflict. If an Indian kills a Colonist's family member, the deceased's family develops a hatred that is not easily forgotten. It makes it very difficult for people to live and work together when this much bad blood is present. In my Scottish Dreams, Henry Sinclair lived peacefully with the Mi'kmaq Nation. They had a common respect for each other."

Hannah said, "One thing is certain, you have a different view of many subjects. Your past life experiences give you a totally different perspective."

She paused and said, "How about some present life experiences. It's time for dancing."

The General had hired professional musicians for this occasion. They included a Pianist, several string instruments, and several horns.

For the first hour, the dancing was the traditional Waltz style dancing I had learned back at Peace Field. I was very comfortable with this style of dancing. The latter half of the night was dedicated to what they called Country dancing. This ended up where you would exchange partners throughout the entire song. It was great fun until somehow I ended up dancing with Alex. The entire room was laughing. After that, we continued to dance the night away. I could tell that Hannah was really enjoying herself.

The night ended with us playing billiards in the study again. I finally sat down. Hannah joined me. She grabbed my hand and put her head on my shoulder. This was her way of saying it was time for bed. We both headed up the stairs, gave each other a goodnight kiss, and headed to our separate bedrooms. I thought about the ring that was hidden in my satchel. Soon enough, Hannah and I would be heading to the same bedroom as man and wife.

CHAPTER 52

LAST EVENING'S FESTIVITIES

WE ALL WOKE up just after sunrise. Marquis and his lovely wife Marie needed to get off to an early start. They needed to be in Boston by the next afternoon to catch their scheduled ship that would return them to Paris. The long and arduous journey to France would often take six to eight weeks. Mr. Adams advised them to head back to France as soon as possible, or he feared that Marquis and Marie would be forced to stay in the Colonies for the entire winter. It was getting pretty late in the year for this sail. He also knew that a Tea Party was about to take place. Mr. Adams didn't want Marquis and Marie to get tangled in that matter. The return trip to Europe was generally quicker than the trip to the Colonies. The currents favored travel in the easterly direction. One never knew how the weather or seas were going to cooperate. We began to say our goodbyes.

Alex said, "Please write to me and let me know when you plan on returning to the Colonies. I suspect that you and I have many more great times ahead of us." The two exchanged addresses.

Hannah said, "It is wonderful to meet both of you. I wish that you didn't live so far away. We all had such a wonderful time. Please come again."

Marquis said, "You can visit Paris any time you wish. My home is your home."

I said, "I have a feeling you will be back very soon. The war is upon us. We could use a great man such as you. Next time, you must visit the Compound."

General Schuyler said, "Please speak with your family. Make them understand our plight. France and this new fledging nation could be wonderful allies. Bring your countrymen. We have a common enemy."

They climbed aboard their carriage and set out to Boston. We all went back into the dining room, where breakfast was about to be served.

The servers brought in a large bowl of scrambled eggs, bacon, sausage, fresh bread, and an assortment of marmalades. The entire meal was served with tea and coffee. I had heard of coffee but had never tried it. There were parts of Europe where coffee was the latest craze.

Mrs. Schuyler said, "It was so nice to have a younger crowd here last night. Not that I don't enjoy the company of our usual guests, but most of them are usually nodding off before the music even starts. Last night I laughed harder than I have in years. And the dancing was just divine."

I looked at Hannah and said, "Well, it helps when you have such a lovely dance partner."

Alex said, "Well, thank you, Jeremiah."

I said, "I was talking about Hannah." Everyone was laughing.

Mrs. Schuyler stated, "I wish you didn't have to leave."

Alex said, "Well, Mrs. Schuyler, I have good news. We are not leaving. Ever! We took a secret vote last night and have decided that we should stay. Even the horses voted to stay. Where else are they going to find a barn made of mahogany?"

Mrs. Schuyler was laughing. She said, "Alex, my side hurts from laughing so much."

General Schuyler said, "Seriously, you three have a special gift. Ben Franklin had spoken of it last week at the lodge. I didn't quite understand what he was referring to until last night. Alex, I watched you win over Arthur St. Clair. He is usually as stubborn as a mule. He hasn't changed his mind on anything in twenty years. The combination of your charm and wit broke through the wall into his mind last night. You were convincing him about the problems facing the Indian Nations. He has been steadfast on that subject as long as I have known him. He seemed to be swayed by your discussion. The entire matter only lasted a few minutes. Once you finish your schooling, I predict you will be one of the leaders of our new nation."

Alex said, "Thank you, sir."

General Schuyler continued, "Jeremiah and Hannah. Mr. Franklin considers you two the most important people in our revolution. He calls you "Very wise and old souls." Our new nation is in good hands. Samuel, you should be very proud of your daughter."

Mr. Adams said, "Indeed I am. From the time she was a little girl, I knew she was special."

Hannah said, "Thank you, Father."

Mr. Adams said, "Jeremiah has been a surprise. He was right under my nose the whole time at the Compound. He surpassed all of the other leaders there in short order. Now, he is like another son to me. I also believe that our new nation is in great shape."

Alex said, "We best be going before I start to blubber." We all burst out in laughter.

I sensed that Alex was very sad to be leaving Eliza. He said to the General, "Sir, would it be okay if I come back and visit Eliza."

The General said, "Alex, of course, you are always welcome in our home. Naturally, I will serve as the chaperone."

Hannah said, "We should probably start preparing the horses."

I said, "Yes. It is that time. I will join you."

Alex said, "Eliza, why don't you join us."

The four of us went to the barn. As soon as they were out of sight. Alex grabbed Eliza and kissed her.

I told Hannah, "I think he learned that move of going to check on the horses from me."

She put her arms around my neck. Before she kissed me, she said, "Actually, I believe that was my move."

CHAPTER 53

BACK AT THE COMPOUND

We had several long days on our way back to the Compound. Mr. Adams knew of several Indian trails that took us on more of a direct route. We finally arrived just after sunset. We had ridden on horseback for a total of ten days.

As we passed the sign that read, "Welcome to the Adams Trading Company," I told Hannah, "That was quite an adventure. I am so glad that you were able to join me. I will always cherish our time together on this trip, but also I think I learned something about the Colonies along the way. There is a spirit amongst thus Colonists that the British don't understand. I feel more strongly than ever that we can win."

She said, "I feel it too."

We pulled up to the main office and dismounted the horses. Mrs. Williams ran out. She was so happy to see us. She looked at Hannah and said, "Is this Hannah? The last time I saw you were just a little girl. What a beautiful young lady you have grown to be." She then looked at me and said, "The days you were gone were very uneventful. Your leaders did a superb job in your absence."

From down the way and across the street, I could hear Mrs. Adams and young Samuel. "Oh, Samuel. I am so glad that you made it safely." She hugged him and then moved on to Hannah. She hugged her and said, "Were they able to keep up with you?" We all laughed.

Hannah said, "Yes. We had a wonderful trip. We had a few bumps on the first day, but the rest of the ride was splendid."

Mrs. Adams said, "Those few bumps wouldn't have anything to do with a few bounty hunters in Milton, did it?"

Hannah said, "Who knew that the news could travel so fast."

Mrs. Adams said, "I was in Binghamton the other day. Your exploits are becoming legendary."

She recalled her and young Samuel's trip. She went on to say, "As we left Quincy, we were stopped by a troop of Redcoats. Your nephew Gordon was among them. He mentioned something about tea. I told them that we were of no interest to them. I further told them to get out of the way. They let us pass. I am concerned that he knows we were headed to the Compound."

I made eye contact with Mr. Adams. It was now confirmed that there was no trader from within our ranks. It was Gordon the entire time. We would have to be more careful. Gordon probably would have guessed that we are all at the Compound. When Mr. Adams was away from everyone, I said, "We need to consider security here at the Compound. We have many important Patriots coming and going from here."

Mr. Adams said, "I should have done the right thing and hung Gordon for killing Mr. Walker. Unfortunately, we may need to deal with him sooner or later." He thought quietly and then said, "I will need to get a message out tomorrow to my cousin John. No doubt by now that he has cross-examined several innocent Patriots."

Alex, Hannah, and I led the horses to their new home. Hannah said, "This horse farm is much bigger than I remember.

Mark and Cleo are going to love it. There are many acres for them to graze."

We showed the horses to their stalls. They looked like they needed food, water, and a long rest.

We all agreed to meet at the tavern for Dinner.

Later that evening, we walked into the tavern, and I said, "Alex, I don't believe you know of a place such as this, but this is called a tavern."

Alex said, "Oh, whatever shall we do here?"

Hannah said, "I think you will somehow figure it out."

I told Hannah, "After all the places we have been to, I now realize that our tavern needs renovation. There is plenty of room. We could place the billiards table on one side of the room and even have a dance floor on the other side."

She said, "I am sure you have never thought you would want a dance floor before."

I said, "No, but sometimes change is good."

We dined and then said good night. I have never been so grateful to be in my own bed.

The next morning both Hannah woke up early and made our way to the horse barn. Cleo and Mark were very happy to see Hannah. She walked over and rubbed the sides of both of their heads. This was a sign of affection to the horses. I placed more hay in their stalls. Hannah said, "Let's walk around and see the rest of the ranch."

Just then, our Ranch Manager, Henry Jones, appeared. I introduced him to Hannah. She then walked him over to the new horses. Hannah introduced him to the horses just as you would introduce someone to a person. The horses were paying perfect attention.

Mr. Jones said, "These are beautiful Morgans. Mr. Adams had always told me about you and your horses. They will be very happy here. I will fit them into the grazing schedule."

He then looked at me and said, "We should add some fencing so that I can let more horses graze for longer periods."

I said, "Henry, I need to speak with Mr. Adams, but we have much bigger plans for the ranch that I am sure you will love."

Henry said, "That sounds great. Let me know how I can be of assistance."

We both thanked Henry, and Hannah said goodbye to the horses.

We walked around the Compound for several hours. I introduced her to everyone that we encountered. We ran into Miss Katherine Crawford. She saw Hannah and me holding hands and seemed very dismayed. I introduced her to Hannah. She was courteous but parted quickly.

Hannah said, "I am sure there will be a long line of broken-hearted young ladies after they see you walking hand in hand with me."

I said, "None that I am aware of. I have been preoccupied with my work, and deep down inside, I knew someone very special awaited me."

She said, "Obviously, you didn't have to wait for me, but I thank the Lord that you did."

I said, "They may seem disappointed now, but wait until they hear the news of Alex meeting Eliza."

She laughed, "Speaking of Alex. Where is he?"

I said, "He likes his sleep. I have had to threaten him with pouring a bucket of ice-cold water over his head to make him wake up. He barely would flinch."

We walked to the office, where we found Mr. Adams discussing some financial matters with Mrs. Williams. Hannah and I helped ourselves to some tea while we waited.

A few minutes later, Mr. Adams summoned Hannah and me to his office. I said, "Good morning Sir. I showed Hannah the ranch, and we discussed my thoughts on expanding the horse ranch. We have roughly four weeks before the snowfall is here to stay. I'm sure the men who call the Compound home would like the extra earnings. I think we could clear at least ten acres for grazing. Also, we have enough wood left over from the missed shipment to add on to the barn."

Mr. Adams sat quietly considering the idea. He knew that the men would like the additional earnings. The men that lived at the Compound year-round typically had no wintertime earnings. Their housing was free. They had all hunted all fall and had plenty of food, but I'm sure they would welcome the expansion and the extra money. The Compound has not expanded anything other than the Mill in years. The permanent residents of the Compound would see the expansion as a positive. Winter can cause cabin fever. This project, plus the additions of the billiards table and dance floor, would make the residents more upbeat.

Finally, Mr. Adams spoke. He said, "I like the idea, but there are two things to consider. First, Ben is scheduled to arrive tomorrow. I don't think Alex and you two will have any free time. What he has planned will be a full-time affair. Secondly, Hannah, your mother is already asking when we can return to Boston. You are of age to decide for yourself, but she will pressure you to return to Boston."

Hannah said, "Mother and I are very different people. I love being out in the country. She loves the city. I will discuss this with her."

Mr. Adams said, "Let's proceed with clearing the fields. Line up as many men as possible and place the best man in a leadership position. We will talk about fencing and expanding the barn at a later date. I think you should make haste and get everyone lined up for the task before Ben's arrival."

Hannah and I left the office. I could tell that she was upset. She said, "I have no desire to go back to Boston. First of all, I think it will become the site of a battle soon, and second I want to be here with you."

I said, "Hannah, I just found you. I am not going to let you go. If you are forced to go to Boston, I will quit my job and go with you."

She smiled and said, "Thank you for saying that. It means the world to me."

Just then, Alex walked up to us. I said, "Look, Hannah, the mid-morning shift has arrived. Alex, get some tea and a biscuit. We have a very busy day ahead of us."

Alex went into the office to have a quick breakfast. My thoughts went quickly back to Hannah's dilemma. Christmas could not get here soon enough.

Uh oh, here comes that smile. She said, "With everything that we have going on here, why are you thinking of Christmas?"

Ok. I had to think quickly. I said, "It just dawned on me that I have never really had anyone to celebrate Christmas with since I was a young child."

She said, "I like watching you try to dance around a topic that concerns me. I find it very romantic."

What would happen next would shock me. Even though it shouldn't have. Maria walked up. She gave me a hug. She looked at Hannah and said with a big smile, "You found her. I prayed for this day."

Hannah just looked at Maria with shock. Then the tears began to flow. She hugged Maria for what seemed like an eternity. Both women were crying.

I said, "I would introduce you two, but it seems as if you already know each other."

Maria said, "Yes, we have known each other seemingly forever, but this is the first time in this lifetime that we have met." She looked at Hannah and said, "My name is Maria. Would you two like to join me for supper this evening? We have much to talk about."

I looked at Hannah and then back at Maria and said, "Yes, we would love to join you."

Maria said, "See you at six o'clock. Also, bring Alex. This involves him as well."

CHAPTER 54

MARIA

SPENT THE BALANCE of the day getting things lined up for the land clearing project. I met with all the leaders to discuss the worker's needs. I instructed them to put the word out that we were looking for men who would like to participate and earn extra wages. The plan was to have everyone that is interested meet at the barn the following morning at eight o'clock sharp.

Even though I was extremely busy, my thoughts kept wandering back to Maria. How was she intertwined with this epic journey that I find myself on? How does she know Hannah? What can she tell us about the future?

Hannah had spent the entire afternoon with her mother. I do not doubt that Hannah's mother tried to convince Hannah to go back to Boston or Quincy with her and young Samuel. However, I know that Hannah's place is here with me. Hannah's home is out in the country, even if I hadn't come into the picture.

Hannah found time to purchase some fresh bread, wine, and cheese during the day for this evening's supper. Hannah and

Alex were in for a real treat. Maria was a fantastic cook. She had learned how to cook many classic Italian dishes as a child back in Rome. She was raised by her grandmother, who was a noted cook in her village outside of Rome.

Alex and I arrived at the Adams' home to pick up Hannah. We were greeted by Mr. Adams. He said, "I understand that you will be dining with Maria this evening. Please give her my regards." Just then, Hannah joined us and motioned us towards the door. I could tell that she was frustrated. Once we were outside and out of earshot, she finally spoke.

She said, "I have been arguing with my mother all day. I have been trying to point out that my father would be arrested very quickly in Quincy. Wasn't that why we left in complete darkness a few weeks ago?" She paused briefly, then continued, "I need to unwind a bit before I see Maria. She is such a special person. I don't want to enter her home angry." We walked around the Compound for a few extra minutes to let Hannah unwind.

A short while later we arrived at Maria's home. She very warmly greeted us. I handed her the wine, cheese, and bread we had brought. Hannah's demeanor changed immediately. Maria had a calming effect on her. We started with small talk, which led Alex to ask, "How did you end up at the Compound?"

Maria said, "Mr. Franklin is the one who brought me here. I was very close with his late wife, Debby. Their marriage was unlike any that I had ever seen. They were in a long-term Common Law Marriage. Debby was his wife of 35 years before she passed after having a stroke. Her name was Deborah Read. It seems that she was married to another man before Ben. His name was John Rogers. He was not a good man. He spent the dowry from their wedding shortly after their marriage. He was a drunkard who constantly lied to her. While a friend was visiting her family from England, he informed Debby that Rogers was married to another woman in England. This caused Debby to throw Rogers out of their house. Rogers took what was left of their money and moved to the British West Indies, where he was killed in a fight, although she could never prove it. She could only claim desertion, which in the Colony of Pennsylvania was not considered grounds for divorce. In steps Ben. He had wanted to marry Debby in his younger days, but her family wouldn't allow it. Her family thought that Ben would spend too much time overseas, and at the time, he seemed financially unstable. Her mother was correct on the spending too much time traveling abroad part. Ben spent 17 of their 35-year marriage abroad. He hadn't seen her during the last ten years of her life. Even though they were apart, Debby ran Ben's businesses in Philadelphia very successfully. They communicated through letters very often."

I said, "That's a very sad story."

Maria went on to say, "They had two children together. His son Francis died of Small Pox at the age of four. Ben never forgave himself because he delayed getting the boy the Small Pox Vaccine. Ben had waited too long. When Ben was going to take the boy for his vaccination, Francis had already contracted the disease. It was too late. They also had a daughter named Sally, who is active with the Patriot's cause in Philadelphia. Ben also had an illegitimate son named William, whom I have no idea as to the identity of the mother. Debby raised this William as her own.

I said, "It sounds like Mr. Franklin is a very complicated man."

Maria continued, "Ben has been married to the Patriot cause and his scientific discoveries for most of his life. A traditional marriage did not fit him well." She paused briefly, then continued, "At the same time, I began to get the attention of the Catholic Priests in Philadelphia. They understood that I had certain gifts that they couldn't explain. Some were saying that I was a witch. I went to Ben for guidance. He said, "I know of a place where you will be accepted and appreciated for your gifts." I packed my belongings very quickly and escaped to the Compound."

Hannah said, "It troubles me that so many supposed religious people can spew such negativity and hatred."

Maria replied, "There are so many small-minded people in

this life. I often wonder how your mission will be accomplished with all this ignorance surrounding us at every turn." She continued, "Having said all of this, I understand that there is a larger goal in front of all of us. I believe that destiny and fate have guided us to this very time and place. Jeremiah, you were born and raised in England; Hannah, you are from Boston; Alex, you are from the Caribbean; and I am from Rome. Destiny and fate have drawn us together, just like our previous lifetimes. No matter how far apart, we have been drawn together again because you three are the Children of the Flood, and I am your Guide."

Alex said, "I think the Watchers just like a challenge." We all laughed.

Hannah said, "Normally, this would be a lot to understand, but we have had Dreams about our past that tell us what you are saying is true."

Alex said, "We all understood that we were grandchildren of Noah. So where did you fit in?"

"In the times of Noah, I was your Grandmother, Na'amah. When your Mothers' were ready, I was the one whose face you first saw when you entered this world." Maria said. We were all shocked by this revelation, even though we shouldn't have been.

Finally, I said, "Every set of Dreams has you as a guide to steer us to the Secret of Eden, and for this life it's you"

Maria said, "This lifetime will be special. You will be moving the Secret of Eden to this great land. The Watchers spoke of this land thousands of years ago. It will be the land of the just and righteous. No matter how much of an uphill climb appears before you, never forget that you have the Watchers and the Almighty behind you."

This was a lot to take in, but we all knew it to be true.

Maria continued, "I sense that you have seen your enemy or, as he has been called, "The Child of Canaan"? Do not underestimate him. He defeated you many times in the past. As always, he is unaware of the Secret of Eden. All that he knows is that he must stop you. He doesn't know why and probably doesn't care what the reason is. He is taking direction from the evil one."

I explained the encounter with Anders that we had a few days ago. Maria said, "Count this as a blessing. At least you know who the adversary is for this lifetime. Although come to think of it, you usually have a preliminary encounter with the adversary in each lifetime. It is as if the Watchers want you to know who and what you are up against."

I said, "Neither Alex nor I have any memories of the adversary that Hannah referred to as Simon de Montfort. Why is that?"

Maria responded, "Hannah, do you want me to explain this to them?"

Hannah said, "Please go ahead."

Maria paused for a minute and then explained, "During the 13th century, Hannah was a Priestess within the Cathar community. Her husband, Jeremiah, who went by the name Francis in that lifetime, was killed shortly after their marriage, as was his entire family, including you, Alex. It seems that the Cathars were a threat to the Church in Rome. While the Cathars believed in Jesus Christ and the Trinity of God, they had other beliefs, such as the belief in reincarnation, which were contrary to the Church's message. They also believed that women could rise to the level of Priesthood. One of the tenets of their faith was that Jesus somehow escaped the cross and traveled to France with his wife Mary Magdalene. Obviously, this did not sit well with the Church in Rome. Pope Innocent III ordered one of his armies to wipe out the Cathars. He ordered every man, woman, and child was to be struck down. In fact, when one of his leaders was asked which of the Villagers were the Cathars? The Leader's response was to kill them all. The Lord will determine which ones were Cathars and which weren't. This Pope and his henchmen were pure evil. To think that this man, who ironically called himself Innocent, was supposed to be the Vicar of the Church and to be walking in the footsteps of Jesus Christ. He was an abomination. His men killed your entire family." Maria paused to collect herself. This memory was very overwhelming for her.

After a few minutes, she continued, "Miraculously, Helena, your name back then, escaped to northern France to the town of Gisor. You went there because of a secret that you had learned. Your mission was to protect the secret. You were a Guardian of the Secret of Eden. The adversary in that lifetime was a man known as Simon de Montfort. He was the Leader that killed all of the Cathars, including Helena's loved ones. He became aware that you knew a secret. The secret promised riches beyond anything that he could imagine. He captured, tortured, and finally killed you. However, you never gave up the secret. Had you given up the secret, the world would probably be a different place."

She painfully finished the story. She said, "The Knights Templar were aware that the forces working for the Pope were getting close to the treasure. There were also rumors of their impending arrests. So the Templars decided to move the treasure to Scotland. The Templars secretly held you in high regard. There is a statue dedicated to you in a small chapel in Rosslyn, Scotland. There is a special area within the Chapel that is called the Lady Chapel. The common belief is that the statue is to honor Mary, the mother of Jesus, but as with many things in the Rosslyn Chapel, it has a hidden meaning. It is a dedication to Helena. You will not find a written history of Helena, but I assure you that it is true, for I was with her during this time. I was a young aide to her. Helena was able to get word to me, even though she was imprisoned, that the Templars were going to be arrested and the treasure was about to fall into the hands of our adversaries. I was the one who informed the Templars of the impending arrests. So they very quickly moved the treasure to Scotland."

Alex said, "Without your decisive action, the treasure would have been lost, and the Almighty probably would have stricken the world with another flood or similar tragedy."

Maria said, "Perhaps, but I was only doing what the Priestess Helena told me to do."

We all sat quietly and thought about what we had just learned. Now, I understand why Hannah had the look of terror on her face when she first encountered Anders.

We all finally ate a delicious meal that Maria called Chicken Parmigiana. I felt that Hannah, Alex, and I gained a Grandmother this evening. Our bond was beyond explanation.

CHAPTER 55

JUSTICE

THE NEXT MORNING all of the men that wanted the extra earnings were waiting for me as Alex and I walked up to the barn. I told them of the plans to expand the ranch. They all seemed excited. I appointed Mr. Michael Hayes to be in charge of the project. Mr. Hayes was in charge when we expanded the mill. He had managed the project with order and proficiency. I gave them the entire concept. I said, "For right now let's focus on clearing the land. Let's move the stumps to a location on the northern edge of the lot. We will have a large bonfire as soon as the stumps are clear. Let's move the boulders to a location near the mill. They may come in handy on any future projects at the mill. They serve as a great foundation for a new structure. Let's plan on starting immediately. Mr. Hayes, if you need to purchase any materials please see Mrs. Williams. I will be tied up with another matter for the foreseeable future. As always, Mr. Hayes has my full confidence."

One of the men joked. He said, "Would that other matter

happen to be named Hannah?" Everyone heard it and laughed.

I said, "Very funny."

Alex said, "That is hilarious." I told him to be quiet before I substitute him for one of the workhorses.

Alex and I met Hannah back at the office. She had spent a few hours unpacking and getting settled. We sat down with Mr. Adams to discuss Mr. Franklin's arrival. Just then a carriage arrived with supplies from Binghamton. As always, this week's edition of the Boston Gazette was included. I looked at it and was shocked. The headline read Justice served. The article said:

JUSTICE SERVED

It has been rumored for a while now that several Redcoats were brutally raping young women in our community. Ten young girls under the age of 16 have come forward. We believe that there were more. Two of the young women have been impregnated. They were able to successfully identify the perpetrators. On Wednesday night, a trap was set for these scoundrels. They were lured to a place where they were told some young girls would be unprotected. Several Patriots ambushed the unsuspecting Redcoats and proceeded to strip them down and Hang them. Attached to one of the men was a note that said "This is what happens to you if you touch any one of our girls." This vigilante justice caused celebration in the streets of Boston. The Redcoats promised retribution."

We all knew something was going to happen. It was a good thing that we were not in Boston. There was no doubt that the British would blame Mr. Adams for this act.

Alex said, "Look at this article on page two."

EXTRAVAGANZA IN ALBANY

On Wednesday night, War Hero General Schuyler hosted a large party for some guests from France and some well-known Patriots that included Mr. Samuel Adams. The guests dined and enjoyed spirits and dancing until the wee hours of the night. All of the dignitaries from the Albany area were in attendance.

Obviously, someone who was in attendance at the party was also a writer for the Gazette. Mr. Adams said, "I don't condone this violence, but I understand it. We needed to make a statement to the British. Now they have it. Even though General Howe is our enemy, he is a decent man who I believe will recognize that his men received justice. He won't like it, but I think it will pass over time. In the meantime, our friends in the Sons of Liberty will be prime suspects. Hopefully, they will be able to verify their whereabouts on Wednesday night. The fathers of these girls will also be suspects."

I couldn't help but wonder if Gordon was among the three.

CHAPTER 56

THE TRAINING

That afternoon we continued to discuss the retribution against the three Redcoats. Mr. Adams said, "You can't help but feel for the girls and their families. I'm unsure how I would react if anyone tried to harm Hannah."

Alex said, "If anyone tried to harm Hannah, my guess is that we would be praying for their souls to be forgiven. Hannah is the last girl that they want to harm." The subject wasn't funny, but, as always, the way Alex delivered it was. Our conversation then moved to Mr. Franklin and his upcoming lessons.

I asked Mr. Adams, "How long will Mr. Franklin be here?"

He replied, "Quite a while. Winter is almost upon us. I think he will be here through Christmas." There was that word again. Hannah smiled at me.

We all decided to go freshen up for supper. Once again, we would be meeting at the tavern.

About thirty minutes later, I stood outside the Adams home. A few minutes later, Hannah walked out looking beautiful as always. I said, "Madame, may I escort you to our fine dining establishment."

She chuckled and said, "It will cost you." She leaned up and kissed me. We walked arm in arm down the street to the tavern. When we arrived, Mr. Franklin and Alex were well into their third or fourth pint of Ale.

I said, "Good evening. Thank you, Mr. Franklin, for keeping an eye on Alex."

Mr. Franklin said, "You're welcome, but who will be keeping an eye on him when you three make your journey to Nova Scotia?"

Hannah said, "Nova Scotia? That is our destination?"

Mr. Franklin said, "Yes. We have much to discuss over the next few weeks."

I said to Hannah, "We both wanted adventure. I think we are about to get it."

Alex said, "Do they have taverns there?" We all laughed.

Shortly after that, Mr. and Mrs. Adams entered the tavern with Maria.

I said, "Isn't young Samuel going to join us?"

Mrs. Adams said, "No, he already ate. He is doing his bible studies tonight."

They sat down. Hannah and I were sitting across from Maria.

Mr. Franklin was speaking to Mr. Adams. I overheard him saying, "I met with our associates in Philadelphia last week. There is no consensus regarding which Colonies will revolt. Many wish to try to negotiate with the British first."

Mr. Adams replied, "Those who oppose us should come and live in Boston for a while. They would quickly change their feelings."

Mr. Franklin then directed his conversation towards Alex, Hannah, and me. He said, "I am very excited to begin your training. Our future depends on your success."

I said, «We now must learn what we are being asked to do. Why have we all been called together for this moment?» This was the question that had been on my mind for weeks.

After supper, we all called it a night. Tomorrow was going to be a big day.

Mr. Franklin said, "Tomorrow, I have many things to go over with Samuel. So let's plan on meeting at the Freemason's Hall at three o'clock. But, first, we will need to go over your Freemason orientation before we can discuss any plans in detail."

Hannah said, "I am told that women aren't allowed in the Freemason Hall?"

Mr. Franklin said, "We will meet in the lobby for now. I will try to convince the members to allow you in. There are several Freemason organizations worldwide that allow women. We need to change our ways here in the Colonies."

I walked to check on the horses with Hannah.

I said, "I anticipated we would start our meetings with Mr. Franklin early in the morning. But, since we have the entire morning, let's take Cleo and Mark out for a ride. I have a very special place that I want to take you to."

She said, "That sounds great. I will pack a lunch for us, so we don't have to rush back."

I said, "Then it's a date."

THE MORNING CHILL

WOKE UP JUST before sunrise the next morning. I was very excited to show Hannah my special place on the bluff. I often ride out to this spot. Sometimes, for a few moments of peace. Other times when I am pondering a big decision regarding the Compound. I walked to the office, where I found Mrs. Williams making the tea. I said, "Mrs. Williams, do you ever go home?"

She laughed and said, "I like being here. It makes me happy."

I said, "Then, on behalf of the entire Compound, we are happy when you are happy."

She said, "Actually, I am so happy that you have found Hannah. Life on the Compound can be very lonely."

I said, "Thank you. She is wonderful."

She said, "Hopefully, she can stay awhile. Mrs. Adams is already inquiring about carriages back to Boston."

I said, "So I have heard. Trust me. I am doing my best to keep her here."

She said, "There is only one sure-fire way to keep her here.

But, I think we both know what that is."

I said, "Can you keep a secret?"

She said, "Of course."

I said, "While we were in Albany, I managed to buy her a ring. But, trust me when I say it is very difficult to keep anything secret from her."

She said, "Oh. I am so excited for the both of you."

I said, "I am waiting for Christmas. I will do it the proper way by first asking her father."

She said, "I can already tell that he loves you like a son. So I wouldn't be too worried about his reply."

Just then, Hannah walked in. She had a big smile on her face. Did I already give up the secret? How am I going to make it another month?

She said, "Good morning. Are you ready for our big adventure?"

I said, "Yes. Let's be on our way."

Once we got outside, Hannah said with a big smile, "Hopefully, I didn't interrupt an important discussion with Mrs. Williams."

I said, "No, we were just talking about the men starting the field clearing project today."

She said, "Uh-huh."

We walked arm in arm to the stable. The horses became excited when they saw us. It was almost like Cleo, and Mark knew they were heading out for a ride. I said, "There is plenty of grass for grazing where we are heading."

She said, "The horses' thank you."

We saddled the horses and exited the barn. The men were gathering outside the barn.

I told them that I would be back sometime this afternoon.

We set out on our way. One of the men yelled, "Good luck with your very important matter." They all laughed.

I then explained to Hannah that I told the men that I couldn't meet with them today because I had a very important matter to tend to. I thought we would be meeting with Mr. Franklin this morning. One of them asked me if the very important matter was named Hannah.

She started laughing and said, "Then I appeared this morning. You may not live that one down for a while."

I said, "That's ok. No offense to Mr. Franklin, but I would rather be spending time with you this morning."

We rode with me in the lead for the first and probably the last time.

Eventually, we ended up at the spot that I call "My Solitude." The spot was up on a bluff overlooking the Susquehanna River. There were Pine Trees everywhere. The long grass was blowing in the wind.

This spot has always had a special place in my heart. It signified the freedom that the New World represented to its new residents. From this river, one could reach anywhere in the world. It flowed to the Chesapeake Bay, which opened up into the Atlantic Ocean and then anywhere you wished. This great land and its abundant resources could be shared with mankind. Flowing water has always given me the feeling that an opportunity awaited. Whether it was boarding a ship in England bound for my new life or watching a load of lumber flowing away from the Compound, I often wondered where each log would end up. I usually draw a parallel between these logs and the new immigrants arriving in the Colonies. Adventure was in their future.

Even though it was only November, I kept thinking of spring. Springtime was always my favorite time here. The snowmelt would often cause the Susquehanna to rise above its banks. The water seemed to be in a hurry, much like the farmer who quickly prepared his fields for the new growth. A new opportunity was coming fast. For me, I thought that my opportunity was to be the Leader of the Compound. However, I recently realized that my real calling was to be with Hannah and continue the ageless mission of being a Guardian of the Secret of Eden.

We tied the horses up to a tree where there was a significant amount of long grass for them to graze on.

Hannah said, "This is magnificent. I will have to paint this scene."

I said, "Yes, we will have it above my writing table in our, I mean my, home."

She said, "I like the sound of our home better."

I said, "Oh, look. There is a Bald Eagle. Aren't they majestic?"

She said, "Saved by the Bald Eagle."

I said, "Trust me. It will be our home."

I sat down, leaning up against a large willow tree. She sat in front of me with her back leaning against my chest. Just then, I smelled that wonderful fragrance again. Instantly, we were both whisked away to the many scenes where we were looking out onto the water. First, it was on the deck of the Ark. Then it was on the Irish Coast, then Scotland, then the Mediterranean, then the cliffs of Quincy. Suddenly, we were talking without moving our lips again. She said, "The answer is yes." We then kissed. All of a sudden, we were back staring at the Susquehanna River. I suppose that we should not speak of those moments. They speak for themselves.

I said, "Now I know why this was my favorite spot."

We just sat there together for quite a while. She was leaning against me. My arms around her waist.

She finally said, "Do you remember the Dream where the Scottish version of you, Ian, and Clara were on their first date."

I said, "Yes, the one where he is trying to show off and falls into the water?"

She said, "Yes. That's the one where I, I mean Clara, fell in love with Ian."

I said, "Well, I fell in love with you when I first saw you on that staircase." So that was my awkward way of telling Hannah how I felt.

She turned and looked at me and said, "I love you too." I would have this moment and scene etched in my brain for the rest of my days. Christmas could not come soon enough.

We enjoyed the lunch that Hannah had brought. It was then time to lead the horses to some water. We did just that and then returned to the Compound.

FREEMASONRY

LATER THAT AFTERNOON, Alex joined Hannah and me outside the Freemason Hall. It's funny that this building was off-limits to talk about for most of my time here at the Compound. But now, it is about to be the center of my world for the foreseeable future.

Mr. Franklin walked out of the building to welcome us. We went into the lobby, where he had a teapot and fresh rolls with marmalade waiting for us. We all took our seats. Several very old books were waiting for Mr. Franklin to use to make a point.

He started by asking a question. He said, "What do you think the term Freemasonry means?"

Alex spoke first, "I believe that originally it was formed by skilled artisans to build structures and examine history."

Mr. Franklin said, "You are partially correct. Freemasons examine history through a lens that is not clogged by prejudices or unproven beliefs. It is a place where the Church in Rome cannot guide our thoughts. If they had their way, we would all be tagged as heretics and be burned at the stake. We are free thinkers. There are no wrong ideas."

He went on to say, "The subject of Freemasonry cannot be completely taught in a matter of days. It is a lifetime commitment. A Master Mason such as myself must study Freemasonry for years, if not decades, to truly understand its meaning. That is why there are only a handful of us Master Masons worldwide. We have a belief that is at our core. The first time you hear it, you will say, "That is why they have all of the secrecy?"

Freemasonry is built on metaphors and allegories. Our initiates program, which includes you three, teaches the lessons of that core story."

He poured each of us a cup of tea and said, "This marmalade is wonderful. I will say one thing about the Compound; we always eat very well."

He sat down and continued. He said, "Freemasonry is centered on the Temple of Solomon and its architect Hiram Abiff. I know that you three have had Dreams about the Knights Templar and their infamous dig underneath the Temple of Solomon. I'm sure this will sound confusing, but that Temple is not the one that the Freemasons speak of. The physical Temple of Solomon is still a mystery. The Temple in which the Knights did their digging was considered the Second Temple of Solomon. There is no historical evidence outside of the Holy Bible that the First Temple ever existed. As an exercise this evening, I would like you to read both the book of Kings Chapter 7:23–26 and the book of Chronicles Chapter 4:2–5. These books not only describe the Temple of Solomon but also give the exact dimensions to which it is to be built. The Temple was said to house a very sacred place called the Holy of Holies and the fabled Arch of the Covenant.

I said, "I vividly remember a special room under the Holy of Holies where the secrets were hidden. Furthermore, this hidden room was directly underneath the Foundation stone where Abraham had offered up his son Isaac as a sacrifice."

Alex said, "There was a symbol in which a stone carving was

hidden behind that told the tale of the Secret of Eden."

Hannah said, "I only have brief visions of this event. I believe that I was only there in spirit."

Mr. Franklin continued, "This may seem very confusing, but the Temple of Solomon that the Freemasons speak of is only a metaphor. The Temple that we are still building today is that of the Temple of the perfect soul. We believe that the soul is re-born, goes through its lifecycle, and repeats its cycle until its goal is achieved. Only at that point can it join the creator in Heaven. For the Freemasons, our mission is to find the truth. We believe that there were ancient mysteries that were known at the dawn of man that were either forgotten or clouded over by power-hungry leaders that wanted to control the message and thus control the masses.

Alex asked, "Are you saying that the message given by the Bible is incorrect?"

Mr. Franklin said, "Incomplete would be the better description. I will give you what I consider the most egregious example of a leader trying to control the message. I am speaking of Emperor Constantine and his First Council of Nicaea in 325 AD. Before he called for the First Council, Constantine could see the growing threat of Christianity. The Romans had been persecuting the Christians since the time of Jesus. He could see that even though they were being persecuted, their movement grew larger by the day. At some point, the Christians could threaten the Roman Empire. Even his mother, Helena, had converted to Christianity. His first move was to outlaw the persecution of Christians. Then in the year 325 AD, Constantine called the first Nicaea Council. His scholars and scribes hand-selected the attendees. They picked Bishops and Religious Scholars that could be controlled. At the Council meetings, they selected which stories would be included in the Holy Bible. The other story that came out of this Council was regarding the Divinity of Jesus Christ."

Mr. Franklin paused, sipped his tea, and said, "What I'm about to say is not meant to change your faith or opinions of what you believe in. As we have learned through independent studies, many factions of early Christianity existed. There was no clear consensus regarding the life and times of Jesus Christ. The Council decided on the Gospels of Matthew, Mark, Luke, and John. All other Gospels and writings were discarded and ordered to be destroyed. The Council also declared that Jesus was a Deity."

We took a break for a few minutes to freshen up. We all were amazed by what we were hearing. I couldn't wait to hear more.

We all took our seats again, and Mr. Franklin said, "Let's get back to Constantine. The Council that he assembled selected which books were to be included in the Bible and which ones were to be not only thrown out, but all copies were to be destroyed. Only sixty-some books were selected out of over seven hundred. Constantine wanted to transform the message of Christianity into his own message, which he could control. In fact, he had transformed the Roman Empire into the Holy Roman Empire. In actuality, Constantine didn't convert to Christianity until his deathbed. During his days as Emperor after the Council of Nicaea, history shows that he still prayed to the Pagan Gods."

I asked, "Do the Freemasons know the true history?"

Mr. Franklin said, "There are no absolutes in this discussion. We know many of the stories that were considered taboo throughout history. One of our main missions is to continue studying all possibilities and keep an open mind."

He continued, "Another story which has been left out of most Bibles is the Book of Enoch. The book itself has never been found, but many searchers are currently scouring the deserts of the Holy Land for it. There are brief mentions of Enoch in the Old Testament. Both Ancient Greek and Egyptian stories discuss the Book of Enoch. We have gained most of our knowledge from these stories. I believe that when the Book of Enoch is finally discovered, many of your recollections will be confirmed. What we do know of Enoch is that he spoke of the Watchers. Enoch said the Watchers were Angels sent down from Heaven. The Jews did not include the Book of Enoch in the Torah because it spoke of a Messiah that would come down to Earth as a simple man of peace. Many scholars now believe that Enoch was foretelling the coming of Jesus Christ. Anyways, this story of this Messiah didn't fit the narrative that the Jews wished to put forward. So they purposely excluded it.

Alex said, "I have many Dreams from different time frames that show an ancient carving that is said to be a message from the Watchers. This message is at the core of my Dreams."

I said, "From my Dreams, I have discerned that the message from the Watchers is a warning that includes a list of expectations. If the expectations are completed, the greatest of the Secrets, The Secret of Eden, will be revealed."

Everyone finished their tea, and Mr. Franklin said, "We have covered much today, but I would like to leave you with a critical thought that describes the beliefs of the Freemasons very well. I would love to take credit for it, but one of my brother Master Masons, told it best. He said, 'In the beginning, picture God being a glowing ball of fire that is rotating very fast. As it rotates, shards of light fly off of the glowing ball. Those shards of light are souls. The point is that each and every one of us has a piece of God within us. How we use this gift is how we are measured.'"

In closing, Mr. Franklin said, "We will meet tomorrow right after lunch. I have given you much to consider today. Now it is time for me to adjourn to the tavern where the barkeep is undoubtedly becoming very lonely."

Alex said, "What a glorious idea." We all laughed.

I said, "I am sure we will see you for supper."

We walked out, and Hannah said, "Some of what we heard today is shocking, but deep down, I know it to be true."

I said, "I feel the same way, but let's keep our thoughts between us. I don't think your brother would agree with some of what we heard."

She said, "I agree. I am unsure how my father keeps all these thoughts to himself. He has never said anything like what we heard today. Not to me, at least."

I walked Hannah to her parents' home. We agreed to freshen up for about thirty minutes. I said I would come back and get her for the short walk to the tavern.

Later that afternoon, Hannah and I joined Mr. Franklin and Alex at the tavern. Mr. and Mrs. Adams decided to stay home this evening.

Hannah said, "I think the long journey has finally caught up with my father."

Alex asked Mr. Franklin, "When do we begin talking about the Secret of Eden?"

Mr. Franklin said, "Soon. I must first establish the background that will help you better understand the Secret."

We enjoyed supper, and then Hannah and I did what was becoming a ritual for us. We walked to the Barn.

She said, "Someday, it would be nice to live at the ranch. My Dream is to run a horse ranch, and it would be much easier if I lived closer."

I said, "Someday after our mission, whatever that is, is complete, we could build a dream home at the ranch."

We walked arm in arm quietly after visiting the horses. It would be nice to Dream about something other than past life experiences and focus on the future.

I kissed Hannah good night and headed to my home, where I would collapse in my bed.

Day Two

THE NEXT MORNING, we again met Mr. Franklin at the Freemason's Hall.

We sat and sipped tea while Mr. Franklin prepared his notes for today's lesson.

Suddenly, Mr. Adams burst through the door and stated, "Redcoats are entering the Compound."

Mr. Franklin said, "How many?"

"About thirty or forty. I must hide in the cavern." Said Mr. Adams.

Unbeknownst to Hannah, Alex, and myself, there was a cavern below the Freemason's Hall that could only be accessed through a hidden door in the main study.

Mr. Franklin, "We must dispense with formalities of this hall. Please follow Samuel and me."

We went to the main study, where Mr. Adams removed some books from the bookshelf. Then, he showed us a lever that was hidden behind the books. He pulled on the lever, and suddenly a wall to our left opened. Mr. Adams quickly entered the opening and disappeared. We pushed the wall back to its closed position and returned the books to the bookshelf.

We then returned to the lobby and exited the building. We found the Redcoat Commander harassing Mrs. Williams. He said, "I know that you are hiding Samuel Adams here. I will burn down each and every building until I find him."

Mr. Franklin shouted, "Commander, you will do nothing of the sort. Do you have a warrant?"

The Commander said, "Who do you think you are talking to, old man."

Mr. Franklin grew angry. He said, "I am the Postmaster for North America. I was appointed by the King himself. Once again, I will ask you again. Do you have a warrant?"

The Commander said, "I am sorry, sir, but we have intelligence that suggests Samuel Adams is hiding here. He is wanted for questioning."

"Commander, if I have to ask you again for your warrant, I will see to your Court Marshall. I am meeting General Gage next week. He will hear of your indiscretions." Said Mr. Franklin.

The Commander said, "I apologize for this incursion. The next time I will be certain to have a warrant."

"Commander, the person you are searching for is not here. I read in the Gazette that he was in Albany several nights ago. I presume that he is back at his home in Boston by now. Incursions such as this are only causing the Colonists to want to rise up against us. This is a very peaceful Industrial community. They have no reason to fight the British. But, unfortunately, I'm afraid you may have just given them one."

The Redcoats exited the Compound. We returned to the Freemason Hall. We were all stunned at what had just taken place.

I said, "I was shocked when I saw this in Boston or Quincy, but to see this at the Compound is far worse."

"We must form an armory here. I have heard of the British

burning down farms to send a message. We cannot just stand idly by and watch them burn down our homes." Said Alex.

About twenty minutes later, Mr. Adams came through the front door. Evidently, there is an exit into the woods from the cavern. He said, "I must return to Boston and make my whereabouts known. I need to take the heat off of the Compound. I will return shortly after that. Once the winter starts, I should be safe here at the Compound until spring at least."

For most people, this would scare them into submission. Alex, Hannah, and I are not most people. This only strengthened our resolve.

Mr. Franklin said, "I think that we should stop for today. Let's resume at the same time tomorrow morning."

Hannah, Alex, and I spent the balance of the day talking with Mr. Adams about forming an armory. Mr. Adams said, "I agree, but please be reminded that it is illegal for anyone to own guns other than for hunting. I know some people that can get us what we need. I will reach out tomorrow."

"I don't mean to sound disrespectful, but it is also very illegal to plan a revolution," Alex said.

Hannah said, "Father, it is too dangerous for you to go anywhere right now. We will go get the guns."

"It is far more important that you three stay unknown. I promise you that I will be careful."

We met the next morning as planned. It was good to know that Mr. Franklin was here to chase away any Redcoats.

Mr. Franklin began by saying, "The day before yesterday, we started our lesson by talking about the Temple of Solomon and its architect Hiram Abiff. I explained that this allegory doesn't pertain to the actual physical construction of a temple. Instead, it pertains to perfecting the tabernacle of the soul. Many of the initiations into the Freemasons are simply a metaphorical play on the building of the Temple of Solomon."

He went on to say, "After your initiation into the Freemasons, you will be introduced to a study of the ancient traditions that go back to the beginning of Man. The stories of the ancient traditions are told through Egyptian Hermeticism, Pythaorean-Orphic Mystery Schools, and the Jewish Kabbalistic Traditions. Hermeticism centers on the belief that all religions, at their core, have a common belief. For instance, the Jews, Muslims, and Christians all pray to the same God. Their differences lie in how they teach their doctrines and what expectations are laid upon their worshippers. The important point is that they all believe in the Creation Story and the God of Abraham. The Pythaorean-Orphic Schools center their beliefs on the Greek Gods, such as Zeus and his wife, Hera. They refer to the common person as Titans, whereas the eternal soul, which they call the Dionysus, is considered Divine. The Dionysus is trapped within a Titan for ten lifetimes which they call the wheel of rebirth. The Jewish Kabbalistic Traditions believe in esoteric teachings describing the all-knowing God and his earth-bound mortals. The Old Testament is made up of Kabbalistic Stories. Many are meant to be simply allegories. The meaning behind the allegories is meant to be a lesson."

He took a sip of his tea and continued, "Freemasonry takes something from all of these traditions. We are interested in their beliefs regarding the reincarnation of the soul. The ancient traditions have come from the place referred to as Atlantis and then later from Egypt. Very little has captured the imagination as much as Atlantis. Plato detailed Atlantis in his Timaeus and Critias Works. Some thought of Atlantis as an allegory, while others believe that it really existed. Some people think that this land that we call America was once Atlantis.

Furthermore, its inhabitants had turned bad, and God set forth a great cataclysm that destroyed most of the world and its cultures. The Bible tells of this cataclysm in the story of Noah. Many researchers are trying to find Noah's Ark, but as of today, they have come up empty. For those of us that wish to see empirical evidence of the Ark and the great flood, we are left unsatisfied. There is no proof of any of this, only legends. I have often wondered what other wonders are part of your Dreams. You three may hold the keys to many unsolved mysteries. Anyways, forgive me as I digress into other subjects. We will save that conversation for a later time. As for ancient Egypt, we are reminded that a great civilization once existed there just by looking at the Great Pyramids and the Sphinx. No one can answer the question regarding how these structures were built. Certainly, today, mankind is not capable of such a feat. Many of the ancient secrets that Freemasons study have come out of Egypt. It is no coincidence that Moses came out of Egypt. As you have learned from your Bible Studies, the stories of Solomon and the Ark of the Covenant are a direct result of Moses's Exodus Story. The bottom line is that we believe that these ancient cultures have been in possession of secrets regarding the creator and the birth of humanity."

He paused and said, "Let's take a break for a minute or two."

I said to Hannah, "My head is spinning with all of this knowledge."

"I am trying to piece together what all of this has to do with us," Hannah said.

I said, "I think the Dreams that we all have go back to the time of these ancient secrets. Mr. Franklin thinks that we are a link to the past not only because of the Secret of Eden, but also as witnesses to history. Usually, throughout history, anything that is written generally was written a considerable length of time after the events actually happened. We are possibly witnesses to actual events."

Hannah said, "My Dreams very rarely go back before the Scottish Dreams."

I said, "Maybe Maria can help us go deeper into our memories. First, we should talk to Mr. Franklin and see what he thinks."

Mr. Franklin must have overheard our conversation. He said, "My reasons for bringing Maria here were twofold. First, I wanted to protect her from the small-minded religious types that seem to condemn anything they don't understand, and the second reason is that I knew she has special skills that would help me clarify matters regarding death, reincarnation, and unlocking the ancient mysteries."

I said, "Mr. Franklin, I don't mean to startle you, but it goes much deeper than that. There is some cosmic force that has drawn Alex, Hannah, and myself together. It has worked again. Maria was with us in our Dreams."

Mr. Franklin looked startled. He said, "Good heavens, what have we uncovered."

Hannah said, "I believe that a higher power guides our path. We have been brought together for a very specific reason."

"We have been together for a specific reason for many lifetimes," I said.

After a ten-minute break, Mr. Franklin started the next session by saying, "If Constantine, along with many others, has destroyed the evidence regarding the ancient wisdom, how do you think we can be sitting here having this discussion?"

Alex answered, "The ancient knowledge has been passed down by secret teachings and secret organizations."

Mr. Franklin said, "Absolutely correct, Alex."

Mr. Franklin continued, "Let's first talk about Jesus Christ. His real name was Yeshua. The Name Christ was given to him at a much later date. It was taken from the Greek word Christos which means "the anointed one." Many of us in Freemasonry believe that Yeshua had mastered his soul, and he fully understood the ancient mysteries. Some of this we do on pure faith. Some of it is because of the secret societies. The Church in Rome has recognized the Gospels of Matthew, Mark, Luke, and John as the only recounting of Yeshua's entire life. One of the problems with this is that they were all written well after the death and resurrection of Yeshua. The other problem is what happened to Yeshua from the age of thirteen to thirty? The closest that we have to an eyewitness is St. Paul. St. Paul knew some of the Disciples. St. Paul's writings have been historically certified to have been written by his hand. Many other writings, some of which were attributed to St. Peter but cannot be authenticated. This doesn't mean that they were not true or accurate. It means that it may not have been written by St. Peter's hand. They may have been written many years later by some of St. Peter's followers."

Mr. Franklin paused momentarily and then resumed, "Anyways, St. Paul writes of having spent fifteen days at the home of St. Peter. His writings and letters tell some of the facts regarding Yeshua. Through the secret societies, we have learned about other written stories from this time. They tell a slightly different story. Constantine and his scholars chose to throw out and destroy these other stories. These stories are known collectively as Gnosticism. The Gnostics speak of Yeshua as being divine, but he was also human. Yeshua's teachings, according to the Gnostics, included the ancient mysteries. The scholars advising Constantine could not control the Gnostic message, so they made it forbidden. The message that the Church of Rome would go forward with was a clear-cut message of the teachings of Yeshua or Jesus Christ as told by Matthew, Mark, Luke, and John. They also accepted the various teachings of the Apostles and St. Paul because they centered on the life of Yeshua and not his ties to the ancient mysteries."

The other issue that I mention regarding Yeshua's missing years is even less clear. I have Brother Master Masons, who reside in the Far East that will tell you lively tales of how Yeshua spent those missing years in Buddhist Monasteries, learning of the ancient wisdom and trying to rectify his Judaic upbringing with the beliefs in the East. In fact, my Brothers claim that there are great memorials to Yeshua if you know where to look. I haven't been able to confirm whether any of this is true or not, but at the same time, I cannot absolutely rule it out. There is a commonality between certain Buddhist teachings and the teachings of Yeshua. Both teachings are beholden to what is referred to as the Golden Rule. It simply means, "Treat others as you would like to be treated yourself."

Mr. Franklin continued, "As I mentioned earlier, many of us

in Freemasonry believe that Yeshua had mastered his soul, and he fully understood the ancient mysteries. I believe that he did not achieve these lofty pursuits in Palestine. Where did he gain this knowledge? The obvious answer from the Christians is that he was the Son of God. He did not have to learn everything. This answer is too simple. I think other explanations are being withheld from us."

Alex said, "Should we stop believing the stories from the Bible?"

Mr. Franklin said, "Not at all. Just remember that there is more to the story. Over the next few days, we will discuss a great man that I consider to be my mentor. I speak of Sir Francis Bacon. Sir Francis once said, and I paraphrase, "Many young men set out to study Philosophy with the belief that they are devout atheists. As they become a master Philosopher, they transform and become a believer in God. Logic dictates to them that there is no other explanation for this wondrous universe we live in."

We all took a moment to get a cup of tea.

We were all seated again, and Mr. Franklin said, "We will conclude this afternoon with a discussion about secret societies. I will give you a brief overview of most of them. There are two very important secret societies. As I mentioned earlier, many had some understanding of the ancient mysteries at the time of Yeshua. As Christianity spread for the next fifteen hundred years, the Gnostic message, aligned with the ancient mysteries, had spread throughout the Middle East, then onto Greece and westward to what we now call Europe. The most notable of these societies were the Manichaeans, the Paulicians, the Albigenses, the Knights Templar, the Hermetics, the Rosicrucians, and finally, the Freemasons. The two that we must examine most closely are the Templars and the Rosicrucians."

I said, "I believe that Alex and I could teach a class on the Knights. I Dream of them almost nightly, no pun intended." We all laughed.

"Yes. Jeremiah. I plan on spending many days and nights with you three to pull from your memories. I will happily have quill in hand and plenty of parchment at the ready." Mr. Franklin said.

He continued, "As far as the Templars are concerned. The Church did not know that the Templars were in possession of the secrets of the ancient mysteries. The Pope probably wouldn't have granted them their Charter to protect Jerusalem and its pilgrims if he had known their secret knowledge. The Pope was also unaware of their knowledge of a secret treasure map buried underneath the Temple of Solomon. As you three already know, the Templars found the Cross of Yeshua and the sacred Menorah that Moses carried on his famous Exodus from Egypt. They also found the secret treasure map, which led them to the Sphinx in Egypt where they uncovered the Secret of Eden and many other treasures."

Mr. Franklin continued, "Over the next 180 years, the Templars became the most powerful organization in Europe and throughout the Middle East. The Knights had moved their treasures several times. The Pope and the King of France, King Philip IV, felt that the Knights had become too powerful. They devised a plan to destroy the Knights. On Friday, October 13, 1307, the King and his henchman rounded up the Knights and imprisoned them. The Leader of the Templars, Jacques de Molay, had advance warning of the arrest. He didn't think it would happen, but decided to play it safe and have the treasure moved to Scotland, where the Knights had a favorable relationship with the Bruces, who were the rulers of Scotland at the time. The Knights were all tortured and executed shortly after that. Some of the Knights escaped to Scotland, as well as several other places where they regrouped into one of many other groups such as the Knights Hospitaller, the Knights of Rhodes, the Knights of Malta, or the Order of Saint John."

"I think I know what happens to the treasure next," Alex said.

Mr. Franklin, "I'm sure you do, Alex."

Mr. Franklin continued, "The secret groups remained very quiet for the next few hundred years. This time was very dark for much of Europe. The church and the various Kings were brutal to anyone or any groups that questioned them or brought forward new thoughts. Our sacred knowledge had to be passed from generation to generation under the cloak of hidden messages and secret codes. Fortunately, this era was also known for the great geniuses such as Leonardo DaVinci and Michelangelo. They were the Masters of Art World. Very few knew that they were also masters of hiding messages within their artwork. At the same time, another secret society emerged that was known as the Rosicrucians. A leading member of this new secret society came into prominence. His name was Sir Francis Bacon."

Mr. Franklin gathered his papers and said, "I think that is enough for today. If you allow me to keep talking about Sir Francis, I fear we will still be sitting here tomorrow morning. I look forward to meeting any of you who would like to join me at the tavern for a pint and supper."

I knew that Alex was going to join Mr. Franklin. So I said to Hannah, "Would you like to join them. I have many questions."

She said, "Sure, but I would like to freshen up first."

I said, "Of course."

I went to my house and did the same. Soon after that, I walked to Hannah's Parents' house, where she joined me. Then, we walked arm in arm down the street to the tavern.

Alex and Mr. Franklin were seated at our usual table. We joined them and began making small talk when I said to Hannah, "Do you find it ironic that Mr. Franklin spoke of DaVinci and Michelangelo when just last week I bought you that art book in Albany that included the works of those two gentlemen. I have heard of those names maybe once or twice, but I don't know much about them. I find it very interesting that they should come into play so quickly."

"I thought of that myself. I don't believe that it is a coincidence. This is the same force that has brought us together with Alex and Maria. But, I feel that there is another higher level that we cannot see that knows exactly what we need at any instant."

Hannah said.

I said, "It goes hand in hand with the fact that you can read my thoughts. Is there a higher purpose for your ability?"

She said, "I certainly would like to know the entirety of this purpose. I understand that it involves the Secret of Eden, but I think there is more."

CHAPTER 60

SIR FRANCIS BACON

T HE FOLLOWING MORNING, we all met once again at the Freemason Hall. Today we were only going to meet for half of the day. I had many Compound matters that I needed to tend to, not the least of which was the progress of the clearing of the land at the horse ranch.

I said to Hannah, "I would also like to sit down and review your new art book."

Mr. Franklin heard my comment and said, "New art book?"

Hannah said, "Yes. Jeremiah was kind enough to buy me a large art book that has prints of the famous works of the European Masters."

Mr. Franklin said, "I would love to see it. Please bring it to one of our upcoming sessions. I love the works of the Masters, but seeing that my primary trade is that of a printer, I am intrigued by the new techniques that allow us to bring these masterpieces into everyone's daily lives."

Hannah said, "Surely. I would love to share it with all of you."

Mr. Franklin gathered his notes and said, "Today, we will talk about one of my favorite subjects, Sir Francis Bacon. When I spoke with Thomas Jefferson back in Quincy, he stated, 'The three greatest men that have ever lived were John Locke, Isaac Newton, and Francis Bacon.' I wholeheartedly agree, but I would add a few more like Galileo, DaVinci, Copernicus, Plato, and Socrates, to name a few."

He continued, "Sir Francis Bacon was one of the world's greatest philosophers, scientists, and statesmen. He was also the father of what we call the Scientific Method. This is a process where one experiments and observes and then repeats and then repeats again. Only then can you begin to understand science. Until you perform these experimentation exercises, you cannot pretend to understand the science of whatever topic you are researching. The Royals and the Church in Rome considered this thought process to be heresy. After all, they had already discovered and defined everything that society needed. To experiment in such a way was to question their authority. I will give you an example. The great Galileo wrote a book called the *Dialogue Concerning Two Chief World Systems*. In this book, he compared the Copernican system, where the Earth and other planets orbit the Sun, to the Ptolemaic system, where everything in the universe circles around the Earth. He published this book in Italy, which was the Church's stronghold. The Church considered this blasphemy. They had already ruled that the Ptolemaic system was correct. In 1633, Galileo was found to be "vehemently suspect of heresy" and was placed under house arrest. By this point, Bacon had already died, but his students and successors took notice that while Sir Frances was correct about the Scientific Method, he was also correct about keeping his heretical thoughts contained within the confines of the Rosicrucian movement. This was nothing new to Sir Francis. His entire life was a secret. He was the secret son of Queen Elizabeth I and Robert Dudley. He was raised from birth by Sir Nicholas Bacon. He spent most of his public life working for the Crown, even though he secretly despised them. He developed secret codes and ciphers to express his dismay. Many believe that he was the genius playwright behind the Shakespeare plays. Many of the plays poked fun at the Crown and would have caused Bacon a hardship in his political career if the true identity of Shakespeare had been revealed. He was also said to have inserted secret messages within the plays. After Bacon's death, it was discovered that Sir Francis possessed a great library that included many of his own sayings and thoughts. Many of these writings found their way into Shakespeare's Plays. They had been written roughly twenty years before the plays were made public. Oddly, many of these notes were written in French, Italian, and Greek and did not offer a translation. Mr. Shakespeare only spoke English, and there is no record of him traveling outside England. It seems that Sir Francis would always keep a notebook with him. As he had creative thoughts, he would record them in this notebook. Many times they were nothing more than a sentence. They were seemingly meaningless unless you were a student of Shakespeare. Some think he buried the secret Shakespeare Manuscripts somewhere in the New World. Perhaps they were hidden in Nova Scotia, or New Scotland as he called it. Maybe, someday that will be our new mission. That will be a thought for another day. We need to focus on one treasure at a time."

We took a break and refreshed our tea. After we sat back down, Mr. Franklin continued. He said, "There are two reasons why we are discussing Sir Francis Bacon. The first is that he was considered the head of the Rosicrucians. His actual mother, Queen Elizabeth I, apparently shipped young Francis off to France in 1576. He was only fifteen, but he was well beyond his years. It is unclear why she did this. Some claim that it was due to the rumors circulating about young Francis being her son. While others believe she did this for an entirely different reason. It seems that she placed Francis under the tutelage of Mr. John Dee. He was always thought to have been a spy for England, who lived in France. The truth was that Mr. Dee was the pre-eminent scholar on the ancient mysteries that were only known by the secret societies. It turns out that Mr. Dee was the head of the Rosicrucians. By age 17, Sir Francis was initiated into the Rosicrucians, which he would later refer to as the Order of the Masons. Mr. Dee taught Francis the art of codes and ciphers. At this time, there were Operative Masons and Symbolic Masons. Operative Masons actually did masonry work. They were credited with the construction of many famous Cathedrals around Europe. The Symbolic Masons were more in line with Freemasonry as we know it today. As time went on, Mr. Dee passed on the Rosicrucian torch to Sir Francis. This is depicted in a famous engraving where the elderly John Dee stands over an open grave while passing the lantern to a young Francis Bacon.

As Mr. Franklin showed us this image, he said, "Take note that Francis Bacon's feet are at a right angle from one another. Symbols meant everything to the Rosicrucians. This depiction is similar to the compass that the Freemasons use. Most paintings or pieces of artwork from the era known as the Renaissance contained hidden messages. Again, this was driven by the Rosicrucian movement. For artists like Leonardo DaVinci, hiding secret messages within their artwork allowed them to strike out at the people in charge."

We took a break for a few minutes. Midday was fast approaching. When we returned, Mr. Franklin stated, "I will wrap up my first lesson regarding Sir Francis Bacon by simply stating that he spent his life trying to get humanity to restore the ancient beliefs that have been lost over the centuries. He felt that they had been lost purposefully because there were those in power who were threatened by the supposed heretical message. He summarized his beliefs in a collection of books that were known as the Great Instauration. They were meant to be a guide for man to return to the old ways."

Mr. Franklin continued, "As I said, there are two reasons for which I want you to understand the life and times of Sir Francis Bacon. The first is because he was the head man for the

Rosicrucians. The second reason is that I have direct evidence that Sir Francis Bacon knew of the Secret of Eden. Not only did he know of it, but he also knew where in Nova Scotia it had been hidden. We will meet again tomorrow morning and start to discuss the Secret of Eden. As usual, anyone who would like to join me to discuss these matters can find me at the tavern later this evening."

As Hannah, Alex, and I walked out of the Freemason's Hall. Alex said, "Just to play devil's advocate, if they know where the treasure is buried, what do they need us for?"

I said, "They probably don't have specific knowledge of the treasure's location. Nova Scotia is a big place. They may believe that we have more specific knowledge in our Dreams."

CHAPTER 61

THE DISCLOSURE

HANNAH AND I spent the rest of the afternoon at the horse ranch. We tracked down the leader of the ranch project, Michael Hayes. We could see that at least half of the field was cleared. Mr. Hayes reported that the boulders were so heavy that two of the work carts had broken an axle. The blacksmith was working on repairing the axles. He was trying to make the axles stronger so that it wouldn't happen again. Hannah and I started walking towards a clearing on the area opposite side of where the barn is.

Hannah said, "This would be a beautiful site for a home. Look at the view to the east."

I said, "It is spectacular and you would be close to Cleo and Mark. Perhaps, we can start making plans this winter and begin construction next spring."

She said, "Thank you."

Just then Mr. Adams rode up on horseback. He said, "Today is December 8th and the East India Tea shipment is scheduled to arrive any day. I will be heading to Boston tomorrow morning. Hannah, I need you to keep a close eye on your mother. She is going crazy here. I would rather be out in the country, but she is a city girl. Always has been. Anyways, I will be meeting Mr. Franklin for dinner this evening. I have asked Ben to bring Maria. I would like both of you to be there as well. Perhaps she can keep your mother busy during my absence."

I said, "Are you sure that you don't want us to join you on the Boston trip?"

He said, "No. It is too important for you to stay here and complete your studies with Ben."

Hannah said, "Don't worry about mother. Tonight at dinner I will make some plans with her. Maybe Jeremiah and I could accompany her into Binghamton for a day."

Mr. Adams said, "That sounds good. Thank you." He then rode off.

Michael Hayes walked up and gave us the report for the day. He then asked, "Are we going to be working on Christmas Day? I was planning on taking my family to Hanover to see my wife's family."

I said, "Go ahead and visit your in-laws. The snow should start soon and we will have to curtail our efforts at the ranch anyway." Michael seemed happy with my reply. He walked off with a smile on his face.

Hannah asked, "What type of Christmas traditions do you have here at the Compound?"

I said, "Many do as Michael is doing. They go visit family wherever that may be. I have been on my own for so long that I usually have a quiet restful day by myself maybe reading a book or breaking out the snowshoes and go for a long hike."

Hannah said, "Well, I have news for you, Mr. Briggs. This is going to be the best Christmas ever. We are going to decorate all of the buildings in the Compound." She paused for a few seconds and continued, "I just had a thought about my mother. She loves Christmas. This will give her a project. When we go to Binghamton, she can help pick out the garlands and other decorations."

I said, "That sounds exciting. Maybe, we can have a party at the tavern for all of the people that are going to stay for Christmas. I am sure that Alex will be on board." We both laughed.

I did my absolute best to keep my mind off of a certain subject. So far so good.

The next morning came early. We had a rousing good time after dinner last night. Alex led us all in song late into the night. Hannah had disclosed her ideas about Christmas and this just set the mood for the rest of the evening.

Mr. Franklin began today's lesson by speaking about himself. I found this very interesting because he spent much of our time together with him asking about us. He, after all, is the one who has the fascinating life story, not us.

He began by saying, "Back in 1730, I was trying to find my way through life. I was the third youngest of seventeen children. I had many interests and a very strong desire to learn. I was invited to join the Grand Lodge of the Freemasons in Philadelphia that same year. Virtually no one had heard of the Freemasons back in 1730. They were only founded thirteen years earlier in 1717. After my initiation, I found myself amongst like-minded individuals. We were all on a quest for the truth. One negative outcome for the British throne was that as the British Empire expanded worldwide, so did the reach of Freemasonry. All of the Masons had a common belief that all that we had learned in church and school was not always true. We had only heard the message that the church and various crowns wanted us to learn. I always felt that there were other explanations. Freemasonry opened up those new doors for me."

He continued, "Anyways, the Rosicrucian movement went somewhat dormant after the death of Sir Francis Bacon. As you

can see, it took 91 years before the secrets of the ancient mysteries found a new home. I quickly embraced the Freemasons and
the brotherhood of those seeking the truth that surrounded me.
I quickly rose through the Masonry Degrees and was appointed
Grand Master of the Philadelphia Lodge in 1734. I have spent
the last 39 years splitting my time between the studies of the ancient mysteries, scientific experiments, and making a living as a
printer. I have shared much of what I have learned from my science experiments with the public. My skills as a printer helped
me spread the word of my discoveries rather quickly. I did not
do this to become rich. However, I do wish I had made a little
more profit than I have. Life has not always been easy. Thank the
Lord for my wife Debby, may she rest in peace. She always kept
my printing business in good standing while I traveled abroad
in search of the truths that we have been discussing for the past
few days. My quest was for truth and was not for wealth. My feeling has always been that none of this gathered wealth gets to go
with you when you pass. I would rather be remembered for my
discoveries and as a man that has stood in the truth. My selfish
side has recently thought, 'Maybe I will be reborn, as you three
have so that I can continue right where I left off'. Since I cannot
guarantee any future for myself, I have chosen to make the most
of this lifetime. Enough preaching about me."

We all took a minute and refreshed our tea. Mr. Franklin
continued, "I spent my years as Grand Master searching for the
truth of the ancient mysteries. I have heard many theories over
the years, some true but many were just fantasy. This continued
until I made a life-altering journey to England in 1759. I went
there to attend a meeting that included all of the other Grand
Masters from all over the globe. While there, I had the great
honor of meeting the Grand Master of the London and West-
minster Freemasons where the Order was founded. His name
was Sir William Byron. Upon meeting me, he referred to me as
the worthy one who is the Protector of Arcadia. As you can imagine, I had no idea what he was referring to. Had this old man

gone mad or was there something there that I needed to learn? Obviously, I chose the latter option. He asked me to join him for supper the following evening. I accepted. For this was a great honor. I had been singled out while in the company of some of the world's greatest minds. The next evening, I met him as scheduled. He told me that the great Rosicrucian has left clues to a great secret that has been hidden in Arcadia. I knew instantly that the great Rosicrucian that he was referring to was Sir Francis Bacon. Sir William continued to say that as he has grown older he has been able to see things that he could not see in his younger days. He said that when he first met me years earlier, he knew that I was one of the worthy, as he called it. He said that the great secret has been with us since the dawn of man. It tells of our past and includes a dire warning from the ones who Enoch referred to as the Watchers. He further stated that he was just a messenger and was not one that is considered worthy. He stated that the secret, as well as a vast treasure, had been hidden under the Sphinx of Giza, then moved to a Cathar Castle, then a Cemetery in Scotland, and now rests in Arcadia. The great Rosicrucian has left a trail for the worthy that exists in church sculptures, paintings, and hidden codes and ciphers. He finished by saying that I must find the Guardians. They will be required to uncover the Secret of Eden."

This story sent chills down my spine. For the first time, I understood the importance that Alex, Hannah, and I represented. We then took a lunch break.

Hannah said, "We must do a deep analysis of all of our Dreams."

"Maria should be able to assist us with this endeavor." I said.

CHAPTER 62

THE ROSSLYN CONNECTION

We RECONVENED AFTER lunch. Mr. Franklin continued where he had left off. He said, "Sir William Bryan told me that he thinks that I should travel to Scotland and visit the Village of Rosslyn. He believed that I would find some answers regarding the hidden secrets. Furthermore, he wanted me to meet the Scottish Grand Master, Sir Alexander Stewart, who was the 6th Earl of Galloway. Since Sir Alexander was still in London for the Grand Master's Meeting, I decided to track him down. Upon meeting him, he said I needed to travel to Scotland to meet Sir William St. Clair. Sir William was a Freemason and was a Grand Master of the Scottish Lodge from 1736-1737. Sir William was the most recent Baron of Rosslyn. He also told me that the Clan Sinclair was one of the most powerful clans in Scotland, but had an internal split during the Jacobite Rebellion of 1745. Most of the Clansman supported the Jacobite cause, but the Earl of Sinclair decided to side with the British. I decided to take Mr. Stewart's advice and travel to Rosslyn. I made the long and difficult trip. It was like traveling back in time. Much of Scotland was still living within the remnants of the Clan System. I finally arrived in Rosslyn. It was a beautiful village set deep in Scotland's hills. I was taken to Rosslyn Castle. The Castle was ancient and was in desperate need of repair. Although it was falling apart, I could see that this place had a deep history. I had heard of the Sinclairs. As the story goes, they were friends of Robert the Bruce, who was probably the last successful King of Scotland. I was led to meet with Sir William St. Clair. He was waiting for me in a sitting room deep within the Castle. I handed him a letter from the Head Grand Master, Sir William Bryan. I had no idea what the letter said. The seal on the letter itself was unbroken. He opened the letter and read it. He said, "Our esteemed Grand Master believes that you are one of the worthy."

Mr. Franklin said, "I told him that this whole concept of worthy or un-worthy was new to me. I was simply attending a meeting of the Grand Masters."

Mr. St. Clair said, "There is a very closely held secret in my family regarding a certain treasure. I will give you several of the clues while you are on this journey. You must do your own research and find the rest of the clues. If you are indeed worthy, then I will give you the exact location of the Secret of Eden at a future time."

Mr. Franklin said, "I will give it my very best effort."

Sir William said, "My ancestor, Henry Sinclair was the Earl of Rosslyn until he died in 1404. He was handed the prime responsibility of protecting the secret treasure just as the Earl before him, namely his father and grandfather, had done. This treasure had at its core a message that instructed its Guardians to transport it to what was referred to as the New World. At the time, very few knew of this New World. One such person was King Haakon IV of Norway. Haakon handed this knowledge of the New World to Henry in return for Henry's promise to continue to fight the Norse Warlords that had been attacking Norway. Haakon knew of a land that was past Greenland that was vast and full of natural resources. If you look within the archives of the Freemasons, you will find ancient texts that refer to a great continent that flows in gold and silver. Much of this knowledge came from the Vikings and, subsequently, the Norwegians. Many called it Arcadia because it sounded like the utopian place the Greeks talked about when referring to their Gods. The name seemed fitting. After the death of Robert the Bruce, the Clan Sinclair lost some of its protections. The new leaders of Scotland had heard rumors of a treasure and would soon start pressuring Henry to give up its whereabouts. Henry decided to hide the great treasure in this New World. The Knights Templar originally discovered this treasure. They had discovered the treasure under the Sphinx in Egypt as well as a very special artifact that has been passed down through the Sinclairs since their days as Merovingian Kings." I then had the following conversation with Sir William St. Clair:

Mr. Franklin said, "I didn't know that the Sinclairs were descendants of the Merovingians."

Mr. St. Clair said, "Yes. The St. Clair's had married into that line. Are you aware of the legend of Mary Magdalene?"

Mr. Franklin said, "I said no. I only know the stories from the Bible."

Mr. St. Clair said, "There is a legend that dictates at its core that Mary Magdalene was married to Jesus Christ. In fact, they had a child who became the first in what is known as the Merovingian Bloodline after Mary's move to France. I have no idea whether this legend is true or not, but one of the items included in the treasure is what is referred to as the Holy Grail. It was the chalice used by Jesus at the Last Supper. Mary had brought it with her when she left Jerusalem. Therefore, I believe that if you ever locate the treasure, you will also locate the Holy Grail."

Mr. Franklin said, "I said. Is the Holy Grail not the treasure?"

Mr. St Clair said, "As a matter of fact, there is another item in this treasure that is known as the Secret of Eden. No one is sure of what it is, but it is said to contain a power that is greater than all humanity combined. This item comes with a warning that if humanity doesn't correct their ways, they will suffer the same type of cataclysm that Noah encountered with the flood. All of humanity would be wiped out. After Henry Sinclair returned home from the New World, he tasked a young man who had traveled with him to record the story in such a way that only, what Henry had called, the worthy would understand. Our Chapel here in town that my ancestors built is supposed to contain many clues. Other clues reside in famous artwork. Move forward a hundred or more years, and one of the worthy came forward. His name was Sir Francis Bacon. Sir Francis spent years studying the legend. Then with some assistance from my forefathers, Sir Francis had solved the entire mystery and traveled to the New World where he saw the treasure with his own eyes."

Mr. Franklin said, "After this meeting ended, I spent the next two months analyzing the Rosslyn Chapel. It was the strangest Chapel that I have ever seen. It almost seemed as though it was there to worship something other than Jesus Christ. The carvings and sculptures overwhelmed anyone attempting to understand the secrets the Chapel was hiding. I surmised that the Chapel was built to honor both the Sinclairs and the Templars."

Mr. Franklin continued, "I left Rosslyn more confused than ever. I then traveled back to England, where I met with Sir Francis Bacon's descendants. His family was kind enough to let me review his notes and belongings. I had discovered many hidden messages in Sir Francis Bacon's archives. I came away convinced that Sir Francis had buried a second treasure in the New World himself. It was as if he did this to distract any would-be treasure hunters from the Secret of Eden. However, I was no closer to figuring out the location of the Secret of Eden. I was very disheartened. All of a sudden, I didn't feel so worthy. I spent the next years trying to understand this treasure hunt."

We decided to take a break for a few minutes.

After we sat back down, Mr. Franklin continued, "I kept trying to find every clue that there was. I would receive notices that associates would send me that said certain paintings had messages about secret items in Arcadia. The fact was, I already knew that the treasure was hidden in Arcadia. The term Arcadia was very vague. The continent of North America was very large. It could be anywhere. I finally had my big breakthrough on my second trip to Scotland in 1771. Once again, I traveled to Rosslyn to meet with Sir William St. Clair. This time I found him in a greatly weakened condition. Age had not been kind. After our pleasantries were concluded, we began to speak of the treasure. I had to ask a question that bothered me. I said, "Sir William. You are at an advanced age. Have you passed on your knowledge to an offspring?"

Sir William said, "No, but it is written down. My son will be handed the notes when my Last Will and Testament are read, just as I had received the startling revelation when my father passed. But, to be honest, I was hoping that you would have found it by now. So let's get on with it." We both had a good laugh.

Mr. Franklin said, "I told him what I have discovered, which wasn't much. Most of my knowledge had come from him."

Sir William said, "Well, you have been at it for 12 years. That in itself is an accomplishment. You have proven yourself to be worthy indeed, so I will be giving you the story as it was handed down by the young man who had accompanied Henry on the mission. His name was Francis MacIntyre."

Mr. Franklin noticed that both Hannah and I were startled.

Mr. Franklin said, "You two look as though you have just seen a ghost."

I said, "In a way, we have. Francis MacIntyre was the son of Ian and Clara MacIntyre."

Mr. Franklin said, "Good heavens. That was the two of you in that lifetime? Correct?"

I said, "Yes, these are some of the most difficult Dreams that I encounter. In one Dream I witnessed, Francis was almost mortally wounded in battle. Henry Sinclair had saved his life by killing Francis's attacker. As a result, Francis lost his leg due to the wound he had suffered that day. He was a mountain of a young man that seemed to have lost everything."

Hannah said, "I only remember a faint vision because I had already passed."

Mr. Franklin said, "Well, there is a happy ending. Young Francis became a well-known scholar, businessman, and philosopher. He was the pride of Rosslyn. This was no doubt due to good parenting."

I could see tears rolling down Hannah's face.

She said, "Excuse me, but this is a little overwhelming."

Alex said, "My Dreams showed Francis to be a very brave young man. He took on his assignment of being the Recorder of the Events very seriously. He had many people telling him how to go about protecting the secret, but he did it his way. The two of you should be very proud."

Mr. Franklin continued, "Well anyway, Sir William, handed me an old parchment which had one line written on it. It said, 'The treasure you seek is buried under the Holy Well.' Once again, I had a clue that meant absolutely nothing to me, but it was something. After returning to Philadelphia, I continued my research, which revealed that the Mi'kmaq Indian Tribe still has a stronghold in Nova Scotia. I traveled there and met with the Chief. He talked of legends of ships coming to their shores. When I mentioned the Holy Well, he just said the Holy Well was the home of Goosecap. I thought to myself, who in the blazes is Goosecap?"

Mr. Franklin noticed both Alex and I stir. He said, "Does the term Goosecap mean anything to either of you?"

Alex said, "Yes. He was an English Nobleman who was shipwrecked in the New World and made a home for himself amongst the Indians. They called him Goosecap, but his real name was Glouchester. Somehow, the Indians changed it to Goosecap. As far as the Holy Well goes, it was a spring located inland where we built a small Castle for Glouchester, Malcolm, Agatha – which was Maria, Angus – which was me, and Angus's wife, Abigail.

After Henry and young Francis departed, they stayed behind in the New World."

Mr. Franklin said, "Do you know where this castle or Holy Well are located?"

Alex said, "If I was near it, perhaps I could find it, but if you get me to the area of the castle, I know exactly where the treasure is hidden."

I said, "You know exactly where it was hidden?"

Alex said, "I hope so. For I, I mean Angus, was the one who hid the treasure."

Mr. Franklin was smiling from ear to ear. He said, "Alex, you have made my day. We should be able to find out where a castle is located in Nova Scotia. How many castles can there be? Now we have reason to celebrate."

Mr. Franklin and Alex left the Freemason's Hall and headed to the tavern.

Hannah said, "You don't remember hiding the treasure, do you?"

I said, "No, I have no memory of hiding the treasure."

Hannah said, "As with all of the other instances when I was watching from the spirit world, the visions are vague, but I do remember a feeling of happiness when you joined me. This must mean that you were killed or died in some other manner."

We both stood up and hugged each other. This had been a very emotional day. We were told the good news about our son from that lifetime, and I learned that I was killed while finding a home for the treasure.

CHAPTER 63

DECEMBER 24TH

TODAY WAS GOING to be one of the most memorable days of my life. The day started with my usual rounds around the Compound. All of the Compound buildings were decorated. Most of the homes were also decorated except for several Puritans who still lived by the ways the Pilgrims who first traveled here on the Mayflower had set forth. We all respected their beliefs, but we also hoped they would respect ours. This would be a special couple of days not only because it was the celebration of the birth of Jesus Christ, but because of the proposal I was about to make. As I walked, I thought about everything I had learned about the Freemasons and the ancient secrets. Somehow the Church had commandeered the pagan holiday away from the Scandinavians, who celebrated the Winter Solstice, and had assigned the birth of Christ to it. As with many traditions celebrated by the Church in Rome, it was decided during the reign of Constantine that the birth of Jesus would be celebrated in December. The fact that the pagan holiday was already in place made it easy for the Romans to transition the pagan day to the birth of Jesus Day. The fact is that very little is known about Jesus's birth or early life. Perhaps someday, someone will find a hidden scroll that will complete the story for all of us Christians.

Everywhere around the Compound were signs that read, "Christmas Celebration tonight at the Tavern – Food, Music, and Dancing. All are welcome. Festivities begin at Six O'clock." This meant that I would pick up Hannah at around 5:30. I would ask to speak with Mr. Adams shortly before that.

Finally, I came upon the Freemason's Hall. Mr. Franklin had asked me to stop in after I made my rounds. I walked in to find Mr. Adams and Mr. Franklin in a heated debate. They were discussing the aftermath of what was being called the Boston Tea Party. On the table in front of them were newspapers from all over the Colonies that described the Tea Party. This story was traveling like wildfire.

Mr. Franklin was upset because some of the men who destroyed the tea were dressed up as Indians. He said, "We are trying to get the various Indian Nations to stay neutral or join us in our cause. They had nothing to do with the planning or execution of this deed. Why would we do such a thing? This only hinders our efforts. We will have to make peace with Indians. We will need much tighter control of our missions going forward."

Mr. Adams said, "I had no idea that anyone would try to disguise themselves as Indians. As you know, I tried to keep some separation between myself and the team that carried out the attack. I was unaware of the details. The good news is that I was speaking to a large gathering at Faneuil Hall when the attack occurred. I was urging restraint. Many Redcoats present can testify that I was not part of the attack."

Mr. Franklin said, "This upcoming spring, we need to gather the entire collection of Patriots together to hash out our differences and put a plan in place. I believe that the British will continue to try to quell our efforts. Some have suggested that we put a Congress in place to set forth rules and guidelines."

Mr. Adams said, "We must be able to set aside our differences. The southern Colonies have a significantly different structure than we do in the north. One thing is certain, most of us in the north will not accept slavery no matter the cost. Our fledgling nation will be scarred forever if we don't correct this wrong."

Mr. Franklin said, "I understand. The southerners have backed themselves into a corner. The northerners have secured workers through Indentured Servitude Contracts. This practice has caused many good men to move to America. Jeremiah is a great example. He was given an opportunity, and he has made the most of it. Unfortunately, the southerners chose to take a shortcut. They chose slave labor over paid labor. Their businesses became successful overnight. But at what cost? Having human beings serve as slaves. This will have to change, but we must gain our independence first for this to happen. There will be many hard decisions in the days to come. The Abolition of Slavery is the most important and also the most difficult issue that we will face."

Just then, Alex walked in. Mr. Franklin said, "Good timing Alex. I have wonderful news. You have been accepted into King's College for the winter semester. So you will start your classes in mid-January in New York City." Everyone congratulated Alex. We all knew that Kings College would be a stepping stone for this brilliant young man.

The subject then turned to our studies of Freemasonry and the treasure. Mr. Franklin updated Mr. Adams with all that we have learned. He also discussed Alex's thoughts regarding the location of the treasure. He detailed how Alex knows precisely where the treasure is located in reference to a certain castle but is unsure of the exact location of the small castle itself.

Mr. Franklin said, "As of now, we have two considerable difficulties to overcome. The first is that we don't know where this castle or Holy Well resides. Perhaps I could meet with the Mi'kmaq Chief again, and he could help us pinpoint its location. Especially now that I know precisely who Goosecap is. Once we find the location, we can lean on our friends that reside in Nova Scotia. It turns out that many Nova Scotia residents helped the British in the French and Indian War. After the war, the British fell well short of the promises they made to the people who fought alongside them. This caused a lot of ill will. The second obstacle we face is that the largest military force in the world is currently stationed in Halifax, Nova Scotia. I speak of the British Royal Navy. It will be nearly impossible to sneak by them with a large treasure. We have much intelligence to uncover on both of these subjects. Over the winter, I will secure a large map of Nova Scotia. Then, we can start looking at all of our options. The good news is that the British forces will probably move once the revolution starts. The bad news is that they will be moving towards the Colonies."

The meeting was adjourning. Mr. Franklin said, "I am looking forward to our celebration this evening. I'm sure that I will see all of you there."

As we were walking out, I pulled Mr. Adams aside and said, "Sir, I plan on picking Hannah up for the party at 5:30 this evening. I would like to have a private moment with you and Mrs. Adams when I arrive. Please don't tell Hannah about this conversation or my meeting with you this evening."

Mr. Adams said, "Can we talk about it now. You are not planning on leaving the Compound, I hope."

I laughed, and I said, "No. I am not leaving the Compound. This is my home. But I would prefer to have Mrs. Adams present for our meeting."

He said, "Very well. I will see you then, and my lips are sealed regarding Hannah."

After the meeting at the Freemason's Hall, Alex and I went to the tavern where Hannah and several other ladies were finishing decorations for this evening's Party.

I said, "Hello. How can Alex and I help?"

Hannah said, "I think we are all set. It should be a great evening. You can imagine how many people have stopped by to offer help. They said that nothing like this has happened before at the Compound."

I said, "We need to have these events regularly. It's great for morale."

Alex said, "I am leaving, and you decide that you are going to have regular parties. I'm hurt."

I said, "I'm sure you will have plenty of parties in New York City."

"It's bittersweet. I'm excited to go to King's College, but there is so much going on with everything that I can't talk about." Alex said.

Hannah said, "Well, Jeremiah and I will have to visit you. I have never been to New York City."

"Our lives have become so exciting. It seems like we go from one adventure to the next." Hannah said.

We helped with the rest of the decorations. A few minutes later, the musicians showed up. Alex showed them to the cottage while I led the band leader to the piano, which he was ready to tune up.

Hannah came and kissed me goodbye and said, "See you at five thirty?"

I said, "Sounds great. But, when I first get there, I need to have a word with your father about an incorrect shipment that came in today."

She said, "Okay. See you then."

I thought, "Okay, the stage is set. I am almost home free."

Alex and I went back to my house to prepare for the night. As the afternoon went on, I started to get more nervous by the minute.

"Why are you so nervous? It's just another party." Alex said.

I decided that it might calm my nerves if I talked about it.

I said, "Alex, I need you to keep a secret. The big surprise is not the Christmas Party." I pulled the Ring Box from my pocket and showed it to Alex.

He said, "Is this for me?" I laughed for the first time today.

He then said, "Is this what I think it is?"

"Yes. I am going to ask Mr. Adams for his daughter's hand." I said.

Alex said, "Now I am nervous. However, there is no question about how she is going to reply."

I said, "I know. I don't have anything to worry about."

"Oh. I meant that she was going to say no," Alex said.

I said, "Very funny. Believe it or not, you have helped calm me down."

I finished getting dressed. I wore the outfit I was wearing the night I met Hannah."

It was five thirty, and it was time to go.

Alex said, "Good luck. I am very excited for both of you."

I walked over to the Adams House. It seemed to take forever. I checked my pocket for the fourth time in the last two minutes.

I knocked on the door. Mrs. Adams answered. She said, "Hi Jeremiah. So good to see you. I'm so excited for tonight. We have worked very hard."

I said, "And everyone here at the Compound appreciates it."

I then said, "I need to speak with Mr. Adams. Is he available?"

She said, "Yes. Let me get him."

Just then, Mr. Adams walked into the study where I was waiting. He said, "Jeremiah. You seemed so nervous today. Is everything alright?"

I said, "Yes. It's better than alright. I'm actually here to ask you something."

I collected my thoughts for a minute and finally said, "I know that I just came into Hannah's life, but we have a special bond."

Mr. Adams said, "Yes. I am aware that both of you seem to know each other from what Hannah claims are previous lives."

I said, "I know it sounds crazy, but it is true. The reason that I wanted to speak with you is to ask you for your daughter's hand in marriage."

Mrs. Adams said with a huge smile, "I knew it."

Mr. Adams said, "Never question a woman's intuition."

I said, "Especially with Hannah."

Mr. Adams said, "Yes. I would be delighted to have you as my son-in-law. I already have a son, but having two would be a great thrill."

Mrs. Adams said, "Are you going to ask her tonight."

I said, "Right now." Hannah had just appeared.

She said, "Ask me what?"

I said, "Hannah, please take a seat." Which she did. She had a smile on her face.

I got down on one knee and said, "Hannah, the best day of my life was when I met you at Peace Field. Please make today even better. Hannah, will you marry me?"

I pulled the ring box from my pocket. I opened it and showed her the ring.

She said, "You bought that ring that I tried on in Albany." She appeared to be in shock.

I said, "Yes."

She said, "Yes. Of course, I will marry you."

We all shed a tear. Mr. and Mrs. Adams were overwhelmed. Hannah gave me a hug that went on forever.

Just then, the door opened, and it was Alex. He said, "I couldn't wait to congratulate both of you. Jeremiah, did she say yes?"

Hannah said, "Of course, I said yes."

Alex said, "Hannah, are you sure you don't want to think about it for a while."

Everyone laughed.

"Very funny," I said.

Alex said, "I knew the night you met each other that you would be married."

CHAPTER 64

THE PARTY

I WAS SO HAPPY. I have found the woman of my Dreams, Literally. And now I am engaged to marry her. I often think back to
my days in England. I was destitute. I just happened to notice
the posting for the job at the Adams Trading Company in the
Colonies. What if I had walked a different route that day? Did
fate and destiny play a hand? Someday, I hope to understand
the force that has been guiding Hannah, Alex, and me for so
long. Anyways, here I am in the Colonies. I am in charge of a
large mill town. I believe that I will play an important role in the
upcoming revolution. And to top it off, I am getting married to
the most beautiful, kindest, and smartest woman in the world.
Life has been good to me. I must fulfill the purpose for which
a higher power has granted me this wonderful life. No matter
what hardships may lie ahead, at least I will have Hannah at my
side.

We all arrived at the tavern. Mr. and Mrs. Adams stood by the
door to greet everyone as they arrived. Mr. Franklin was the first

to arrive. He walked over to Hannah and me and said, "Hannah, your father is in such a jovial mood. We should have had a party like this a while ago." We laughed.

I said, "I think he is happy because of today's big news."

Mr. Franklin said, "Did I miss something. I love hearing news. Especially good news."

Hannah held out her hand and showed him the ring.

Mr. Franklin said, "This is wonderful. Over my many years, I have acquired the skill of recognizing good versus bad or right versus wrong. I knew back in that fateful moment when you spilled wine on General Washington's shoes that you and Hannah were meant to be together. Together, you two are both right and good. You will be the face of the Colonies. Neither of you comes from Royal bloodlines, but both of you are willing to work to become leaders. You will serve as role models for young Americans everywhere."

He looked at the ring and said, "Jeremiah, there is enough ring here for three women."

I said, "I thought the same thing myself, but Hannah deserves only the best. There is a band that goes with the engagement ring that she adds to her finger at the Wedding Ceremony."

Mr. Franklin said, "Wait until this word gets out. Everyone will be so excited. Martha Washington couldn't stop talking about you two that fateful morning. Her senses were working overtime. I know it is early, but have you thought of a date or place."

Hannah said, "We haven't even spoken about that yet. Whenever and wherever are not a concern just yet. I am just ecstatic that it is on the horizon."

Mr. Franklin said, "Let me be so bold as to say that this will be a major event that every Patriot will want to be part of. You two are the future of our movement."

Maria was next to join us. She had a smile on her face that went from ear to ear. She said, "I knew this day would come. I have watched both of you find each other in each lifetime, and I must tell you, it never gets old."

Hannah said, "Thank you for being a special person in our lives."

Just then, Alex walked up with drinks for everyone. He said, "This will probably be the first of many toasts to Jeremiah and Hannah this evening, but here's to giving us a Christmas to remember."

Mr. Franklin said, "Here here."

The news of our engagement made its way around the room. All in attendance came over to Hannah and me to express their good wishes. Dinner was served after everyone arrived. The main dish was the cut of beef that I had tried at the Schuyler Mansion. It was called Prime Rib, I believe. Everyone raved about the food. After supper, Alex led everyone in a series of Christmas Carols. He actually has a beautiful voice.

After that, the hired musicians were ready to start. Most of the men were like me. They had never danced before. Hannah was not having any of this "I have never danced before excuse." We showed everyone exactly how to dance. The women dragged their men out on the floor. Once they got the hang of it, they were all dancing beautifully. Even Mr. Franklin was dancing with Maria. The evening was a delight for all in attendance."

At the end of the evening, we said goodbye and wished everyone a Merry Christmas. They all thanked us for arranging the party.

I said, "This will be a regular event going forward."

Hannah and I walked back to her parent's home. I said, "Thank you for such a memorable night. Soon you will be walking with me back to our home."

"I can hardly wait." She said.

I said, "What time should I arrive tomorrow for the Christmas celebration."

She said, "Around nine o'clock sounds good."

I said, "Goodnight, future, Mrs. Briggs."

She said, "I like the sound of that, and thank you for giving me a night that little girls dream of. It was magical. I am not sure

I will get any sleep tonight. I am so excited."

I said, "Same here."

She said, "I love you."

I said, "I love you too."

I walked back to my home and quickly fell asleep.

CHAPTER 65

CHRISTMAS DAY

T HE WAR WAS *not going very well. The British had forced General Washington out of New York. We needed to do something decisive. The men were losing faith. I wrote to Hannah to tell her that since the roads were impassable for a carriage, I would stay and help out wherever I could. As soon as the roads dried up or froze, I would make my way back to the Compound.*

The General asked me to travel to the front line and get a report. He was not trusting what he was hearing. I did so. I found that on the other side of the Delaware River, there were Hessian forces and not British forces. After I told this to the General, he made a crucial decision. He was going to order a surprise attack and overtake the Hessians on Christmas Day and then attack the arsenal at Trenton. The General knew that he needed to give the French a victory that would help entice them into the conflict. I made the journey across the Delaware with the General. I briefly saw Alex leading his men into battle. I am not sure if he even saw me. He looked like a true warrior. His men followed him with valor. He lost several men that day. Suddenly, a cannonball landed near my position …

I woke up in a cold sweat. I just had one of those rare Dreams that involve the future. Was this a warning of some kind? Would this cannon ball kill me? Then it dawned on me. It was Christmas day in my Dream, and today was also Christmas day. I must tell Hannah of my Dream. Also, maybe Maria will be able to give me some answers.

I had slept in until about eight o'clock. Last night was very special, but also very exhausting. I'm relieved that the engagement is on, and the future looks bright for Hannah and me despite what my Dream was trying to tell me. I looked outside to discover about six inches of new snow. The entire landscape around the Compound was beautiful. I made some tea and quickly dressed for the day. The plan is to spend the entire day with Hannah's family, which I'm sure includes Mr. Franklin, Maria, and Alex.

I had to dig out my snowshoes for my daily walk around the Compound. It was so picturesque that I could hardly resist. I'm sure Hannah would like to join me on the excursion. While I was sure she didn't bring snowshoes with her from Boston, I was certain that there were a couple of extra pairs at the main office. So I retrieved a pair and went directly to the Adams' House. I knocked on the door and was greeted by Young Samuel. We exchanged pleasantries, and then Hannah appeared. I said, "Good morning. How would you like to join me on a brisk walk around the Compound? We can go visit the horses."

She said, "Sounds wonderful. Let me get changed into something warmer."

Moments later, she appeared. She is far better prepared for the winter than I am. I said, "On our trip to New York, I must make a point to get some proper winter clothing." She just gave me that devilish smile that I have come to know. I better change the subject.

We set out towards the horse ranch when she said, "My parents have spent the entire morning planning our wedding. I'm not sure how much input we will have."

"Hannah, it's our wedding. First and foremost, I want you to be happy. So let's make sure that your feelings are known as well." I said.

She said, "Do you have any special requests?"

I said, "If it were up to me, I would carry you over to the Chapel, and we would be married within the next hour."

She said, "Wouldn't that be funny if we showed up in an hour and said we're married." We both laughed.

"I think that all of the Patriots are going to want to be there. Mr. Franklin has expressed his thoughts on how you and I are to become the face of the future. It's all very exciting, but I want you to be happy with whatever we choose." I said.

Hannah said, "I think they will want us to exchange our vows in a grand affair. It will be the event of the year. I just want to make sure that you are comfortable with it."

"Then a grand affair it will be. We can make the Compound look presentable." I said.

Hannah said, "Not a chance. They were talking about General Washington's Estate at Mount Vernon or perhaps General Schuyler's Mansion. I am sure that either would welcome such an event. To be perfectly honest, though, I am not sure how comfortable I will be knowing that slaves are serving our guests, so I think Mount Vernon is out."

"I agree with you wholeheartedly," I said.

Just then, we arrived at the barn. The horses saw us as we walked in and seemed excited.

I said, "I have been thinking about the horse ranch. First, we need to build our home as we have discussed, and then we should build an inside riding barn large enough to give the horses some room to run in the winter."

She said, "We need to propose this as a business opportunity to my father. I know he currently does not have the funds, but some of his friends certainly do."

I said, "We can turn this into a thriving enterprise that will be in our family for generations to come."

I took this opportunity while no one was within earshot to tell Hannah about my Dream. She said, "The universe is speaking very loudly to you."

I said, "I know, but what does it mean?"

She said, "It is no different than the Dream that you had about me being washed overboard." Then, she paused and continued, "We can change the future. We can avoid certain circumstances."

I said, "I know that you are right. We can avoid being in these predicaments."

Mr. Hayes, who normally feeds the horses during the winter, left two days ago to be with his wife's family in Hanover. So Hannah and I fed them together. We said goodbye to the horses. We then walked back to her parent's house, where we were greeted by Hannah's parents. Mrs. Adams said, "There's the happy couple. We are so excited about the wedding."

I said, "So are we. Also, thank you for inviting me to your home for Christmas."

Mrs. Adams said, "You don't need to thank us. We are going to be family very soon. This will be the first of many Christmases we will spend together."

We sat and enjoyed the fire that Mr. Adams had built. He told stories about Christmas when Hannah and her brother, Samuel, were very young. He said, "The anticipation was more fun than the actual Christmas day."

Later that afternoon, Maria, Alex, and Mr. Franklin arrived for the Christmas feast. Mrs. Adams had marinated and cooked four whole chickens for supper. It was wonderful. The meal was followed by apple pie.

After dinner, we exchanged gifts. Hannah was surprised by not only the artist's desk and easels but colored pencils as well. I said, "We are going to have the finest horse ranch/artist studio in the Colonies." Everyone laughed.

I opened my gifts from Hannah. She had given me a new black greatcoat that was wonderful for the harsh winter we were seemingly going to have. She then handed me a package that contained new dress boots and fur mittens. I leaned over and gave Hannah a thank-you hug. Everyone else opened their gifts and celebrated this wonderful day.

I thought to myself, "Let's enjoy this day. We have much uncertainty ahead. War and a dangerous mission to Nova Scotia are on the horizon. We need to enjoy special days like this."

After all of the Christmas festivities had concluded, the subject quickly turned to the wedding. Hannah said, "Jeremiah and I spoke about our special day. We both are okay with having a large gathering that includes all of your and Mr. Franklin's associates. We are very proud that you think of us as the face of the new America. We only request that we don't have the wedding in a Colony where slavery is permitted."

Mr. Adams said, "We definitely will respect your wishes. Is there any objection to me reaching out to General Schuyler to ask him to let us host the wedding at his home?"

Alex replied, "None whatsoever." Everyone laughed.

Mr. Adams said, "Does anyone other than Alex have any issue?"

Hannah and I both said no.

Hannah said, "I have always wanted a spring wedding. How about late May or early June?"

Everyone agreed that those days would work.

Mr. Adams said, "Then it is settled. I will reach out to General Schuyler tomorrow."

CHAPTER 66

NEW YORK CITY

FOR THE FIRST time since I met Hannah back at Peace Field, we had several days just to relax. These were some of my most memorable days. We made ourselves comfortable at Mr. and Mrs. Adams' house. Hannah worked on her sketches while I sat at the table and got caught up on my Diary. I was weeks behind. I had much to write. We did this for several days while the fire roared and the tea flowed.

The past couple of months have been a whirlwind. Everything from taking over the leadership position at the Compound to Freemason studies, Sons of Liberty meetings, parties, the tour across Massachusetts, and to top it off, I found the woman of my Dreams, and now I'm engaged. I could write a six hundred-page book about my last year.

Mr. Adams had sent General Schuyler a letter requesting his Mansion's use for our wedding. Amazingly, we received a response two days later. It helps to own a carriage company that regularly travels between Binghamton and Albany. General and

Mrs. Schuyler gladly accepted our request. They were very excited. They recommended we wait until mid-June for weather reasons. The General said, "The rainy season ends around the first week of June."

Hannah and I looked at a calendar and decided on June 11th. That would be our special day. Mr. Adams responded to General Schuyler, thanking him and requesting the June 11th date. He proposed that Mr. and Mrs. Adams would accompany Hannah and me to Albany at some point in March to finalize the plans.

A month later we made the journey with Mr. Franklin and Mr. Adams to New York City to visit Alex. There was to be a meeting of the Sons of Liberty while we were there. After several long days we arrived at Alex's living quarters in the south end of Manhattan Island. He seemed very well settled. As we walked around it became apparent that Alex already knew everyone at King's College. The shocking part was that everyone referred to him as Alexander.

Hannah said, "That sounds so formal. I hope you understand that you are always going to be Alex to us."

Alex laughed and said, "Everyone thinks I some sort of a genius here. The school is not that difficult, but it is very time-consuming. I barely have any time for a social life."

I had never went to College so I could not relate. I said, "I'm sure that you will do great here. Your social life will be there waiting for when school ends."

We ate supper with Alex in King's College's dining hall. The food was average at best. I suppose if all of your time is going towards studying then food is just not that important. We walked over to the Inn and left a note for Mr. Franklin and Mr. Adams. Alex detailed the names of four taverns that we could possibly be at if they cared to join us.

Alex kept carrying on about how little free time he had. We

walked into the first Tavern which was extremely crowded with college students and professors. Everyone had to come up and greet "Alexander" as they called him. We had several ales and went to the next tavern with the hopes that we could at least secure a table. The same thing happened. Everyone shouted "Alexander" as we entered. I said, "I was almost feeling sorry for you about the lack of free time and no social life. Everyone seems to know you well at these taverns. It has only been a month!"

Alex said, "Well you know that I sometimes leave an impression." We all laughed. I could see that Alex was adjusting very well to his new circumstances.

Shortly thereafter, Mr. Franklin and Mr. Adams joined us. I had forgotten that Mr. Franklin was somewhat of a celebrity. This was especially true around the College Professors. They all wished to speak with him. It was hard to tell who had the larger audience that evening, Mr. Franklin or Alex.

We stayed at that tavern until the wee hours of the night. Mr. Franklin spent most of the night talking to the Science Professors about his experiments. Alex spent most of the night just being Alex. Hannah and I just sat back holding hands and taking the whole thing in.

The next morning we agreed to meet at nine o'clock for tea. Mr. Franklin had some questions regarding symbols. He had brought a very old book with him. He opened it to the Chapter on Ancient Judaism. He showed all of the symbols in the Chapter to Alex, Hannah, and I. He then said, "Do any of these symbols mean anything to any of you.

Alex said, "Yes. The Star of David and the Secret Seal of Solomon."

Mr. Franklin said, "How so?"

Alex replied, "The Star of David was prevalent throughout my Dreams of the ancient world. With reference to the treasure, it was a decoy or a trap for the unworthy. The Secret Seal of Solomon was used to guide you to the treasure."

The Star Of David

Secret Seal of Solomon

I said, "I agree. I distinctly remember the Secret Seal. The Secret of Eden was hidden behind it under the Great Sphinx."

Alex added, "There is one very important vision I need to verify. I believe the treasure is again buried behind the Secret Seal of Solomon. The Secret Seal is hidden underneath a thin layer of clay. The Star of David, however, is out in the open. We rigged the stone that has the Star of David on it. Both symbols are about four feet across from one another in a narrow cavern within a larger cavern. This Dream always includes the sound of running water nearby. Anyways, if you move the stone that has the Star of David on it, death will reign upon you."

Mr. Adams said, "Please explain exactly what that means."

Alex said, "It means that a large boulder is lying in wait above the robber's head. As the stone with the Star of David is moved, the large boulder rolls over. It has a flat side where we inserted at least twenty long blades. The boulder will then fall on the perpetrators' blade side first. The weight is enough to kill someone. The blades finish the job if necessary."

I said to Hannah, "Obviously, I was dead by the time that the treasure was hidden in that lifetime. I don't recall that at all. So we better remember that little tidbit."

We finished our tea. It was time to board our carriage and begin the long journey back to the Compound. Hannah said to Alex, "We are traveling to Albany in March to meet with General and Mrs. Schuyler to make the wedding arrangements. You should try to join us."

Alex said, "My semester ends after the first week in March. I have two weeks off before the next semester starts. Let me know if those dates work. I would love to see Eliza and all of you, of course."

Hannah said, "We will send you a letter with the dates."

We all gave Alex a hug and boarded our carriage.

CHAPTER 67

WINTER AT THE COMPOUND

WINTER IS PASSING before my eyes. The sheer beauty that a fresh snowfall brings is breathtaking. Hannah and I have made it a daily habit to walk the grounds of the Compound and venture far down the trails. One Saturday, we set out to the place I call 'My Solitude.' This was a long walk. As it turns out, the top of the snow was hard enough to walk on top of it without using the snow shoes. We knew this could change instantly depending on sunlight and wind, so we brought the snowshoes just in case. We packed enough food for the day. It was one of those perfect days when there wasn't a cloud in the sky. We both wore billed hats that helped to protect our eyes. Everything was so bright. It took us several hours to get there. Finally, we arrived. The Susquehanna River was as beautiful as I remembered. I stood behind Hannah and draped my arms around her.

Once again, we were both taken to somewhere in the Middle East. We were standing there staring at the Mediterranean Sea when someone approached us. This person's face kept changing. First, it was the Seer in the Rug Store in Jerusalem, then the face changed to that of Agatha from the Henry Sinclair Dreams, and then it was Maria. She finally said, "Your future may seem set, but beware that you have an adversary lurking out there that looks to do you harm. Just as you seek to guard the Secret of Eden, they seek to destroy you and the secret. There always has to be an opposite. The ancients used to say, "As above, so below." You must prepare this time. In previous lives, he has destroyed you but failed to attain the Secret of Eden. You must not let him destroy you this time. The secret needs to be guarded for future generations. This lifetime is just a mere stepping stone. Future generations will be the ones to finally understand the secret and all of its powers. You must help prepare the way for the next in line, for I can tell you now that it will be your great-grandson and his beloved soulmate who will be the next Guardians. You must help prepare the way for them."

Every time we have experienced this usual moment of bliss in the past, we have come overjoyed with the sense that Hannah and I are one. This time was different.

Hannah said, "There was a lot of information just handed to us. We must digest this slowly. We have already met the adversary. His name is Anders. He is what they call a Pirate. We must not underestimate him. Simon de Montfort was pure evil but was very cunning at the same time."

I said, "She mentioned that the next Guardian would be our great-grandson and his soulmate. Does that mean that they will be the next incarnation of us?"

Hannah said, "I suppose it does. You must guide our great-grandson with your Diary. There must be coded messages that only he will understand. We can't risk your Diary falling into the wrong hands, so we must keep it hidden. Then, when the time is right, our great-grandson will receive the message."

We walked back to the Compound mostly in silence. Then, finally, I said, "We should speak with Maria and Mr. Franklin."

Hannah said, "I agree. Maybe she will have some additional insight."

Later that afternoon, I found Mr. Franklin at the Freemason's Hall.

He said, "We had some troubling news today. There is an entire Company of Redcoats in Binghamton."

I said, "That is troubling. Why would they be making such a move in the dead of winter?"

Mr. Franklin said, "That is the question. We have several informants who live in Binghamton and are currently looking for answers."

I said, "For safety sake, we must assume they plan to come to the Compound."

Just then, Mr. Adams walked in. He said, "Good timing Jeremiah. I assume that Ben has told you the news regarding the Redcoats?"

I said, "Yes. Do you think that they are looking for you?"

Mr. Franklin said, "You don't need that kind of force to capture one man. This could be just a show of force. This area offers no strategic reason for their presence. The Susquehanna River does not exactly fall into the category of strategic. It suits our purpose well, but that's it."

Mr. Adams said, "Let's see if our informants can tell us what kind of encampment they are setting up. We should ask if it looks temporary or somewhat permanent."

Mr. Franklin said, "We feel it is time to further discuss this building. Obviously, you know that there is a secret cavern below this building. There also is a small armory so that whoever needs to escape will be armed."

I said, "That's all well and good, but you need to hear what happened to us today." I went on, "It was disturbing. I would prefer if Hannah were here also. In case I miss any details. I will go get her right now."

Mr. Franklin said, "Dear God, we are having one of those days. Jeremiah, make sure to tell the barkeep at the tavern that I may be there extra early today."

I laughed. A little levity helps to break the stress.

I went to the horse barn. I knew that Hannah was there shoeing the horses. Winter was about to end, and the horses needed to be ready for some exercise. I told her about the news from Binghamton and that Mr. Franklin and her father were waiting for us at the Freemason's Hall.

We rushed over there. Mr. Franklin wanted to hear about our experience first. I said, "Hannah, please tell them what happened."

She went on to say, "Jeremiah and I often have experiences where we are whisked away to mostly romantic places where we are usually staring out over a body of water. In this instance, we were joined by the Seer that has been with us on our past journeys together. This time the messenger changed faces many times, but the one that spoke was Maria. She had a dire warning about a mortal enemy that had destroyed both of us in past lives. She also said that we must prepare the way for our great-grandson and his soulmate, for they will be the next Guardians. We wanted to speak with you first, but we think that we should meet with Maria to see if she has any recollection of this meeting."

Mr. Franklin said, "Let's plan on meeting with her tomorrow. Jeremiah, can we have the meeting at your home tomorrow? I would like to have the setting as peaceful as possible. Some of these discussions seem to upset Maria."

I said, "Sure." Knowing full well that I need to give my house a thorough cleaning. I have been meeting Hannah at her parents' home up until now. It appears that it is time that my home finally gets a woman's touch.

Mr. Adams finally spoke. He said, "Hannah, I want you to continue your Tai Chi. You can defend yourself against any attack as long as they don't have guns." He said, "For those of us who don't know Tai Chi, you are allowed to use the secret escape. Let's review the escape again. Please follow me."

He led us to the bookshelf in the main library. The shelves were very thick because of the weight of the books. Mr. Adams said, "I will show you one more time. A loose board is exposed when you remove the books on the left side of the second shelf. Under the loose board is a lever. It requires a little force, but when the lever shifts, a wall opens."

We looked into the space behind the wall. It led to a hallway. At the end of the hallway, there was a set of stairs that led to a cavern below the building. We all walked down the stairs. We lit several pre-positioned lanterns, and the entire cavern lit up. Across the room was a tunnel that seemingly went on forever.

Mr. Adams said, "This tunnel leads to a secret exit that lies deep within the woods to the south of the Compound. We have staged a small armory of guns, swords, and knives near the exit. In addition, a large boulder that is designed to block the exit swings on a pivot only from the inside. After you swing the pivot, you can make your exit into the woods undetected."

I asked, "Did Gordon know of this secret exit?"

Mr. Adams said, "No. There was no need to tell him. The only ones who know of this secret exit are some of us Freemasons and you two. But, of course, we will share this with Alex when he returns."

I said, "Is this to be the new hiding place of the treasure after we retrieve it?"

Mr. Franklin said, "Yes. We will follow the same Symbology used for thousands of years. We will also include a trap should the unworthy ever make it this far."

After supper that evening, Hannah and I spent the entire evening cleaning up my house. I must confess that I haven't exactly been very tidy. The last time the house had a thorough cleaning was before Alex lived here.

Hannah said, "How did you and Alex live like this?

I said, "I don't know, but part of the issue is that I met a special someone I would rather spend my time with instead of cleaning my house."

She said, "Nice try. Soon I will be moving in here. We need to convert this from the house where two single men lived into our home."

I said, "I can hardly wait."

We finally finished. I said, "We are going to need some new furniture. We barely have enough seats for our meeting with Maria tomorrow."

I had one comfortable chair that actually had padding. So I sat down in it and said, "You seemingly only have one choice for a seat. That would be on my lap."

She sat on my lap and put her arms around my neck. I said, "Now, this works for me."

I said, "I was thinking about what Maria had said to us in the vision today about our great-grandson. So, since my soul will be present in our descendant, I would like to request that my soulmate has long blond curly hair with blue eyes and a devilish smile when she is up to something."

She said, "That sounds a lot like me. Would you be upset if I was a brunette?"

I said, "Not a chance as long as you are in there. Also, this means that we will have at least one child if we are to have a great-grandson."

She said, "Yes. I suppose that is true. We haven't discussed it yet, but how many children would you like to have?"

I said, "Well, Mr. Franklin is one of seventeen. I think that we should try for eighteen then."

She said, "That means I would be pregnant for twenty years."

I said, "I am teasing, of course. I would like to have as many as the Dear Lord allows us. How many would you like?"

She said, "Three or four."

I said, "We should consider this as we plan our new home."

CHAPTER 68

A Look into the Past, Present, and Future

THE FOLLOWING DAY began with Hannah knocking on my door. I answered it and said, "Is everything alright?"

She said, "Yes. I didn't mean to alarm you, but the only inside place large enough for my Tai Chi exercises is the main room at the Freemason's Hall. However, once the snow is gone, I can do it outside. Do you think anyone will care if I do my exercises there?"

I said, "Let's see. You are training for a mission that will save everyone on the planet, including all of the Freemasons. I think they will get over it."

She said, "I suppose you are right. Will you go with me and keep a lookout?"

I said, "Sure. Maybe you could teach me a few moves. After all, look how well you taught me to dance."

We arrived at the Hall a few minutes later. I watched her go through her exercises. It looked like she was doing a form of ballet with defensive fighting skills and religious overtones. She worked up quite a sweat in the process.

I said, "After the wedding and our mission to Nova Scotia is complete, you should teach the young women of the Compound some of these skills."

She said, "That's an excellent idea. These women need to be able to protect themselves and not be so dependent on men."

She showed me some basics. The art of defending yourself is about managing your leverage. If you have the upper hand in the battle for leverage, you have the superior position.

She said, "I am going to go home and take a bath. My muscles are going to be very sore today. I need to get back in shape."

I said, "Well, your shape looks perfect to me."

She said, "You are too kind. I will see you at your house after I bathe. I will bring some food to snack on while we meet with Maria."

I said, "Sounds great. I will have tea ready and perhaps something stronger."

She kissed me and I headed out of the Freemason's Hall.

Around noon Hannah arrived first with several dishes full of Marinated Beef, Roasted Potatoes, and some heavenly-looking cake. I said, "Thank you for going to all of this trouble."

She said, "Don't thank me. Thank my mother. I just carried it over here."

"But you carried it with such style and elegance," I said.

She said, "You sound just like Alex."

"It really is a skill. It took me a little while to appreciate it." I said.

Maria and Mr. Franklin arrived a few minutes later. We made small talk for the first twenty minutes or so. Then, finally, I said, "Well, we are happy to have both of you here." I continued, "We have made Mr. Franklin aware of our common past."

Mr. Franklin said, "Just so I am clear on this matter, in the time of Noah, you were the grandmother to Alex, Hannah, and Jeremiah."

Maria said, "Yes. I was the wife of Noah. Alex and Jeremiah were my grandsons, Joktan and Peleg, and Hannah was my granddaughter Tytea. Noah often said that these three were special. At the time, I didn't understand why they were special, but, as always, Noah had insight that I could not explain."

Mr. Franklin said, "I have many questions about the flood, but we shall save that for another day."

After a short pause, I said, "Hannah and I had an extraordinary experience yesterday which involved you, Maria." I explained the encounter by stating that we were in what I would call a Dream state, but we were awake. I continued, "We are on a beach looking out at what we believe was the Mediterranean Sea. You gave us a dire warning about an adversary that has plagued us throughout the centuries."

Maria said, "I had this Dream several weeks ago. The adversary that we speak of was the Muslim Warrior who killed Jacques in the times of the Knights Templar and was a Norse Warlord who killed Ian in the time of Henry Sinclair."

Hannah said, "Fortunately or unfortunately, we believe that we have met the adversary for this lifetime. His name is Anders. In the past, we would have referred to him as a Pirate. The evil was very present with this man."

Mr. Franklin said, "How can you be so sure it was him?"

I said, "When I looked at him, he suddenly changed to Abdul the Muslim and then to Oleg the Norse Warlord. These were characters that both Alex and my previous incarnations had fought with. I was certain it was him because he killed me in those lifetimes. His being was etched upon my soul."

Hannah said, "When I looked into his eyes, I saw Simon de Montfort. He was the beast that tortured and killed me in the early fourteenth century."

Mr. Franklin said, "I have heard the Templar and Henry Sinclair stories from Jeremiah and Alex, but I have not heard Hannah's story."

I said, "I didn't know it because Montfort had killed me earlier in the story. This story causes Hannah much anguish. Maybe Maria could summarize it for you." Hannah nodded to Maria.

Maria paused for a minute and said, "During the 13th century, Hannah's previous incarnation was named Helena. She was a Priestess within the Cathar community. Her husband was killed shortly after their marriage. The Cathars were a threat to the Church in Rome. While the Cathars believed in Jesus Christ and his resurrection, they had other beliefs, such as the belief in reincarnation that were contrary to the Church's message. They also believed that women could rise to the level of Priesthood."

Mr. Franklin said, "I am aware of the Cathars. The Freemasons are in possession of a very recent discovery known as the *Pistis Sophia* that we believe was part of the Cathar dogma. This document details the revelations made by Jesus after his resurrection to his Disciples and his wife, Mary Magdalene and his mother, Mary. We have kept this document hidden due to the fact that the Church in Rome would have it destroyed immediately."

Maria continued, "Pope Innocent III ordered one of his armies to wipe out the Cathars. He ordered every man, woman, and child was to be struck down. He was an abomination. His men killed Helena's entire family." Maria paused to collect herself. This memory was very overwhelming for her.

After a few minutes, she continued, "Miraculously, Helena escaped to northern France to the town of Gisor. She went there because of a secret that she had learned of. Her mission was to protect this secret. She was a Guardian of the Secret of Eden. The adversary in that lifetime was a man known as Simon de Montfort. He was the Leader that killed all of the Cathars, including her loved ones. As the leader, he became aware that she knew of this secret. The secret promised riches beyond anything that he could imagine. He captured, tortured, and finally killed

Helena. However, she never gave up the secret. Had she given up the secret, the world would probably be a different place."

She painfully finished the story. She said, "The Knights Templar were aware that the forces working for the Pope were getting close to the treasure. They had been told of their impending downfall. There were also rumors of their forthcoming arrests. So the Templars decided to move the treasure to Scotland. The Templars secretly held Helena in high regard. There is a statue dedicated to Helena in a small chapel in Rosslyn, Scotland. There is a special area within the Chapel that is called the Lady Chapel. The common belief is that the statue is to honor Mary, the mother of Jesus, but as with many things in the Rosslyn Chapel, it has a hidden meaning. It is actually a dedication to Helena. You will not find a written history of Helena, but I assure you that it is true, for I was with her during this time. I was a young aide to Helena. I was trying to follow in her footsteps. I was the one who delivered the message to the Templars that they were about to be arrested."

Mr. Franklin said, "This is astounding. The forces that have drawn all of you together are supernatural. We must accomplish this mission. It is larger than any of us or a new nation for that matter. We live in a special time. You are being guided by something I can only begin to understand."

He took a sip of tea and continued, "I have spent several months studying this Chapel. There are so many sculptures and statues in that Chapel that it is hard to find anything. I will look the next time I am there."

Maria took a sip of her tea and continued, "Just as I believe that Hannah, Jeremiah, and Alex are Angels for the most high. The adversaries, such as Simon de Montfort, are the Children of Canaan. They answer only to the fallen Angel who we call Lucifer."

Mr. Franklin said, "Maria, do you have any insight into the future?"

Maria said, "That is much more difficult. People have free

will, which can cause them to change directions, whether it is from guilt, being on the wrong side of the law, pressure from friends, and many other forces. But I can tell you this. I see the treasure making it here. However, I believe that the new America is going down a wrong path right from the start. The practice of slavery must end, or the Secret of Eden will show its wrath. Those who promote slavery are working in lockstep with Lucifer, whether they intend to or not."

Mr. Franklin said, "We are addressing the issue of slavery, but the feeling is that we must win our independence first." He paused briefly, then continued, "Maria, you have just given us an incredible insight into Hannah's past. Your abilities are a treasure that I shall never forget. But, I have one more question. Do you know what awaits those living by the rules handed down with the Secret of Eden?"

Maria said, "A rise in the level of consciousness that equals that of the Spirit World and access to the Universal Knowledge."

Mr. Franklin said, "The Universal Knowledge?"

Maria said, "I don't know what that means. I'm sorry."

Mr. Franklin said, "Jeremiah, I have one question for you. Where do you keep the spirits?" We all laughed.

After that session, I think we could all use a drink.

CHAPTER 69

THE AFTERMATH
OF HELENA

THE NEXT SEVERAL months were filled with many happy days and a few solemn days. The story of Helena has weighed heavy on both Hannah's and my mind. I knew that our past lives were filled with many harrowing moments, but the story of Helena put it all in perspective. It highlighted the fact that we were going to embark on a very dangerous mission against an enemy that has plagued us for centuries. Often times destroying us. This enemy is strong and brutal.

One particular morning Hannah and I were on our usual morning walk around the Compound. It was sunny but very brisk. Winter had not quite left us yet. We started to talk about Helena. Hannah said, "There were many times when I would hear you and Alex talk about your Dreams and I felt that something was missing. I thought it must have been because I was in the spirit world at that time. But that thought didn't seem to make sense. Once Maria told the story of Helena, everything came together. I have had some Dreams about that particular life. The Dreams are very sad so I think I always try to forget them. They were more like nightmares in a way. Part of me believes that as a result of this Cathar life, I have learned how to ride a horse, shoot a gun, and mastered the art of Tai Chi. One thing is certain, I am not going to go without a fight this time. Being a pacifist in my days as a Cathar might have been fitting at the time, but I assure you that it will not work in this life. If anyone tries to bring harm to me or my family, they will find themselves wishing that they never met me."

I said, "I believe that with every fiber of my being. I have always thought it was special that you have self-defense skills. I never bothered to ask you why. Now I know why."

She said, "Promise me this. After we secure the treasure and our mission to help win the revolution is over, we will have a peaceful existence here raising our family and of course raising our horses. I don't want any more conquests or secret missions. I simply want to be a wife, mother, and a rancher."

I said, "You have my promise."

We continued our walk around the Compound in complete silence. I could tell that the revelation about Helena was causing some pain for Hannah. I didn't dare bring up the fact that I had the ship Dream, or nightmare in actuality, again where Hannah gets washed overboard in a major storm. Once again I woke up from the Dream at that point. I never get to see what happens next. I know that if this happened in real life I would definitely go after her. I would never allow her to be taken from me in this manner. Thankfully, we didn't have any plans to travel on a ship anytime soon. Then it hit me. Nova Scotia. Was it an Island? Could we get there by traveling exclusively on land?

We were heading to meet Hannah's mother at the office. Hannah and her mother were going to discuss the wedding plans. This was a mother-daughter bonding moment. I would tell them that I had to go meet Mr. Franklin at the Freemason

Hall. I knew that he had purchased a map of Nova Scotia while we were in New York. I dropped Hannah off at the office and said I would return shortly. I needed to look at the map.

A few minutes after dropping Hannah off at the office, I raced over to the Freemason Hall. Mr. Franklin was there writing letters as he had done most days recently. I often wondered to who all these letters were being sent to. There were at least ten to twelve letters heading to the Post Office in Binghamton every day. I asked him for the Map of Nova Scotia. He handed it to me. I laid it out on the table. I could see that there was a land route to and from Nova Scotia that was much longer. While Nova Scotia was not truly an Island, the best route from the Colonies to Nova Scotia was by the sea. It was quite a large area. There was no place marked as the Holy Well. Hopefully, Mr. Franklin's contacts in Halifax would know where this Holy Well is.

Mr. Franklin said, "I am trying to resolve this issue regarding the location of the Holy Well by going down several roads. First, I have written to my contacts in Halifax. I am asking them if the Mi'kmaq Chief will show him where the Holy Well, or as he calls it, the home of Goosecap, is. Second, we will require a map showing all roads to and from this place. Third, I have written to Former Grand Master William St Clair of Rosslyn. I asked him what he knows of this place. Is the castle still inhabited? What is the best way to get there?"

I said, "I am hopeful we can travel by land."

Mr. Franklin said, "Why, do you get seasick?"

I said, "No, but as you know, the Dreams that Alex, Hannah, and I endure mostly have meaning. Most of them are a look into our past lives. But, occasionally, we also have Dreams that look into our future. I believe that many of them are warnings. Somehow, our minds seem to know the future. No matter how I try to explain it, none of this makes sense. What it boils down to is I have a recurring Dream where we are out to sea in extremely rough water, and a wave comes over the bow and washes everything and almost everyone overboard, including Hannah. Then

I always abruptly wake up. Someone is trying to warn me. So, therefore, I am avoiding traveling by sea."

Mr. Franklin said, "That's extraordinary. I fully understand your concerns. Maybe after the treasure is secured, you and Hannah could travel back by land. However, it would take a significant amount of time to do so. With the abundance of British forces in Nova Scotia, I'm not sure it would be any safer."

Mr. Franklin continued, "If you made your escape on the inside route through what they call the Bay of Fundy, maybe the waters would be less treacherous. But, first, we must learn where the treasure is, then we can plan an escape that keeps you away from open water."

I said, "Thank you. Please don't say anything to Hannah. She already knows of this Dream, but I usually avoid this topic because it upsets her. I don't want to put any weight on her mind."

Mr. Franklin said, "That's very understandable. Both of you have been through so many experiences. Sometimes, I think the rest of us are lucky because we don't remember our past lives. But, I'm sure that we all have had bad experiences. One thing that is certain is that in each and every life, you must go through death. I'm sure that it is not easy."

I said, "No, it's not, but at least Hannah and I have had each other."

Mr. Franklin said, "I have another item I want to speak to you about. As we discussed previously, we will include both General Schuyler and General Washington in the planning of the Nova Scotia expedition. These men are both very busy and getting busier by the day. I would like to lock down the days when we will get together to start the Nova Scotia planning. This may require a trip to Philadelphia to meet with General Washington. I think General Schuyler should be there as well."

I said, "I will discuss this with Hannah. I don't see a problem. I will have to make sure that all Compound business is in order. Spring can be a hectic time around here."

Mr. Franklin said, "Perhaps. I will reach out to General

Washington to see if he can join us for the wedding a few days early."

I said, "I will speak to Hannah about it this evening. Mr. Adams may also want to be there."

Mr. Franklin said, "I was planning on asking him as well."

CHAPTER 70

THE OLSEN'S OF NORWAY

S SPRING APPROACHED we made the journey to Albany to finalize the weddings plans. Alex was on leave from college for a few days so he joined us in Albany. We traveled back to the Compound after what had been a joyous few days in Albany. Alex made his return to Kings College in New York City to finish off his first year of college. It was always good to return to what had become Hannah's and my home. Life here had become rather mundane over the winter, even though we attempted to make the long and cold winter months more eventful. The sunshine that spring brought was a welcome sight to behold. As the ground thawed, I reviewed the new grazing land that had been cleared the previous fall. Very soon, we would be planting the grass seeds that would grow into the feed for the horses. After reviewing the fields, I went to the office to discuss the seeds and new fencing required.

As always, Mrs. Williams was two steps ahead of me. She said, "While you were gone, I picked up the necessary hardware to build the fencing for the new grazing fields. The men at the mill began to cut all of the wood required. We should be ready to install the fencing by next week."

I said, "Once again, you have outdone yourself. I came here to discuss how we need to prepare for the fencing project, and you basically have it completed."

Just then, a carriage pulled up, and out stepped Mr. Franklin. I walked out of the office and greeted him. I said, "I didn't expect you back at the Compound so soon. Is everything alright?"

Mr. Franklin replied, "Yes. I received some information regarding your adversary. The news is more sinister than I expected."

I said, "I will find Hannah so that we can meet to discuss your findings."

He said, "Let me get settled, and then let's meet in the Freemason's hall in one hour. Oh, and please bring Maria as well."

An hour later, Hannah, Maria, and I joined Mr. Franklin in the lobby of the Freemason Hall. I explained to Maria that only Freemasons were permitted to go beyond the lobby.

Mr. Franklin said, "Thank you all for joining me today. On my recent trip to Philadelphia, I met with a man named Robert Mackenzie. I was referred to Mr. Mackenzie by Sir William St. Clair of Rosslyn, Scotland. Sir William had instructed Mr. Mackenzie to speak with me regarding the Clan Sinclair. Upon our meeting in Philadelphia, Mr. Mackenzie gave me copies of the story of Lord Henry Sinclair, the Baron of the Rosslyn and the Ornkey Islands. I am sure all of you could have probably written the story yourselves, but this story was written by the hand of your son in that lifetime, Francis Macintyre."

I held Hannah's hand as Mr. Franklin produced a scroll that our son had written during that lifetime.

Mr. Franklin said, "I had to have this document translated

into English from Gaelic, so I will be paraphrasing some of the translation. The header on the document read "The Viking Family of Oleg Olsen." The document reads:

For centuries, Viking blood has flowed through the veins of the men of the Olsen Family. The Vikings lost their power hundreds of years ago because of leadership that had different ideas. The way of the Vikings was one of conquest and pillage. They believed that their gods had blessed them with these sacred duties. If a Viking lived by the code, they believed that when they passed, they would go to a place called Valhalla and drink at the same table as their gods and their forefathers. Oleg Olsen was a proud Viking."

Mr. Franklin paused, then continued, *"All was well with the Vikings until the mid-eleventh century when Christianity had gained a foothold throughout Scandinavia. The Christian message forbids the taking of life and stealing from others. The Viking Kingdoms gave way to more Christian-like nations such as Norway and Finland. This didn't happen immediately. It took several hundred years for all of the Vikings to change their ways. Some never did. They simply moved to the sea. They lived on Islands from the coast of Norway through areas of Iceland and Greenland. As time went on, some ventured to the New World, which was called Vinland. Legends had told of this vast land to the west that had an abundance of everything from game, lumber, and fortunes for those willing to make a sacrifice. Leif Eriksson discovered this land in 1000 AD. He started a settlement that was called L'Anse aux Meadows in Vinland. This New World didn't exactly fit the narrative of the Vikings because there was little or nothing to conquer and pillage. The only people here were the natives. The natives had little that the Vikings would want; thus, the Vikings opted to look for greener pastures back in Europe."*

"In the late 14th century, the King of Norway, King Haakon IV, made an agreement with a Scottish Earl named Henry Sinclair. Sinclair's exploits were noted throughout the region. The King offered Sinclair a lordship over the Ornkey Islands, which were critical shipping routes. All he had to do was rid the Ornkeys of the Norse Warlords that called the area home. The Norse were pirating shipments that were supposed to be headed to Norway. This angered the King. The Norse Warlords

had to be eradicated. One such Warlord was Oleg Olsen III. Sinclair engaged Olsen in battle and wiped out Olsen and his entire following. The only exception was Oleg IV and his younger brother Hans who were on a mission at that time. Oleg IV returned to the Ornkeys to find his family and friends dead. From then on, young Oleg's mission was to avenge his father's death. He knew how to find Sinclair. When Sinclair sailed, he always sailed under white sail with the Red Cross, which was made famous by the Knights Templar. Once you saw a fleet of ships flying the Red Cross, you knew that Sinclair was not far away. One such mission involved Sinclair and his fleet of ships sailing port to port to Vinland. Oleg had followed Sinclair at great cost. He lost three of his ships, and his younger brother Hans was captured by Sinclair. Oleg knew the only chance he had to avenge his father's death was on land. Sinclair made landfall at a remote Island just off the coast of Vinland. Oleg knew that this was the land of the Mi'kmaq. They were fierce warriors and were very protective of their lands. Sinclair kept making trips inland to a place that was a two-day hike into the countryside. Oleg had never figured out why Sinclair and his soldiers kept traveling to this spot. Then on one fateful day, Oleg decided to make his move against Sinclair. There was a large caravan of materials being shipped inland. Henry Sinclair and several of his aides were ahead of the shipment when Oleg attacked the carriage carrying the shipment. My father, Ian Macintyre, killed Oleg in an instant that I will remember forever. Sadly, my father was also killed in the melee. He died a hero's death that few would ever know about." Mr. Franklin paused and continued, *"Sinclair thought that this was the end of Oleg. I discovered years later that Oleg's younger brother Hans, who was being held prisoner aboard one of Sinclair's ships, watched a great treasure of at least ten treasure chests being offloaded from another ship. Apparently, Hans surmised that the reason for the trips inland was to hide the treasure. Thankfully, no one from Oleg's landing party survived to tell where the treasure had been taken."*

Mr. Franklin said, "Jeremiah, now you know how you died in that lifetime."

Hannah said, "You were a hero. You were the one that killed Oleg."

Mr. Franklin said, "There is more to this story. The one that you have called your adversary. The one that goes by the name Anders is a descendant of Oleg Olsen. He may know of the treasure. However, he probably doesn't know its exact location but may be waiting for you to lead him there."

Mr. Franklin then returned to the story. He read, "*Eventually, after the winter season ended, Sinclair made the journey back to Scotland, Hans was handed over to Norwegian officials where he was placed in jail. Several years later, Hans escaped during a prisoner uprising. We assumed that he never forgot what he witnessed back on that Island. He found another Viking community that took him in. He was married and had a family. The story of the hidden treasure would be passed from generation to generation.*"

Mr. Franklin reached for another document and said, "Robert Mackenzie wrote this next document. He states that one of the current Olsen's confided the following to him. The document says, "*The Vikings that had taken Hans in were a seafaring people. Instead of plundering kingdoms, they took to plundering shipments. Over the centuries, the Viking name had died off, and they were now known as Pirates. The Pirates had mainly migrated to the Caribbean. There were regular shipments going to and from Europe which could be plundered. The greatest heist was to locate one of the ships that was taking silver from South America back to Spain. This was every Pirate's dream. The ironic thing about piracy was that if you aligned yourself with the right nation, piracy was not only legal but it was revered. The British, French, and Spanish were in a constant battle over territories and shipping rights. These one-time outlaws were no longer called Pirates, but with their newly found legitimacy, they were called Privateers. The Olsens' prospered during this era. They had worked with famous Pirates such as Edward Thatch, who was known as Blackbeard, and Bartholomew Roberts, who was called Black Bart. Blackbeard was believed to have buried treasures up and down the coast of the Colonies. The Olsen's kept their families secret to themselves. Over the centuries, many of the Olsens had searched Nova Scotia for the treasure that their ancestor had seen. The only thing they could find was a small castle whose inhabitants had died off years earlier. The castle was a hunting retreat for British Royals during the 1500-1600s. After the British stopped using this place as a retreat, the Olsen's had swarmed upon it in search of the fabled treasure. They came up empty-handed. There was no sign of a treasure anywhere. Even though they couldn't find any treasure, the Olsen's knew that someday someone would come for the treasure."*

Mr. Franklin said, "One of my associates in Halifax was able to get me the following information regarding Anders Olsen." Mr. Franklin read from the letter that he received. It said, *"Anders Olsen is the latest family patriarch. He calls Halifax his home even though he has worked in ports from South America all the way back up the coast of the Colonies. He finally settled in Nova Scotia. The conflicts between England, France, and Spain over the rights to the islands of the Caribbean had been settled, effectively knocking the Pirates out of business. Anders then developed a trading company in Halifax that collected large fees for security and didn't bother paying any taxes. This was a glorified business of being a land-based Pirate. They would steal a portion of what they were hired to protect and sell it on the black market. This would be anything from liquor, teas, clothing, and armaments. Recently, they have been seen stealing shipments and armaments on both the Hudson and Connecticut Rivers."*

Mr. Franklin read the forthcoming last paragraph of this communication from Mr. Mackenzie with great despair. He continued to read, *"Anders Olsen and his family are employed by a warlord from Crimea. Crimea is part of an ancient civilization known as the Khazarians. They are worshippers of Satan and also go by the name of the Children of Canaan."*

This sent shivers down both Hannah's and my spines.

Maria finally spoke. She said, "The fight between Good and Evil will happen soon."

CHAPTER 71

THE DOWNPOUR

Winter had finally receded which gave way to a beautiful spring. Everything was in bloom. The seeds that we had planted for our new grazing fields were taking root and were beginning to show. The Compound had never looked better. June had finally arrived and it was time for Hannah and me to begin the journey on horseback to Albany for our wedding. The next morning we set out on our journey bright and early. Despite the early hour, we had many well-wishers there to send us off. To both of our surprise, Alex was one of them. The morning started clear and crisp. The plan was to make it to Oneonta and spend the night. There wasn't much to this old Indian village, but we knew that we would get a meal and hopefully get two rooms above the tavern. We both took in the beautiful views along the way. We had stopped mid-day near a stream so that the horses could take a break and get a drink from the stream for a few minutes.

Hannah said, "Do you have any Dreams about the upcoming revolution?"

I said, "I have had visions. As a matter of fact. The morning after we met, I walked to the top of a hill near Peace Field and had a vision of a great battle taking place in the distance."

She said, "I know that hill very well. I have walked up there many times with my parents as a young child."

I went on. Further, I said, "Then recently, actually it was on Christmas morning, that I had a Dream where I was on an exploratory mission for General Washington, and I was hit by shrapnel. I was so startled that I woke up. It terrified me."

She said, "Were you hurt?"

I said, "Yes, but it was not fatal." I continued after a momentary reflection. I said, "I think there will be a great hardship, but we will win. These thoughts about the future are nowhere near as clear as the Dreams from the past."

She said, "I have dreamed about great celebrations in Philadelphia and hardships in New York. But I also believe that we will succeed."

I said, "I just want our children to grow up in a nation where they feel like they are important. A nation governed by its people and not some faraway King who has never even been here."

She said, "As soon as the revolution is completed, we must work on ending slavery next."

I said, "I agree."

We saddled back up and continued to Oneonta. The day became unusually warm and humid for this time of year. I knew what that meant. Thunderstorms were on the way. We decided to pick up the pace. We were still a few hours from Oneonta. Suddenly the rain started. What seemed like a sprinkle at first turned into a major thunderstorm after a few minutes. The area where we were only had a handful of trees. There was nowhere to take cover. We had to persevere.

Hannah said, "Aren't you glad I suggested this ride?"

I laughed and replied, "This will be one of those stories we tell our children."

The horses seem to enjoy the coolness of the rain. I thought it would eventually stop soon, but that is what I get for thinking. It didn't seem possible, but the rain started to come down even harder, and this time the storm was accompanied by strong winds. Through the haze of the rain, I could finally see the town. I have never been so happy to see civilization. We pulled into the stable that was beside the tavern. We checked the horses in with the Indian stable mater. He laughed when he saw us. We were a sight for sore eyes. We went into the tavern to inquire about a room. The barkeep said that he only had one room available. He said, "The foul weather has caused people to take shelter." I told him that we would take it.

Hannah looked at me and started laughing. I said, "I will stay with the horses."

She said, "You are not staying with the horses. We will figure something out. Let's get out of these wet clothes."

We went to the room, which was pretty spacious. There was a fireplace. Hannah said, "We could take turns using the bed."

I said, "Not a chance. I will sleep on the floor." There was at least a rug in front of the fireplace. I said, "I will ask the barkeep for an extra blanket."

I started a fire which felt terrific. "I said, "We should try to dry our clothes."

Hannah said, "I will transform the bedspread into a fine evening gown. The women of Paris will be very jealous." We both were going to enjoy this time together no matter the conditions. I went down to the tavern and ordered supper for both of us and a large bottle of wine. I waited for our meal.

Meanwhile, Hannah was hanging all of her clothing near the fire. A little while later, I arrived with the supper and the bottle of wine. It was my turn to change. Hannah turned around to give me some privacy. I quickly wrapped a sheet around me, making me look like a Roman emperor. Hannah saw me and started laughing. She referred to me as 'Julius Caesar.'

I said, "Wouldn't it be funny if we showed up at the wedding dressed like this." She laughed.

We opened the bottle of wine and drank it with our supper of Beef Stew. It wasn't the greatest, but the fact that it was piping hot made it very enjoyable. We dined and laughed about our crazy day.

We had one of the most incredible nights since I have known Hannah. We both laughed quite a bit that evening.

The next morning, I woke up. Hannah was lying next to me on the floor. Neither of us used the bed. There was never a better feeling than waking up and having her lying next to me. A fire has never felt this good.

CHAPTER 72

BACK IN ALBANY

J UST AFTER SUNRISE, we were back on the road again. The horses were fed and well-rested. We should be able to make it the rest of the way to Albany today unless there is another monsoon lurking out there somewhere. There were several towns on the way where we could take a break when we needed one.

Hannah kept referring to me as Julius Caesar because of my appearance the previous night. I said, "We probably should keep it between us that we shared a room last night."

Hannah said, "I know, but it's too bad. It was an amusing situation. Alex would have found it very funny."

I said, "Yes. He would have. The problem is that he would have to tell every one of our guests at the wedding."

"Then it's our little secret." She said.

We rode on for hours through the hills. The views were breathtaking. Finally, just before sunset, we arrived at the Schuyler Mansion. One of the servants made General and Mrs. Schuyler aware of our arrival. Suddenly, we were greeted by General and Mrs. Schuyler, Mr. Franklin, General and Mrs. Washington, and Eliza. Everyone was so happy to see us.

Mrs. Washington said, "I have been so excited since we received your Engagement Announcement. I knew from the moment I saw you at Peace Field that you were meant to be together. It was right out of a fairy tale."

Hannah said, "Thank you for traveling here from Virginia for our special day. It means so much to us."

Mrs. Washington said, "We wouldn't miss it for the world."

We all entered the house. They had already eaten supper by the time we arrived. General Schuyler summoned the Chef and instructed him to reheat some food for us."

We all sat at the dining room table and shared stories. I told the gathering how we had been caught in a massive thunderstorm the previous day. I said, "All you could do was make the best of it. It turned out to be one of those nights that we will tell our children about."

The subject changed to the overall political climate in the Colonies. Mr. Franklin asked the Generals what their overall opinion was.

General Schuyler spoke first. He said, "The British are uneasy. They don't fear a threat from the rebels. They believe there is no way that the Colonies could muster up a fighting force that could inflict much damage on their forces. However, malaise is creeping into the soldiers on the ground. The hangings in Boston have them alarmed. Collectively, they are mighty, but they tend to travel in small enough units that they feel that they are vulnerable. Please understand, these men are trained to fight. Not to sit and play the role of Constable."

General Washington said, "What the British are not considering is that during the French and Indian War, our enemies, namely the various Indian Tribes deployed very successful tactics. Some refer to these tactics as Guerilla Warfare. They are small pointed attacks on supply lines and troops while they sleep or are otherwise not ready for battle. The British Infantry are trained to fight an orderly battle where troops stand in formation and fight. The hope is to outnumber the enemy and, at some point, outflank them. This usually results in the weaker combatant being surrounded. The Indians fought a different type of warfare. They were unsuccessful because their numbers were inadequate, and there was no specific Command and Control. If we resort to warfare to gain our freedom, we will have to deploy similar strategies. Our attacks will have to be strategic and precise."

General Schuyler said, "The General has succinctly described what needs to take place. The question is, "Are the Farmers and townspeople up to the task?"."

CHAPTER 73

THE PLAN TO CAPTURE THE SECRET

T HE NEXT MORNING Hannah and I enjoyed an early break-fast and then went on a brisk walk into the City Center of Albany. We headed to Mr. Hannity's Emporium, where I had purchased Hannah's Ring. We walked in and were very warmly greeted by Mr. Hannity. He said to Hannah, "May I see your hand?"

She showed him the ring. He said, "That looks absolutely beautiful. From the moment I met you, I knew that that ring belonged on your finger."

Hannah blushed and said, "Thank you. I get many compliments. Everyone asks where it came from, and I always give them your name."

He said, "Thank you. Also thank you for extending me the invitation to your wedding. It will be the event of the year here in Albany."

We spent some time looking at the artwork. It was all quite exquisite. Eventually, we made our way out of the store.

I said, "Up until now, I wasn't nervous about the wedding, but when you hear comments like the one we just heard from Mr. Hannity, I began to start to overthink things."

She said, "Same here. I am not used to being the center of attention like this."

"Hannah, whenever you walk into a room, all of the people turn their attention towards you. Whether you know it or not is the question." I said.

She said, "Thank you. That's nice and all, but I don't want the attention. I just want a normal life. As you know, in our past lives, something usually comes between us. Everything from the Black Plague to murdering Crusaders to vows of celibacy. That weighs heavily on my mind even though my future-based Dreams show me nothing of the sort."

I said, "Then don't let it bother you. These Dreams we have are usually never wrong. The Dreams regarding the future can be just a warning. We can alter the future by making changes. Let's make the most of every day together in this lifetime." The part I kept to myself was my repetitive Dream regarding Hannah being washed overboard in a rough storm. She wasn't going to like it, but whenever we head out to sea, she will have a rope tied around her which will also be tied to me. If we both go overboard, then we will perish together. I am going to alter the future, and that is certain.

We returned to the Mansion just as the carriage carrying Mr. and Mrs. Adams, Mrs. Williams, Maria, young Samuel, and Alex arrived."

We greeted everyone. Mrs. Adams was once again beside herself with excitement. She said, "The big day is almost here."

We all entered the Mansion where everyone else from the previous night was waiting. Everyone took a few minutes to get settled, and then it was time for lunch. We all enjoyed a meal that consisted of chicken and vegetables.

After lunch, General Schuyler said, "Well, let's retire to the study so that Ben can explain the predicament that has caused us to gather a day earlier than everyone else attending the Wedding."

General Washington, General Schuyler, Mr. Adams, Mr. Franklin, Alex, Hannah, and I all sat around a large mahogany table in the study. Mr. Franklin started by saying, "This story starts in the time of Adam and Eve."

General Washington interrupted, "Ben, you are the world's premier storyteller, but any story that starts with Adam and Eve will find me dead and gone by the time it reaches the halfway point." Everyone laughed. On first meeting, I thought General Washington to be a very stern man, but now I am seeing a different side of him. Perhaps, he was stern because I spilled wine all over his perfectly shined boots.

Mr. Franklin replied, "George, I will be as succinct as I possibly can." He went on, "This story is as old as humanity itself. As we have learned from our studies as Freemasons, the Book of Enoch details a set of Angels that have come down from heaven. Some good, some bad. The great flood rid the planet of the bad Angels, and only the good ones survived. The good Angels refer to themselves as the Watchers. Throughout history, there has been a legend that the Watchers have left us both a message and a chest made of metals that no earthling has ever seen. The message is said to detail how a land exists to the west that shall become the beacon of freedom and will represent all that is right and good. I believe it refers to America. The Knights Templar found the fabled message under the stone in which Abraham was willing to offer his son Isaac up for sacrifice. This was underneath the Temple of Solomon. This message led them to the Great Sphinx of Egypt, where they found what is known as the Secret of Eden. The Secret has been passed down through the generations where it was moved from Giza to the Seaport of Acre, then to France, then onto Scotland, where a Scottish Nobleman named Henry Sinclair moved it to the New World. He hid it in the place we now call Nova Scotia. Our mission is to find the treasure and move it here to the Colonies to be seated in its rightful home."

General Washington said, "Ben, that is quite a story. Pirates have combed the coastlines here in North America looking for treasures and found very little. How do we know that this story is true?"

Mr. Franklin said, "I will get to that. You haven't heard the truly important part yet. George, you also know from our Freemasons studies that the ancients believed that the soul must complete its mission before heaven can be achieved. We refer to this as reincarnation. This is where a soul is reborn into a new body after the previous body dies. In this case, there are a set of Guardians that have followed the treasure since the time of Noah. After each lifetime, they are continually reincarnated to protect the secret. They serve to protect it and make way for the treasure to open up and unveil its secrets. We refer to them as the Guardians of the Secret of Eden." After a long pause, Mr. Franklin continued, "Three of these Guardians are sitting in this room with us today."

General Washington and General Schuyler both had a look of shock on their faces. General Washington looked around and said, "I assume you are speaking of Alex, Hannah, and Jeremiah?"

Mr. Franklin said, "Yes. These young people are actually not young at all. Their souls are very old. These three have explicit Dreams about their past lives that detail everything I am telling you. Their stories have been corroborated with written histories. Alex and Jeremiah were two of the Knights who first discovered the treasure under the Great Sphinx. Hannah was a fabled Priestess in France who was tortured and gave her life to keep the Secret secure. All three were present in one form or another during the times of Henry Sinclair. Alex's previous incarnation was the one who hid the treasure in Nova Scotia. They have been reunited in this lifetime to continue their quest, which is unimaginable because they were born in different parts of the world. Hannah was born in Boston, Jerimiah in England, and Alex in the Caribbean. Yet they once again have found each other. It is quite extraordinary. Furthermore, Hannah and Jeremiah have been together as soulmates since their grandfather Noah paired them together. Now they are to be married once again."

General Washington said, "This is a lot to digest. So now you look to Phillip and me to devise a plan to retrieve the treasure."

Mr. Franklin said, "Yes."

General Washington said, "Ben, there is never a dull moment with you, but this clearly tops them all."

Alex stood up and went over to retrieve the whiskey container and some glasses. He said, "Every time this story is told, it ends up with someone needing a drink. So I'm just getting prepared." Everyone laughed.

Mr. Franklin, "Let's talk about the treasure itself. The treasure includes the typical silver and gold items that one usually expects to find with a treasure, but this treasure also includes the Golden Menorah that Moses led the Jews out of Egypt with and also the Goblet that Jesus used for the Last Supper."

General Schuyler said, "You are telling me this treasure includes what the King Arthur Tales referred to as the Holy Grail?"

Mr. Franklin said, "Yes, but there is more."

General Washington said, "There is more? What could be more than the Holy Grail?"

Mr. Franklin said, "There has been an ancient legend that predates the Egyptians. The chest that I previously mentioned that was discovered underneath the Great Sphinx also includes an ancient message that is a warning. It seems that the Watchers have set down a set of rules that humanity is supposed to follow. If mankind does not follow these rules, the Watchers will reign down a catastrophe as they did with the Great Flood in the Noah Story. The message further states that when mankind proves himself worthy, the Secret of Eden will reveal itself, unleashing the Secrets of the Universe."

General Schuyler said, "Is that it. Whenever I think the story is complete, you deliver an even crazier item."

Mr. Franklin said, "Let's come back to the past later. Let's talk about Nova Scotia."

General Washington said, "The British forces are split between Halifax and Boston. Therefore, it would be difficult to land a team anywhere on the eastern coast of Nova Scotia."

Mr. Franklin said, "Let me back up and tell you that somehow I blend into this tale. At a meeting of my fellow Grand Masters in London, our Supreme Leader requested a meeting with me where he referred to me as the Protector of Arcadia. This title startled me. This conversation led me to the village of Rosslyn in Scotland, where I met a descendant of Henry Sinclair by the name of Sir William St. Clair, who, over the years, has begun to tell me more and more about the treasure. It seems that the Great Master, as I like to call him, Sir Francis Bacon, was involved in the tale. He is said to have traveled to Nova Scotia and laid his own eyes on the treasure. He began through art and coded messages to leave a trail that leads the worthy, as they call these special people, to the treasure. I have been given many of these clues already."

Mr. Franklin took a sip of his whiskey and continued, "I traveled to Nova Scotia last summer and was introduced to the Mi'kmaq Chief, Jean-Baptiste Cope. This meeting was an achievement in itself. There have been many trying times between the British and the Mi'kmaq. I had to portray my sympathies as being towards the French, which is not far from the truth. My analysis of the clues handed to me by Sir William St. Clair led me to the understanding that the treasure was hidden under something known as the Holy Well. When I asked the Chief, he simply said that the Holy Well was at the home of Goosecap. I left more bewildered than ever. I had no idea who Goosecap was. Then, recently, while I was conducting some training for our three Guardians here, I mentioned Goosecap. Both Alex and Jeremiah lit up. It seems that they became acquainted with him during the Henry Sinclair mission."

General Washington said, "You two knew this fellow?"

Alex, "Knew him? I shared a home with him for some twenty years. He was one of the smartest people that I have ever come across. His real name was Sir James Glouchester. He was a Royal who was a University Professor who set out on a mission to find the land that the Vikings called Vinland. The Mi'kmaq took him in and revered him. He taught them new ways to grow food and how to increase their daily fish catches. They guarded him as though he was a deity to them. I became very close with him."

I said, "I knew him briefly. It seems that I was killed by an adversary who is in opposition to us in every lifetime. During the Templar lifetime, he killed both myself and Alex's former self. He made his presence known to us on our previous journey to Albany. He is a Pirate who goes by the name of Anders. Maria has stated that this man is a fallen angel and is on a mission for Satan himself."

General Washington said, "Maria? The same Maria that I just met this morning?"

Mr. Franklin said, "Yes. I was going to get to her shortly. It seems that she is a Seer who has guided the Guardians in the past lifetimes. She was the wife of Noah. Her name was Na'amah."

I said, "I was very close with her during the Sinclair years. She came with us on the mission because Henry Sinclair believed that the Mi'kmaq would revere her because of her spiritual skills. Her name in that incarnation was Agatha."

Alex continued the story, "She died of natural causes after about ten years in Nova Scotia. She was dearly missed. She is every bit as important as Hannah, Jeremiah, and me."

Mr. Franklin said, "I did some checking on this Sir James Glouchester. He was indeed a Professor who went missing and was presumed dead. He was a lesser-known Royal who was the second cousin to the throne at the time. I have been thinking about performing a ruse and having these three pose as lesser-known Royals who are in search of their ancestor. This would help us get by the British, and then we would tell the Mi'kmaq

Chief that they are the descendants of Goosecap and are here to pay homage. This would take considerable skills of coercion by these three."

General Washington said, "Let me make sure that I have it straight. These three are Guardians of a Secret treasure that was given to us by the Watchers of the fabled Book of Enoch. They have an age-old ongoing battle with one of Satan's Angels. We are going to go behind the lines of the largest military in the world to dig up the treasure. But, oh, I almost left out the most important part. We are going to do this with the hope that some of the most fierce Indians in North America won't try to take our scalps."

Mr. Franklin said, "In a nutshell, that is correct."

General Washington said, "Seceding from the British Empire will seem like child's play in comparison. Now I understand why Alex brought the whiskey to us."

I said, "Please understand that every event surrounding this treasure is wrought with battle and loss. During the Templar years, we were getting attacked on every front by Muslim Warriors. We were Crusaders, after all. We were Frenchmen laying siege in a foreign land in search of a fable. The fable became a reality, and the attacks became ruthless. Keep in mind we also found the Cross of Jesus Christ and his Burial Cloth on that mission. We were part of history."

Alex said, "In the Sinclair years, we were constantly battling the remnants of the Vikings. Their mission was to take lives and conquer lands. It was in their blood."

Hannah said, "May I be excused. I am going to join the ladies and discuss the wedding. All of this death and war talk makes me very sad. The ladies are discussing much happier things."

I said, "No worries. I will fill you in later."

She left the study, and I said, "Hannah is a very upbeat person, but all of this talk just reminds her of the great sadness that her soul has endured."

Everyone completely understood.

Mr. Franklin said, "The gold and silver can be used to underwrite our finances for the revolution and the expenses of the new fledgling nation."

General Washington said, "This indeed is a battle that we must win."

We decided to take a break. It was getting close to dinner time. The servants served us some food in the study. I went to check on Hannah. I found her with the other ladies. They were all smiles. It seems that the whiskey had found its way into their discussion as well. There was nothing but smiles in that room. Hannah excused herself. We walked out onto the Veranda. I could see that she had imbibed in the spirits. She put her arms around me and began to kiss me passionately. Then, she pulled away and said, "Two more nights." I knew exactly what she was referring to.

I said, "I can hardly wait." We hugged for a few minutes. I continued, "Are you enjoying yourself?"

She said, "Eliza and I have had several glasses of whiskey. Alex may have met his match with her."

"I will pull Alex out after a little while, and we will join you and Eliza. Then, maybe we will head into Albany for a bit." I said.

She said, "That sounds great. I will let Eliza know."

I said, "See you in a little while."

I returned to the study, where the two Generals were in a deep discussion on tactics.

I found Alex and said to him, "It seems that our two ladies have found the whiskey and wish to peel us away from this conversation. I suggested that we visit a few taverns in town. Hannah liked the idea. I'm sure Eliza will as well."

Alex replied, "You know, you really are a genius. I don't care what anyone else says."

"What does anyone else say?" I said.

Alex said, "It's just a joke. When should we take our leave? If we wait too long, the ladies will be passed out."

I said, "Hannah says that Eliza can hold her own, but let's get out of here soon."

Mr. Franklin said, "Generals, you now know the entire story of the Secret of Eden. I would like to hear what you know of the British forces in Nova Scotia. Where are they stationed? Are they centralized? Or spread out?"

General Washington spoke first. He said, "The British forces here are split into two commands. The first is referred to as the Commander-in-Chief or CIC America. This Leader commands everything in the Colonies up through Newfoundland. This Commander is General William Howe. The second CIC commands Quebec and Ontario. This position was recently handed to General Guy Carleton. The two of them report directly to General Thomas Gage, who currently has his Command Headquarters in Boston. As far as Nova Scotia is concerned, it is a large area that is still in control of the various Indian Nations. The British forces are centralized in Halifax with many outposts up and down the Coast."

Mr. Franklin said, "We are trying to pinpoint a particular area where we will need to send a landing party." General Schuyler produced a map of Nova Scotia. Mr. Franklin pointed to an area in a bay that was known as Mahone Bay. He said, "The Mi'kmaq Chief I met with lives nearby. He seemed to know of the place that we will be looking for. I suspect that it is within a day's hike."

Mr. Franklin said, "Alex knows exactly where the treasure is once he gets there but is unsure of its exact location within Nova Scotia. Therefore, we will need to hire guides from the Mi'kmaq to take us to this place."

Alex said, "This place has a small castle that was built by Henry Sinclair's builders and me. If you get me to the castle, I know exactly where the treasure is located."

Mr. Franklin said, "I also did some checking on this castle. It was used as a retreat for the Royals during the reign of the Stewarts. It seems that no one currently uses the estate because it has fallen into a state of disrepair. Perhaps I can get information about the castle's whereabouts from my historian friends in London."

General Washington said, "We must devise a convincing scheme so that a landing party can be dropped off safely and retrieved after the treasure is secured. This will be no small feat."

General Schuyler said, "I have traveled this coastline several times. There are many Islands where our party could take cover. Some of them have natural harbors. The British forces will have patrols traveling up and down this Coast. A ship would have to be hidden. Perhaps the mast should be taken down."

After about an hour or so, I said, "You have been given much to think about. I propose that we adjourn for the night. Hannah was hoping to head into town for a little while."

Mr. Franklin said, "I have much to tell you regarding this adversary that we spoke of. Through my contacts in Europe and Nova Scotia, I have learned much about this man and who he works for. Perhaps the three of us should meet early tomorrow morning. You both need to know who we are up against."

Both Generals agreed to meet Mr. Franklin shortly after sunrise.

General Schuyler said, "I haven't discussed it yet, but I think we should all head into town this evening. Our friends from all over the Colonies will be arriving today. I think we should all have some social time together before tomorrow's heated debates start."

Everyone liked the idea. We raised our glasses, and Mr. Franklin said, "To the Secret of Eden."

CHAPTER 74

THE FORMING OF A NATION

FTER THE GENTLEMAN left the study, they found their wives out on the veranda having a great time.

General Washington said, "It is good to see the women having such fun. We will have many dark days ahead. Let today be one of those joyful days that we all need."

Mr. Franklin said, "I agree. If we succeed in our mission, we will be considered the fathers of the new nation. These women should not be held in any less standing, for they will be the mothers of this nation."

General Washington said, "Somehow, you always have the proper words."

The ladies all saw us and collectively tried to put on a serious face. Then, suddenly, Hannah started giggling, and all of the other women started laughing."

Martha Washington said, "Excuse us, George, us ladies are having a wonderful time."

General Washington said, "That is why we are all here. We

are going to celebrate the special day of a special young couple."

What proceeded was the most light-hearted gathering of these souls that I would ever see. Of course, there were tough times ahead, but today was going to be fun.

We all loaded onto the carriages and made our way into town. We walked into the first tavern and were greeted by the Boston contingent of Patriots. Hannah and I were greeted by Hannah's Uncles John and Peter Adams, John Hancock, Paul Revere, and Patrick Henry.

Martha Washington gathered everyone around and said, "I notice that your wives aren't here. So every one of you march back to your Inn and retrieve your wife. Tonight is for all of us."

All of the men made their exit and returned with their wives shortly after that.

The celebration then started. Alex was in his glory. We all laughed and carried on for hours. Hannah and I went from table to table. Everyone here has known Hannah since she was a young child. Soon after that, some of the other Patriots made their way in. Thomas Jefferson and his wife Martha soon arrived, as did Robert Morris and his wife, Mary. Mr. Haym Salomon accompanied them. Next to arrive was Mr. John Jay and his wife, Sarah. They were also recently married. Mr. Jay said he was looking to speak with Alexander. He mentioned that Alexander was making a name for himself at King's College. It turns out Mr. Jay was a recent graduate himself from Kings College. I waved Alex over. The two men instantly seemed to have a bond which is not uncommon for Alex. Before long, the tavern was completely full of Patriots. Hannah and I were making the rounds. We knew most of these Patriots. Some were meeting us for the first time. Everyone was very friendly and was wishing us well.

About halfway through the night, several British Officers walked into the tavern. They made their way over to Generals Schuyler and Washington. The men were all friends, At least for now.

General Washington introduced General Thomas Gage,

the Commander of all British forces in Albany, to everyone he was seated with. Everyone played their role beautifully. General Washington told General Gage that he was in town staying with General Schuyler for a few days for a wedding. He said that his nephew Jeremiah was to be wed on Saturday night. I was honored that the General thought of me as his nephew, but we all knew the truth that he needed to keep the name of Samuel Adams out of the conversation. Therefore, Hannah's name was never mentioned. The Generals exchanged pleasantries, and General Gage moved on because there was no available seating. Typically, someone would give up their table for a British Commander. However, that was not true for this group.

I looked around the room at this collection of Patriots. I knew I was looking at the new nation for the first time.

The evening came to an end a few hours later. Hannah was dozing off in her seat. It had been a long and emotional day. However, it was a day that would be remembered because of the new bonds that had been formed.

Hannah and I walked back to the mansion by ourselves. Unfortunately, we ran into a group of Redcoats that were looking to give us a hard time. They said, "Do you dare to cross our line. You should be walking on the other side of the street."

I said, "Since when do you own the road. We are loyal subjects of the Crown. As a matter of fact, we just enjoyed a few drinks with General Gage. Should I go back and ask him which side of the road we should walk on?"

The Leader replied, "No, sir. Please ignore my soldier's lack of intelligence."

We kept walking, and Hannah said, "Hopefully, they won't disturb our wedding."

I said, "That is the beauty of having our wedding at the Schuyler's Mansion. He is a war hero to the Redcoats. No one will even think of causing a situation at his home."

The next day seemed to arrive extra early. The meeting with all of the Patriots was to take place at the Schuyler's home. Since the main subject was secession from Britain, there was nowhere safe in Albany to conduct such a meeting. There were hundreds of British forces milling about the town.

When I came downstairs for breakfast, I was greeted by Mr. Franklin. He said, "I met with the Generals this morning and told them everything that I know about your adversary. They both agreed that the employer from Crimea was a shock. History has proven that some of the most unsavory characters have come out of that part of the world. General Schuyler stated that he had heard of drunken malfeasants making their way up and down the Connecticut River. He said that he would investigate the situation.

Mr. Franklin said, "It would be advantageous to have this adversary sitting behind bars when you, Hannah, and Alex set out to retrieve the treasure."

I said, "Yes. That would certainly make all of us happy." Even though I believe that the Generals will have the best of intentions, fate will keep our confrontation with the reincarnation of Canaan intact.

CHAPTER 75

THE FORMING OF A NATION – DAY TWO

THE SONS OF Liberty once again had a morning meeting at the Schuyler Mansion. Seemingly, the meetings were moving slow. There were many contrasting opinions in this group. Later that evening we met everyone in town at one of the taverns. Hannah and I visited once again with all of the Patriots as they gathered in the City of Albany. We made a point of trying to speak with the people that we had not spoken with the previous night. Maria sat with us at one particular table. We made small talk, and finally, I asked her if she had any further insight into how our Nova Scotia mission would go. She said, "You will battle your great enemy just as you battled his ancestor."

I said, "I'm curious why you chose the term ancestor. Our adversaries in the past were not related to each other in any way?"

Maria said, "He is from the family of Oleg. So naturally, his motive will be to avenge his ancestor, but as we have learned from Mr. Franklin, he knows of the treasure."

Hannah said, "Does he know what the treasure is?"

Maria said, "I cannot say for sure, but I believe the treasure story has been passed down through his family. Also, there is a word that I keep seeing. It is Vegvisir. I have no idea what it means, but every time I think of Nova Scotia, I see this word."

I said, "That was on the medal that Oleg wore around his neck during the Sinclair days. It was the last thing that I saw as I was dying."

Hannah said, "Vegvisir. What in heavens does that mean?"

Maria said, "We will have to study this word and its meaning."

I said, "It sounds like we will be making our mission probably next summer. So we will have a year to plan for the mission and perhaps decipher the meaning of Vegvisir. Maybe Mr. Franklin will know what it means."

Maria said, "I will try to focus my thoughts on the mission. Sometimes the visions come easily. Sometimes they don't come at all."

The night was delightful, but Hannah and I were very tired, so we decided to head back to the mansion. As I walked her to her room, I said, "After the wedding, while we are touring the Adirondacks, we may have to take one day and just sleep all day."

She said, "That sounds great. I can hardly wait."

I kissed her good night and went to my room, where I quickly fell asleep.

The following day arrived, and I awoke completely refreshed. I think both Hannah and I needed the additional sleep. I am not sure how Alex does it. I'm sure he was one of the last ones to leave the Tavern last night.

The schedule for this day was for the Patriots to reconvene at ten o'clock to continue the discussion regarding the Continental Congress. I went to get some tea and was greeted by Mrs. Adams and Hannah. Mrs. Adams once again had that glow of anticipation. I sat down and joined them. Mrs. Adams said, "Now, today we are to meet with the Preacher at three o'clock to review and practice the ceremony. You tell Mr. Franklin that he is not allowed to go long in his meeting today."

I said, "Why don't you tell him yourself."

She turned around to find Mr. Franklin standing right behind her.

Mr. Franklin said, "Good morning, and fear not. I will finish our meeting by two or earlier today."

He added, "The Generals would like to see you and Hannah in the study."

I said, "What about Alex?"

Mr. Franklin said, "General Washington already has wakened Alexander as he is now called. He looks as though he has been run over by a quarter horse." We all laughed.

I poured another tea for both Hannah and me, and we ventured into the study.

The Generals, Mr. Franklin, and a very unhappy-looking Alex, or should I say, Alexander, greeted us.

General Washington spoke first. He said, "Phillip and I have spoken at great length of the Nova Scotia mission and have the following conclusions. First, we believe that as hostilities start here in the Colonies, the British Forces will leave Nova Scotia and head to somewhere in the Colonies. If I were making this decision, I would choose New York because it would cut our rebellion in half. Whoever controls the Hudson River will be in the superior tactical position."

General Schuyler said, "I concur. I believe the forces here in Albany will make their way to several outposts along the Hudson River."

General Washington said, "This will leave the Nova Scotia Command Center without very little in the way of forces to patrol the coast. Therefore, this will be the opportune time to locate and secure the treasure."

General Washington continued, "Secondly, we must assume that you will be spotted when you return. We should not try to land in Boston. There may still be a large presence of British ships there. We think that the port of Falmouth should be the port of reentry. We will have ships ready to escort you back from Nova Scotia and take the battle to the British. This should allow you to quietly sail behind the battle back to Falmouth Harbor. We will have a company of soldiers to help you offload the treasure. We will have carriages with well-rested horses waiting at all stops on the way back to the Compound. This must be a very carefully planned mission. The execution of the plan must be ready for all contingencies."

Mr. Franklin said, "By then, I will have the additional information from Sir William St. Clair, and I am going to make another visit to the Mi'kmaq Chief. We must have a highly skilled guide to lead the team to the Holy Well. I will make arrangements with the Chief."

General Washington concluded the impromptu meeting by saying, "Plan on the mission taking place next June. Almost a year from right now."

Alex, Hannah, and I nodded in agreement.

General Washington said, "One other thing. If I am taking on this assignment of Military Commander, I would like Alexander and Jeremiah to be my aides. From your historical past lives, you possess knowledge that cannot be taught. Therefore, I think that you could be very important to our campaign."

Hannah was just about to give the General an earful for leaving her out when Mr. Franklin said, "General, Jeremiah and Hannah have already accepted positions as Emissaries for me. Their historical knowledge will pay dividends in many facets of our conflict. In addition, they will serve as Diplomats within the Colonies. As we all know, they are the face of the revolution. I predict that I will be in France soon after hostilities break out. Hannah and Jeremiah will be delivering messages to you and our other leaders regarding the French and the Spanish assistance. They will also focus on maintaining a close relationship with our independent financial sponsors such as Robert Morris."

General Washington said, "Very well. Alexander, I would like you to be a Senior Aide, but first, you will need some infantry experience. This may cause a break in your education, but you can go back to school after the revolution is complete."

Alex said, "It would be an honor, Sir."

General Washington said to Alex, "After the wedding, return to college and take in as much as you can. I don't have a crystal ball, but I will speculate that I will need you at some point next spring. Obviously, you will temporarily leave my leadership team when you head to Nova Scotia."

Alex said, "Yes, sir."

As Mr. Franklin predicted, the meeting of the Sons of Liberty concluded around noon. I went and sat next to Hannah at the table on the veranda. It was just the two of us. She looked nervous. I said, "What's wrong? You look distressed."

She said, "Sitting here with nothing but idle time on my hands is just making me nervous."

I said, "Nervous. You didn't look nervous when you donned the bedspread like a fashion mogul in Paris a few nights ago." She started laughing.

She said, "Thank you. Nothing cures nervousness like some laughter."

I said, "You are welcome. My turn will be tomorrow."

She said, "You know that we could sneak out the back door and go off to a faraway chapel and get married without all of the guests."

I said, "As inviting as that sounds, we would disappoint all our friends. They are here for us. I could sense today that while the business was critically important, most of the men here today were ready for our celebration."

We ate lunch with the others, and then Hannah said, "Let's go out and check on Cleo and Mark."

Alex must have heard Hannah. He said, "Not again. You

know after tomorrow, you won't have to sneak off anymore." Hannah started to blush because suddenly, everyone at the table now knew our secret.

Hannah said, "Alex, I can hardly wait for your wedding. I have so many stories that I am just dying to tell."

Alex said, "Then I probably should choose to stay quiet." Everyone laughed.

I said, "Alex and Eliza, why don't you join us on our walk. It is a beautiful day. Way too nice to be cooped up inside all day."

We all walked for a few hours. Eliza showed us her favorite spot, which was right on the shore of the Hudson River. It reminded Hannah and me of our special place that she calls "Jeremiah's Solitude" back home at the Compound. There is a major connection for both Hannah and myself to water. It always seems to bring calm to both of us. We were now ready to go back to the mansion, meet with Reverend Maclean, and prepare for our big day.

Hannah reminded Alex that he has the special duty of bringing the ring, or should I say the wedding band.

Alex responded, "No worries. Also, I have the special duty of taking care of Jeremiah this evening. So I will make sure that he doesn't drink too much and gets to bed early."

Hannah said, "I hadn't even thought about that yet."

I said, "Alex when we leave after the rehearsal, we need to make sure that we have everything ready. Once we leave today, we won't be back until tomorrow."

We arrived back at the mansion and were warmly greeted by Reverend Maclean. We walked out into the garden where the ceremony would take place. The Reverend showed Alex and me exactly where he would like us to stand. Hannah would then be escorted out of the house by her father and brought to where I would be standing. It was hard to imagine this garden jam-packed with all of our guests. Behind the house, a large tent was being assembled where everyone would be seated for dinner. A temporary wood floor was installed to serve as the dance floor. A team of musicians from Albany had been hired to play music after the dinner was complete. I said to Hannah, "It is incredible that all of this is for us."

She said, "We are fortunate to have family and friends who care very much for us. I feel very blessed."

I said, "Coming from where I started in England. You could never have convinced me that I would ever have a wedding as special as this, and I would be marrying someone as special as you."

Hannah said, "You are too kind."

And just like that, the rehearsal was over. We all sat down and shared an early supper. Mr. Franklin and the Washington's joined us. Mrs. Washington said, "This wedding is going to be right from a fairy tale." We all agreed.

Mr. Franklin said, "It has been a privilege to spend so much time with this young couple and Alex, of course. They are keeping me young."

I said, "Sir, it has been my honor to work so closely with you. I hope that we have many days together going forward."

Mr. Franklin said, "At some point, I will be relocating to France. My role will be there. I will be writing to both you and Hannah nearly every week. Some will be social letters, and many will be messages for our leaders."

Hannah said, "I am looking forward to our travels through the Colonies to deliver the good word to our new nation."

We continued to speak in reflection on the last year's activities. My past life now seems mundane compared to what I face daily. The sun started to lower as the afternoon went on. Finally, it was time for Alex and me to board the carriage for the Inn. I gathered my new clothing and freshly laundered clothes that had been neatly packed for me. Alex did the same. Hannah handed me her bag for the wedding night.

Hannah kissed me goodbye and said, "Until we meet at the altar."

I said, "Yes. It's hard to believe that our big day is almost upon us. I'm not sure if I will be able to sleep tonight."

We boarded the carriage and headed to the Inn.

CHAPTER 76

THE 11TH OF JUNE, OUR WEDDING DAY

LEX AND I went to a few taverns and shared some laughs. We ran into many of the Patriots who wanted to toast me on my last night of bachelorhood. Alex and I did share a special moment where we discussed how our lives have changed over the past year. I brought up the story of the day when Mr. Adams delivered him to the Compound. I said, "I wasn't sure what to make of you at first, but when I look back, it seems like a very well-orchestrated play. After all, you were the one who introduced me to Hannah."

Alex said, "It is hard to imagine, but I think it was my assignment to introduce you two. If I told that to anyone other than you or Hannah, they would think that I have gone mad."

He went on to say, "It does sadden me that I don't seem to have a soulmate. I was deeply in love with my wife Abigail back in the Henry Sinclair times."

I said, "Is there no chance that she is Eliza."

Alex said, "I don't believe so. Don't get me wrong. I care for Eliza very much, but the connection is just not like what you and Hannah have."

I said, "Give it time. You and Eliza have barely spent any time together. You two are at a different time in your life. You have college and then your assignment with General Washington. Perhaps something will trigger within Eliza that will bring back her memory of the past. Hannah and I often talk about the fact that we felt we were on a mission before we met. Neither of us knew what that mission was until we came together. You and Eliza may have an awakening yet to come, or perhaps this is something new that will go on for many lifetimes."

Alex said, "Well, let's drink to new awakenings." I laughed.

I said, "Now that's the Alex that I know."

We stayed out later than I planned, but it was good to have some time with Alex. Since I met Hannah, virtually all my time has been with her. Alex clearly understood. He knows that he is not only my closest friend but Hannah's as well.

The next morning I laid in bed as I usually do. I tried to think about what I needed to accomplish for the day. Then it hit me like a tidal wave. I am getting married today! I jumped out of bed and realized that I didn't need to do anything other than get ready for the ceremony today. I have become accustomed to waking up with a long list of things that need to happen on any given day. Today was different. I dressed and went downstairs, where the Innkeeper was waiting with tea.

I sat on the porch for a while and watched as the city of Albany came alive for another day. I began to reflect on my childhood in England. I never knew my mother, Ellen. She passed while giving birth to me. As a child, I had guilty feelings about this. I thought, "If it weren't for me, she would still be alive." As I grew older and started to understand that I had a larger mission in front of me, I realized that my mother's sacrifice was just another part of the play that I find myself in. I also thought about my father. He had died way too early, as did my brothers, Abraham Jr. and Lemuel. It was kind of sad that I wouldn't have any family at my wedding today. Hopefully, they are watching from above. I presume that they would be very proud of how far I have come. We were basically peasants in England.

Joining the military for families like mine was just a way to ensure that you were fed daily. Now, here I am in the New World, about to marry a beautiful woman who is the daughter of a very prominent businessman. The guests at our wedding are the leaders of the New World. Since I can envision the Colonies being victorious, I can boldly say that men like Benjamin Franklin, George Washington, and even Alex, or should I say, Alexander Hamilton, shall become some of the most famous names in history. I have the good fortune of calling these men my friends. My parents would never have dreamed of such success. For the first time, I understand what Mr. Franklin means when he says we are the face of the new nation. I came from what was a bleak future as a peasant to become a leader in the New World. That is why this new nation will be a beacon to the rest of the world.

Soon Alex joined me, and I shared my thoughts with him. His situation was strangely similar. He was an orphan that barely knew his parents. He has a brother somewhere that he hasn't spoken to in years. Hannah and I are his family, and he is part of ours. I said, "All this free time has caused me to reflect on my life. I'm not sure if that's good or bad." We both laughed.

Alex said, "Yesterday when General Washington offered me a position as an Aide, I thought to myself, 'Does he know that less than a year ago I burned down John Adam's Barn.' Everything is happening very fast. It seems like yesterday that you met Hannah. Now it is your wedding day." I agreed that things were moving quickly.

I said, "Yes, but remember how fast things have happened in our past lives. I remember from the Henry Sinclair days how we celebrated St. Andrews Day in Rosslyn one day, and seemingly the next day, we were in the King of Norway's home asking for his blessing."

Alex said, "For some reason, we have been chosen for a very crazy mission. If you told this to a stranger, they would call the constable to have you locked up." We both laughed.

We walked around town for a few hours. We ran into several Patriots who wished me good luck today. I spent the next few hours writing in my Diary. There was much to report to whoever was to read this someday. Hopefully, my great-grandson will find this Diary and learn about his destiny.

The Inn had a small bath house. Alex and I used it to get ready. The sauna felt terrific. Every time I visit a bathhouse, I feel a great cleansing of the body and mind. I wondered how much it would cost to have one at the Compound.

It was finally time to get dressed. The Bridal Carriage would pick up Alex and me at precisely five fifteen. The ceremony was scheduled to start at six o'clock. We dressed in the new suits we purchased on our last visit to Albany. We then boarded the carriage right on time. Well-wishers recognized the carriage and waved. Alex stuck his head out the window and yelled, "Honestly, I'm not the Bride. She is much prettier." This helped break down my nervousness for a minute, at least. The driver turned the corner, and I could finally see the Mansion. This site will be engrained in my memory forever. There were the usual orchards on my right and the Mansion in the foreground on my left. There were carriages lined up as far as I could see. All of these people had traveled great distances to witness our wedding. Finally, the Bridal Carriage pulled up to the side of the Mansion, where Alex and I hopped out. As rehearsed, we waited for our cue to walk out to the altar that had been set up for today. We watched through the bushes as Mrs. Adams was seated with Samuel Jr. Behind her was the entire Adams Clan, led by John Adams and his brother Peter. On the other side of the aisle, which was usually reserved for the Groom's family, was Mr. Franklin, Maria, General and Mrs. Washington, General and Mrs. Schuyler, and Mrs. Williams. The rest of our friends filled the next thirty rows.

Suddenly, Alex and I were given our cue. I said to Alex, "I know it is a little late to ask, but did you bring the ring?"

Alex said, "What ring?" He paused for a second and pulled the ring out of his chest pocket.

Next, the Maid of Honor, Eliza, walked slowly down the aisle towards us.

Alex and I stood there at the altar as instructed. I looked out at all of the smiling faces. I must have looked terrified. Eliza made a face at me that meant, "You need to smile."

Suddenly, the three Flautists began to play the Wedding March, and everyone stood up. Suddenly, I could again smell that fragrance that was part of Hannah's spirit. It always brought me peace and happiness. The door to the Mansion opened, and Mr. Adams appeared, and then came Hannah. She looked like an angel that had just come down from heaven. Her dress and headpiece were stunning. Mr. Adams and Hannah approached the altar, where he hugged me and gave me Hannah's hand. She looked at me and gave me that devilish smile that I had come to love. Then, she whispered, "Hello, Julius Caesar." I nearly burst out laughing. All of the nervousness that I felt was gone. Only Hannah could have this effect on me. She is truly an angel.

Reverend Maclean welcomed everyone. He said, "I get to officiate in many weddings, but few like this one. Even I was getting nervous today." Everyone laughed. He went on to say, "It is a rarity that I get to meet people like Hannah and Jeremiah. Obviously, from the large crowd here today, you also believe these two are special."

The reverend read from the gospel story where Jesus converts the water to wine at a wedding. He said, "He did this because he knew the importance of celebrating a marriage that was consecrated in the presence of the Holy Father. It truly is a reason to celebrate."

Next, we exchanged our vows. I suddenly had a flashback to several of our previous weddings. Hannah was beautiful in each and every one of them.

The reverend then received the ring from Alex, which he blessed, and then handed it to me. He said a few more words and then instructed me to place the ring on Hannah's Finger, which I did. It looked stunning next to the engagement ring. He then said, "Jeremiah, you may now kiss your bride." I did, and I could hear everyone cheering. The reverend then said, "It is my distinct honor and privilege to be the first to introduce you to Mr. and Mrs. Jeremiah Briggs." Everyone stood and cheered. The reverend then led us back down the aisle to the tent area, where we greeted all of our guests.

One by one, Hannah and I greeted all of our friends. Everyone was so happy. We all knew that there would be tough days ahead, but today was just about this celebration.

Finally, everyone was seated, and Alex stood up and asked everyone to raise their glass. He said, "Many of you know me as someone who was always involved in mischief. Yes, Mr. John Adams, I am speaking to you." Everyone laughed. Alex continued, "I was a lost soul. Then I met Hannah first. She was the sister that I never had. Even though she was my sister, she was a better shot with the bow and the rifle than I would ever be. On several occasions, she stepped in and stopped me from taking a beating from some of the other boys. Those boys knew her and were afraid of her. She knew that my mouth was always getting me into trouble and that someone had to help me. Then one day, after an unfortunate mishap in Mr. John Adams' Barn, I was told that I was going to move to someplace that was only known as the Compound. Originally, I thought this was a prison sentence." Everyone laughed. He continued, "I would no longer have Hannah to keep me out of trouble. I arrived at the Compound and was taken in by Jeremiah. I quickly realized that he was the other half of Hannah that would keep me on the straight and narrow. Then, as fate would have it, Jeremiah and I were invited to the Annual Party at Peace Field. I introduced Jeremiah to Hannah, and it was love at first sight. If you believe in fairy tales, you would have if you witnessed what I have for the last year. It is truly a fairy tale.

I have had the great fortune to have my two closest friends fall in love with each other. Their relationship is one for the ages. I don't mean to put you two on the spot, but the title of Uncle Alex suits me very well. Anyways, I could go on all night if you let me, but now I need a drink. To Hannah and Jeremiah." Everyone said, "Here. Here."

Shortly after that, dinner was served. It was the Schuyler's signature dish of Prime Rib. As usual, everyone raved about the food. After dinner was finished, Hannah's parents pulled Hannah and me aside. Mr. Adams said, "This truly was a glorious day." Mrs. Adams started by telling me that they want me to refer to them as Mother and Father going forward.

I said, "I have felt like you have been my parents for some time. So it will seem very comforting to refer to both of you as my parents."

Mr. Adams said, "The next matter is that of my shares of the Compound. I would like to pass it on to you as our gift. I will stay on as a broker as I always have done. Unfortunately, the British have inhibited my ability to earn, so I would still like to get my salary. I believe my Cousin Peter would also like to sell you his shares. He only became involved with the Compound as a favor to me. I know you two have big plans for the Compound, and nothing would make us happier than to see you two realize your dreams."

I said, "That is a wonderful gift. Of course, we will need you to continue as a broker, but more importantly, to be a mentor to me."

Mr. Adams said, "I look forward to it. But, don't forget you always will have Mrs. Williams to run the operation. She is the one that keeps everything moving forward." Just then, if as on cue, Mrs. Williams walked up. First, she congratulated us both on such a beautiful wedding. Then, she said, "Don't forget. We need to do this all over again back at the Compound."

Hannah said, "That means I will get a chance to wear this beautiful dress one more time."

I said, "I wish that we could capture the image of you and your father walking down the aisle. You truly looked like an angel."

The evening went on. Everyone danced the night away. It amazed me that I was now actually not terrified to dance. Hannah and I tried to make it to every table to thank our guests. Everyone said that they look forward to seeing us in Philadelphia in September.

We made our way over to Mr. Franklin and General Washington. I said, "Before Hannah and I leave on our holiday tomorrow, let's talk about the timing of everything so that we can plan accordingly."

Mr. Franklin said, "Sounds good. Maria has told me of her vision of the word 'Vegvisir.' I think it sounds Norwegian or Viking in nature. I will research this word and have some answers when I see you after your holiday. Also, we have one more lesson to complete: coding and Hidden Messages. When I am in France, I will send you coded messages that will need to make it to General Washington and the other leaders. The British will no doubt be intercepting my correspondence, so we must plan accordingly."

The night was drawing to a close. At least for everyone except Alex. He was challenging all takers to a billiards match in the Mansion.

Both Hannah and I were suddenly exhausted. The nervousness and the pressure of the day finally had caught up with us. We boarded the Bridal Carriage and made our way to the Inn. We had a night to remember, and it wasn't quite over yet.

CHAPTER 77

THE SUMMER OF 1774

The months following our wedding were perfect. We focused on nothing but the ranch and the future expansion plans. There was virtually no talk of the revolution or the upcoming trip to Nova Scotia. Our focus was on enjoying each day one at a time. This is something that has eluded Hannah and me throughout our history together. There was always some major calamity that would garner all of our attention. Neither of us has any recollection of the simple times in our past. Maybe that is how the soul works. We have had many discussions with Maria on this subject. Her response is that we are thinking too much. She says, "Just enjoy each day like it is your last." Not exactly the most uplifting viewpoint, but we understand her point.

One particular day started as every morning had since our wedding. I rolled over to find Hannah lying next to me. What a fantastic way to start the day. I rose and made my way over to the Compound Office. Mrs. Williams and I went through the Compound's finances when a rider on horseback appeared. It was Edward McGillicutty. He is a Scot who manages Mr. Adams's Carriage Company in Binghamton. He greeted me and said, "I have a very important message from General Schuyler in Albany."

I thanked him, and he waited as I read the letter just in case I needed to send a response. I broke the seal and quickly read the scroll. I was startled as to what I was reading. I asked Mr. McGillicutty to have an express carriage ready this afternoon. Then I ran to get Hannah and Alex. I explained that we had received correspondence from General Schuyler. I read the following letter:

Jeremiah, Hannah, and Alex,

I hope this letter finds you well. I have been doing some investigation on your adversary. It seems that his ship is currently docked in Hartford in the Colony of Connecticut. He has been making his way through the countryside, stealing and causing heartache to the locals for at least a month. For some reason, the local Redcoats are looking the other way regarding his crimes. I believe that he has bribed his way up and down the Connecticut River.

As you know, I have high-level contacts within the British Military ranks. I have informed them what is taking place in Connecticut, and they are sending a regiment of Dragoons there to arrest your adversary and the complicit Redcoats. I need the three of you to meet me at the home of Benjamin Roberts in Hartford this coming Saturday. Mr. Roberts is a trusted Patriot. You will also be welcome to stay at his home. I need you three to positively identify your adversary so he can be arrested. The evidence that we have will place him behind bars for years to come.

Sincerely,

General Phillip Schuyler

CHAPTER 78

THE TRAP

For the rest of the morning, I reviewed Compound matters with Michael Hayes and Mrs. Williams. Everything was in order. The seed on the new grazing fields had been planted, and the fencing was well underway. Afterward, I returned home to pack for the upcoming journey to Hartford. Finally, the carriage arrived, and we began our journey. The mood between the three of us was tense but focused. We were going to come face to face again with our enemy. Several nights ago, I had a Dream that went back to the days of Noah once again. I needed to share it with Hannah and Alex. It went as follows:

Canaan's evil thoughts had cast a dark blanket over Noah and his people. Peleg and Tytea tried to speak with Canaan. They said it was not too late to ask for forgiveness from the Almighty. Canaan would just laugh at them. It was as though the words coming from him were no longer his. Peleg felt as if he was now speaking with the evil one directly. On one occasion, Canaan grabbed a large rock and prepared to throw it at Tytea's head. Out of nowhere appeared Joktan. He tackled Canaan and told him that it was time for him to move on from this settlement. Joktan said, "If you ever raise a hand in anger against anyone in our Grandfather's family again, I will personally kill you. I assure you that even your evil master will not be able to spare you. For I will have the Almighty giving me my strength."

Later that day, Peleg and Tytea told their Grandfather, Noah, what had occurred. Noah responded, "This brings me to a very difficult decision. Even though Canaan is my flesh and blood, I must cast him from our settlement." Both Peleg and Tytea knew that this day was coming. It probably should have happened already.

Later that day, Noah called everyone to the gathering area and asked them to form a circle. Then several of our other cousins escorted Canaan to the center of the ring. Canaan was forced to the ground. Noah said, "Canaan, you are of my flesh. It brings great sadness to me to see you turn to the evil spirit. I give you one last chance to change your ways."

Canaan then spit in the direction of Noah. That was his answer. Noah then said, "Canaan, I banish you from our tribe. If you ever appear amongst us again, it will result in your death."

Canaan looked at Noah and said, "I will go forward and tell tales of your drunkenness and debauchery. You will be despised by my followers. Even though you led us through the great rains, your name will be tarnished forever."

Peleg said, "But those are lies. Our Grandfather has done nothing but love you since the day you were born."

Canaan looked at Peleg and just stared. His face began to look more evil by the minute. It was no longer Canaan's face. It was now the face of Satan. He finally said, "I am aware of what the Watchers have asked you, your brother, and your whore wife to do. I will always be there to destroy you." Canaan or you might call him Satan, stood up and walked away, never to be heard from again.

Created with Sketch.

We sat quietly for a few minutes. Then Hannah finally spoke. She said, "None of us should find it shocking, but I had the same Dream recently. The only difference was that it was through Tytea's eyes."

Alex said, "I also had the Dream. This is the reason why we are traveling to Hartford with so many weapons." He paused, then continued, "Hannah, this is a battle I cannot have you fight for me. I must be prepared to confront this evil."

Hannah said, "If we stick together, there is no way that he can defeat us."

Created with Sketch.

Several days later, we arrived in Hartford. As we entered the small town, Hannah said, "I have an overwhelming feeling that we are being watched." Both Alex and I knew that if Hannah was sensing something, then it was absolutely true.

As we approached the center of the town, a Dragoon approached the carriage. He said, "Are you the guests of General Schuyler?"

I said, "Yes. Do you know where he is?"

The Dragoon replied, "He is meeting with my Commander in the back room of the tavern."

We exited the carriage, and I instructed the driver to feed and water the horses. Our meeting with the General would likely take a few minutes. We then entered the Benjamin Hickok Tavern and headed to a back room where we found General Schuyler. He was in full British Military dress. He was wrapping up his meeting with the Commander of the Dragoons. He introduced us to the Commander. He said, "Commander Charles Elliott, I would like you to meet Mr. and Mrs. Jeremiah Briggs and their associate Mr. Alexander Hamilton. They are the witnesses to the many crimes of Mr. Olsen and his band of malfeasants."

We shook hands and exchanged pleasantries. The Commander said, "I have much to do. General, I will let you inform your witnesses of our plan." The Commander then left the room.

The General started our meeting by saying, "Your enemy has been making his way through the nearby villages stealing everything he can. He always offers the villagers a token payment that is far less in value than the stolen materials are actually worth. He caught the attention of the British when he raided an armory less than a day's ride from here. Even the bribes that he has paid to the local Redcoats would not help to give him cover when it comes to stealing armaments. The British leadership in Boston got word of this treachery and ordered several units of Dragoons to Hartford. Every evening after sundown, the Pirates, as I like to call them, make their way to this tavern. The plan is to have the Dragoons surround the tavern, and the Constable will go in and make the arrest. We don't expect him to go peacefully, so we will be heavily armed." He paused briefly to take a sip of his tea and then continued, "I would like you three to positively identify Mr. Olsen to me. The British have evidence of enough crimes to imprison him for the rest of his life. But, as you know, we have other reasons to want this man behind bars. If the British Commander asks you to identify Mr. Olsen, please do so. Once this beast is safely in custody, you may begin your journey back to the Compound."

We all acknowledged our assignment for this evening's arrest. General Schuyler had made arrangements for us to freshen up at an Inn on the outskirts of the village. The General concluded our meeting by stating, "A platoon of Dragoons will arrive just before sundown to escort you to the tavern where you will meet me outside."

Several hours later, a platoon of six Dragoons arrived to escort us to the tavern. The hours spent at the Inn were stressful because we knew that an encounter with Canaan, or I should say, Anders Olsen, would happen this evening. I thought about many of the encounters with this evil presence. One or more of the three of us had been killed during some of these encounters. I couldn't get my thoughts away from the Dream where Oleg secretly attacked our caravan in Nova Scotia. I had killed Oleg in this Dream, but as I have learned recently, Oleg also managed to kill me in this occurrence. For some reason, my Dream always ended before I met my demise.

We rode in the carriage in the utmost silence. The only thing I could hear was the sound of the horses trotting and, of course, my own heartbeat. When we had reached the halfway point, the silence was broken by the unmistakable sound of musket fire. Our caravan of carriage and Dragoons stopped immediately. The Dragoons spoke amongst themselves. Then, finally, the Dragoon Commander said to us, "Wait here. We are going to ride in the direction of the musket fire. I will leave two of my men here with you."

The Dragoons then rode off to investigate. Hannah, Alex, and I have been through so many traumatic situations over our many lifetimes. We knew that this was about to be another one of them. Suddenly, Anders and his men started running from the nearby woods. They quickly overwhelmed the two Dragoons. Hannah leaped from the carriage and went into a full warrior mode. She took down three of Anders's men instantly. I joined the melee and was able to disarm one of them. Anders quickly recognized that we were a formidable opponent and did the only thing that he knew would stop us. He grabbed Alex and held a knife to his throat. Everyone stopped moving.

Anders finally spoke. He said, "The Angel of Death. We meet once again." He paused, looked around at his men, and continued, "If my men could fight the way you fight, I could conquer the world. I am not whether I should kill you or hire you." All of Anders' men laughed.

Hannah responded, "I have trained my entire life for this moment, Canaan. In the end, you will lose. That is a certainty." Being referred to as Canaan seemed to cause some confusion for Anders. Hannah continued, "Surely, you know who you really are?"

Anders replied, "Of course, I know who I really am. You and I will have much time to speak of our past on our voyage to Nova Scotia."

I said, "Why Nova Scotia?" Of course, I already knew the answer.

Anders said, "You will lead me to what my family has been trying to find for hundreds of years."

Alex said, "If you harm any one of the three of us, then your mission will fail. Each of us possesses a portion of the information required to find what you are looking for."

Anders pondered the situation and said, "If you three cooperate, I will release you after we make our discovery."

Hannah said, "I will kill you before then." Usually, if a woman threatened a man of Anders enormous size and strength, the people within earshot would laugh. That did not happen in this case. All of Anders' men had seen Hannah's formidable skills a few minutes earlier.

Anders finally responded. He said, "I am certain that you will try, but only the Gods know whether you will succeed or not." He then looked at his men and said, "Let's take these three to the ship and set sail immediately."

As we began our walk to Anders' ship, suddenly, a musket went off just to our rear. This was our chance. In the resulting confusion, Alex wrestled himself free of Anders' grip. Hannah had overpowered the men guarding her, and I was able to grab the knife that was strapped to my calf.

Anders knew that the musket fire would quickly draw the Dragoons to this location. So he yelled to his men, "Back to the ship. Don't worry about the prisoners. They will soon come to us."

Anders men began to run through the woods to the nearby harbor. Just then, General Schuyler rode up to us. He was the one who fired the musket a few moments ago. He said, "Is everyone alright?"

I said, "Yes, we are fine."

Just then, several platoons of Dragoons appeared. General Schuyler instructed them to give chase to Anders and his men. We boarded the carriage again and followed the trail leading us to the Harbor.

As we reached the harbor, we could see Anders ship in the distance. It was raising its sails. Unfortunately, the British Frigate in the harbor was no match for Anders' ship but gave chase anyway.

The Dragoon Commander came over where Hannah, Alex, and I were talking to General Schuyler. He said, "Do we have any idea where they are heading?"

I said, "If I were them, I would be returning to their home port of Halifax, Nova Scotia."

General Schuyler concurred. He said, "Yes. I would agree. My sources tell me that he has bribed nearly everyone in charge in Halifax."

The Dragoon Commander said, "We have several Battleships stationed in the Harbor of Newport just north of here in the Colony of Rhode Island. I will send several Dragoons there to inform the Admiral of what has transpired. Their black sails should not be too difficult to spot."

General Schuyler said, "You three have done your part. Let's go to the tavern and discuss what just happened. Tomorrow, you can start your journey back to the Compound."

For the rest of that evening and the following months, I couldn't get an image out of my thoughts. It was the image of Anders as he was running out of the woods. He had a large silver medal around his neck. It had a strange symbol on it that I had never seen before. The word underneath the symbol was the word that Maria had foreseen. It said, "Vegsivir."

Vegsivir

CHAPTER 79

FALL OF 1774

I T WAS LATE in August 1774. We had returned from our journey to Hartford about six weeks ago. We still had not heard any news about whether Anders had been captured. We chose not to talk about Anders until we heard something definitive about his capture.

Hannah and I sat down for supper on Alex's last night at the Compound. He was returning to King's College the following day. Also, Hannah's and my mission as emissaries for Mr. Franklin was about to begin with a trip to Philadelphia. We knew this mission would cause us to be away from the Compound for extended periods. We were both excited and sad at the same time. Hannah said, "I hate to leave the Compound now. Everything is going so well. I am so happy here. I can hardly wait until this revolution is over, and we can just focus on raising a family and, of course, raising our horses."

I said, "I know. The problem is that we are giving a substantial part of our profits to the throne, and nothing is stopping the

Redcoats from seizing all of our horses at any time. We must do our part to stop this tyranny."

Hannah said, "I know, but as soon as this ends, we will start our family and live the lives that most people only dream of."

I said, "Sounds wonderful to me."

Just then, I heard a knock on the door. I knew it was Alex. Don't ask me how I knew that, but even his knock was entertaining. Alex entered and sat down at the table. Even though Alex said he wasn't hungry, Hannah served him a plate. We mostly made small talk about daily life at the Compound. Then the subject turned to Alex's return to New York City.

I said, "I'm sure there will be some tavern owners that will be very happy to have you back in New York City." We all laughed.

Alex said, "I am excited to go back to college, but I think this year may be my last for a while. If General Washington is correct, the British will seize New York City when the fighting starts. It will not be safe for me there."

I said, "This may be true, but you still need to focus this year. When the school year ends, we will be making our trip to Nova Scotia. This treasure-hunting expedition is why we are all here. It is part of our destiny."

I said, "I almost forgot. Mr. Adams had informed me that the Annual Harvest Festival was being moved to Philadelphia because Quincy was no longer safe."

Hannah and I were disappointed, but we understood. We promised each other to visit Peace Field someday after the hostilities stopped. This place would always hold a special place in our hearts. This led us into the discussion of our long-term plans with the Compound. I went on to tell Alex that Hannah and I only wanted a quiet life after the war.

Alex then said something that I hadn't considered. He said, "Don't forget that after we secure the treasure, its new home will probably be here at the Compound. So for the first time in our long histories, you two will be living in close proximity to the Secret of Eden."

This caused a long pause in the conversation. Then, finally, after a minute, I said, "It will be much easier to protect here. Only a very few people will know of the Secret's whereabouts."

The conversation then moved on to Alex's future after the revolution. I was caught off guard by what I heard next, although I shouldn't have been. Alex said, "I believe my life's mission will be in government. Perhaps I will work myself into a leadership position. I intend to learn much from General Washington while I am his aide. After the war, I would like to dedicate my life to setting up a government where all men have an equal chance to succeed."

Hannah said to Alex, "Although most of my Dreams are about our past lives, occasionally I have visions of the future. I have had visions where you are one of the new nation's leaders."

I said, "I also see you as becoming a great leader, but you will always be the Alex who was the life of the party. I will never forget our trip to Boston or our ride here with Hannah and Mr. Adams."

Alex finished his supper and said, "Speaking of being the life of the party. What are we doing here? We have many friends who are waiting for us at the tavern. They are throwing me a going-away party. That is why I stopped by. You certainly don't want to disappoint our friends."

I helped Hannah clean up after supper, and then we met Alex at the tavern. The night was very lively, with everyone toasting Alex's departure. Hannah and I knew this was probably Alex's last night at the Compound. After that, he would probably move on to one of the big cities where he would assume his role in the founding of this New Nation.

The following day I woke up at dawn as usual. It had only been a few months since our marriage, so I was still surprised to find Hannah lying beside me every morning. What a great joy this is. Every day is exciting because I know that we will be together. I always start the day by hugging and kissing her on the cheek. Some days we lay there for quite a while. Today, however, was the day Alex would leave for college. We walked to the Compound Office, where Alex was waiting for the carriage. Finally, the carriage arrived. The Driver said, "Mr. Edward McGillicutty asked me to deliver this letter. It is addressed to Mr. and Mrs. Jeremiah Briggs and Mr. Alexander Hamilton."

I said, "That's the three of us." The driver handed me the sealed letter. It was from General Schuyler. I read it to Hannah and Alex. It said the following:

Hannah, Jeremiah, and Alex,

I hope this letter finds you well. I received this notice from the Dragoon Commander, Charles Elliott. He has received word from the Admiral in Newport regarding the Pirate Ship, as he calls it. The Pirate Ship was chased down the Connecticut River, leading them to Long Island Sound's open waters. The Pirate Ship changed its course to the northeast and headed to the open seas. Two Battleships from Newport Harbor approached the black sailed ship as it was heading northeast off the coast of Newport. One of the Battleships fired a warning shot across the Pirate Ship's bow and directed them to drop their sails and prepare to be boarded. The Pirate Ship, instead, returned fire which did minor damage to one of the Battleships. Both Battleships immediately opened fire on the Pirate Ship, which was completely destroyed in the barrage. The Pirate Ship sank shortly after that. There were no survivors.

Hopefully, this will help ease your fears as you prepare for your journey next summer.

Your Friend,
General Phillip Schuyler

This was indeed good news. Alex and I were ecstatic over this news.

Hannah seemed troubled by what she had heard. She said, "Why would Anders fire on two British Battleships? It seems to me this would happen to someone who is on a suicide mission."

Alex responded, "Maybe he would rather face death than be captured by the British."

We said our goodbyes to Alex and wished him a safe journey and a good school year.

CHAPTER 80

PHILADELPHIA

THE LEAVES WERE beginning to change and I was reminded how Maria had so eloquently stated that autumn is her favorite time of the year. That fact that all of the animals and trees in the forest knew that the transition to winter was coming was astounding. There is no other time of the year where the transition is so stark. Also, this was the time of the year when I met Hannah. It is a great reminder of how blessed I truly am.

Mr. and Mrs. Adams were going to join us on our journey to Philadelphia. This was a multi-faceted trip. The First Continental Congress was to convene on September 5, 1774 and was expected to last until some point in October. Secondly, since many of the Patriots would be in Philadelphia for the Congress, it seemed appropriate to celebrate the Annual Harvest Festival while everyone was present.

Mr. and Mrs. Adams, Hannah, and I climbed aboard the carriage for the long ride. We were going to go straight through to Stroudsburg, Pennsylvania Colony. We would spend one night there and then continue on to Philadelphia. In honor of Alex who was, no doubt, studying in New York City, I brought a keg of ale for the ride. The ride was a joy for the first day. The second day was tiresome, but we managed to sleep a little. Finally, on the morning of the third day, we pulled into Stroudsburg. The town was named after a man named Jacob Stroud. It seems that his family had settled this area back in the mid-1700s. Many in the area were Dutch or Quakers. They did not believe in war. They believe that nations were divinely granted and the British throne met this criteria. At the meeting before the wedding, it was discussed that somehow the large Dutch and Quaker communities needed to be engaged about joining the revolution. After supper that evening, the locals had gathered to hear Mr. Adams speak about the hardships that the Redcoats were placing on the Colonies. Everyone was gathered in the town center waiting for Mr. Adams. The crowd of roughly one hundred was relatively quiet as compared to the other speeches that Mr. Adams had given.

The speech started with a summary of the taxes and Acts that have been levied onto the Colonies by the British. He noted that these taxes have caused many businesses to fail. He detailed how the British seized ships from business people that have simply spoken out about the policies. He also spent time discussing how the Colonists have no say in their own futures. He said, "Many of those making decisions on our behalf have never even been here before. They are unwilling to even listen to our pleas. The crowd was largely unmoved by what Mr. Adams had said so far. He closed the speech by telling how Redcoats were seizing homes, horses, and raping young girls in Boston. This drew a reaction. One person yelled, "What are you asking of us?"

Mr. Adams responded, "For now, we only ask that you boycott British goods. We will be making every effort to bring American grown products to your town. We have been making great strides in developing routes for all of these products."

Another person yelled, "Are you going to put an end to slavery?"

Mr. Adams replied, "There is nothing that I would like more than to rid this continent of slavery. We are debating this issue every time we gather. Everyone agrees that it is an atrocity, but we are not sure how to put an end to it. Many in the south claim that society would completely fall apart if slavery was abolished. We must come up with a solution that assists the southern plantation owners financially while they acquire paid farm hands." He paused momentarily then continued, "I assure you that this is at the top of our list on what needs to change."

The crowd applauded and then dispersed. I think Mr. Adams won some of the people over. He would have won more over if he had a more certain answer on the slavery issue. We discussed slavery at the tavern and he said privately, "Truth be told, there are some from the southern Colonies that don't think slavery should end. We must first attain our independence and then conquer this abomination."

The next morning we set out early for Philadelphia. We arrived on the outskirts of the city just as the sun was setting. A few minutes later we arrived Mr. Franklin's Market Street home. Mr. Franklin was there waiting for our arrival. He showed us to our rooms and then invited for drinks before dinner.

We discussed our findings about the people of Stroudsburg over a few drinks. Mr. Franklin said, "Our cause will be a tough sell to the Quakers."

It was time for dinner so we headed to the City Tavern. This was a newly opened business. I believe that their timing was perfect due to the fact that all of the Patriots were about to descend onto Philadelphia. This tavern was just around the block from Carpenter's Hall, where the Continental Congress meetings were scheduled to take place. Upon arrival, we noticed that many Patriots were dining there. Most of these people here tonight had attended our wedding several months earlier. Everyone came to say hello. Not the least of which was General and Mrs. Washington. We exchanged pleasantries with everyone. This was going to be quite a reunion. All of the ladies wanted to talk to Hannah about married life. Someone asked if there were any young ones in the near future. Hannah said, "Yes. My horse is expecting." Everyone cheered and laughed.

General Washington introduced us to a husband and wife that were looking to join our cause. He said, "Jeremiah and Hannah, I would like you to meet my upholsterer Mr. John Ross and his lovely wife, Betsy Ross. I am refurbishing the home that I will be living in here in Philadelphia and they are doing most of the work. John is well versed on the Patriot movement and has offered his services to our cause."

I said, "Very nice to meet both of you. We will accept all of the help that we can get. We are facing an uphill battle, but our cause is noble and just."

We enjoyed this evening very much. It was nice to see all of our friends without the pressure of a wedding. We spent several hours there and then made our way back to Mr. Franklin's home. Life on the road was taking its toll on us.

The night ended with Mr. Franklin giving instructions to communicate with Hannah and me. He then said, "They will code the messages and send them to wherever I am at."

Hannah asked Mr. Franklin, "At some point are you going to teach us how to code messages?"

Mr. Franklin responded, "Yes. I plan on spending an ample amount of time tomorrow teaching you the Book Cipher method. This method is very simple but highly effective."

The subject then turned to the Continental Congress. A big surprise came in the form of Mr. Franklin stating that he would not be at the First Continental Congress meeting. He would be boarding a ship bound for England on September 4th the day before the Congress started their meetings. He felt that he needed to keep separation from the rebellion. After all, he was still the Post Master General for the Colonies. The plan was to have Mr. Franklin deliver the Continental Congress's request directly to King George III. The notes from the Congress would be sent to Mr. Franklin at the conclusion of the Congress. I assumed that

General Washington would also stay away because, even though he was retired from the British Military, he felt that he could be called back at any moment. I asked Mr. Franklin, "Will the General be staying away from the Continental Congress meetings also?"

Mr. Franklin said, "No. He will be attending. He is almost daring the British to accuse him of treason. I believe in my heart that the great general is already convinced that war is inevitable."

The next morning we rose early as we usually did. We went downstairs where Mr. Franklin had been waiting for us. He said, "After breakfast let's meet in my study. We can start your training on Coded Messages." We ate some biscuits with our tea and then joined Mr. Franklin in his study.

Mr. Franklin said, "You are not to share what I am about to teach you with anyone. That includes Alex, your parents, any of the other Patriots. The reason for the secrecy is simple. If they are captured, they can't tell what they don't know. Tactics and methods can be more valuable than the coded messages themselves."

He took a sip of his tea and continued. He said, "The Coding method that we will deploy between us is called the Book Cipher. The two of you and I will possess the same scroll. I will send you a list of numbers. These numbers refer to words in the scroll. The scroll will contain what is known as the Regius Poem. It is one of the guidebooks of the Freemasons. The version that we will both have is the English translation version. The original was written in the early Anglo-Saxon language and it very hard to understand. He handed us two copies of a scroll that contain the translation of the Regius Poem."

Mr. Franklin had a handwritten list of numbers that seemingly were random. He said, "If I send you the following list that read's 3,1,12,22,1(3),12,41,36,1,7,1(3),12,4(4),12,41,12(6),42,9 6,9(7),25,27,44(4),4(4) 42,41,21,7,9(8)

The numbers represent a word within the Regius Poem. Not the entire word, but the first letter of the word. You will see that some of the numbers are in parenthesis. The number in the parenthesis represents the position of the letter within the word in the case where it is not the first letter. If you look at 1(3). The word in the Poem is Here, so 1(3) represents the letter R."

He went on to say, "This Coded Message states 'THE FRENCH ARE SENDING TROOPS IN MAY'".

I said, "This seems simple enough."

Mr. Franklin said, "Don't take the shortcut and number the sheet that contains the poem. If you are captured, you would be handing over messages that will imperil our entire operation. Keep the scroll in a separate location. When you travel it can be in your bags. The British will understand that since you are a Freemason that it is logical that you will keep the Regius Poem with you at all times. Many of the British Officers are also Freemasons."

He took another sip of tea and said, "My messages will be far lengthier than the one we just deciphered, so be patient. If you have to write the message down, make sure it is destroyed after the message is delivered. When I arrive in London, I will send you a test message to the Post Office in Binghamton in Jeremiah's name. My letter will have my return address. Please send me a coded message stating that you received my message. I will return before you make your journey to Nova Scotia. We will plan future communications at that point. For now, have a courier check the Post Office every week. The letters will look like a shipping manifest. The sheet with the numbers on it will be somewhere in the manifest."

He stated furthermore, "I would like you to stay in touch with both Robert Morris and General Washington. If an emergency arises and we have to speed up our plans then you will turn to Robert for financial matters and the General for military matters. If this should happen, send me a coded message as soon as possible. The General will be making all of the decisions. Do not tell anyone this, but it is certain that he will accept the responsibility of becoming the Commander-in-Chief of all of our forces."

After Mr. Franklin left the room, Hannah said, "If you told anyone that a simple girl who loves horses and a man who runs a Milltown are to play such a critical role in this nation's future, they would think that you have lost your mind."

I said, "It really is amazing."

Both Hannah and I sat quietly pondering our lives. From my meager existence in England and her happy deep woods upbringing, the two of us, along with Alex, are about to have a role in world history. Even though our actions would be essential to the forming of this new nation, no one would ever know of the two of us. We were both perfectly comfortable with that.

CHAPTER 81

THE ANNUAL HARVEST CELEBRATION

THE CONGRESS HAD been meeting for twelve days with little in the way of a consensus on how to proceed. That all changed on September 16th, 1774, when Paul Revere arrived in Philadelphia with the news that the British had seized over two hundred barrels of gunpowder from the stores located in Charlestown. He detailed how two hundred and fifty British Soldiers had sailed on longboats to make the seizure. They accomplished this without a shot being fired. The truly amazing part was what he said next.

Mr. Paul Revere said, "The word spread through the countryside very quickly. The story was quickly embellished as it traveled from farm to farm. In a matter of days, four thousand Militiamen descended on Boston to protest this seizure. They demanded that the British appointed 'Mandamus Councilors' resign. The Councilors finally resigned due to the threat of violence.

The British were shocked at how quickly these Militiamen had gathered. The British Commanders retreated to their Forts to reconsider their next moves."

Everyone sat in shock at first, but as the reality sank in, it became apparent that a primary question that the Congress had been debating had been answered. The question during the debate was whether or not the Colonists would join the fight. The answer was an astounding yes. The leaders of Congress celebrated this development. Many supporters of what was known as the Suffolk Resolves had received a boost. The Suffolk Resolves was a resolution put forward by the leaders of Suffolk County, Massachusetts. The resolution rejected the government that had been put forward by the British for the Colony of Massachusetts. It also called for the boycott of all British goods until all of what was referred to as the Intolerable Acts had been repealed. The Suffolk Resolves was headed for passage in the Continental Congress.

After exploring Philadelphia again, Hannah and I returned to Mr. Franklin's home, where we had a surprise waiting for us. Alex was hiding behind a door in the study. Just as Hannah and I entered the room, he jumped out and surprised us. We were both so happy to see him. He poured us a glass of wine and recanted all that had happened so far in his fall semester at King's College. He had taken a hefty class load because he felt that he might not be returning the following year. In addition, he said, "The rumors of war are running rampant. The presence of Redcoats is definitely on the rise."

I went on to tell him of the day's news. We were both elated about the resolution but were also resigned to the fact that war was imminent. We were also aware that our excursion to Nova Scotia was quickly approaching.

Alex said, "Let's put all this behind us for a few days and enjoy the Annual Harvest Celebration. If I'm not mistaken, this also is the first anniversary of something very special."

I said, "Yes. It is hard to believe that I have known my love, Hannah, for a year. It has gone by so quickly."

Alex said, "Oh, I was referring to how you destroyed Jeremiah in a horse race a year ago. Also, it was the night you helped him overcome his dancing fears." We all laughed.

Hannah said, "If I am not mistaken, Eliza dragged you onto the dance floor as well."

Alex said, "That reminds me. Eliza and her parents should be arriving for the celebration in a few hours."

I said, "Tonight should be a very festive night at the City Tavern. All of the Patriots will be there celebrating the good news from Boston. "

Alex said, "On the way, let's stop at the Inn where the Schuylers are staying to leave a note that tells them to join the Patriots at the City Tavern."

Alex, Hannah, and I made our way to the City Tavern, where many of the Patriots were already well into their celebration. Alex, or Alexander as many of the Patriots called him, was becoming a celebrity. He was a larger-than-life character who would play a prominent role in the revolution. So naturally, everyone wanted to share a toast with Alexander.

We made our way over to General Washington's table. He was joined by his wife Martha, as well as Thomas Jefferson and his wife, Martha. The General invited us to join them, which we quickly did. I told Hannah, "It's nice to be seated with the most important men in the room."

She quietly said, "I assume you are talking about Alex?"

I laughed and said, "I was talking about the General."

General Washington wanted to hear about Alex's studies. Alex told him not only about his classwork but also about his observations of the situation in New York City. Alex knew that General Washington was of the viewpoint that New York City would soon be in the crosshairs of the British Empire. They were discussing the strategic importance of the city. It had become the main entry point for all of the future citizens of America. It is evident that the General had great respect for Alex's intellect. He could see beyond the lively, youthful exterior that most people saw with Alex. For those of us who were close to the situation, it was apparent that the General already considered Alex to be an aide.

This was the first time that I had an extensive conversation with Thomas Jefferson. Everyone referred to him as a visionary. We talked at length about his vision of the expansion of the Colonies. I said, "I have heard it said that the Great Lakes area is rich in minerals, especially copper."

Mr. Jefferson responded, "Yes. That is absolutely true. The problem is that Michigan is currently managed by Quebec, which is a British territory. Ben Franklin has thoughts of asking Quebec to become the fourteenth Colony. That would solve many of our future issues." He paused briefly, then continued, "Obviously, we must first win our Independence here in the Colonies. Then, at some point in the future, we must purchase or fight for the Great Lakes Region. Businessmen will invest in the infrastructure required to mine the minerals that are present in abundance around the Great Lakes. The next question is how to reach the world from the Great Lakes. Several of the Lakes are separated by a waterfall or a substantial set of non-navigable rapids. I assure you that great minds are working on solving this dilemma."

I said, "These are huge obstacles for sure, but one thing that has always proven itself throughout history is that humanity will unleash its ingenuity if there is opportunity. As we have all heard, 'Necessity is the mother of invention.'"

Mr. Jefferson said, "Truer words have never been spoken. It is hard to express my thoughts on future expansion to a Congress that can't agree on some basic requirements. Hopefully, today's news may have finally changed that."

Alex said, "Mr. Jefferson, I like hearing your thoughts on the future of the Colonies. I believe that our new government must help industrious entrepreneurs to facilitate this growth. This great land's massive offering of natural resources must be opened up for trade with the world. This will require the government to invest heavily but judiciously in infrastructure."

I noticed that both General Washington and Mr. Jefferson were listening intently to Alex's every word. Thinking that this young man who was just turning twenty could grab the attention of two of the greatest minds of our times was overwhelming. The General was already well aware of Alex's intellect. Mr. Jefferson now understands why the elders make such a fuss about Alex.

Hannah was deep in conversation with Mrs. Washington and Mrs. Jefferson. They were very curious about Hannah's desire to live on a ranch. Most women of this time period wanted nothing to do with life on a ranch. As usual, Hannah was winning them over. I continued my conversation with Mr. Jefferson. I said, "When I look at a map, I see all of the land west of the Great Lakes that is largely unexplored. Access to the western shore of this continent would allow shipments to the Orient. Throughout history, Europeans have often tried to export and import goods to the Orient. Many obstacles always prevented trade with the Orient. Men like Genghis Khan often controlled what was called the Silk Road. The Pacific Ocean offers a chance to ship directly to the Orient and bypass the warlords."

Mr. Jefferson said, "You have very studiously summarized the opportunity that this land offers. I believe that a waterway exists that will lead us to the Pacific. We must explore this someday."

One sure thing is that many great geniuses had been called to this New World. But, back in Europe in the middle ages, many of these thoughts and dreams would be considered heresy simply because the Church in Rome had not thought of them first.

After supper, Hannah and I made our way around the room to greet all of our friends. We saw that General and Mrs. Schuyler had arrived. They brought Eliza with them, which made Alex very happy. We exchanged pleasantries, and I thanked General Schuyler for his efforts regarding our adversary.

Alex said to Hannah and me, "General Washington and General Schuyler would like to meet with us tomorrow afternoon before the party to discuss Nova Scotia. It sounds like they have a detailed plan that includes dates, warships to escort us, and battled hardened soldiers to accompany us."

I said, "We will be there."

The night began to grow old. Hannah and I snuck out of the tavern to return to Mr. Franklin's home. Today has given us much news to consider. It was a very good day.

The next morning started slowly. We were scheduled to meet with the Generals at noon in Mr. Franklin's Study. Alex was still sleeping at 11:00 when we decided to wake him up. We had some coffee on hand that would bring Alex back to life. The conversation that we were about to have was very important. We had two of the greatest military minds about to deliver a plan that would give us a great chance of success. We needed Alex to be fully engaged.

The two Generals arrived separately within minutes of each other. We all sat in the study. General Washington said, "I have often sat in this study listening to Ben's ideas. Some were brilliant, and some were bat shit crazy." We all laughed. He continued, "The funny part of the bat-shit crazy ideas is that many of them turned out to be worthwhile. Not the least was his notion that connecting a copper rod to a Church Spire would reduce the risk of fire. I laughed at him. Nowadays, all new churches are built with the copper rod installed. Anyways, General Schuyler and I wanted to sit down with you to discuss the tactical plans of delivering you three to a beachfront in Nova Scotia and getting you out after your mission is complete. General Schuyler is going to go over the details."

General Schuyler said, "I have assigned a very experienced Sea Captain to this mission. His name is John Paul Jones. He has spent significant time in Nova Scotia and knows the area of the Gold River well. He states that he gets along with the Mi'kmaq. Evidently, they consider him to be a great trading partner. He has a crew that also wants to join our Navy.

The plan is to leave from Falmouth, Maine. Captain Jones will lead a fleet of four ships that will escort you to and from

Nova Scotia. These men have pledged their allegiance to General Washington and myself. We will finalize the details with Ben when he returns from France. Captain Jones said that the Island with the tall oak trees would serve as the perfect cover while you go on your excursion. General Washington will send six very well-seasoned warriors with you to secure the treasure. After you load the treasure onto the ship, you will set sail back to Falmouth. Along the way. Captain Jones' ships will escort you back safely. When you arrive back in Falmouth, we will have forces that will help you unload the treasure and send you on your way back to the Compound. In some ways, this will be the most troublesome part of the journey. We fully expect you to encounter British forces on the way back. We plan to have decoys along the way in the same carriages as the one holding the treasure. We are still considering whether or not we should give you a military escort."

General Washington said, "I prefer causing a conflict near Boston that will draw the British Commander's attention. We will give you a final plan when we meet in June. The target date is June 14th for your departure. The seas typically are calmer by that point."

Alex said, "Well, at least you two will be going to a far way Island for your first anniversary." We all laughed.

The Generals both departed Mr. Franklin's home. We will be seeing them shortly with their wives at the Annual Harvest Celebration.

Several hours later, Alex, Hannah, and I walked to the Powel House. This was the home of the Mayor of Philadelphia, Samuel Powel.

His wife Elizabeth was one of the most prominent figures in Philadelphia during the 1770s. She was known throughout the Colonies as a great host and Statesman in her own right. She had become a great friend to the Washington's, Franklin's, and Adams families. So when the opportunity came up to host the Annual Harvest Festival, she immediately offered her home.

Martha Washington introduced us to Mrs. Powel upon our arrival. She said, "I have heard much about the three of you. Please make yourself at home."

We thanked her for her hospitality.

The next to greet us was young John Quincy Adams. He had grown at least two inches since last summer when he visited us at the Compound. I could see that he would enjoy this year's festival much more than previous years because there were so many children to play with.

Hannah and I recounted that fateful walk down the staircase at Peace Field. I told her that the world had stopped. I still haven't placed that aroma that seems to accompany her presence. She said, "Search your Dreams. It is the same essence that Tytea told Peleg would be a signal of her presence after she had passed. It has been with my soul ever since. In the Sinclair times, we called it Lavender. The funny thing is that you are the only one that can smell it." She paused as we both thought about the essence. We then returned our thoughts to that fateful night at Peace Field. Hannah continued, "I remember talking to Alex, and then I turned to greet you, and I was speechless. There you were. All the visions from my previous lives passed right before my eyes. I never thought about meeting my soulmate until that moment, and then there you were. The funny part is that I had a disagreement with my mother just before I came downstairs. She insisted that I could meet my Prince Charming at any instant and that I needed to be prepared. I didn't believe her. Little did she know that it would be five minutes later?"

I said, "The entire night, I was thinking of clever things to say to you. I have never been so nervous."

She said, "One thing is for sure I hope General Washington is wearing his old boots tonight." I laughed.

The dinner was lovely. They served Prime Rib, which was outstanding. After the dinner was completed, everyone moved into the ballroom. I had never seen a room as large and stunning as this one.

The Band was comprised of a piano, complete string section, and horn section. Finally, the music started, and everyone started to dance. Hannah said, "This brings back many memories."

We danced the night away. What a wonderful experience. I said, "Hopefully, we will be able to introduce our children to this wonderful event."

She said, "Yes. It is one of those memorable events that you will remember for the rest of your life. I miss Peace Field, but this year's celebration has to go down as one of the best. Let's hope that our good fortunes continue."

I said, "I know my good fortunes will continue as long as you are at my side."

The next morning we said goodbye to Alex and Mr. and Mrs. Adams. Then, we boarded a carriage and started the journey back to the Compound.

Hannah said, "I'm so excited. I will get to see Cleo soon."

CHAPTER 82

THE SPRING OF 1775

T HE WAVES WERE *gradually building. Waves that started with a spray were breaking over the ship's bow. Every drop of water that hit the wound on my leg was causing excruciating pain as the saltwater entered the wound. From wave to wave, I could see the bow dipping further into the wave's trough. Loose items such as ropes, rags, and a mop went overboard. In the distance, I could see a huge wave beginning to crest. As the wave approached the ship, our bow kept dipping to the point where I thought the ship would flip over. The Captain had done a spectacular job keeping the bow into the waves. If the ship was to be caught sideways by a wave, it would be over for all of us. As the huge wave broke over the bow, we were all underwater for a brief moment. As the wave subsided, I watched as the water carried Hannah towards the side and then pulled her over the side. I was screaming her name but could hear nothing in return....*

Then I woke with Hannah leaning over me, telling me she was right there. I was dripping wet with sweat. I had the nightmare again.

We both walked over to the couch. The fire that we had lit the previous evening was still burning. Hannah threw several more logs on the fire. We needed to discuss the recurring nightmare. It was May 31st. Our trip to Nova Scotia was just two weeks away. She needed to hear this.

Hannah sat down next to me, and I said, "I have told you that I have this recurring Dream where you are washed overboard in a storm. Each time that I have this Dream becomes clearer than the previous one. In this Dream, I had a serious wound on my leg. The saltwater hitting the wound caused excruciating pain. I would always wake up to realize that it was just a Dream. As you undoubtedly know, Dreams mean more to us than other people. Was you washing overboard going to be a reality, or was this just a warning? Could I defy destiny by saving you? The only thing I can think of is that whenever we are on a boat together, I will tie us together and then to the ship. I would never forgive myself if I failed to do anything after all of these warnings. If we are tied together, then if one washed overboard, then the other is also going. At least we would die together."

Hannah said, "If it means that much to you, then we will tie ourselves together. We should also tie Alex down. I can hear him complaining already." This caused me to laugh.

I said, "We keep meaning to talk with Maria. Today is the day. The tavern won't be private enough. Let's invite her over for supper."

Hannah said, "Sounds good. I will stop by her house and invite her on the way to the stable this morning."

I could not go back to sleep at this point. The sun would be up in an hour or so. I warmed up some tea and decided to write in my diary. I have not written anything in quite a while. It wasn't because nothing had happened. It was the other way around. Hannah and I were very busy. We were completing the addition to the stables. They had turned out just as we had hoped. We worked so many hours that we would come home and collapse at the end of the day. I am not complaining. It wasn't all work.

My last journal entry was just after the Christmas Party. It had been five months since I had recorded anything. We had a huge Christmas Party at the tavern. It was our second annual Christmas party. Alex had returned from King's College for a few days. As usual, he made the party very memorable. The balance of his time off was spent in Albany visiting with Eliza. We also had several dance parties at the tavern over the winter.

The next item that I needed to add to the journal was the wonderful news about Cleo. In Mid-March, Cleo had given birth to a beautiful filly. She was dark brown with a diamond-shaped white marking on her head. Hannah named her Joanie because her favorite character from history was Joan of Arc. We watched this miracle happen. It took longer than I had imagined. The Veterinarian was there the entire time. We watched the filly stand within minutes of being born. Mother and Foal had come through the birth with no complications. Hannah and I decided that this was what we wanted to do with our lives. This was very rewarding. Mark and Cleo were part of our family. Now our family was just a little bit bigger. Watching Mother and Foal run in the pasture was very special. We could sit and watch this all day long.

In April of that year, I received the test communication from Mr. Franklin. After consulting the Regius Poem, we discovered the message, "All is well here in jolly old England. Happy Spring."

The Continental Congress had formulated its message that was to be delivered to King George III. This was sent to Mr. Franklin uncoded and for all to see. It offered an olive branch. In short, it requested that the King repeal what the Colonists referred to as the Intolerable Acts that the Parliament had perpetrated on the Colonies. If the King agreed, there would be no further boycotts of British Goods.

After several months, word had traveled back from Mr. Franklin that the King would not even look at the requests. The decree from the First Congressional Congress had gone largely ignored. Back in the Colonies, this set many things in motion.

I felt as though the war had already started when the British had seized the weapons at Charlestown. Not a shot was fired, but clear messages were sent. Months earlier, at the first Congressional Congress meeting, Hannah and I heard General Washington tell the Delegates that under no circumstances would the British be allowed to seize our weapons without a fight. He felt that weapons seizure would be their first move, as it had been for many centuries.

Back in Boston, the militias began to add men. At the onset, the war was very popular. The speed with which the militiamen reacted astounded even their leaders. The men of the militias in Massachusetts earned the name 'Minutemen' because of their speed.

On April 19th, 1775, General Washington's words rang true. Around seven hundred British troops under the command of Lieutenant Colonel Francis Smith began marching on the city of Concord, where a large cache of weapons was supposed to reside. Several days prior, several spies got word to Paul Revere, who raced to Concord and had the militia leaders move the weapons caches to various other towns. On the morning of the 19th, Paul Revere raced to tell the Minutemen that the British were on the way. A battle ensued in both Lexington and Concord. Militarily, neither side won on this day. In terms of confidence, the Minutemen won because they caused the British troops to turn around and return to Boston without the weapons they set out to seize. The Militias and Minutemen grew to fifteen thousand strong and surrounded Boston. For the British, this was intolerable. General Gage would order all his forces in Nova Scotia to deploy to Boston. The stage was set for our mission.

After the Battles of Concord and Lexington, a Second Congressional Congress was convened in Philadelphia on May 10th, 1775. There were two noticeable faces present at this Congress that were not at the first Congress. The first was John Hancock, and the other was Benjamin Franklin. The purpose of this Congress was to establish a de facto government that could print money and conscript soldiers. The Militia and the Military leadership were still being decided. Mr. Franklin told Hannah and me secretly that General Washington was already declared the Supreme Commander. The only thing that was still being decided was how to mesh all of the Militias together into one cohesive Army. The announcement would come sometime in June.

Mr. Franklin was scheduled to arrive back at the Compound any day. From there, he would travel to Albany with Hannah, Alex, and myself. The plan was for Mr. Franklin, General Washington, and General Schuyler to meet in Albany, where our mission would be finalized. After that, the Mission to Nova Scotia would start in Albany.

Later that afternoon, Maria arrived at our home for supper. She was such a pleasant person. We needed to have her over more often. She brought a loaf of fresh bread with her. She was such a fantastic cook that we were sure the bread would be outstanding. We made small talk for most of the meal, much centered on what she called the 'Baby Horse.' Finally, she asked, "When is your mission to Nova Scotia?"

I said, "We leave for Albany in a week and then leave for Nova Scotia a week after that."

She said, "I have had many Dreams about your trip. There are many negative turns that could happen. You must not trust anyone, especially when they discover treasure is involved. Gold and silver will cause a man to change in a moment. Even though Canaan appears to have been killed in this life, please be aware that he has many followers. They could be family or anyone for that matter. Keep in mind that the followers of Canaan were the ones who built up the hedonistic cities of Sodom and Gomorrah. All his followers weren't born evil, but Canaan always has an ever-present charisma that makes seemingly normal people want to be his followers."

I said, "Do you have any more thoughts about the word Vegvisir?"

She said, "It will be on the body of your true adversary."

I said, "Mr. Franklin was able to understand its meaning. It is a Viking Medal that was used as a sort of a compass. Whoever wears this symbol will never be lost. Many Vikings wore this symbol."

I said, "Do you see a castle?"

Maria said," Of course. Don't forget that I lived at this place for many years before my death in that lifetime. It is a beautiful setting. I had many happy years there."

Hannah said, "Is there anything else."

Maria said, "Also, do not fear the Island. The spirits that reside there know both of your souls. They are your friends. Please pass this on to Alex. I have visions of him being on the Island."

I said, "Do you see us being successful?"

Maria said, "Success is a relative term. I see success, but I also see great cost. Please keep in mind that my Dreams are not absolute. You can change your future."

I said, "Do you see any shipwreck or rough seas?"

She said, "No. I see a great battle ensuing on the water."

I went on to tell her of my Dreams. I finished by telling her that I planned on tying the three of us to the ship.

She said, "Maybe the warnings you have received in your Dreams are enough to change the future already. It sounds like you have a plan. I see a great race that includes a battle where men will die. The treasure that you will be carrying is enough to affect the future. It has great power. Men have died trying to obtain it. You three are the Guardians of this Secret treasure in the past, present, and future. Everything you have learned and trained for will culminate in one very special moment. Trust your intuitions. They will always guide you properly, for they are the sum of all of your decisions in past lives. They have learned the proper path forward."

I said, "As with every one of our lifetimes, we are very fortunate to have you."

CHAPTER 83

DESTINY IS UPON US

T WAS SUNDAY, June 5th, 1775. Today is the day that Alex and Mr. Franklin are scheduled to arrive at the Compound. Tomorrow will be when we commence our Nova Scotia mission. The plan is for us to rest for a night, and then we will set out on the two-day journey to Albany. We would probably be gone for at least three to five weeks. There was much to get done. Not the least of which was to meet with Michael Hayes and discuss all of the summer requirements around the Compound. I found him at the Saw Mill. I said, "Good morning. As you know, Hannah and I will be departing tomorrow for Albany. I am sure that you know all of the tasks for summer around here. Let's press to see if we can increase our output here at the mill. I spoke with our trading partners in New York. They said that they would take as much lumber as we could provide. Everyone is worried about losing workers to the war effort. That hasn't happened yet, but I believe it will, so let's sell as much as possible. Rainy days are ahead."

Just then, Hannah walked up and joined our conversation.

She said, "I have been asked about the war efforts by several of our young men. They ask questions like if they leave the Compound to join the Patriots, will their job be waiting for them when they get back? One of the married men asked if his family could stay here while he is away fighting the war."

I said, "The answer is yes on both questions. We must keep an eye on how many men we are losing. There is no doubt that business will suffer during the war."

Hannah said, "While these men are away, why don't we train the able-bodied women how to work these tasks. That way, we can stay productive as a workforce and help these women get their minds off the war."

I said, "That's an excellent idea. Let's evaluate each case on its own merits. If, for instance, there is a mother with an infant, then working at the mill is not a proper fit."

Hannah said, "When we were in Philadelphia, I spoke at length with Mrs. Betsy Ross about how there will be a shortage of uniforms and clothing for our military men. Perhaps we can put the women of the Compound to work in that endeavor."

I said, "Let's walk to the office and speak to Mrs. Williams about this. What equipment do we need to make this happen?"

Mr. Hayes said, "Henry Walker's widow and her mother-in-law were seamstresses before they came to the Compound. We should also talk to them."

I said, "That sounds great. Nothing would help that poor woman more than having something to focus on."

Hannah said, "This would give the women of the Compound a chance to be part of the war effort. This would also allow us to be productive in the winter."

I said, "Let's look at the business side first. What equipment do we need? What raw materials?"

This project was quickly set into motion. I gave Mrs. Williams guidelines on how much to spend. I made it clear to everyone involved that we must keep this quiet. If the British heard that we supported the Colonists during the war, there would be hell to pay.

Later that afternoon, Mr. Franklin and Alex arrived. It was always a joyous occasion for either of these men to be at the Compound. This also meant that our excursion to Nova Scotia was that much closer.

Mr. Franklin told Hannah and me, "It is always great to see the both of you."

Hannah said, "Alex, how was school?"

Alex said, "It ended very well. It is unclear at present whether Kings College will reopen in the fall. I am of the mindset that it is time for me to join General Washington's Staff. I can finish my studies after the war is over."

Mr. Franklin said, "We must be victorious. Over the next month, you three will perform a task that will give our cause a chance to be successful. Your efforts will be considered secret and probably will never be told to the public, but God will know what you have done."

I said, "Well, why don't you freshen up and meet us at the tavern in a few hours to continue our discussion."

Everyone agreed. Alex said, "I probably don't need a couple of hours, so I will go to the tavern earlier and make sure it is safe for all of you." Everyone laughed.

I said, "Alex, I know you always have our back. Especially when there is a tavern involved."

Hannah and I went to our home and finished packing.

I said, "We are supposed to be members of a Royal Family when we travel to Nova Scotia. How should we dress?"

Hannah said, "I would think hunting attire would be appropriate."

I said, "In that case, I will need to visit General Schuyler's tailor when we are in Albany. I have nice suits for parties and scruffy work clothes for dirty projects here at the Compound."

Hannah agreed and said, "I have the same issue. I have several riding outfits, but that's about it."

Several hours later, we finished our packing and made our way over to the tavern. We found Alex and Mr. Franklin there. I said, "Is it clear for us to enter?"

Alex replied, "Mr. Franklin and I had to fend off several Redcoats and a unit from Genghis Khan's army, but it appears all-clear for the time being."

We all laughed. I said, "Genghis Khan? Really."

Alex said, "I just finished studying him in my Eastern Studies class, so it was fresh on my mind."

We were then joined by Maria. As we were about to set out on this glorious mission, we wanted to hear her perspective.

Mr. Franklin said, "You can learn so much from history. One thing that is usually found is that history repeats itself." He paused for a moment and continued, "Look at me sitting here lecturing you three about history when you have already lived it."

Hannah said, "Even though we may have lived it, we still need reminders."

I said, "Also, you must remember that history is written by the victors. Some of life's most important lessons were never recorded."

Maria said, "Even though history is written by the victors, everyone has the ability to understand the real truth. It is in all of our souls. During our previous lives, we have witnessed the real history. We must learn how to access it. Hannah, Jeremiah, Alex, and I are living testimonials to this fact."

We all sat and pondered the deep message that Maria had just expressed. She truly is a gift for all of us. I said, "Not to change the subject, but we have several pressing matters to discuss." I paused briefly then continued. "Mr. Franklin, The women of the Compound wish to do their part for the war effort. They would like to produce military uniforms here at the Compound."

Mr. Franklin replied, "That's wonderful. There will definitely be a need. I will get word to Mrs. Betsy Ross. She is coordinating these efforts. Your help will be greatly appreciated."

I said to Maria, "Please tell Mr. Franklin your thoughts on the word Vegvisir."

Maria said, "It will be on the body of your adversary. Possibly a tattoo. You must attack this person immediately. You must get the upper hand even though you believe that Anders is dead. The battle could be with a relative of his. He will be a seasoned warrior. I see a great race and a significant sea battle taking place. There will be a significant losses on this mission. I see great bloodshed. Mainly, the British and others will be the ones to suffer." She paused then added, "Alex, do not to be afraid of the Island. She said those spirits are our friends."

Alex said, "I remember that from when Henry Sinclair's party first arrived in Nova Scotia. The men were terrified because they kept having images of ancient warriors. This Island is a burial ground for the Mi'kmaq. Their spirits are everywhere. Agnes communicated with them and made sure that they knew our intentions. We never had an issue after that."

Mr. Franklin said, "You three are the right choice for this mission. Let's discuss the great treasure hunt and subsequent sea battle with the Generals when we arrive in Albany. I have been told that you will be joined by the best of the best when it comes to warriors."

Maria said, "Trust no one other than you three. Treasure will cause men to change."

Mr. Franklin said, "Point noted. We must arm you three with the ability to fend off any enemies."

Mr. Franklin said, "I have news regarding the treasure. I would like to wait until our carriage ride to tell you. The news that I have could also change ordinary men."

CHAPTER 84

ALCHEMY

THE NEXT MORNING came very quickly. I knew that Hannah would have the difficult task of saying goodbye to the horses. We took our bags to the office where the carriages always pick us up. Then we walked to the ranch. The horses were all grazing. Mark and Cleo immediately noticed us and walked over to us. Joanie continued to run around and play. This always warmed our hearts. This young filly didn't have a care in the world. Hannah had tears streaming down her face. These horses were her life. She hated leaving them. Just then, Alex walked up.

After watching Joanie run around, he said, "So this your new granddaughter?"

Hannah laughed, looked at Cleo and Mark, and said, "Yes, and these are my children."

Hannah continued, "Part of me wishes they were going with us. These two horses can outrun anything."

I said, "You would never forgive yourself if these horses were in harm's way."

Alex and I gave Hannah a few moments with the horses. We could see that the carriage had arrived, and Mr. Franklin was already aboard. We walked to the carriage and loaded our bags. Alex had one bag filled with his clothing and another container that included a keg of ale. Leave it to Alex to always be prepared.

Hannah soon joined us, and we set out for Albany.

Hannah commented, "I'm glad my parents are still in Philadelphia. This goodbye would have been very difficult."

Mr. Franklin said, "Now that I have you three together with no one else within earshot, I want to tell you of my meeting with Sir William St. Clair in Rosslyn. First, I think he is finally comfortable with the treasure being moved. I explained to him the concept of you three being Guardians. He was astonished. He now knows that the treasure will end up exactly where it belongs, in America. I told him that unless someone has already moved it, you three know exactly where to find it. He said as long as they stay away from the Star of David, everything will be alright. Alex, I know that you have mentioned the Secret Seal of Solomon in the past, but are you comfortable with its location. Sir William said that the Secret Seal is hidden."

Alex replied, "Yes. I hid it."

Mr. Franklin replied, "Oh yes. I keep forgetting. Two things happen when you get older. The first is your memory goes, and (he pauses for effect) I can't remember what the second thing is." We all laughed.

Hannah said, "Mr. Franklin. You have been spending too much time with Alex."

Mr. Franklin replied, "You three are keeping me young. Oh, how I would love to be your age again." He paused briefly, then continued, "Anyway, Sir William was very concerned about your safety. He believes that the Secret has been safe within his family, but he worries that Sir Francis Bacon's party may have left clues. Not to mention, Sir Francis did not travel alone. How many others knew of the treasure?" He paused and continued, "Sir William went on to say that Sir Francis was so concerned about protecting the treasure that he buried a second treasure of his own possessions as a decoy. He believed that most treasure hunters would see the signs and spend all of their efforts to find the second treasure. He set all assortments of traps and hidden tunnels that lead nowhere to confound the treasure hunters. The second treasure is of both significant historic and monetary value."

I said, "Is this second treasure near the castle?"

Mr. Franklin said, "No. It is on the Island of the large oak trees. He even went on to say that he left messages there in code that only a Freemason or Rosicrucian, back in those times, would be able to decipher. He said that this mystery could take men lifetimes to decipher the clues. He said that there is a map on the Island if one knows where to look and where the map starts."

Hannah said, "This is all to distract treasure hunters from the real treasure at the castle?"

Mr. Franklin said, "Yes, This is quite extraordinary, but Sir Francis was an extraordinary man."

I asked, "Do we know where this starting point on the map is?"

Mr. Franklin said, "This is where it gets a little sketchy. Please remember that Sir William is a very old and sick man. He was hard to understand. When I pressed him on this matter, he kept speaking of an Altar. I was dumbfounded by this. I thanked Sir William for his help and returned to London. I spent days in various Royal Libraries looking for clues."

Alex said, "Perhaps there is a rock formation on the island that looks like an Altar."

Mr. Franklin said, "Perhaps. I think it has something to do with Sir Francis's study of Alchemy. He wrote extensively on the subject. He always concluded that heat or fire is at the core of Alchemy. He wrote several allegories, such as 'Strange Fire at the Altar of the Lord'. This is a study of mankind that often uses an Altar for sacrifice or Alchemy-related activities. I believe that the Altar he referred to has to do with a great Fire pit. I wonder if the Mi'kmaq have an Altar there since it was a burial ground."

Alex said, "This is all interesting, but we are in on the charade. This is all a decoy because what lies at the castle is the real treasure. What Sir Francis has left on the Island is there to confound the unworthy."

Mr. Franklin said, "Agreed. Our mission is the real treasure."

Alex said, "Maybe after the war is over, we could make a second trip to find Sir Francis's treasure."

I said, "See, Sir Francis has already sucked you into his mayhem." We all laughed.

Alex said, "I know one thing for certain. All this thinking has made me rather parched. It is time for the Keg of Ale."

We enjoyed the ride with Mr. Franklin. None of us knew if we would ever again be able to spend so much time with this brilliant man? Every time we were with him, we learned something that would never be found in a book.

CHAPTER 85

THE PLAN

THE NEXT AFTERNOON we arrived at this place that has become so near and dear to Hannah and myself. The Schuyler Mansion had become such a focal point of our lives. We had so many enjoyable visits there and who could forget, we were married there. As our carriage pulled up, General and Mrs. Schuyler, General Washington, and Eliza came out to greet us. It was always so good to see our new extended family. Their servants took our bags to our respective rooms. This would be the first time Hannah and I would share a room here at the mansion. We all met in the foyer. General Schuyler poured drinks for all of us in his study.

General Schuyler said, "Here is to our Guardians."

General Schuyler went on to say that tomorrow morning, we would meet to discuss the Nova Scotia mission. Tonight would be about enjoying ourselves.

General Washington said, "Martha sends her regards. Of course, she wishes she could be with us, but I thought the more prudent move would be to keep her safe at Mount Vernon. After all, we are now at war with the British."

Mr. Franklin said, "It is my turn to propose a toast. You are the first ones to learn the big news. General Washington has accepted the position of Commander In Chief of the Continental Army. It will not be made public until the 17th, so please keep the news to yourself. Here is to the new Supreme Commander."

Everyone raised their glass and toasted this great man. We all knew that we were now part of history, some recorded and some unrecorded.

Alex said to General Washington, "Sir, I will not be returning to King's College until the war is over. I would like to start my assignment of being an aide to you as soon as I return from Nova Scotia."

General Washington said, "Alexander Hamilton, I accept your request. I will have your commission drawn up as soon as you return."

General Washington said, "The other major announcement that will come out very soon is that our host General Schuyler has accepted the position of Commander of the Northern Continental Army. His mission will be to protect the Colonies from an attack from Canada. As we all know, a large contingent of British troops is staged in Canada. The General will see to it that they don't attack." Everyone cheered for General Schuyler.

There were no more announcements. Instead, we all made small talk for a few minutes. Then, Hannah and I made our way out onto the courtyard that was the sight of our wedding.

I wrapped my arms around Hannah and said, "Can we do it all over again. That wedding was one for the ages."

Hannah said, "Yes, but not until the next lifetime."

I said, "Then it's a plan."

Hannah said, "You still have to ask me in that lifetime, but you already know the answer."

The others joined us. It was a beautiful June afternoon. The servants set up a dining table for us. We all sat and talked and laughed the night away. Alex was on his best behavior. It probably was a combination of the fact that his girlfriend was there with her parents and his new boss.

Hannah mentioned to Mrs. Schuyler that the two of us need to do some shopping for hunting clothing. She said, "We need to look like we are British Royals setting out on a safari."

Mrs. Schuyler said, "I have just the store for you. Phillip can steer Jeremiah to the proper men's store."

General Schuyler said, "You must be careful on the streets of Albany. We are at war now. There still are many British soldiers and loyalists here."

I said, "Understood. We will complete our shopping and then quickly return to the mansion."

General Washington said, "Tomorrow, I should like to review all the operational details of the Nova Scotia mission. Then I will travel to Cambridge, Massachusetts, to assume my new role."

We spent the rest of the evening talking about softer subjects, such as our new foal at the Compound. We all kept it light, but everyone knew that tough days were ahead. After supper, the men sipped brandy and played billiards. Mr. Franklin sat with the ladies and discussed news from Paris. It seems that Mr. Franklin had his ear to the latest trends. He said, "I do look forward to traveling across France. It is one of my favorite places. Hopefully, they will honor our request of support in our efforts against the British."

Hannah and I both started yawning at the same time. That was our cue that it was time for bed. We were going to have some sleepless nights ahead, and we needed to take advantage of the comforts afforded us by the Schuylers.

As we said goodnight to everyone, General Washington said, "Let's meet at eight o'clock sharp in the General's study.

The following day Hannah and I woke up around six am or whenever that rooster decided it was time for us to wake up. We dressed and proceeded downstairs, where we found the Generals and Mr. Franklin discussing strategies. I said, "Would you like us to come back later?" General Washington said, "No, you are just witnessing two old soldiers going over every last detail in excess. The problem is that both of us are seasoned enough to know that the best-laid plans are usually discarded as the musket balls begin to fly."

General Schuyler agreed. He said, "From then on, it comes down to instincts and training."

We enjoyed our tea and rolls with the Generals and Mr. Franklin. I could see they were ready for us, so I woke Alex up. To my surprise, he was up and already on his way down. This was good to see. As soon as Alex poured his tea, General Schuyler pulled out a large scroll that listed all of the events of our mission. The steps were as follows:

1. Leave Albany on the morning of June 13th.

2. Arrive in the Port City of Falmouth late in the day on the 14th.

3. Proceed to Paoli's Tavern in Falmouth. You will be met at eight o'clock by Lieutenant Captain William Palfrey. He will lead you to the harbor where you will board our new ship, the Alfred, and meet Captain John Paul Jones. He will be your Captain that will sail you to and from Nova Scotia. You will also meet your six other seasoned warriors that have been hand-picked by General Washington and Captain Palfrey.

4. Your ship will be escorted by three of our finest ships. If you are under attack, their orders are to maneuver between you and the attacking vessel. Then, they are to engage the attacker while you make your escape.

5. You will make landfall on the landward side of the island with the tall oak trees. There you will wait for your guide to signal you with two lanterns on the shore adjacent to the mouth of the Gold River.

6. When your guide is spotted, you three will join Captain Palfrey and his soldiers in two of the lifeboats and row to the mainland to meet the guide.

7. When you meet the guide, he must say the phrase, "The

early bird catches the worm." You are to return to the ship if he does not say this. The guide's name will be Gregor.

8. Assuming that the guide correctly states the phrase, you are to confirm that Gregor has arranged for the two dual horse carriages. They should be strong enough to hold nine heavy chests.

9. The following morning, the guide will lead you on a one-day journey to the castle that is home to the Holy Well. After that, you will have three days to complete your mission. If you have not returned by the third day, the crew of the Alfred will go ashore and begin to search for you.

10. Upon arrival, you will secure the perimeter and enter the castle.

11. At this point, Alexander is to locate the treasure vault. Then, the soldiers will help load the chests onto the carriages.

12. After the chests are secured, the guide will lead you back to your ship.

13. Captain Jones and his crewmen will be waiting on the shore on the third day to help load the chests into the lifeboats and make their way back to the Alfred.

14. The Alfred and the escort ships will set sail for the return journey to Falmouth.

15. Upon entering the Falmouth harbor, you will light two lanterns on your bow. This will signal our forces to secure the harbor and assist with offloading the chests.

16. The chests and you three will be loaded onto two carriages that will travel on a pre-planned route back to the Compound. The drivers will know the routes. There will be many turns that probably won't make sense, but please be assured that our soldiers will be guarding these routes. You will receive fresh horses and drivers twice during this two-day journey.

17. Once you have arrived back at the Compound, the chests will be taken to the hidden cavern under the basement of the Freemasons Hall.

General Washington said, "Good luck on this sacred mission.

Rest assured that General Schuyler and myself hand-picked Captain Palfrey and Captain Jones. They are trusted warriors and friends. The soldiers accompanying you are the best our Army has to offer in hand-to-hand combat and marksmanship. Are there any questions?"

I asked, "What do we say if we are captured by the British?"

Mr. Franklin said, "You are to stick with the story that you are members of the Glouchester family and wish to learn of his fate and the fate of his family heirlooms. I have planted this story all over Halifax. So no one will be surprised by your presence."

Mr. Franklin said, "There is another matter which we must discuss. When I am in France trying to negotiate the French's assistance, I will send coded messages to Jeremiah and Hannah as to my progress and, hopefully, my breakthroughs. These messages will need to make it to you, George, I mean General. I assume you may wish to have Alexander serve as the intermediary."

General Washington said, "Yes, do not bring the messages directly to me. You may endanger yourselves. Bring the messages to Alexander."

Alex said, "I will work this out with Jeremiah and Hannah. We will establish meeting spots. They will send me a letter stating that all is well or some other mundane topic. This will be my cue to meet them at a predetermined location."

General Washington said, "Commit your messages to memory. Do not carry any written messages with you. I assume that you two will travel under the guise of being owners of the Compound and are on your way to meet with your customers."

I said, "Yes, Sir. That is the plan."

This was a lot to take in. Finally, General Washington bid us farewell. We had no idea when the next time we would see this great man. Hannah and I both bid the General "Godspeed."

CHAPTER 86

FALMOUTH

I slept well for a few hours, but the overwhelming feeling of anxiety woke me up. I laid there and stared at the ceiling for hours, seemingly. I thought about the Dreams that I have had about my previous lives. Every life had a focal point where all of our actions pertained to guarding the treasure. Sometimes the mission was to hide the treasure, and other times we were moving the treasure to a new secure location. It seemed like every mission ended successfully but usually involved a tragedy where one or more of us were killed. I believe that we are very well prepared for this mission. No one more so than Hannah. She is an absolute warrior who is hidden in this beautiful body. I also believe that Alex and I have relived these past lives for a reason. The lesson of our Dreams was that we must be ready for an attack at all times, and when we do respond, it must be quick and merciless. This enemy has no greater goal than to kill us all. Therefore, we must ensure that the warriors which the Generals have assigned to this mission understand the nature of our adversary.

Finally, I heard the rooster crow. It was time to get up and head out on our mission. The previous day included a short but productive shopping trip into Albany. The attire we purchased looked like hunting attire that a Royal would wear on a fox or bird hunt. We all purchased two outfits for the mission.

We ate a quick breakfast and boarded the carriage that would take us to Falmouth in the Colony of Maine. The first day was just like every other carriage ride. We enjoyed each other's company. As usual, Alex brought a Keg of Ale. Today would be the last day for any kind of levity for a while. On the second day, we made a stop in Lebanon, New Hampshire Colony, to change out the horses and the driver. We grabbed a quick meal at the tavern. Then it was time to arm ourselves. We each had a musket, a pistol, a bow with a quiver of twenty arrows, and two large knives. I wasn't sure how to carry all of this, but I am certain I would figure it out. Hannah strapped her knives to her legs under her dress.

We set out from Lebanon for the final leg of the journey to Falmouth. At roughly seven-thirty, the driver pulled up to Paoli's Tavern. This was step one on the large scroll presented by the Generals. We were waiting until precisely eight o'clock to make our entrance. The driver was instructed to wait outside. We would gather Captain William Palfrey and then head to the Harbor. We went in and sat down. We didn't order anything. Captain Palfrey's first test would be his ability to follow a schedule. A minute after we sat down, a burly man who appeared to be a farmer walked up and asked us to step outside. I asked the man, "Are you Captain Palfrey?"

He said, "No. He is waiting for you outside."

We went outside and met a tall, slender man who appeared to be a warrior. He walked up to us and said, "I am Captain Palfrey. I will be your guide on this mission."

I said, "Very nice to meet you. My name is Jeremiah Briggs, my wife Hannah, and this is our associate Alexander Hamilton."

Captain Palfrey said, "Very nice to meet all of you. General

Washington speaks very highly of you three."

Hannah said, "There is something I need to ask you and all of your men. Please remove your coat and roll up your sleeves."

He said, "Ma'am?"

Alex said, "I strongly advise you to do as she asks."

The Captain removed his coat and rolled up his sleeves. There was no sign of any tattoo.

He said, "My men are not accustomed to being ordered around by a lady. So please let me ask them to expose their arms."

She said, "Very well."

The Captain said, "What would have happened if I had a tattoo."

Hannah said, "It's not just any tattoo. It is an old Viking symbol with the word Vegvisir written under it. A very competent person advised us that our enemy on this mission would have this tattoo. We already know their leader, but we believe that he has many associates. If you had had this tattoo, I would have instantly slit your throat."

The Captain laughed and said, "Ma'am, with all due respect, this is not my first battle. Please refrain from speaking to my men this way."

Alex said, "Captain, have you heard the tales of the woman that is called the Angel of Death."

The Captain said, "Of course, but I assume that's all embellishment."

Alex said, "I have witnessed those events with my own eyes. I assure you that the tales have not been embellished. Sir, please let me introduce you to the Angel of Death."

The Captain said, "Understood. I am only here to help you complete your mission."

Hannah said, "Thank you, Sir. I despise that name but I have spent my entire life training for this mission."

I said, "Sir, we believe that our adversary was killed in a sea battle with the Redcoats, but please be assured that he still has a following that is more than capable."

The Captain said, "Let's discuss this in detail when we leave the harbor. I don't trust anyone around here. There are many British Loyalists in this area."

We arrived at the harbor moments later. The Captain asked to have a few minutes with his men before we board. I think Hannah definitely made an impression on him.

Moments later, the Captain returned and escorted us on the ship. The men had all removed their coats and had their sleeves rolled up. There were no signs of the Vegvisir tattoo on any of the men. The Sailors, however, had many tattoos. The Captain introduced us to the Ship's Captain, John Paul Jones. He said, "Pretty tough to find an experienced sailor that doesn't have any tattoos."

Hannah said, "We are looking for a particular tattoo." She went on to describe it. One of the men said that he had seen that tattoo years ago in Jamaica. Captain Jones ushered the man over to us. I asked the sailor, "You have seen the Vegvisir tattoo?"

He said, "Yes, but it was long ago, but I remember it clearly because I had no idea what it meant. The place where I saw the tattoo was not the type of place where you should ask a lot of questions."

I said, "Do you remember anything about the man with the tattoo?"

The seaman said, "No, he was a typical swashbuckler that frequented the Caribbean during those days."

I said, "Please let us know if you remember any details regarding this man. The fact that you are escorting us makes you his enemy. He will think nothing of killing you to get to us."

As soon as we were on board, the Captain ordered his sailors to untie the ship. The men rowed us out to the mouth of the harbor, where the men raised the sails. We were headed on a northeast heading.

I asked the Captain for some rope so I could secure ourselves. He said, "I expect calm seas, but suit yourself." He ordered one of his men to get us some rope. The man returned shortly with about 30 feet of rope.

Alex, Hannah, and I found a place to be seated near the Aft. I tied one end of the rope to one of the ship's cleats, then tied the other end around all three of our waists.

I heard one of the men say, "It seems that the Angel of Death is a landlubber." The men all laughed.

We ignored their comments. If the storm I had seen in my Dreams appeared, they would all be washed overboard. We were sitting on sacks of seed that were to be offered to the Mi'kmaq. They were very comfortable.

We finally lost sight of land. The sky was full of stars. There were so many that it was hard to locate any of the stars that I was familiar with back at the Compound. I thought back to the ancient Mariners who navigated these waters using the stars. I was immediately taken back to the time of Henry Sinclair. He had been instructed by the lost fisherman named Antonio to "Follow the Great Swan to the New World." Where was this Great Swan? A few months back, I had asked Mr. Franklin about this. I asked, "Is this a real star formation?"

He said, "The Greek Philosopher Ptolemy was the first to identify this constellation. The Greeks called it Cygnus, which translates to the Swan. The Swan plays heavily in the stories of the Greek God Zeus. Since the onset of Christianity, the Swan has been renamed the Northern Cross."

As I looked up into the sky, the Stars forming the Northern Cross became brighter for a few seconds. It was like some eternal force wanted me to see the Northern Cross. Once again, the feeling that Alex, Hannah, and I are being guided has never felt stronger.

As the night went on, we all fell asleep. The rocking of the ocean waves was enough to lull us to sleep.

I woke up when the sun came up. The colors of the water were out of one of my Dreams. As the sun crested the horizon, I saw blue, violet, orange, lavender, turquoise, and various shades of whites. I still could not see land in any direction. The sea looked eternal. It reminded me of Mr. Franklin's statement of God being a giant rotating ball of light and energy with souls being thrust off. What could be more God-like than the ocean this morning? Its eternal nature reminded me of the many lifetimes I have endured with Hannah in my arms, as she is right now, and Alex at my side. I believe that being a mariner is the true nature of my soul. Many of my past lives were near or on the sea. I am fortunate that my previous incarnations used the sea to travel and protect the Secret of Eden. It is no coincidence that most of the out-of-body experiences that I have had with Hannah have taken place while we looked out at our true home, the sea.

Finally, I began to see a small point of land dead ahead. As we drew nearer, the point became larger and started to look like a large peninsula. I asked the Captain, and he said that the land ahead was the southern end of Nova Scotia. Captain Jones said, "I expect to make landfall at the Island of yours later this afternoon. The current is at our back, and the winds are coming out of the west. I expect the water to remain calm."

Alex and Hannah woke up a few minutes later. Hannah and I stood and stared as the sun was well over the horizon to the East. I held her hand, and we instantly had one of those moments where we were transported back to another life. I believe this lifetime was when she was the heroine known as Helena. We were on a ship leaving a Mediterranean port. We were constantly on the run in this lifetime. Once again, we were sailing on the sea. We quickly returned to the present. The water was perfectly calm, so we untied the ropes from our waists. We decided to go into the cabin to get some tea and food. The food was pretty basic. There was an abundant supply of jerky and tea. We returned topside to take our seats once again. Several hours later, we were running parallel to the coast of Nova Scotia.

Captain Jones said, "I am trying to stay as close to shore as possible. Any British ships will be farther out. If we are close to shore, the British ships would have a more difficult time spotting us."

Sometime after lunch, the Captain pointed to a large expense of water. The shoreline moved farther away. He said, "This is Mahone Bay. Your Island is deep within this bay." We shall start heading to the Island as soon as we spot the oak trees. This Island must have been special to someone. To plant all of these trees not indigenous to this part of the world really says something. What is so important here that anyone would go through all this trouble?"

Alex said, "In a few days, you will know the answer to your question."

CHAPTER 87

LANDFALL

OUR SHIP, THE Alfred, made its way through Mahone Bay. The large oak trees could be seen from twenty miles or more. Alex said, "I have had the Dream where my wife, Abigail, planted those young Saplings. She would have been very proud of how they all turned out."

Hannah said, "I don't believe I ever heard of what became of Angus and Abigail after Ian was killed. I know you hid the treasure, and then Henry Sinclair and, Ian and Clara's son, Francis sailed back to Scotland, but I never heard anymore."

Alex said, "From what I know, the group of Angus, Abigail, Malcolm, Agatha, and Sir Glouchester lived out their days at the castle. The older people passed on first, and then just Angus and Abigail were left. I faintly remember Angus and Abigail living their final days in Halifax. The winters had become too much, and they needed to see people. Being isolated for a long time is not good for a person. I believe that they had strict instructions that when they passed, they were to be buried out at the castle beside Ian, Malcolm, Agatha, and Sir Glouchester."

I said, "We may see the graves of our former selves. That will be an odd feeling."

Alex said, "I remember all of this like it was yesterday even though it was over three hundred years ago."

Our ship pulled up next to the Island. The plan was to set anchor on the landward side of the Island. Alex noticed that the Island appeared a little different. He said, "I don't remember a pond on the Island. It appears to have the shape of a triangle. Maybe this is Sir Francis Bacon's handiwork. Mr. Franklin will find this interesting."

All four ships set anchor behind the Island. I don't think anyone could see the ships from the sea.

The ships were only about two hundred yards from the mainland. Suddenly, a man with two lanterns appeared on the shore. At least twenty Mi'kmaq Warriors surrounded him.

We formed a landing party that consisted of Alex, Hannah, myself, Captain Palfrey, and his team. We rowed our way to the mainland.

We reached land and disembarked from the lifeboats. Captain Palfrey led the way. He said to the white man, "Do you have a message for us?"

The white man said, "The early bird gets the worm."

Captain Palfrey replied, "Are you, Gregor?"

The man replied, "Yes. The Mi'kmaq would like to meet with you. Please follow us."

Hannah said, "Wait, Gregor, please roll up your sleeves and hold out your arms."

Gregor replied, "I don't take orders from a woman."

Alex said, "If you don't do as your told, I guarantee you that you will not be among the living much longer."

Gregor begrudgingly said, "Ok." He rolled up his sleeves and presented his arms. There were no tattoos.

Gregor said, "Please follow us. The Mi'kmaq encampment is a five-minute walk."

We walked to the encampment. I was shocked at how large it was. There must have been five hundred natives living here. We entered a large tent. There was an older woman there who had a very peaceful quality to her. She went right to Hannah. One of the young Mi'kmaq men served as a translator. She said through the translator, "You are a very old soul. We have known each other in several past lives. I knew you as Helena. After your death, your memory lived on through folklore. Songs were sung about you."

She then looked at Alex and me. She said, "You two are also very old souls."

I said, "Yes. The three of us have been together through many lifetimes. One of those lifetimes was here with Goosecap."

Just then, the Chief entered the tent. He introduced himself as Jean-Baptiste Cope. He spoke to the older women in their native tongue. He said, "Aiyana tells me that you three are sacred souls and should be considered our friends."

Hannah said, "Aiyana is a beautiful person. I could see that before she spoke. What does Aiyana mean?"

Jean-Baptiste said, "It means Forever Flowering."

Hannah said, "That is beautiful and very fitting." Her eyes were welling up.

Jean-Baptiste said, "Please join us for our evening meal."

I said, "Thank you. That is most kind of you."

We all were seated, and we passed around a drink that tasted like a very strong wine. This was followed by a meal of elk. This was very flavorful.

Jean-Baptiste said, "Mr. Ben Franklin said that you were descendants of Goosecap. I sense that this is not true."

Alex said, "As Aiyana instantly knew, we are very old souls. We have been reincarnated many times to protect a certain message and treasure. In a previous life, I lived here with my wife amongst the Mi'kmaq. I fought beside the Mi'kmaq as invaders tried many times to conquer this land." Alex went on to detail many of the battles that have beleaguered the Mi'kmaq Nation.

He continued, "When I died, the Mi'kmaq buried me and later my wife at the castle. I was known as Angus and my wife, Abigail. The Mi'kmaq were our brothers."

Jean-Baptiste looked at Aiyana. She nodded that everything Alex had said was true.

Jean-Baptiste said, "So now you wish to move these items buried at the castle?"

Alex said, "Yes. Our spirit guides are telling us that this Message must not fall into the hands of the British."

Jean-Baptiste said, "There have been many that have traveled here in search of this treasure. The Mi'kmaq also believe that this treasure should not be here. We cannot keep it secure. Year after year, men have come here to find this treasure. We can see that they are not worthy. Aiyana says that you are indeed worthy."

Alex said, "With your permission, we would like to travel through your lands to secure this treasure."

Jean-Baptiste said, "Please tell me of this new nation of yours."

Alex said, "We are trying to break away from British tyranny. We want a society where all men are created equal. We want a country where your efforts will decide your future, not someone's surname. I have studied the Constitution of the Iroquois Nation. They have created a document that we can use as a model. It is well thought out."

Jean-Baptiste said, "The various tribes are not in agreement whether or not to support your revolution."

Alex said, "I know that. We hope we can convince your brethren that our way is much more in line with the freedoms that the creator has set forth."

Jean-Baptiste said, "You have made your points here today. Go forth and retrieve the message. We will not stand in your way."

We stood up to exit the tent, and Hannah went over to Aiyana and said, "I hope to see you again."

Aiyana replied, "You and I will know each other in each lifetime."

Hannah said, "Let's try to be nearer to each other in the next lifetime."

Aiyana said, "I would like that very much."

We exited the tent. Gregor was waiting there for us. He said, "We shall meet here tomorrow morning just after sunrise for our journey."

Aiyana stood quietly nearby. She gave Gregor a cold stare. It was as if she knew something. I would discuss this with Captain Palfrey, Hannah, and Alex when we returned to the ship.

CHAPTER 88

THE JOURNEY

A
LEX, HANNAH, AND I sat on the bow of our ship, recanting the day's activities.

Hannah said, "I am always amazed when someone from a past life surfaces. I believe that these encounters are messages from above. Our encounter was not just a coincidence. From what I recall, she was an aide to Helena. In yet another life, she was my sister. I wish that I could spend more time with her."

I said, "Maybe after the war is over, we could travel back here to visit."

Hannah said, "I don't think she will be much longer in this life. But, I am sure that she will appear at some point in a future life."

Alex said, "What do you think of our guide."

"I think he is a bit of a scoundrel. We need to watch his every move." I said.

Alex said, "You are picking up on the same feeling that I have had. I saw many similar men as this Gregor while traveling through the Caribbean in my younger years. If this was a hundred years ago, I think that we would be calling him a pirate. I think we should make Captain Palfrey aware of our concerns."

Hannah said, "Throughout the ages, we have encountered these situations. We have been chosen for this mission. We need to trust our intuitions. We have been blessed with these capabilities and must use them to guide us."

The sun was just falling below the tree line to the west. We were all tired. Nothing would do us more good than to get a good night's sleep. So we proceeded to our quarters below deck. The plan was to meet the guide, Gregor, just after sunrise.

I slept very peacefully until just before sunrise. I had no dreams. I think it was my mind letting me rest. I woke up and heated some tea in the ship's galley. Alex and Hannah soon joined me. The men accompanying us were also awake and loading their packs with jerky for the trip. We did the same. We had no idea when we would get our next meal.

Shortly after that, we boarded the lifeboats and headed to shore. We walked to the Mi'kmaq Village. Aiyana was there to greet us. She hugged Hannah and said, "The Mi'kmaq will be with you. Do not fear what you cannot see. They are your friends."

Hannah was shocked because Aiyana said this in English. It was like she used the translator for show last night. For some reason, she didn't want to let her fellow Mi'kmaq know that she had learned English.

We boarded the carriages and set forth down a wildly overgrown trail. We had to stop several times to cut the overgrowth so the carriages could pass. We had traveled for about two hours when I had my first sensation that I had been here before. I could tell that Alex felt it as well.

Alex said, "This is the spot where it happened."

Hannah said, "What happened."

Alex said, "Ian was attacked by Oleg."

It was a surreal feeling to return to the spot of one's demise in a previous life. Hannah held my hand even tighter. This reminder actually had a calming effect on me. I was ready for anything that this adversary was going to bring at us. In that past life, I had let my guard down long enough for Oleg to attack. This would not happen again.

After about six hours, we stopped to give the horses a break. Captain Palfrey insisted that we stop in a clearing. He felt that the openness of the clearing made us safer.

I told Alex and Hannah, "I have the sensation that we are being watched."

Hannah said, "When Aiyana hugged me, she whispered in my ear that the Mi'kmaq would be with us. She knows what we are up against. I believe that we are being watched by friends."

Alex said, "I feel it as well. But, I am not afraid because somehow I knew that these people watching us mean us no harm."

Gregor stood off by himself. He seemed nervous. We all picked up on it.

I said, "We need him to get us to the castle, that's it. We can send him on his way after we arrive."

We all boarded the carriages once again and headed to the castle. Gregor said that we still had about two hours to go.

Alex said, "All of this looks so familiar. I don't think it is from any of my Dreams. It is though my spirit knows the way."

We sat quietly for the rest of the ride. I knew we were getting close because I could see the lake to our right. I had forgotten how beautiful this view was. Off in the distance, I could see a stone wall.

Alex said, "There is the castle. Just as I remember it."

As we approached, there was a bluff that had a spectacular view of the lake. I asked the driver to stop. We all climbed out. You could never prepare for what lay in front of us. There were four tombstones, as well as two unmarked graves. Each had the name and year of their death on them. I instantly saw the tomb of Ian. It said that he died in the year 1400. Next to him were the tombstones of Malcolm, Agatha, and Sir James Glouchester. A few yards away were two graves that were different. They appeared like several Indian Graves I had seen near the Compound.

Alex finally spoke. He said, "There lie the bodies of Angus and Abigail."

Hannah said, "Let's keep our wits about us. If there is to be an attack. It will probably happen shortly."

We opened the castle gates and entered the grounds. Once everyone had entered the grounds, we closed the gates. We had an impromptu meeting with Captain Palfrey.

Alex said, "The treasure is hidden in a cavern underneath the castle. There is a hidden stairway within the castle."

Captain Palfrey said, "Do you know how to access this hidden stairway?"

Alex said, "Yes. I built it."

Captain Palfrey said, "Someday, when we are back home, we must have a sit down where you explain this entire matter. But, for now, as General Washington has instructed me, I will take you at your word."

Alex continued, "There is another entrance in a ravine behind the castle. This entrance can only be opened from the inside. There is a boulder that is on a pivot rod that must be released from the inside. Once this boulder is moved, we will have a clear way to carry the treasure out to the carriages. We should stage the carriages back by the ravine."

Captain Palfrey agreed. We had about three or four hours of daylight left. We decided to get the treasure out of the cavern tonight and bring the carriages back within the castle walls. Several of the soldiers performed a sweep of the castle and the surrounding grounds. After a few minutes, they gave the all-clear signal.

CHAPTER 89

AVENGING OLEG

ALEX GUIDED CAPTAIN Palfrey and his men to the ravine behind the castle. The Captain left two of his men with Hannah and myself near the castle's main entrance. Two of the soldiers drove the carriages to the ravine where they could be loaded. Alex walked the Captain down the ravine to show him the entrance that was currently blocked by the large boulder.

The Captain and Alex decided to have the Captain wait here for no longer than thirty minutes. If the thirty minutes went by and the boulder was still in place, the men would meet back at the main entrance to the castle.

Alex and one of Captain Palfrey's men walked back around the castle and through the gate. The men closed and locked the gates. They had strict instructions to only open the gate if Captain Palfrey instructed them to do so.

Alex walked over to Hannah and me and said, "Captain Palfrey is waiting for us to open the rear entrance to the cavern. We have only thirty minutes to do so."

The three of us entered the castle. It was built almost entirely from stone. The roof was wood and was in a state of disrepair. This was a beautiful place at one time. Supposedly British Royals had used this as a hunting retreat in the 1600s. It dawned on me that we were also walking in the footsteps of Sir Francis Bacon. Mr. Franklin told us that Sir Francis saw the treasure. Hopefully, he returned the hiding place to precisely the same state in which he found it. Knowing that Sir Francis was a man of great detail assured me that he would leave the treasure appearing like it had not been touched.

Alex, Hannah, and I went to the room that was the study at one time. I had the image in my mind of Angus and his castle mates sitting in this vast room, sharing stories and talking about history.

Alex leaned into a bookcase to find the lever. The lever would release the secret door. Suddenly, we heard what sounded like a cawing noise from a Crow.

Hannah said, "I haven't seen a crow anywhere near here. Draw your pistols and be ready for anything."

Alex found the lever and pulled it. We heard a clicking noise, but the device probably had frozen up over the last three hundred years. Alex pointed to where the hidden wall was. He threw his shoulder into it, and suddenly the wall opened up and exposed a stairway that led down into darkness. We lit the three lanterns that we had brought into the castle. Finally, we looked at each other and decided to walk down the staircase. The steps were feeble and about to break. It was obvious that we could not bring the treasure up this staircase. It could not take the weight.

Alex led us to the area where we could hear the rushing water that led to what the Mi'kmaq called the Holy Well. As Mr. Franklin had explained, this well was simply a natural spring.

We set down the lanterns strategically where there would provide light to the entire space.

Just then, we heard footsteps coming down the staircase. It

was Gregor and three other men. They had pistols and swords drawn. This was the moment we all feared. They must have been hiding somewhere in the castle. Gregor grabbed Hannah and held a knife to her throat. Then suddenly, there were more squeaks coming from the staircase. Someone else was walking down the stairs. Finally, the person reached the bottom of the stairs and entered the cavern. It was Anders Olsen. Alex, Hannah, and I should have been shocked, but we weren't. Over the generations, Canaan had proven himself to be very cunning.

Hannah said, "Back from the dead?"

Anders laughed and said, "Those feeble-minded Redcoats never bothered to search the harbor back in Hartford. I convinced my Captain that he would be joined by my other ships in the Long Island Sound. I told him to attack the Redcoats and never surrender. I further told him that help was on the way, which it never was. I needed you to believe that I was dead."

Alex said, "Obviously, we never bought into your ruse. We have an army of the finest warriors in the Colonies here expecting your every move."

Anders said, "Yet, I am the one holding knives to your throats."

Just then, both Hannah and I saw the mark of the devil. Anders had the Vegvisir Tattoo on his arm for all to see. He also had a similar medal around his neck that prominently displayed the Vegvisir symbol. Maria's vision was correct.

Alex pointed his pistol in the direction of the men and said, "There is one thing that you don't understand."

Anders said, "No, there is one thing you don't understand. You know my name is Anders Olsen, but you don't understand how I fit into this situation. Several centuries ago, my ancestor, the Great Oleg, was killed by Henry Sinclair while the treasure was being transported. My family has been searching for this treasure for centuries, and now you three have led us to it."

Hannah then said, "I must know. Do you understand that you are the reincarnated soul of Canaan? Our cousin from the time of Noah." Anders's men seemed utterly baffled by this revelation.

Anders said, "Yes, I have these Dreams, but my mission is to avenge the Great Oleg and bring wealth and power to my family."

Alex put his knife to his own throat and said, "The treasure in this vault requires a secret code to open it. If anyone tries to open it without the code, then poison will be spread across the treasure. Touching the treasure would mean instant death to anyone who dares to touch it. The fumes from the poison would kill everyone nearby. The people who placed this treasure here were smarter than you or that beast Oleg." Alex paused for a moment and continued, "I am the only one who knows how to access the chamber, and I am the only one who knows the secret code. If any harm comes to either of my friends, I will slit my throat, and all will be lost."

Anders said, "You seem like a reasonable man. I will cut you in on the treasure."

Alex said, "I would rather die than make a deal with you." He edged the knife closer to his throat.

Anders said, "Lead us to the treasure, and I will let you three live."

Alex said, "I will agree to lead you to the vault, but I will not give you the code until my friends, and I are out of harm's way."

Anders said, "You have a deal, but understand that I have twenty men surrounding the castle. The soldiers that you have brought with you may perish. My orders to my men were to attack at sundown."

Alex said, "Then you better get moving. If any of those men are harmed, then our deal is off."

I was amazed at how Alex had negotiated this situation. The part that these men did not know was that we had Hannah on our side. She could probably kill these men all by herself. The problem was that Alex or I might be hurt in the crossfire. I made eye contact with her. She looked calm. I knew her well enough to know that she was ready to attack at any instant. Then came the moment where I knew we had the upper hand. I tried not to smile.

Alex said, "I will move over to the side. I will instruct your men on how to open the vault. Any moves against my friends, and all will be lost. Agreed?"

Anders said, "Agreed."

Alex then said, "Go into the narrow gap in the wall and turn to your right and look for the Star of David."

One of Anders' men said, "What is the Star of David?"

The other man said, "I know what the Star of David is. Didn't you ever study the Bible?"

The first man said, "No."

Anders said, "Sven, be quiet and look for the Star."

Sven said, "I have found it!"

He held a lantern up to the Star and asked Alex, "Is this it?"

Alex said, "Yes. Now the stone in front of you must be slid out towards the cavern.

I looked over at Hannah as to say, be ready.

Suddenly, I heard her voice in my head just as I did on that fateful day back at Peace Field. She was talking to me without moving her lips. She said, "When the trap is set, go after Anders. I will make quick work of Gregor and join you to finish off Anders."

The two men had to push the stone wall with all of their might. Then, finally, it began to move. The stone slid a few inches when one of the men reached into the gap and said, "I only feel more rock behind this stone.

Alex said, "The opening is further to the right. If you push it a little farther, you will find the beginning of the opening."

The men pushed and heard a clicking noise as if a trap had been triggered."

Anders said, "If this is some trick, I will make you watch me kill your friends."

Alex said, "This is no trick. Just keep pushing."

The men pushed a little further, and we heard the rumble of a large stone rolling. Suddenly the boulder dropped from above with at least ten sharpened stakes leading the way. The men were instantly killed. I looked over at Hannah as she pulled her knife from its sheath attached to her thigh and slit Gregor's throat. Anders let out a roar that would awaken the dead. I lunged my sword into his midsection and said, "This is for Ian and Jacques."

Anders tried to reach for his gun, but Alex thrust his knife into Anders' eye.

The three of us caught our breath. I hugged Hannah. We had conquered our demons. Hannah said to Alex, "That was brilliant."

Alex said, "Never a doubt." We all laughed.

Alex said, "I believe Anders has men posted in the nearby woods. We must open the secret entrance and get the treasure moved before they attack."

We went to the far end of the cavern and found the boulder. Alex released the lever that was off to the right side of the boulder. We heard a loud click. The three of us put all our weight into the boulder, and it began to move. It finally started to pivot on the metal rod with ease.

We climbed up the ravine and told Captain Palfrey what had happened.

I said, "Anders stated that his men were to attack at sunset."

It was almost sunset. Captain Palfrey ordered his soldiers to return the carriages to the gate. They quickly began to move.

Alex, Hannah, and I returned to the cavern and moved the boulder to the closed position. We walked back to the vault area under the Holy Well. What we saw was a blood bath. The four men had bled out. The floor was completely covered with blood. We climbed the staircase and went out to the courtyard. The carriages were just entering the gate. The men quickly closed the gate.

Captain Palfrey gave his soldiers their instructions. I said, "What do you want us to do?"

He said, "Gather your arms and stand at the ready inside the castle. If anyone of the enemy makes it into the castle, you are to shoot to kill."

Hannah said, "Captain, I am an expert marksman with the rifle and the bow. Let me position myself where I can safely get a shot off."

The Captain said, "Very well. Try to ascend to that birdhouse at the peak of the Castle."

The birdhouse, as the Captain called it, was built to be a lookout for this situation.

Alex said, "I built that birdhouse. There are holes in the side of it where you can get your rifle through and shoot at your enemy. The stone structure will protect you from return fire."

I said, "I will go up there with Hannah. Alex, why don't you position yourself near the front entrance so you can fend off anyone who makes it through the gate."

Alex said, "Sounds like a plan."

The Captain ran over to us and asked, "How many men did this Anders fellow say that he had outside the Castle."

I said, "Twenty."

He said, "We must use our ammo carefully. This attack could go on for hours."

We all understood his message. Only shoot if you have a clear shot.

CHAPTER 90

SUNDOWN

T HE SUN BEGAN to quickly set. All was quiet. I reached into my satchel and pulled out some jerky. Neither Hannah nor I had eaten all day. We promptly devoured several pieces of jerky and had several sips of water from Hannah's canteen. This was the proverbial calm before the storm.

Suddenly, we heard a voice from outside the gate yell. "Come out with your hands up. The castle is surrounded."

Hannah said, "I can see him. I can hit him with an arrow."

Hannah and I pondered the situation. Should we be the first to attack?

We agreed that there was no way that we were going to surrender. We hadn't come this far to give up now. So Hannah decided to take the shot.

She got on one knee and drew back the bowstring. She very patiently waited for the perfect moment. As luck would have it. Tonight was a full moon. The attackers would have a difficult time hiding. The man came into the open, and Hannah released the arrow. It was a direct hit into the man's heart. He died instantly. His comrades quickly came to his aid. Hannah was able to pick off two more of these men. Then there was quiet. It seemed like hours, but it was actually only minutes. Finally, we heard gunshots. We could see their flash. The men were perched in the trees. There were also arrows flying in from all directions. We were not safe in this birdhouse. Arrows were the one thing that could hit our position. The upper third of the birdhouse was all windows with no glass. Several arrows found their way into the birdhouse. Suddenly, I felt an excruciating pain in my thigh. I had been hit by an arrow. I broke off the arrow. Part of it was still in my leg. Hannah helped me as we climbed down from the birdhouse.

Hannah said, "Leave the arrow in place for now. It will slow down the bleeding."

When we were out of harm's way, she tore off part of her dress and wrapped it tightly around my upper thigh. This was serving as a tourniquet. I had only heard of this from soldiers that I had known.

I said, "Hannah, you need to rejoin the fight. I will be fine."

She said, "Are you sure?"

I said, "Yes."

The fighting continued for roughly two hours. We had killed or wounded at least ten of their men. The problem was that we were dangerously low on ammunition.

Captain Palfrey said, "Hold your fire. We are going to have to win this fight with our swords."

Suddenly, a voice yelled out from the other side of the gate, "Show us Anders, and we will have a cease-fire."

Well, this wasn't going to work. Anders was lying in the vault in a puddle of his own blood."

Captain Palfrey yelled, "Drop your weapons, and we will allow you to go peacefully."

All that I could do was listen to the banter. From where I was lying, I could hear everything but see nothing. There was quiet for a few minutes, and then I heard massive amounts of gunfire. The strange part was that it was not coming in our direction. Finally, one of the lookouts yelled, "I believe that the Mi'kmaq have joined the fight."

The shooting was over quickly. A few minutes later, the lookout yelled, "The Mi'kmaq Chief and many of his warriors are at the gate. Should I open the gate?"

Captain Palfrey said, "Yes."

The gate opened, and Chief Jean-Baptiste Cope rode in with ten of his warriors who were also on horseback. Aiyana was riding with her son. Hannah ran out of the castle to greet them.

Chief Jean-Baptiste Cope said, "All the men in the woods are dead."

Captain Palfrey said, "Thank you for joining us. Our ammunition was almost depleted." The Chief nodded.

Aiyana said to Hannah, "Remember when I said that the Mi'kmaq were with you?"

Hannah laughed and hugged her old friend. Then Hannah said, "An arrow has struck Jeremiah."

Hannah and Aiyana quickly came to my aid. Aiyana looked at the wound and said, "We must remove the arrow and cauterize the wound."

Alex prepared a fire. Hannah helped me climb onto a table. Captain Palfrey had a flask of whiskey that he carried with him for this very occasion.

Alex said, "Thank you, Captain. I can use a drink right about now." Everyone laughed. Once again, Alex had broken the tension.

Hannah said, "Nice try. This is for Jeremiah, but I promise you we will have one hell of a party back at the Compound."

Alex said, "You all are my witnesses."

"Alex, you were brilliant today," I said.

He said, "Thank you. Now drink up. You are going to need it."

Moments later, Aiyana used a pair of plyers the Captain had

handed her. She poured some of the whiskey on it to sanitize the plyers. Then, she grabbed the arrow and slowly pulled it out of the wound. I screamed in agony. She finally removed the arrow completely. Then she poured some whiskey on the wound. The Chief then handed her the andiron that had been heating up in the fireplace. She placed the flat end of the andiron onto the wound, which caused the most unbearable pain I have ever experienced. She also had to cauterize the exit wound on the back of my thigh.

Finally, Aiyana said, "We are done for now. Back at our village, I have herbs that I will give you that will help fend off infection."

I said, "Thank you. Also, thank you for coming back into Hannah's life. This has meant so much to her."

She said, "It is my honor. Your wife is a true hero."

Alex said, "Well, there is still one thing that we need to do." He paused for effect and said, "Let's go get the treasure."

I said, "Please help me get down there. I didn't come this far to watch others find the treasure."

Aiyana said, "Be careful not to put any pressure on your leg. We will have to re-cauterize the wound if it starts to bleed again."

Alex and Captain Palfrey helped me to navigate my way down the stairs. The Captain's men had moved the bodies of Anders and his henchmen to another part of the cavern. They used dirt from the outside to soak up all of the blood.

I sat on the table that the Captain had brought down. I had to keep my leg elevated.

The men had also cleared the boulder from the vault entrance.

Alex quickly uncovered the Secret Seal of Solomon. He asked the Captain for some help. After a few minutes of pushing the stone, the entrance to the treasure vault was exposed. The men carried out seven chests that were filled with gold and silver. Everyone was amazed.

The next item to come from the vault was the Sacred Menorah. Alex explained to everyone there that Moses used this

Menorah as he led his people out of bondage in Egypt.

The next item was a small chest. When Alex opened the chest, a wine goblet appeared.

Captain Palfrey said, "Is this what I think it is?"

Alex said, "Behold the goblet used by Jesus Christ at the Last Supper. Many of you know this as the Holy Grail." All of the Christians took a knee.

Alex returned the goblet to its chest and closed the latch.

The next thing to be removed from the vault was a stone slab with strange carvings.

Hannah explained, "This is the Message that accompanies the Secret of Eden. It is a Message from the Watchers that is as old as the Adam and Eve story itself. It explains that if mankind lives by the code handed down in this Message, the Secret of Eden will be exposed to all. Once the Secret is revealed, all of the secrets of the universe will be shared with humanity. However, if humanity does not follow the rules, then mankind will be wiped out in a similar fashion to that of the great flood from the Noah Story."

The last item to be removed was a shiny box. The materials used to make this box were like nothing that man had ever seen. I was just as amazed as every other time that I had ever seen it. It was breathtaking.

Alex said, "Behold, the Secret of Eden. Hannah, Jeremiah, and I have been its Guardians throughout the centuries."

That was everything. The men had brought the carriages to the back entrance of the cavern. The chests were all loaded into the carriages.

Captain Palfrey said to Jean-Baptiste, "Should we wait for morning to make our return trip."

Aiyana quickly said, "I must start Hannah's husband on my treatment back at our village."

Chief Jean-Baptiste Cope said, "My men grew up in these woods. The nighttime is their friend. We will guide you through the night."

Alex said to Jean-Baptiste, "We can leave you with some gold and silver coins if you like."

The Chief responded, "No thanks. The only thing that I ask is that you make your new government live by the rules handed down by the ones you call the Watchers. The entire world is counting on it."

The Mi'kmaq said they would return all of the deceased to their families in Halifax.

We all boarded the carriages and headed back to the Mi'kmaq village.

BACK TO FALMOUTH

URING THE RIDE back to the Mi'kmaq village, the horse carrying Jean-Baptiste and his mother Aiyana pulled up to our carriage. Aiyana had a troubled look on her face. First, she said, "We must hurry back, and you must board your ships and leave immediately." Then, she looked at me and said, "I have seen your demons, and they await you in a storm on the seas."

Hannah said, "Aiyana, why should we be in a hurry to get out to sea then?"

"The great storm is still a day away," Aiyana said.

I said, "We are a day early. We told Captain Jones that we would most likely return tomorrow."

Hannah said, "Are you saying that we can make the crossing before the storm hits."

Aiyana said, "Yes."

I said, "I must know. How do you know a storm is coming tomorrow?"

Aiyana said, "All the answers you need are in nature. Watch the birds, watch the trees, and watch all of the creator's miracles. They have intuitions we cannot understand, but I have seen enough to know to follow their leads. The Mi'kmaq have been living through these storms for centuries. We know all of the signs. We will move to higher ground tomorrow."

Hannah got word to Captain Palfrey. We are to head directly to the ship. The Captain said that he would have scouts ride ahead at daybreak to notify Captain Jones that we would need to depart immediately.

Several hours later, we rode through the Mi'kmaq village. Aiyana stopped to get herbs for my wound. She said she would catch up to us at the mouth of the Gold River.

We arrived back at the landing area where the lifeboats awaited us. Captain Jones had ordered the other three ships to wait out in Mahone Bay. He maneuvered the Alfred closer to the mainland so we could transfer the treasure more readily. Alex helped the soldiers load the chests. Hannah and I would be on the last lifeboat. Through the woods, we could see Aiyana and her son, Jean-Baptiste, riding toward us. They arrived and dismounted their horse. Aiyana instructed Hannah to fill her canteen with water from the Gold River. We knew that she did this because the water was spring water that had flowed from the Holy Well area near the castle. This water was as pure as any water you could find.

Aiyana then pulled a mixing bowl from her pouch and poured some ground herbs into the bowl. Then she poured some spring water from Hannah's canteen into the bowl. Finally, she used a makeshift spoon to mix the ingredients into a thick paste.

Meanwhile, Hannah had removed the dressing from my wounds. They looked awful. Hannah said, "At least the cauterization seems to have worked. There is no sign of new bleeding."

Aiyana said, "That's good news."

She then spread the paste onto the wounds. Even though she was very gentle, the pain of anything coming into contact with my wounds was excruciating. Aiyana said to Hannah, "Do this every six hours."

Hannah said, "Okay. Thank you for coming to our aid."

Aiyana said, "It has been my privilege. Since I was a little girl, I have had Dreams about what I could have done differently to help the Great Helena. This is helping to heal me as much as it is healing your husband."

Hannah said, "Well, thank you from the bottom of my heart. You are a great friend. I firmly believe that our souls will be together again."

The two women hugged for the last time. I thanked Chief Jean-Baptiste for his help and friendship. "I will pass your message of following the guidelines instructed by the Watchers on to Mr. Franklin and General Washington."

He said, "Thank you."

Hannah and I boarded the lifeboat and made our way to the Alfred. Several of the men carefully lifted me onto the ship. Alex, Hannah, and I sat in the same spot as before. The bags of seed had been replaced by bags of coconut fiber. Evidently, the Island had mounds of it lying around. The men had no idea where it had come from. The nearest coconut tree is at least a thousand miles away. I am not sure what these men will do with these fibers, but one thing is certain, they make for a comfortable seat.

Captain Jones pulled up the anchor and instructed his men to row the ship out past the Island. Once safely past the Island, he had his sailors set the sails. Once out to sea, we headed on a southwest heading towards the Maine Colony. The return trip wasn't as fast because we were fighting the current.

As I had insisted on the trip to Nova Scotia, Alex, Hannah, and I were tied together and then secured to the ship's cleat.

Alex said, "Is this really necessary? The water is perfectly calm."

Hannah said, "Yes. Aiyana had also seen Jeremiah's Dreams. They are real. We are attempting to outrun them."

Alex said, "Okay if I have learned one thing in this life, it is not to go against the Dreams. They are always right."

We all slept comfortably for most of six hours. We were awakened by the waves. The water was becoming noticeably rougher. Hannah redressed my wounds and administered the paste as Aiyana had instructed.

I said to Captain Jones, "How much further to Falmouth?"

Captain Jones said, "Three or four hours. It's a good thing that we left when we did. There is a Nor'easter brewing. The winds are coming out of the North East. Several British Frigates appeared to be following us but thought better of it. The wind is at our stern. We are moving at about ten knots." He continued, "I am trying to get us on the south side of the Georgetown Islands that you can see at eleven o'clock. Once in there, we should see calmer waters, but I can't guarantee that we won't see any more British Ships."

Roughly two hours later, Captain Jones had two of the three escort ships pass us. If there were British ships, they would engage them. The single ship following us was to protect us from the rear.

An hour later, we came around the eastern point of the Georgetown Islands. As we did, we immediately noticed two British Frigates that were setting anchor in a protected Harbor of Refuge. They immediately saw us and pulled up their anchors. One of our ships that was sailing behind us changed its heading so it could engage the British Ships. They came within one thousand yards and fired upon the closer of the British Ships. The first cannonball missed wildly, as did the second. The third clipped the aft of the British ship and destroyed the helm. The ship was unable to set sail. The second British ship was able to escape. Our ship gave chase. The two ships played a game of cat and mouse. This allowed us to clear the area. As we approached Falmouth Harbor, we spotted two British Frigates heading from the south. Captain Jones signaled the other Captains to allow the Alfred to enter the Falmouth Harbor first. His orders were to not let the British ships into the harbor. This set up what was to be an epic battle. What Captain Jones didn't realize at first was that these two British ships were supply ships. They had cannons and the ability to defend themselves but were not offensive. Oddly enough, one of the ships was called the HMS Halifax.

Once we were in the Harbor, Alex went up to the bow and lit two lanterns. There were two problems. It was daytime. Even though it was cloudy, would anyone be able to see the lanterns? The second problem was that we were arriving a day early? Would anyone even be looking?

The City of Falmouth was a safe haven for the Patriots. The Patriots were mainly from Boston. They had shops here in the Falmouth Harbor. Since the British had controlled the Boston Harbor for years, Falmouth had become the place where one could avoid British taxes and oversight.

General Washington had ordered several platoons of his most trusted soldiers to man the Falmouth Harbor and to be prepared for the arrival of the Alfred. They were instructed that a very special shipment was inbound from Nova Scotia. This shipment was to be protected with their lives. No one knew what could be so important, but it was not the soldier's place to question orders. This group of soldiers was led by none other than Paul Revere. General Washington had the utmost faith that Mr. Revere would faithfully execute his orders.

CHAPTER 92

FALMOUTH HARBOR

APTAIN JONES DIRECTED his men as they secured the Alfred to the dock. Captain Palfrey immediately sprang into action as he saw the carriages arrive. The men offloaded the chests onto the carriages. The men also helped me exit the Alfred. I spotted Captain Jones, "Thank you for getting us this far."

Captain Jones said, "It is my honor. I don't know what's in those chests, but I am happy that General Washington chose me for this assignment."

I said, "Good luck getting out of here."

Captain Jones said, "Those are supply ships. I will sink them if they don't get out of our way."

Suddenly, Paul Revere rode up on horseback. He said, "You are back a day early. I was getting concerned. I have seen these storms arise my entire life. This particular storm looks worse than most." He further explained, "I have six two-horse carriages. Four of the Carriages are filled with vegetables. They are to be decoys. They will distract the British. Do not stop for anything."

Captain Palfrey said, "Pray for the souls of any Redcoats who comes near our friends or their cargo."

Both of the carriages were loaded with the treasure. The two sets of identical carriages left Falmouth Harbor just ahead of us. Captain Palfrey and his men loaded themselves onto our carriages. They were our security for this ride. The drivers were instructed precisely what routes to take and what turns to make. Across the harbor, we could see roughly twenty Redcoats hurrying towards our position. They were probably a mile away. Captain Palfrey's men were given a significant amount of ammunition for the trip. We had hoped for a quiet ride, but we're prepared for anything.

Suddenly, our driver made a right turn down a very narrow path. This path felt like one of the many Indian trails that were shortcuts to the Compound. Alex, Hannah, and I knew those trails rather well. But, with these trails, we were at the mercy of the driver. I just remember what General Schuyler said before we left, "The drivers will make turns that don't make sense."

CHAPTER 93

WESTBOUND TO ALBANY

THE CARRIAGES CARRYING the treasure were headed westbound in the general direction of Albany. We felt that we were safe once we entered the greater Albany area. Most of the Redcoats had moved out of Albany towards the coast. Suddenly the skies started to turn black. I had forgotten that the entire area was about to get hit with a Nor'easter. We needed to find shelter. The rains would soon begin. The driver said we were thirty minutes from Lebanon, New Hampshire. Alex said that he would confer with Captain Palfrey. We thought there was a good chance we would have to take shelter for the night.

We finally made it to Lebanon just before the rain started. It was coming down in buckets. Alex said to Captain Palfrey, "We probably need to take shelter."

The Captain replied, "I understand. The roads will possibly be flooded or too muddy to pass." The Captain continued, "Let's try to find a barn. We can all stay there and protect the treasure."

Alex said, "Let's ask the tavern owner. They always seem to

know everything in these towns."

Alex walked to the tavern. He was startled when he walked in and saw about ten Redcoat officers drinking and carrying on. He knew that there must also be soldiers if there were officers here. He asked the tavern owner if there was a barn anywhere that they could use for the night. The tavern owner responded, "There is nothing here that the British haven't already seized."

Alex came back and told Captain Palfrey what he found. Alex remembered how Mr. Franklin told him that the road to Albany had been paved because it was so heavily used during the French and Indian War. He knew that the road would be safe. He also knew that no one would use it as long as it was raining. Alex and the Captain made a calculated decision to get to the paved road and continue to Albany. After all, Alex knew that they could take shelter at the Schuyler Mansion if they could make it to Albany.

The paved road was south of their current position. Therefore, they would have to travel about an hour south of Lebanon to reach the paved road.

The heavy rains continued for a few more hours. Then it was off and on downpours. Once they reached the paved road, there were several tense moments where they passed small groups of British soldiers. They also passed a carriage that appeared to be carrying a British General. The consensus had been that the British had left Albany weeks ago. Evidently, this wasn't the case. Finally, the next morning we reached Albany. All of us were wet and cold. We knew that we would be welcomed at the Schuyler Mansion.

One of the servants recognized Alex and immediately summoned Mrs. Schuyler. It seems that the General was away on a deployment. We hid the carriages in the horse barn. Once she saw that I was injured, she summoned their Doctor. It took him about twenty minutes to arrive.

He looked at the wound and said, "It's a miracle that you made it this far. Whatever remedy the Indian Sage had used has successfully fended off the infection. At some point, you will have to learn how to walk again. I will recommend a cane for starters."

After the Doctor left, Mrs. Schuyler came and spoke to Alex, Hannah, and me. She said, "Several British Intelligence Officers have stopped by looking for Phillip. I said that he has traveled to New York for business which is a total fabrication."

I said, "I thought the British had cleared out of Albany?"

Mrs. Schuyler said, "Apparently, not all of them."

Hannah said, "We should probably be on our way in the morning. Do you feel safe here?"

Mrs. Schuyler said, "Yes. I don't think they would lay a hand on me or threaten Eliza."

Hannah said, "You can come with us to the Compound."

Mrs. Schuyler said, "I am not running away from my home."

Captain Palfrey let the men enter the Mansion one at a time to get cleaned up and have a hot meal. Alex got cleaned up and spent time with Eliza.

Hannah helped me get cleaned up, and then she treated herself to a hot bath.

We eventually made our way downstairs to join the others for supper.

After supper, we made our way into the General's Study. Captain Palfrey spoke first. He said, "The plan was to have troops stationed periodically along the route. Obviously, the weather changed that plan. We must leave early tomorrow morning and make our way to the Compound. We will change drivers and horses once during the ride. I don't think we will see Redcoats on the way, but remember that I didn't think that we would see any Redcoats in Albany either."

The next morning we made our way out of Albany. We saw several regiments of Redcoats as we were leaving. We made it to Oneonta without incident. We changed out the driver and horses and continued on our way. We were about twenty miles away from the Compound when a small platoon of Redcoats seemingly appeared out of nowhere. There were six of them. Upon closer look, I noticed that they were being led by Gordon. The covers of both of the carriages were closed. Gordon said, "What do you have in the carriages?"

I said, "That's none of your concern. You know what happens next, correct?"

Gordon said, "Are you threatening one of His Majesty's officers?"

I said, "I now know who will win this war if they thought it was a good idea to make you an officer."

Gordon said, "Get out of the carriage."

I said, "I warned you to stay away from here." Just then, an arrow from one of our guards pierced Gordon's heart. In an instant, gunfire erupted, and then it was over." All of the Redcoats were dead. We had to stop and bury these men. We were certain that someone would come looking for them. Some of the Redcoats had shovels. It was kind of ironic that they brought shovels to their own burials. It took about two hours to bury all of the men. We then boarded our carriages and finished the journey to the Compound. I felt relieved that Gordon was finally out of our lives. He finally paid for the death of Henry Walker. The only concern going forward was how much intelligence about the Compound had he passed on to his superiors. A smart man who had committed such a heinous crime would have stayed clear of the Compound. Unfortunately, Gordon was not a smart man.

We pulled in just before dark. Mr. Adams came out first. He said, "We were getting worried. The checkpoint officers said that they hadn't seen you yet."

Hannah said, "We had to make a detour."

Mr. Adams said, "The mission?"

Alex walked him to the carriages and removed the blankets. Mr. Adams looked in astonishment at what he saw. He said, "I must get the message out that the mission was a success."

The soldiers helped Alex carry the treasure into the Freemason's Hall. The men and Captain Palfrey, for that matter, were told that the treasure would be transported to Philadelphia by another team. The truth was that the treasure was going to be hidden in a secret vault underneath the Freemason's Hall.

After everyone went to get cleaned up, Alex and Mr. Adams wrestled the treasure to the hidden chamber. The doors were all locked. A vault would be created similar to the vault that was located beneath the castle.

We all met at the tavern for a night of celebration. The purpose in which Alex, Hannah, and I had been placed here at this time had been accomplished.

Alex told Mr. Adams the entire story from start to finish. Mr. Adams said, "This was one for the ages."

As promised, Alex explained to Captain Palfrey, over many drinks, how the three of us have been Guardians of this Secret for many lifetimes.

As I sat there incapacitated and thus unable to help, I suddenly had an image come into my thoughts. The image was of Noah. He was looking on with a smile and tears of joy streaming down his face. His grandchildren had succeeded in delivering the Secret of Eden to its foretold home. I'm sure Maria was experiencing the same image. After all, Noah was her husband in that lifetime.

CHAPTER 94

MESSENGERS

ENERAL WASHINGTON FORMALLY accepted the position of Commander in Chief of the Continental Army in late June of 1775. After he helped plan our trip to Nova Scotia, he made his way to Cambridge, Massachusetts, where he used the home of Benjamin Wadsworth for his Headquarters. These early days of the war were frantic and frustrating for the General. The British had much in the way of respect for General Washington. Even though they failed to promote him while he was fighting for the British in the French and Indian War, they knew not to underestimate him.

The General always felt disrespected and eventually resigned from his post with the British. He sat and watched as the British House of Commons disrespected the American Colonists at every turn. Finally, he knew that he could sit on the sidelines only for a brief time. He loved America. When duty called, the General answered the call. His biggest issue was who he trusted to carry out his orders.

Even though the General was focused on the matters at hand, he recently spent much of his time worrying about Alex, Hannah, and me. The mission was very dangerous. He wondered, "How close did they follow the schedule that he and General Schuyler had developed?"

After settling in back at the Compound, we sent messengers to General Washington and Mr. Franklin. The messenger that we sent to General Washington arrived back at the Compound several days later. He recalled the delivery of the message as follows:

I walked into the General's Headquarters and told his aide, George Baylor, that I had a message that I must deliver directly to the General. Mr. Baylor walked into the General's Office and informed him that he had a message from the Compound that must be delivered directly to him.

The General said, "Show him in."

I walked into his office and said, "I have a message from Mr. Samuel Adams."

The General said, "Written or verbal?"

"Verbal." The messenger said.

The General said, "Please tell me the message."

"Mr. Adams said to tell you that the gifts from St. Andrew have safely arrived," I said.

The General sat in stunned silence, which was suddenly replaced by a smile that went ear to ear.

Mr. Franklin recalled how he heard about our mission's success after he arrived at the Compound. He told us the following:

I loved to entertain guests at my Philadelphia home. I always try to select a wide array of guests for my dinner parties. This particular night's guests included socialite Elizabeth Powel, her husband Samuel, and Betsy and John Ross. These two women couldn't be from more different worlds. Elizabeth was from the world of high society shops and salons, whereas Betsy was a former Quaker. Her family had vanquished her due to her marriage to John Ross, who was not a Quaker. I loved the spirited conversation. Most centered on the war. Lexington and Concord were fresh on everyone's minds. I stayed pretty tight-lipped regarding my leanings on the subject of the revolution. The evening started with everyone saying kind words to the Powels for hosting the past fall's Annual Harvest Festival.

I was curious to see where my guests landed on the subject of the war. The Ross's were enthusiastic supporters of the cause. The Powels were on the fence. They were concerned about losing the vast fortune that their forefathers had created here in the Colonies. Everyone at the Dinner Party knew that I knew far more than he had let on. Both women pressed for news. As usual, I gracefully avoided answering the question. Instead, I guided the conversation to a more neutral subject, such as my travel exploits in England, Ireland, and Scotland. Everyone seated at the table was from one of these places. Even though they all loved their homes in the Colonies, they longed to hear stories about their ancestral homelands. The subject was easily changed.

I was detailing how I was traveling via carriage through the Scottish Highlands when there was a sudden knock on the door. One of my servants answered the door and then delivered a sealed letter addressed to me. I excused myself and went to my study to open the letter. I read the letter and said to myself, "Never had so few words made me so happy." The letter read, "The gifts from St. Andrew have safely arrived. SA". I began to weep like a young child. The mission had been carried out wonderfully by these three young Patriots, or Guardians as they should be referred to.

I returned to my guests. "Elizabeth Powel asked, "Is everything all right."

I said, "Everything is better than all right." The Dinner Party continued with my friends. I was in an unusually jolly mood. I knew that tough days were ahead, but the task that seemed impossible at one point had been successfully completed. In my mind, I knew that I would need to depart Philadelphia in the morning for the journey to the Compound. I was going to see the Secret of Eden with my own eyes. Then, finally, I could say that I have part of something equal to the exploits of my great mentor, Sir Francis Bacon.

CHAPTER 95

THE MANDATE

HANNAH AND I finally had time to rest and recuperate from the Nova Scotia mission. Dr. McGregor from Binghamton stopped every other day to check on my wounds. The worry of infection had finally passed. Now was the concern of recovery. The Doctor has ordered me to stay off my feet for another week. After that, I would have to learn how to walk again. He thought I would need a cane for a while, possibly a long time. However, I am determined not to let this slow me down.

I was seated in a wheelchair that Mrs. Williams had from her husband's many illnesses. Hannah set up another chair right next to me. We were watching the horses as they grazed on our new pasture. The young foal, Joanie, was a bundle of energy. She was trying to coax the other horses to run with her. One by one, the other horses would run with her for a few minutes, but not much more. Finally, I said, "Joanie needs a brother or sister to play with."

Hannah said, "Easier said than done." She paused briefly and said, "Have you given any thought to our future family?"

I said, "Yes. Of course. We should wait a little while longer to see what our wartime assignments entail. The Lord will give us a beautiful child when he believes the time is right."

Hannah said, "I agree with you, but I do look forward to being a mother."

I said, "You will be a great mother."

Hannah said, "It's difficult to pick a time for a child. But, as far as I know, there is only one sure-fire way to guarantee that I won't become pregnant."

I paused for a moment, knowing full well what she meant. I finally said, "Have you seen how well our cabbages are doing this year. And the new potatoes are better than ever before." I haven't seen Hannah laugh this hard in a while.

She said, "Nice change of subject. I think I got your answer on the sure-fire method."

We enjoyed this afternoon immensely. When it was time for supper, we met Hannah's parents and Alex at the tavern. Alex had not stopped celebrating since we returned. I joined him probably more than usual because the spirits helped take the edge off the pain I was still feeling. We discussed the upcoming days. Many of the Senior Patriots were making their way to the Compound.

Our friends and fellow Patriots started to arrive the following day. By no surprise, the first to arrive was Mr. Franklin. His bags were taken to his usual accommodations above the tavern. After saying hello to Alex, Hannah, and me, Mr. Franklin wanted to see the treasure. We entered the Freemasons Hall, and Alex released the hidden door that led to the cavern below. This would be my first challenge. I was going to take the staircase with just the help of the cane. Hannah protested, but I persevered. It took a while, but after about ten minutes, I cleared the bottom step. Mr. Adams joined us a few minutes later. Alex and Mr. Adams had set up all of the treasure chests. Each had a lantern overhead. Mr. Adams went around and lit the lanterns. Mr.

Franklin had the look on his face like a young child who had just found a stash of cookies. He went from chest to chest and admired the contents. He finally said, "I know we may have to melt some of this down, but there are significant artifacts in these chests." He lifted a Tiara from one of the chests. He continued, "For instance, I believe this Tiara is Egyptian. Its value is beyond calculation."

The good news was that there was still a significant amount of gold and silver coins that can be used to finance the war efforts. Mr. Franklin said, "At some point during my visit, we will have to do a full accounting of these treasures. Next, he made his way over to the Menorah and then onto the Holy Grail. He said, "Wars have been fought over these items. Now they are in our possession."

Last but not least, he went over to an area that was covered by blankets. Alex removed the blankets and said, "This is the Secret of Eden."

Mr. Franklin walked over to his satchel and removed a scroll. He said, "Here is the translation of the message carved onto that stone."

We decided to wait for the others to arrive to carry the conversation any further. Mr. Franklin looked elated but tired. This was a very emotional day for him. We all went back upstairs and left the Freemasons' Hall. I said, "Mr. Franklin, these next two days are going to be very long. Get some rest."

He responded, "Thank you, Jeremiah. I may follow your suggestion. I barely slept on the ride here. The excitement was too much."

I did the same. The hike up and down that staircase had taken all of my energy. I retreated to my home to lay down.

Before I knew it, the sun was starting to set. Hannah woke me up. She said, "My Uncle John and Aunt Abigail just arrived with their children." Everyone decided that since this was such a joyous occasion, everyone would bring their families. There was only one rule. The Patriots were not allowed to tell their spouses what was in the cavern. Instead, we would simply call a meeting of the Freemasons for the disclosure of the treasure.

We walked over to the office area and greeted our guests. I said, "Mr. and Mrs. Adams. Welcome to the Compound. Please make yourself at home."

We exchanged pleasantries. Quincy had found Alex and was telling him of his fishing exploits out on the Cape. Hannah said, "Alex will be a wonderful father someday."

I said, "Yes. He will."

Next to arrive were General and Mrs. Schuyler and Eliza. They were soon followed by a carriage carrying Robert and Mary Morris, Thomas and Martha Jefferson, John Jay and his wife Sarah, and Martha Washington. The General was scheduled to arrive a few hours later. The next carriage carried the Boston contingent of John and Dorothy Hancock and Paul and Rachel Revere. Unfortunately, neither brought any family with them. The Hancock's were pregnant with their first, and the Revere's had eight children. Unfortunately, however, two had died at childbirth. Mrs. Revere spoke so lovingly about her children that I could tell that they were nowhere near finished having children.

Everyone got settled into their accommodations, and then we all met at the tavern. Most of these visitors had never been to the Compound before. Every one of them commented on the sheer beauty of the landscape.

Then, to make a grand entrance, Alex entered the tavern in his new Continental Army Uniform. General Washington had granted him the title of Lieutenant. He wore white knickers with black Army dress boots, a white shirt and collar, and a blue long coat with red trim. Everyone cheered as he approached. It seems that both of us received our commissions and our uniforms while we were in Nova Scotia. I was given the title of Intelligence Officer. I would only wear my uniform while I was at one of the bases or encampments. General Washington wanted me to look like an average businessman while elsewhere. I would have worn my uniform this evening if it wasn't for my injury. We all exchanged pleasantries while we were waiting for General Washington.

We knew he must be getting close because four of his scouts arrived at the Compound as an advance team to assure the General's safety. The Compound had never seen this many dignitaries at one time. It was critical since the Compound was now going to be the new home of the Secret of Eden that no undue attention be given to it. It was to be considered a horse ranch and Milltown. Nothing else.

About twenty minutes later, several carriages arrived. One was carrying guards, and the other was carrying General Washington. He walked into the tavern. Everyone stood up and cheered. He made his way directly to his wife, Martha. The two enjoyed a long hug. The life of a warrior was very difficult. It was even harder on the ones left behind. Everyone was seated, and dinner was served. The tavern's signature dish of Pot Roast was served. Everyone engaged in light and lively conversation.

After dinner, Mr. Samuel Adams stood up and asked the men to adjourn to the Freemason Hall. Hannah would tell the women that she was not feeling well and would leave when the men left. The other women didn't know Hannah's role and that the Freemasons had given her a special dispensation. She was the only woman allowed in the Freemason Hall.

Everyone gathered in the Great Room of the Freemason's Hall, where the General gave an update on the conflict. The battle that I described as death by a thousand cuts was well underway. As the General predicted, the British were setting their sights on New York City. He was planning an offensive to try to catch them off guard.

Mr. Franklin thanked the General for his update and said, "You have all been asked here this evening for the unveiling of a secret. This secret is so powerful that wars have been started over it for centuries. But, finally, we have brought it to its rightful home. This treasure proves that we have a God-given mandate to seek our Independence and develop that shiny city on the hill that Jesus spoke of in his Sermon on the Mount. This treasure goes back to the time of Adam and Eve. Guardians have been assigned through the centuries to guard the treasure and make sure that it doesn't fall into the wrong hands. What I will say next will shock you. These Guardians have lived the life of a Guardian, died a normal death, and then have been reincarnated again to continue their role of being a Guardian. Three of these Guardians are in the room with us tonight. You know them as Alexander Hamilton and Hannah and Jeremiah Briggs. Each lifetime is highlighted by Dreams from previous lives that guide them on their sacred mission." The Patriots that had not heard this before sat in shock.

General Washington spoke next. He said, "I know that some of you sit in disbelief. I was reluctant to believe the story. Then, Ben started to tell me about something that began with Adam and Eve, and I said to Ben, "The way you tell stories, I will be dead and gone before we get to the midway point." Everyone laughed.

The General continued, "I sat down with these three remarkable young people and realized that the entire story was true. We backed up their recollections from their Dreams with written histories. Everything lined up. I welcome you to ask them about this tonight. After tonight, I don't think we should speak of it again. It has been kept secret for a reason. As you can see, this land we fight for is remarkable. It will stand for decency and fairness as an example for the entire world. I will let Ben tell you the details of an amazing journey. I haven't heard about the actual operation yet, so I am hearing some of the details for the first time."

Ben said, "Actually, I would like Alex to tell the story. I don't want to miss any details."

Alex stood up and said, "Yes. Hannah, Jeremiah, and I have been with the secret for centuries. I will be brief; otherwise, we will be here for days. The Message that would guide us to the Secret of Eden, as it has become known, was buried under Solomon's Temple in Jerusalem. In that lifetime, Jeremiah and I were Knights Templars. Our mission was to find the treasure and move it to a safer location. The Muslim Armies were about to overthrow Jerusalem, and our access to the Temple would be lost. We found the Message under the Temple, which led us to the ancient Sphinx of Giza in Egypt. The treasure itself was buried under the Sphinx. We found and loaded it onto ships and were then killed by the Muslims."

Alex continued, "In another time, Hannah was a great Cathar Priestess known as Helena during the Crusades. She was protecting the treasure, which was hidden underneath a Cathar castle at that point. She was tortured and killed but never gave up the whereabouts of the treasure. The three of us came together again in the 1300s. We were aides to a Scottish Nobleman named Henry Sinclair. The Sinclair family had been the treasure's host after the Templars' demise in October of 1307. Henry Sinclair did not think that the treasure was safe in Scotland after the death of Robert the Bruce. Somehow the secret had been revealed to a few French Nobles. Jeremiah and I were senior aides to Henry Sinclair. Hannah had already passed from the Black Plague. Even though she had passed, she was always with us. She could communicate with us through an elderly sage who was with us. Anyways, Henry Sinclair knew that the Message detailed a great land to the west. This land was to become the home to all that was good. So we set out with the treasure to the New World. We landed at what is now known as Nova Scotia, where we hid it under a castle that we built near an ancient Indian site known as the Holy Well."

Some of the gathered men were dumbfounded at what they were hearing. Alex went on, "That brings us to this current lifetime. After carefully planning a mission with Mr. Franklin, General Washington, and General Schuyler, we set out to recover the treasure. We fought several tremendous battles while we were there. Thank goodness that Hannah was with us. For any of you that don't know Hannah very well, she is the one that is known as the "Angel of Death" throughout the colonies. Even though she is the sweetest person that you will ever meet." Everyone laughed.

Hannah blushed and said, "I do hate that name."

Alex continued, "After the long days in Nova Scotia, we were able to secure the Secret of Eden. So, gentlemen, I invite you down to our secret cavern to see the treasure with your own eyes."

Alex released the door. Everyone was very courteous in allowing me to navigate the staircase first. Then, everyone made their way to the cavern. Alex closed the door behind them just in case any Redcoats had followed the guests there.

Mr. Franklin said, "First, we have seven chests filled with gold and silver. We intend to use this to underwrite any currency we intend to print. As you can see, there are priceless pieces in these chests. Maybe someday they can make it into a museum somewhere. Next, I invite you to the table to our right. What you see is the Menorah that Moses used to lead the Hebrews from Egypt. Next, we come to this case." He opened the case, held up the chalice, and said, "Behold the Holy Grail. This is the chalice that Jesus Christ used at the Last Supper." Everyone gasped.

Paul Revere said, "This truly is a special day."

"Paul, we haven't gotten to the Secret of Eden yet." Mr. Franklin said.

Mr. Franklin led everyone across the room, where Alex removed the blankets. Then, Mr. Franklin said, "Gentlemen, this is the Secret of Eden."

Everyone stared, and finally, Mr. Hancock said, "What in the blazes is this?"

Mr. Franklin said, "It is a message from the Creator." He then reached for the scroll which contained the translated message. He continued, "This stone has markings in ancient Aramaic that state the following:

We are the Watchers. We have been here since the dawn of Humanity. We came at the direction of the Almighty Creator. We have instructed many generations of humankind of the Creators will. None have followed our direction. We have the ability to create earthquakes, great storms, and great floods. We have punished the unworthy with death and destruction. We will continue our quest until humankind abides by the Creator's will. The Creator's will was already handed down to the one you call Moses. Somehow several key aspects were neglected to be recorded. The Creator also will send his Son to deliver the message. Humanity has made strides but still falls short of the Creator's expectations. The Creator's wishes are the following:

All Humankind is created equal and will be treated equally

All Wars will cease. Humankind will not kill his brothers and sisters.

All humankind will follow the laws handed to Moses.

Humankind can only honor the Creator by following his rules.

Humankind will share its resources equally.

The Great land to the West will be the home of the righteous and the foundation of the Creator's promises. This will be the Land of Plenty.

The Seal of Solomon is the keeper of the Secret of Eden. The Seal stares at the Secret of Eden as the Great Lion in the Land of the Great River stares at the Great Falcon as he is going to rest on the longest day.

When humankind has successfully mastered the Creator's will, only then will the Secret of Eden be revealed.

Everyone stood in stunned silence. Finally, General Washington spoke. He said, "Gentlemen, we have our mandate. Ben, you spoke of the Declaration that you, Thomas, and John Adams would like to write."

Mr. Franklin said, "Yes. We have ideas on what this document should state. All of us in this room must help convince our Congress to ratify this Declaration. However, you must not divulge what you have seen today." He paused briefly, then said, "Our time is now."

General Washington said, "Everyone in favor says aye." There was a resounding sound of Ayes. Then, the General said, "Anyone says no?" There was silence.

General Washington said, "It is time for the United States of America to announce its Independence." Everyone cheered.

We all returned to the Great Room upstairs. We all sat and talked until the wee hours of the morning. Everyone had so many questions for Alex, Hannah, and me that they needed to get answered that evening.

Once these leaders left the building, they were never to speak of this again.

One of the most intriguing questions came from Robert Morris. He asked, "Where will the treasure be moved to now?"

Mr. Franklin chose to answer. He said, "We are looking for a permanent home near Philadelphia."

Alex, Hannah, and I knew that the treasure was going to stay right here at the Compound. We were designing a vault with traps similar to those deployed at the castle in Nova Scotia.

Epilogue

THE WAR

AFTER THE DISCLOSURE of the Secret of Eden, Hannah and I were sent on many missions that covered most of the following year. Many of the meetings involved finances. We met with Haym Salomon and Robert Morris on several occasions. We would then travel to General Washington's camp to inform him of the discussions. The General then ordered me to Philadelphia to speak with Congress. Upon arrival, it was clear that Congress was head over heels in the debate regarding the Declaration of Independence. Also, the lack of funding for food, payroll, and munitions was troubling. Hannah said, "I would like to see these Congressmen survive for one week under the conditions that the Continental Army is enduring."

She was right. There was a severe disconnect between what was happening in Philadelphia versus the battles in the Northeast Colonies. The good news was that Congress was getting closer on the Declaration. Daily resolutions touted everything from immediate ratification to permanently placing the Declaration on hold. The pro-independence side was winning. Then on July 2th, 1776, Congress ratified the Declaration. The Declaration was formally announced two days later, on July 4. We spent that evening with Mr. Franklin. Philadelphia celebrated with bonfires, fireworks, and parties all over the city. Soon the news would spread across the Colonies.

Mr. Franklin laughed and said, "I think that for the first time since my youth, I find myself unemployed."

Mr. Franklin's unemployment didn't last long. By October of 1776, Benjamin Franklin was heading to France to serve as Ambassador of the United States of America. A short while later, he was joined by John Adams. We met Mr. Franklin one more time in Philadelphia to review our communications. He still felt the best option was to stay at the Compound and wait for his instructions. We had to juggle this with the fact that General Washington was well into forming a network of spies. These spies were posing as Loyalists. Both intelligence activities would keep me very busy.

In late October 1776, we arrived back at the Compound. All of the harvesting activities were now completed. I didn't anticipate any further excursions until next spring. We were both saddened by the thought that there would be no Annual Harvest Celebration this year. Hannah declared that war or no war, the celebration was going to go on. We would have it here at the Compound. Invitations hastily went out. Most sent regrets because their husbands were off fighting for the cause. We had the celebration anyway. The residents of the Compound made all of the work worthwhile. Alex managed to secure a few days' leave to join us. Eliza and her Mother also joined us.

The evening of the party started very early for Hannah and me. She said, "I need to talk to you about something."

I said, "Can it wait until tomorrow?"

She said, "Probably not." She had that devilish smile on her face once again. I knew something very funny or very special was about to follow.

She said, "Remember when we had that conversation which

ended up in you telling me how good the cabbage looked."

I laughed and said, "Of course. I thought that was a very funny comeback, if I say so myself."

She just stood there smiling at me. So I said, "What of the cabbage?"

She said, "You silly man. So this is where you are supposed to figure out that I am expecting!"

I stood there at a loss for words. I grabbed Hannah and hugged her. I said, "This is the greatest news ever."

I was sky-high. We went to find Alex. He was at the tavern helping Eliza and the other ladies set up for the party.

I told him the story about the cabbage conversation a few months ago. He thought it was very funny. I then told him what Hannah had said today. Eliza let out a scream. Eliza said, "Don't you get it? Hannah is pregnant."

Alex said, "That's wonderful news. I am so happy for both of you. So, finish the story, How did the cabbage do this year?"

We were all laughing hysterically. Alex could make you laugh no matter the situation.

We then spotted Hannah's parents. They walked over to us, and Mrs. Adams said, "You two are just beaming with joy. I know that this celebration is very special to you."

Hannah said, "Yes, this day will always be special to us, but today we are especially excited."

Mr. Adams said, "Well, are you going to share your news with us?"

Hannah said, "Well. I will keep it simple by saying that the both of you will be going by the names Grandma and Grandpa."

Mrs. Adams screamed with excitement. Hannah's Father had tears welling up in his eyes. They were very excited.

Mrs. Adams said to Mr. Adams, "See, I told you so." We laughed. This was exactly what she said when we got engaged.

Just then Maria joined us. She was smiling from ear to ear. She already knew. I said, "Maria, we will never be able to surprise you." We all laughed.

We were so happy that we could make this announcement here with our Compound Family. They were the first to know about our engagement a few years ago, and now they were the first to know that we were going to have a baby. The Annual Harvest Celebration went on as planned. This party was very special because we were able to celebrate it with our Compound family.

A few weeks later, we were reviewing the plans for our new home with our Compound builders. Hannah and I discussed staying at our current house for another year. She had a very good point. She said, "If we wait a year, I will have a baby to tend to. If we build the house this year, I will at least be able to focus on telling the builders what we want. We were both thinking that by next March, I would have to go on a mission or two. So we had concluded, let's get the house built this winter.

Just then, I noticed that Mrs. Williams was heading our way. She arrived and said, "This was just delivered to your attention. I recognized the writing on the outside of the package. It was Mr. Franklin's writing. I opened the package and discovered that it was indeed a coded message. Hannah and I returned to our house, where I retrieved the Regius Poem from the lockable chest. We went through the steps as Mr. Franklin had taught us. After we checked the coding twice, the following message was deciphered, "King George was informed recently that if he committed any more troops to war efforts that the Monarchy would go bankrupt."

This was terrific news. One of the concerns held by General Washington and his staff was that if the British were to commit an excessive amount of troops that the war could be over quickly. However, this war could be won if Mr. Franklin could get the French to join us.

I told Hannah, "I need to get this to General Washington immediately."

She said, "Then you need to go."

I said, "I promised you at Peace Field that I would never leave you again."

She said, "I want our child to grow up in a nation where he or she can set their own course. So if you delivering a message helps that cause, then that supersedes all. Just please be careful."

I packed a bag and ordered a carriage. The Continental Army was stationed near Princeton and Trenton in New Jersey. So I would head in that direction.

Hannah and I said our goodbye at the house. We did not want to draw any unnecessary attention. I said, "I will try to come back as soon as possible. Hopefully, the winter will hold off for a few more weeks."

She said, "It is okay. You come back safe and sound. Whenever that is, do not rush. Although, I do expect quite a few letters."

I said, "You know. I have never written you a letter."

She said, "That's because we have always been together."

I said, "I will return soon."

I hugged her for a few minutes and then went to the carriage. Trenton and Princeton, December 1776

I had delivered the message to General Washington's Headquarters. He was quite happy. He said, "Hopefully, the French will smell blood in the water."

Getting here was quite an adventure. The carriage got stuck in the mud on three occasions. The driver said that it was doubtful that I would be able to return before March.

I thought to myself, "I will ride back to the Compound on horseback if I need to."

The war was not going very well. The British had forced General Washington out of New York. We needed to do something decisive. The men were losing faith. I wrote to Hannah to tell her that I would stay and help out wherever I could since the roads were impassable for a carriage. As soon as the roads dried up or froze, I would make my way back to the Compound.

The General asked me to travel to the front line and get a report. He was not trusting what he was hearing. I did so. I found that on the other side of the Delaware River, there were Hessian forces and not British forces. After I told this to the General, he made a very important decision. He was going to order a surprise attack and overtake the Hessians on Christmas Day and then attack the arsenal at Trenton. The General knew that he needed to give the French a victory that would help entice them into the conflict. I made the journey across the Delaware with the General. I briefly saw Alex leading his men into Battle. I am not sure if he even saw me. He looked like a true warrior. His men followed him with valor. He lost several men that day. Suddenly, a cannonball landed near my position, and I was hit with some shrapnel. The cuts were minor, but I feared that I had lost hearing in my left ear. I was transported back across the Delaware to a field hospital.

I recovered for several days, and then General Washington instructed me to return to the Compound. He felt it was more important for me to retrieve messages from Mr. Franklin.

Finally, on January 4, I convinced a carriage driver to make the journey back to the Compound. He charged double the normal rate, but I was in no position to argue. Two days later, I arrived back into Hannah's loving arms.

Hannah and I spent the balance of the winter working on our new home. Finally, the walls and roof were up. Windows and doors would follow soon.

That following spring, I had several messages that had to be delivered to General Washington.

Fortunately, I was home on March 20. Hannah and I welcomed a beautiful baby boy into this world. We named him John Samuel Briggs. He was our pride and joy. As expected, Hannah was a wonderful mother. It also helped that most of the women in the Compound wanted to spend time with the baby.

Many of the messages were relatively benign and required me to deliver them to the General and then return to the Compound. While there, I tracked down Alex to inform him of our fantastic news and also asked him to be Godfather to our son.

Later that summer, a battle had taken place to our north. It involved a small town that was known as Saratoga. The Battle was won by the Continental Army. This was one of the deciding points of the entire war. The British had suffered a stunning defeat. The Boston Gazette had covered this Battle in detail. I knew that Mr. Franklin would soon hear about this.

Valley Forge

In November, I received another message from Mr. Franklin. After Hannah and I completed the deciphering, it read, "France to join the conflict. First financially, then with troops." This was probably the most important message that I delivered. I traveled to a small industrial town in Pennsylvania that was called Valley Forge. Before all of the Continental Army troops arrived, one could say that Valley Forge was very similar to the Compound. This community seemed completely overwhelmed. I suppose that if 12,000 soldiers descended upon the Compound, everyone would think that we were in over our heads.

My goal was to deliver the message and then return home. Shortly after I arrived, heavy freezing rain hit the entire area. The roads were impassable. Once again, I was stuck in some god-forsaken hellhole in November. The difference this time was that Alex was now officially an Aide-de-Camp to General Washington. This is a fancy title that means Alex is a very close confidante to the General. Evidently, Alex had performed so well in the Infantry that the other leaders chose him to be Washington's Aide. I was very proud of him. Although, I always knew that there was greatness in his future.

Even though I arrived with good news, the situation here at Valley Forge was dire. In addition to the fact that the men had not been paid in quite some time, supplies such as food and warm clothing were scarce. How could this be? I am sure that if the good Americans in Philadelphia and Boston knew of this, they would send supplies by the wagon load. But unfortunately, everything had to be appropriated by Congress.

I met with General Washington and asked him if he would like me to travel to nearby Philadelphia and plead with Congress. He said, "Many of them were just here. Our appropriation has been approved. Now, the problem is getting the supplies here." He thanked me for my good intentions.

After being there for a few weeks, I began to feel ill. The camp doctor said I had been infected with the influenza that has been ravaging its way through the camp. I was very feverish and freezing at the same time. The doctor said that I just needed to let it run its course. I would need to be quarantined for at least two weeks. Once again, I found myself in a medical unit at an army encampment. I wrote Hannah several times during these dark days. The fever finally subsided, and the grounds froze. While this was bad news for the men sleeping in tents, it was good news for me. I could hire a carriage to return me to the Compound. It also meant that the needed supplies could make it to Valley Forge.

Yorktown

I spent the next two years traveling back and forth to the various military camps. One very special message said that the French Fleet led by Marshal Jean-Baptiste de Rochambeau was on its way. Our old friend Marquis de Lafayette was already here serving as an advisor to General Washington. I found it ironic that the Marquis and Alex were working together. They bonded back in the early days when we happened to be at the Schuyler Mansion at the same time. This was a sign that a higher power was guiding this entire affair. It was 1780, and the situation had calmed down a bit. Alex was able to travel to Albany to marry Eliza. Once again, the Schuylers put on an extravagant affair. It was a lovely wedding. I was the Best Man, and Hannah was the Maid of Honor. Nothing made us happier than seeing our friends get married.

After the wedding, we traveled back to the Compound. Hannah pulled another surprise on me. She announced that she is expecting again. This was terrific news. John was now three years old and into everything. The news of another baby on the Compound was well received. Hopefully, the upcoming year will require me to take minimal trips to General Washington's Camp.

I was home for the Holidays in 1780. I would not receive another message until March of that year. The message did not come from Mr. Franklin. This time it came from General Washington.

I traveled to General Washington's Headquarters as soon as I could. I met with Alex when I arrived. I told him that he was going to be an uncle again. He was elated. Shortly after that, Alex led me to the General's quarters.

General Washington greeted me warmly. He said that he had made an important decision. The Continental Army was going to travel south with the French forces led by Marshal Rochambeau. The French Naval Fleet would rendezvous with him to effectively trap General Cornwallis and the British Regulars. He felt that a decisive win in the south could effectively end the war.

I said, "That's wonderful. What would you like me to do?"

The General said, "Your mission will involve finances. I will explain shortly. We need to make the British believe that we will still attack New York City. That has been my plan since the beginning of the war. Now I see another way to win this conflict. I joined Alex and General Washington for dinner that evening. The General had devised a ruse that would involve shiploads of militias that would gather in New Jersey and act like they were going to attack. We need them to delay General Howe's forces for at least two days while we make our move. This will require Mr. Morris to requisition the ships necessary to pull off this charade."

I had my marching orders. I wrote Hannah a letter telling her that the General had given me a very important assignment that could help to lead to victory. I assured her that my mission was behind the lines of Battle.

The following day I rode to New Jersey to meet with Robert Morris and the New Jersey Militia leaders.

Upon arrival, I met with Mr. Morris. He said, "Ships I can do. However, more money will prove to be difficult."

I said, "The General is not asking for money. He needs the ships for a short period of time."

I then met with four Militia Commanders. They agreed to play their part. I stressed that secrecy is the key to success. The British must really believe that you are attacking.

The plan was placed in motion.

Meanwhile, General Washington's forces descended on a British Military stronghold in the port town of Yorktown in his home state of Virginia. A significant battle ensued.

The Siege

The sound of cannon fire was relentless. The good news was that most of it was coming from the Patriots. The feeling amongst the soldiers was that victory was within our grasp. This was the first time since this awful war commenced that I could see confidence in the eyes of the soldiers. Most of them have lived through victories at Princeton and the loss of New York City. Some went as far back as Lexington and Concord, but then had to survive sickness and starvation at Valley Forge. Finally, it all seemed worth it. All seemed well for the revolution, but I had a horrible feeling about my situation as this day moved on. The ominous cloud that surrounded me was getting worse as the day went on.

The stage for the final Siege was set. Our leaders had come up with a brilliant strategy of smoke and mirrors that resulted in the British Commander, Lieutenant General Cornwallis, being trapped.

As I stood outside the Command Tent and waited for my orders, I heard an argument ensuing that became very heated between the Marquis de Lafayette and Alex. Since Alex is my closest friend, I naturally favored his opinion in this argument. The two great men went back and forth about who would lead the charge against Redoubt #10. The Redoubts were small, hastily built fortresses where the Redcoats could hunker down and avoid enemy fire. Redoubt #9 and #10 were the last strongholds of the British here at Yorktown. If these Redoubts fell, Cornwallis would be surrounded. I believe that Marquis was trying to protect Alex from a suicide mission. The three of us have been close friends for many years. However, Alex was having none of it. He felt that he had earned the honor of leading the Siege through his exploits in previous battles.

After a few minutes, the tent flap opened, and out stepped General Washington. He was followed by the Commander of the French Troops, Comte de Rochambeau. There was no man anywhere that had the presence of General Washington. Wherever he went, he commanded everyone's attention. The General intervened on behalf of Alex and stated, "Lieutenant Colonel Hamilton has earned this honor and will lead the Siege on Redoubt #10. He will lead roughly four hundred Americans. The Siege of Redoubt #9 will be led by the French Count of Deux-Ponts, who will have four hundred French Infantry. The French will also lead a diversionary attack on the Fusiliers Redoubt. This will draw the attention of the British. I am ordering this camp and all soldiers to silence throughout the night. The attacks on Redoubt 9 and 10 will be commenced in utter silence. No musket is to be loaded during this time. All men are to have bayonets at the ready. This will be a battle won by hand-to-hand combat. Gentlemen, victory is at hand."

This decision would possibly seal my fate and also would explain the darkness that surrounded me. I was officially an Intelligence Officer and reported directly to General Washington. However, I needed to be at Alex's side during the Siege. May my lovely wife, Hannah, and my son John forgive me for what I am about to do. There was no guarantee that I was going to make it out alive.

After nightfall, Alex prepared his men for the Siege on Redoubt #10. The night was very cloudy, and the moon was hidden behind the clouds. The complete darkness allowed our approach to go undetected. This was another sign that we were receiving help from above. We began the March toward the Redoubt. Seemingly, the only sound that I could hear was my own heart beating. Finally, we arrived at the wall without the British spotting us. Alex ordered his men to surround the Redoubt, which they quickly did. We estimated that the British had somewhere between seventy and ninety men. The numbers were clearly in our favor.

Via hand signals, Alex gave the order to attack. What I saw next was a scene from hell. As we began to climb over the wall, the British quickly became aware of our presence and began to fire their muskets. The first volley killed ten of our men. The young private climbing next to me took a musket ball directly to his face, which removed most of his head. I kept trying to move as fast as I could, but the feeling that the next musket ball would hit me at any second gripped me. The fear was overwhelming. Somehow, I needed to survive this and make it back to my family. The good thing about musket fire was that it took about eight seconds to reload. Eight seconds might not seem like much, but it is an eternity when the enemy is sprinting at you with a bayonet. As I breached the crest, I could see the hand-to-hand combat that ensued. We clearly outnumbered the British. Most were surrendering. Through the smoke from the British muskets, I saw a British Colonel making his retreat into the command tent at the center of the Redoubt. I led several men after him. As we entered the tent, several of the men who had joined me were instantly killed by musket fire. That just left me and a very young Private to take on the British Colonel. I had clearly made a mistake. The crazy life that I have led was about to end. Most of the British soldiers were escaping through a tunnel that led from the tent. Everything was going in slow motion. The Private was frantically trying to load his musket. I knew that the Colonel had to kill me, or I would have followed him into the tunnel. I withdrew my knife and tried to get close enough to make an accurate throw at the Colonel. I watched as he raised his musket and placed his finger on the trigger. I attempted to dive, but then I heard that most ghastly sound. His musket had fired. Complete terror took over my being. I hit the floor and then heard a loud thump. I turned my head to see that it was Alex who actually fired the musket. The British Colonel lay in a pool of his own blood near the entrance to the tunnel. Once again, Alex had saved me. I said, "Thank you. I thought that my life was about to end." We both looked at the Private who was in shock. The young man couldn't have been over fourteen years old. I asked the young Private his name.

He replied with a boy's voice, "Sir, my name is Lemuel Cook."

Alex said, "Private Cook, attacking this tent with my friend here has granted you the Almighty's favor. Never forget it."

My mind raced back to the day when Mr. Adams first brought Alex to the Compound. Private Cook actually reminded of the younger Alex. The brash young man named Alex would turn out to be a hero to my family and me. The day I met Alex was the second most important day of my life. It is only surpassed by the day that I met Hannah.

Surrender

Everything worked as planned. The British were completely fooled. General Washington's forces led the Siege on Yorktown for days. The British were waiting for reinforcements to arrive by sea. They didn't know that a large fleet of French ships awaited their arrival. It was checkmate, as they say in chess. The cannons soon turned on Cornwallis's Personal Headquarters. It only took a few hours before the white flag could be seen from his headquarters.

Terms of surrender were agreed to the very next day. Cornwallis would not show up himself for the surrender ceremony. He stated that he was too sick. We all laughed at this. The scene was surreal. There was a line of Continental Army Troops on one side and French Troops on the other. I spotted young Private Cook. He looked at Alex and me as if we were some type of Gods. Both Alex and I just laughed.

The British Troops marched up the middle with all the pomp and circumstance you would expect. Their band was playing "God save the King." They were soon drowned out by the Continental Army Drum and Fife Corps playing "Yankee Doodle Dandy." The British Commander tried to surrender his sword to

Marshal Rochambeau. The Marshal refused and made the Commander surrender his sword to General Washington. The British troops then surrendered their muskets. The Americans had won their Independence. The celebration was crazy that night. As a courtesy, the American Commanders invited their British counterparts to dine with them.

I sent a letter to Hannah. The next few days would involve the Continental Army moving to Philadelphia to celebrate the victory with Congress. I asked her to pack up John and join her mother and father on the trip to Philadelphia so that we could celebrate this victory together. I assumed there was no way that Samuel Adams would miss this celebration.

Roughly a week later, a carriage pulled up to Mr. Franklin's house, where I had been staying. Mr. and Mrs. Adams, Hannah, and young John climbed out of the carriage. Hannah was very clearly showing now. Great days were ahead.

We soon joined Alex and Eliza for the party. The celebrations in Philadelphia went on for weeks.

Hostilities were now over with the British. The terms of the British surrender took two years to finalize. Finally, the Treaty of Paris, where the British Empire formally accepted the Independence of the United States of America, was signed on September 3, 1783.

The Death of the Giant

Since I arrived in this land, we have been perpetually fighting for respect from other nations. We knew that this land represented a great opportunity. We needed to be the ones who controlled this great opportunity. The year was 1789. Congress had turned itself into a divisive collection of opportunists that threatened all that we had fought for. I was hoping to spend some time with Alex so that I could understand what was going on with our young nation.

Meanwhile, at the Compound. All was well. John was now eleven or eleven and three-quarters, as he would say. Hannah had given birth to a beautiful baby girl who we named Katherine

Elizabeth in July of 1781 and another baby girl who we named Marie Sarah in May of 1784. There was never a dull moment at our ranch house. Life with three children ranging from 4 to 11 years old was wonderful. Hannah was a wonderful mother. By the age of 6, she had John riding like he was ready for a Calvary assignment. Katherine, or Katie, as we call her, had just started to learn the various aspects of equestrian riding. Young Marie pleaded with Hannah to allow her to ride the big horses. For now, Marie would stay with the pony we had given a home a few years back.

For me, it was challenging to write in my Diary. Every time that I tried to write, my hands would instantly swell up. Yet, I had to press on so the message would be passed on to our great-grandson.

Hannah and I built a platform near the riding arena where we placed a handful of chairs so that we could watch the children ride. We rarely spoke of past days when we carried out our duties as Guardians of the Secret of Eden. Somehow in this lifetime, we managed to survive to enjoy raising a family. Most people took this for granted. If they only knew what we had endured over the centuries, they probably would have had a different perspective. When the children were younger, Hannah and I decided not to tell them about the treasure located in the cavern below that building across the way. No good would come from it. It was hardly ever mentioned. Then, several years back, Alex visited to discuss the treasure. He said that the nation was on the verge of collapse. He wished to melt down the gold and silver coins in the treasure chests and mint a new currency based on actual coins. The paper money that had been printed and re-printed was no longer of any value. We agreed with Alex. One of the primary reasons we went on the excursion to Nova Scotia was to give our new nation the financial wherewithal to survive. I said, "It's a miracle that the treasure is still intact. After seeing the conditions at Valley Forge, I wondered why we were just letting the gold and silver just sit."

Alex said, "General Washington knew that even harder days were ahead. Thank goodness that we all had the patience to wait."

So Alex came with a carriage and a Company of thirty soldiers and took the gold and silver. He carefully removed the gold and silver without anyone seeing the other religious artifacts or the Secret of Eden. We sealed off the vault once again. This was the last time I laid my eyes on the Secret of Eden.

The news of the day spread like wildfire. General Washington would be inaugurated as the First President of the United States of America. The hope was that he could bring the divisiveness in Congress to an end. John Adams had received the second most votes, so he would be sworn in as the Vice President.

Hannah and I decided that we were not going to miss this Inauguration. These two men were not only legendary Patriots, but they were our good friends.

During April of that year, we packed up the children and traveled to New York for the Inauguration. We stayed at the same Inn across from the famous Bowling Green Park in New York City. We told the children about our many stays here while we were dropping off or visiting with Uncle Alex.

Alex and Eliza brought their children from their home in Philadelphia to witness the great moment. We wished that our children would see each other more often. Alex and I vowed to make it happen more in the future.

We were invited to a special party at the Morris House in Harlem. Most of the surviving Patriots were there. Our children had the great honor of meeting General Washington and his wife, Martha. Martha made a point of telling our children about the famous night at Peace Field where I met General Washington after spilling wine on his shoes. She said, "He did this because he couldn't take his eyes off your mother." The children laughed.

The night was a wonderful trip into our past. The children met all of the Founding Fathers except one. Perhaps the most important one, Benjamin Franklin.

We attended the Inauguration the next day. From that day forward, General Washington was referred to as President Washington.

I talked to Alex about Mr. Franklin. He said that he visited with him recently. He is still consulting Congress. But, he said, "To be honest, his health is failing rapidly."

Later that afternoon, I spoke with Hannah. We both agreed that we needed to visit our old friend.

The next morning we left New York City for Philadelphia. The following day we arrived at the Franklin House. Mr. Franklin was so excited to see us. The children had no idea what a Titan of a man they were meeting. He invited us to spend the night. He joined us for dinner that evening. His servant said that was the first time that he had left his bed in months. Hannah and I could see that he had very little time left. We spoke of the early days of the rebellion. I let Mr. Franklin know that we had not told the children about Nova Scotia or the treasure. He agreed with our decision. We had a very lovely evening. Hannah and I knew that this would be the last time that we would see Mr. Franklin alive.

On April 20th, 1790, we received a notice from Alex that our beloved friend, Benjamin Franklin, had passed.

The Father of the Founding Fathers

The year was 1799. The Compound was still very prosperous. We had grown the horse ranch into a twenty-horse operation. People were bringing their mares to us for our prominent stud services. The mill was still quite active. Our son John took over all of the milling operations. He was a natural at it. John was spending his spare weekends in Hanover, Pennsylvania, visiting his soon-to-be wife, Mary. Our daughter Katie had taken over the Compound operations after Mrs. Williams died suddenly of what the Doctor believed was a heart attack. That was a very sad day. Mrs. Williams had been working at the Compound since 1770.

Our youngest daughter Marie was riding competitively throughout the northeast. Our daughters grew up to be beautiful, strong women, just like Hannah.

The previous month we celebrated the Annual Harvest Festival. The Compound had been the home of the festival ever since the beginning of the war. Families from all over came to enjoy the special day. It often reminded Hannah and me of the fateful festival at Peace Field.

It was December 15th, 1799. We were getting ready for Christmas when a messenger arrived on horseback. Hannah opened the letter and read the message.

"The Founding Father and First President of the United States of America, George Washington, has passed at his home in Mount Vernon, Virginia."

This pronouncement caught both Hannah and me off guard. We hadn't heard any news of ill health or anything of the sort. We both had an empty feeling in our hearts. We spent the rest of the day milling about our everyday activities. Later that afternoon, Hannah said, "Since we can't travel at this time of year, let's have dinner with the children and tell stories about the Great General."

I said, "That sounds great. But, I am torn that we can't go to the funeral. He touched both of us in so many ways."

Later that evening, we all met at the tavern. Coincidentally, John's lady friend Mary was able to make the trip from Hanover. Mr. and Mrs. Adams also joined us. We all sat around and discussed General Washington. All three of our children had pretty extensive knowledge of the great George Washington. I said to everyone, "Now, you are about to hear the real story from your mother and myself, as well as your grandfather."

Mr. Adams said he first met the General at a Sons of Liberty meeting in Boston. The General was a noted military commander who made quite a name for himself in the French and Indian War. He came to our home to share supper with us.

Hannah said she remembered that day very well even though she was young. She said, "There was a very special air about this man. He would walk into a room, and the entire room would stop talking and just pay their respects to the General. Sometimes, the entire room would break out into clapping."

Hannah continued, "You all know how your father met the General, but the part you don't know is how quickly both General Washington and Mr. Franklin recognized the greatness in Uncle Alex and your father."

I said, "He even held your mother in higher esteem than Alex or I." Hannah blushed.

Hannah continued, "Some of my greatest memories are watching him on the ballroom dance floor. He was an enormous man, but he had the grace and elegance of a dancer. The other side of him was very frightful, to say the least. He was not a man to be crossed." She then told of the instance at Peace Field where he dressed down the Dragoon Commander that had come to arrest her father. This led to many questions for Mr. Adams. Like, "Why were they going to arrest you?" Mr. Adams gracefully answered their questions. It was good for Mr. Adams to relive his glory days. He was also a very important man in America's Founding.

The night went on for hours. Our children, who are now adults, learned many things that would never be read in any history books. Finally, I closed the night by saying, "Your family has a very proud history. Please share these stories with your children."

A Living Legend

It was the summer of 1804. All was well at the Compound. Earlier that spring, John and his wife Mary gave birth to our first Grandchild. His name was Andrew. John and Mary live in the home that Hannah and I lived in after we were first married. It was a joyous year.

The previous year was saddened by the death of a great Patriot, my father in law and mentor, Samuel Adams. He died at the age of 81 from a long list of ailments. His last several years were spent mainly in bed. His passing was actually a blessing. Hannah and I gave him a funeral that was befitting the true hero that he was. He wished to be buried at his family's burial plot at the Granary Burial Grounds in Boston. Many of the Patriots that are still with us were there to say goodbye to this great man. His cousin and our second President John Adams, gave a moving eulogy.

Our children kept Mrs. Adams busy with several ongoing projects around the Compound. Life went back to normal at the Compound until that fateful day.

It was late in the evening on July 13th. There was a darkness abound. Both Hannah and I felt it. I saw Maria sitting on her porch in tears. She seemingly did not age. I was not sure why she was so troubled. Could it be the same thing that Hannah and I were feeling? We retired early that night. Both of us hoped that this feeling of melancholy would be gone by the time we woke up the following day.

The next morning arrived, and the feeling was still there. Then we saw a messenger riding into the Compound. I knew that these messages were always bad news. The messenger handed me the message. I opened it and read it aloud.

"Alexander Hamilton was shot during a duel with Aaron Burr on July 12th. Mr. Hamilton succumbed to his wounds on the 13th."

Both Hannah and I broke down in tears. We had a feeling that, at least in this lifetime, the Guardians were invincible. Our glory days of battle were now behind us. How could the Lord take this great man?

Hannah said, "Eliza is left with eight children. We must first comfort her and then offer her our aide."

We broke the sad news to John, Katie, and Marie about their Uncle Alex. Then, we packed a bag and boarded a carriage bound for New York City.

Two days later, we arrived in New York. As usual, we stayed at the Inn across from Bowling Green Park. As we arrived, I saw the building that was the former home of King's College. It brought back some great memories.

Later that afternoon, we went to Alex and Eliza's New York

home. We found a devastated Eliza there trying to console her younger children. We all broke out in tears when we saw each other. Alex had been such an instrumental man in all of our lives.

Friends had been dropping off food all day long. Eliza said, "Even with eight children, there is no way we can eat all of this." So we stayed all day with the Hamilton's. Later that day, we decided to tell all of the children our favorite Alex stories. All of them knew the tales of the great statesman, Alexander Hamilton. So now they were going to learn about the Alex that we knew.

I told them how Alex and I first met. I said, "Your father arrived as a brash young man that within a day had flirted with every young lady at the Compound. That all changed when your father met a beautiful young lady named Eliza on a stopover in Albany on our way to Boston. He was still very fun-loving, but he was no longer interested in any of the young women that seemed to always run into him. Hearts were broken everywhere. Later on that same trip, your father introduced me to the love of my life, Hannah, and the rest was history."

Hannah said, "My favorite memories of Alex were on our escape ride from Quincy back to the Compound. My father would stop in every town to give a speech for Independence. Alex would then entertain everyone at the local tavern. He was fun-loving, but by the end of the evening, everyone in that tavern was ready to join our cause. When I look back on this, I believe that this was just training for what he would later encounter in the halls of Congress."

The stories continued throughout the night. We all laughed so hard, but we were constantly reminded of why we were there. Alex was only 47 years old. He should have had many years left. This loss would hurt for a long time.

The funeral was held the next day. Many of our old friends were in attendance. Alex's elder sons gave a moving tribute. One line in particular that stood out was, "It seemed as if God had called him suddenly into existence, which he might assist to save a world." If everyone only knew how close to reality that this line actually was.

Alexander Hamilton will be remembered as a Founding Father of America. He was a war hero and was cited for his heroic activities in the Battle of Yorktown.

He was a very close friend of Marquis de Lafayette.

He was the first Secretary of the Treasury.

He was one of the three authors of the Federalist Papers with James Madison and his longtime friend and Supreme Court Justice John Jay.

He was credited with the founding of the US Mint.

He was credited with the founding of the Central US Bank

He was a strong proponent of the US developing a strong Industrial base.

He was credited for founding the Federalist Party, which started the two-party system.

To John Adams, he was initially a brash upstart who then grew into a great Statesman even though they were always on different sides of the issues of the day.

To Thomas Jefferson, he was an adversary who he had the utmost respect for.

For George Washington, he was a trusted friend.

For Benjamin Franklin, he was an enormous talent that comes along maybe once every hundred years.

For Hannah and me, Alex is our eternal best friend and fellow Guardian of the Secret of Eden.

Quod Deus recordatur angelum

It was May 26th, 1821. My health has declined to the point where I had to be helped around. A year ago, I had such chest pains that everyone thought I wouldn't last the day. The Doctor told me to get my affairs in order. Hannah was having none of it. She saw to it that I had three meals a day and plenty of exercise. I was only seventy years old. I have known many people who lived into their 80s. On a recent trip to Binghamton, the clerk thought Hannah was actually my daughter. My daughter Katie thought this was hysterical.

Every morning my son, John, would walk with me to the office and back. I enjoyed these moments with him. I was so proud of my children. John took over the Compound operations, and Katie took over the office management. John and his wife Mary had another child who was now eight years old. Her name was Andrea Grace.

Our daughter Katie had worked under Mrs. Williams's tutelage for years. Katie and her husband George were trying to have children but were unsuccessful so far. It didn't help that George had joined the Army and was often away. Our youngest daughter, Marie, had moved to Boston with her husband, James. They had two boys and a girl, Andrew, Alex, and Anna.

Hannah loved having all of the grandchildren around. I still have the image of watching Hannah teach the kids how to ride and jump. Hannah was in amazing shape. She could take the jumps with as much grace as she did when she was 18. She was a timeless beauty. One day last summer, Hannah and I sat and watched the grandkids play. I said to her, "So which one of them was going to have the son that would grow up to be a Guardian of the Secret of Eden." This was a topic that we hadn't discussed in years. My Diary had been locked away for at least ten years.

Without hesitation, she said, "Andrew."

Andrew was the oldest of the grandchildren and seemed to be the one who was drawn to history. He loved to hear our stories about the Founding Fathers. I knew better than to ever doubt Hannah's intuition.

On this particular day, while John and I were on our daily walk, I spotted Maria. She was very old now. Age was finally getting the better of her. I said, "Hello, Maria."

She had the oddest response. She said, "Quod Deus recordatur angelum".

My hearing wasn't all that great, so I said, "I beg your pardon."

She looked at me and said, "Quod Deus recordatur angelum."

Neither John nor I had any idea what she was saying.

We spotted Hannah over at the ranch. We walked to her,

which was more difficult than I thought. I told Hannah what Maria said.

She said, "What does that mean?"

"We were hoping you knew," I said.

Hannah said, "It sounds like Latin. Anyway, we should find out. You know whenever she speaks, it usually has meaning."

John said, "How old is she anyway? 100? 200?"

Hannah said, "Now, John. Be kind. Maria has been a very special person to your father and me."

Hannah looked flush. I said, "Do you feel alright?"

She said, "I have felt better. I think I will go home and lay down for a bit."

I said, "I hope this is not that flu that has been going around the Compound."

She said, "I am sure that I will be fine."

I let Hannah sleep for a few hours. When I checked on her, I could see that she was burning up. She had a high fever.

I walked over to the office to get Katie. On the way back, she ran ahead of me to check on her mother.

She sent one of the children who was passing by to find John. A few minutes later, John arrived. Katie gathered several buckets of cold water and placed cold cloths on Hannah's forehead. She also made some tea.

Katie said, "I think she is very dehydrated. After the tea, we need her to drink some water."

This seemed to help. Her fever was slightly reduced. Katie sat in the chair next to Hannah. This went on past midnight. I woke Katie up and said, "Go get some rest."

She said, "I am not going anywhere." So I retrieved a blanket and pillow for her.

During the night, Hannah began to cough to the point of gagging. Tea helped a little, but the coughing resumed a few minutes later. We forced her to sit up. This helped with the gagging.

In the morning, John directed one of his workers to ride on horseback to Binghamton and retrieve the Doctor.

I could see with my own eyes that she was getting worse. I held her hand all day and prayed. I started to cry. She just looked at me and smiled. She said, "Don't cry. This is just one stop on our magical journey. If I don't make it, please be sure that my ring is passed down to our great-grandson." Even though she was very ill, she still thought of our greater purpose. Both John and Katie had a look of confusion on their faces.

John said, "Great-grandson?"

I said, "Please don't ask why. Just honor your mother's wishes."

I knew she was right, we were part of a larger mission, but that didn't make it any easier. I always thought for sure that I would go first. Hannah was the picture of health. I never saw this coming. I said to myself, "I don't want to live without her." Was I being selfish?

She could see that I was distraught. Even when she was very ill, she could calm me down. She managed to give me one of her devilish smiles and said, "It will be okay, Julius Caesar." I laughed through my tears.

Later that morning, I was awakened by the Doctor. He looked at her and then checked all of her vitals. Next, he listened to her chest. He finally said, "This is the flu that is going through our area. Roughly one hundred people are suffering from this in Binghamton." He went on to say, "It is critical that this does not turn into pneumonia. She must try to sit up and expel the phlegm, so it doesn't settle in her lungs. He said that he would be back in the morning. With the flu going around, he had many stops to make.

John said, "Is there anything else we can do?"

The Doctor said, "No, the flu must run its course. The key is to keep the phlegm out of her lungs. Make sure that she has plenty of fluids. Both tea and water."

The grandkids had heard that Hannah was sick and wanted to see her. Katie brought them in to see her one at a time. She had them stand across the room from Hannah. She managed to smile and wave at them. I could see that they were all terrified.

Hannah was going downhill fast.

Katie did everything as the Doctor had instructed, but Hannah seemed to turn to a shade of gray. The rosy cheeks that she always had were gone. I was terrified. I was having severe pains in my chest again. I didn't say anything, but I felt awful.

That night we were up most of the night. Hannah's breathing became labored. John had asked the Priest who resided in a chapel a few miles from the Compound to stop by. His name was Father O'Shea. He was an Irishman. John had invited him over to say a prayer for Hannah. When he arrived, he knew it was time to administer Hannah her last rights. John's wife, Mary, and Katie's husband, Michael Jr., joined us. Everyone was crying.

Hannah managed to say, "Please don't cry. I have had a wonderful life. I met the man of my Dreams. I have three beautiful children and eight wonderful grandchildren."

I held her hand tightly. Gradually, I could feel her losing her grip. Her breathing was now strained.

Roughly thirty minutes later, Hannah joined the Lord. I was heartbroken. The only woman that I had ever loved had been taken from me. The pain in my chest kept getting worse.

The Doctor arrived a few minutes later and confirmed that Hannah had indeed passed.

Father O'Shea stayed to offer his support for my family.

John thanked him and said, "What does Quod Deus recordatur angelum mean?"

Father O'Shea said, "It means God recalls an Angel."

John explained how Maria had said that to John and me earlier.

Father O'Shea said, "Sometimes elderly or people near death can see supernatural things."

The Doctor checked me out as Katie and John wrapped Hannah's body in several sheets.

He said, "I believe all of this has caused your father to have a stroke."

Both Katie and John were inconsolable. They were in danger

of losing both of their parents in one day. This was not right.

I could hear everything that was being said. I just couldn't talk. I lay there for hours. I was in a slightly different stage of consciousness. I was reliving all of my greatest moments with Hannah. Several of them included Alex as well. Then I would slip into a depressed state. My Hannah was gone. My children could see that I was slipping. I was trying to hold on for them. To lose both parents on the same day was way too much for anyone. No child should have to endure this.

Just then, Katie whispered in my ear. She said, "It's okay. Go be with Mom."

John said the same thing. I squeezed both hands and acknowledged that they felt my grip. Just then, I had the most incredible sensation. I could smell that beautiful fragrance. I knew that could only mean one thing. Hannah was here. Then I saw the most beautiful scene. It was Hannah. She was wearing that blue dress that she wore the first night I met her. Finally, she spoke. She said, "Are you ready, Jeremiah?"

I said, "I just want to be with you wherever you are."

She said, "You will be, but first, only you know if it is your time."

I said, "Yes. It is my time."

Just then, I heard another voice. It was Alex. He was young again. He said, "Boy, you really look old." It hurt to laugh.

I said, "I am really old."

Alex said, "Well, will you please get on with this already." Once again, it hurt to laugh.

Just then, I felt my spirit lifting out of my body. All of the pain was gone. I was young again. I had Hannah in my arms and Alex at my side. We drifted off, and instantly we found ourselves staring down on the Secret of Eden. This brought immense joy to the three of us.

The next thing I knew, we seemed to be drifting higher and higher. We watched as Boston, New York, and Philadelphia grew in size. Buildings were sprouting up that seemed to touch the sky. There was another city that we didn't recognize. It had great structures that looked like they were directly from Greek mythology. We knew we were looking at the new capital city of the nation that we helped found. Behind us, there were more cities to the west. It appeared that our dream of building this nation had worked.

There was one thing that was absolutely certain. The Guardians of the Secret of Eden were together once again. Time to bring on a new mission.

UNTIL NEXT TIME

Letters to Hannah

January 2, 1777

My Dearest Hannah,

I find myself in the Field Hospital in Trenton, New Jersey after I was slightly injured while on a mission with the Great General. The war effort has not been going so well. Morale was very low. The recent brilliant move by the General has changed everything and may change the momentum of the battle. For the first time, I think we are gaining the advantage. I saw Alex for a brief instant. He was leading his men into battle. He never ceases to amaze. Please do not worry. I will heading home as soon as the Weather allows. My mission was extended because the weather caused the roads and trails to be flooded. I wanted to do my part. Our side needs all the help it can get.

I long for the days to be joining you by the fire or simply watching the horses graze. I will be home soon.

I love you
Your adoring husband,
Jeremiah

January 15, 1778

My Dearest Hannah,

Once again I write to you from a Field Hospital. This time I have been stricken with the Influenza that has overrun this encampment. The conditions here at Valley Forge are wretched. There is rationing of food and men are forced to walk barefoot in the snow.

Congress has appropriated the funds, but the roads are too treacherous to bring in any supplies. We can never again let our soldiers suffer in this manner while our politicians rest comfortably in their own homes.

Alex has been promoted to Senior Aide to the Great General. Before I took ill, I was seeing Alex every day. He is the great leader that we both knew he would be.

I will be heading home hopefully after my two week quarantine period has expired.

The vision of watching you take a blank piece of parchment and turning it into a beautiful painting is getting me through this hardship. I hope to be home soon.

I love you
Your adoring husband,
Jeremiah

August 18, 1781

My Dearest Hannah,

The Great General has given me an assignment that hopefully will help end this war. I feel so honored that he has called on me for this most important task. No worries, it is not dangerous. The enemy is beginning to lose its desire to keep fighting. Our men are fighting for a great cause. The British are not. It is becoming evident that our dream of Independence will be a reality.

I believe what the General has planned will be discussed by historians for centuries. I can hardly wait to see you so I can tell you without all of the cloak and dagger. This mission will delay my trip home for probably another month. I'm terribly sorry. Give John a hug for me.

Our desire to live the simple life of raising our children and running a horse ranch is almost a reality.

I love you
Your adoring husband,
Jeremiah

October 19, 1781

My Dearest Hannah,

The War is over. The British have surrendered. Alex and I stood next to the Great General during the Surrender ceremony. The British showed up with their band playing 'God save the King' They were quickly drowned out by our band playing 'Yankee Doodle Dandy' It was a fantastic moment. I know that it may come as a shock but I'm sitting next to Alex in a tavern as I write this letter. He says Hello. He is writing a similar letter to Eliza.

Tomorrow we are heading to Philadelphia. I'm sending this on an express carriage. Please pack up John and yourself and meet me in Philadelphia for the celebration. Meet me at the place we always stay. Also, please tell your parents to join us.

I can't wait to see you and John. I promise you that we will never be apart again.

I love you
Your adoring husband,
Jeremiah